Ophia's Sister-Soul

Ophia's Sister-Soul

Parting the Veils
Book One

Seth Mullins

ISBN: 979-8-9986772-0-5

Any references to historical events, real people, or real places are used fictitiously. Names, characters, and places are products of the author's imagination.

OLD OPHIA

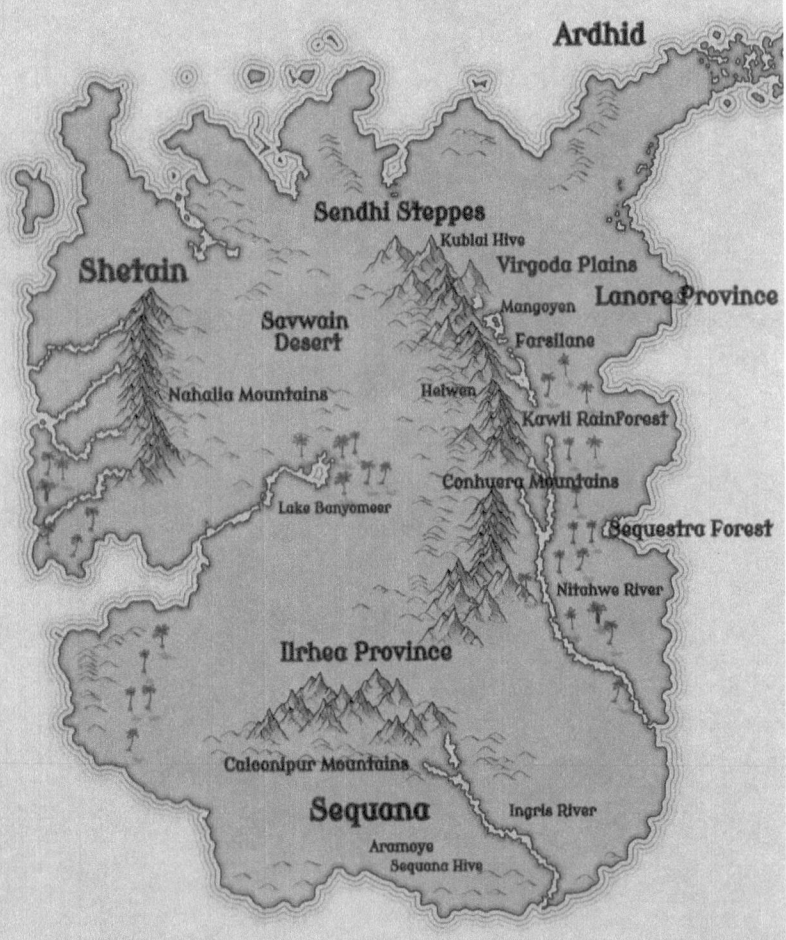

Ardhid

Sendhi Steppes

Kublai Hive

Virgoda Plains

Shetain

Mangoyen

Lanore Province

Savwain
Desert

Farsilane

Nahalia Mountains

Hetwen

Kawii RainForest

Conhuera Mountains

Lake Banyomeer

Sequestra Forest

Nitahwe River

Ilrhea Province

Caleonipur Mountains

Sequana

Ingris River

Aramoye
Sequana Hive

RUDOWINE OCEAN

For the lovers, seekers, and dreamers.
On Earth, Ophia, and Everywhere.

Introduction by Sanyori Mon-Sequestra

The sum of our dreams can be strung into a prop circle, casting our life journeys in the light of a stage production. Within such a play, we may see aspects of the plot that eluded us while we were identified with our roles within that drama. How many times have I witnessed this? The audience yells at the speaker on the stage, trying to awaken him or her to some crucial fact, despite knowing that such a ruckus can never alter the story's trajectory.

The spectators can't help themselves.

I hope you'll forgive me for all this dramatist's jargon. I was—am—a man of the stage, and I speak as my nature and training lean. And I've been conditioned by my tenure as a Sophryne, a Wakeful Dreamer. There are times—particularly during historical moments of great unrest, tension, and change—when the dreams of a multitude coincide, creating an even larger, overarching narrative.

I call that narrative living theater. Many others refer to it as myth.

And perhaps (partly) because I'm accustomed to blurring the distinctions between "dream" and "reality," I've been asked to narrate—as concisely as possible—my people's most beloved myth: "The Twin Souls and the Parting of the Veils."

Within the context of this tale, the lines between

dreams and reality are sometimes in stark contrast and sometimes scarcely discernible. On occasion, I daresay, they even seem to trade places. I've heard this is often a characteristic of twins. Who could resist the temptation to at least try it, to explore—to borrow a phrase from Colleen Addison's world—"how the other half lives"?

For art and dreams are life's twin blessings.

Those not native to my home world of Ophia, who share Colleen's points of reference more intimately than mine, might feel that some information about my people, the Shaini, and the origins of our most revered teachers, the Sophryne, might be in order.

Ah, but I ought rather try and catch a golden mahseer with my bare hands, were I currently possessed of fleshy hands, than try to satisfy this demand. You see, little history survives from our earliest ages. Only the most nebulous clues, clothed in symbolism, are preserved in oral traditions. That's because time itself was (is) malleable. Many possible paths were explored. Each of these, in turn, thrust roots into their own "pasts" and "futures."

During those earliest epochs, the Shaini tangibly felt and participated in Sorsajna, the fire of Creation. Later, when we no longer felt Sorsajna in the pit of our being, our Speakers, the Sophryne, were obliged to find more demonstrable ways to evoke its essence. They had to almost confound and beguile the minds of their kindred in the hopes of awakening them to old inner knowledge.

They reminded us of magical inner movements we felt divorced from in waking. This was the birth of art and drama—and language itself—arising alongside the dreaming life of humankind. Primitive peoples, like the Oskwai tribes you'll hear about, could gesture towards objects in their physical world. But for those more intangible feelings of possibility, magic, and wonder that dreams awaken in us, words were needed.

How else could that wonder be shared when it couldn't be related to anything in one's surroundings?

And so we early humans tried to convey what we'd experienced in our sleep-time excursions using sounds, gestures, and pantomime. Once upon a time, we'd inhabited a living dream. Then, suddenly, we were Ophia-bound, entrenched in material bodies, and subjected to the laws of Space and Time. We clothed ourselves in flesh as Ophia clothed itself in ground.

And now we had to survive, to pluck Her fruits to sustain ourselves. Might humankind (Shaini or Oskwai) forget that the world's manifest beauty was a reflection, albeit a fractured one, of luminous Sorsajna, from which all existence flows? Could we retain the memory of our origins? These questions led to the birth of all the Sophryne arts, which reminded us of that boundless and nameless realm from which we emerged.

Thus, you'll find little "hard history" here. We can only approach any version of truth by chasing the wind trails of our most venerated myths. But it's empowering, methinks, to recall that we all participate in Creation. From the raw stuff of life, we bring forth forms that can be seen, heard, felt, smelt, and tasted. And sometimes, to our eternal enrichment, souls clothe themselves and walk among us to remind us of the dimensions from which we are (seemingly) sundered. The twins I spoke of were—are—two of the most renowned.

Such beings are naturally drawn to Sophrynism, to Wakeful Dreaming, a practice that straddles the lines between life and death, here and hereafter, time and eternity. Powerful Sophrynes can work such an effect upon the minds and souls of those with whom they come into contact that the recipients begin to break through the barriers of the world they know. They begin to perceive and respond to other realms of being. Such epiphanies can also penetrate the sense of separation that we often experience with one another.

A seemingly insurmountable gulf divided the sisters' respective worlds. They needed to experience, in their blessed, fragile bodies, that more pervasive separation I spoke of. Both worlds had lost their sense of magic, and our heroines, Colleen Addison and Esperidi Mon-Sequana, healers at heart for all eternity, instinctively looked for ways to patch the resulting rift. That search carried them through the heart of their mutual bereavement.

In the line of Ophia's tapestry, into which Esperidi became a vital thread, the Sophryne arts were perfected out of necessity. I know because I lived during that cruel and repressive era. It was perilous for any of us to speak our minds. We writhed within a spider's web, our every movement, word, and emotion sending tremors through its strands. To criticize the ruling body with even a whisper... One might as well trumpet protests to a lynch mob.

Such was life under the Cordonne and its Weaving.

Imagine the living conditions of the thousands of Shaini inhabiting Ophia during that age. I, Sanyori, spent my formative years beneath the Weaving's eyes. I knew my community's quiet desperation. Our security came at too steep a price. But who among us would dare raise voices of dissent? The Weaving would expose us. Even plotting rebellion would alert the Cordonne. One could not even get aroused by the prospect of freedom.

What recourse had we?

Ah, but the Weaving, the chief instrument of the Cordonne's control, was still a physical construct within a physical world. It could never reach its fingers into the dreaming dimension. And so it was there that we learned to awaken, congregate, and communicate freely.

We who escaped Old Ophia during its last days, its decaying days, planned our emancipation while we slept. Shadowy omens and premonitions illuminated our way, foreshadowing possible perils and treasures. Abandoning the social compass, we oriented ourselves around inner whispers and nudges. They helped us to regain our bearings when we'd lost sight of all shores.

That's how we came to etch the essential structure of this Sentient Library, where I now inscribe these words and struggle not to feel overwhelmed by the responsibility bequeathed upon me. I must remind myself that a living myth is created by all who partake in it. This relieves some of the burden. It soothes my stage jitters, so to speak.

Some participants in the drama, like Colleen, prefer to relate aspects of their stories in their own ways. Colleen preserves her voice in a physical journal much as I do this more ethereal tome. Sometimes, she speaks in the present tense. Sometimes, she considers her life in hindsight. In either case, the denizens of countless worlds can now understand—and, in some ways, participate in—her journey.

Such magic still astounds me.

But what about those who might be considered our adversaries? Surely, Jain-Toh, Karia, Konatep, and Tumoset, among others, would abhor seeing their deeds so exposed?

Keep in mind that a being's perspective can be profoundly transformed on this side of the Partition, particularly after they've come into contact with the larger entities of which they are a part. The drama we call "Parting the Veils" touched upon many worlds, altering their mental landscape and changing their historical trajectory. This could not have been achieved without every participant's contributions, even if their positions seemed destructive in the limiting field of time.

Do not forget that contrast is often our greatest

teacher within these mortal worlds.

Those reading this testimony with at least a partial knowledge of its underlying myth may grow restless at this juncture. "Yes: We know what the twins achieved in the end. They forged a pathway between the worlds, allowing each to recapture its sense of possibility and wonder. But what did they actually do?"

With that question, the road grows nebulous indeed. How does one recount the travels of two heroines who walked as much in their dreams as in waking? How does one do justice to the supporting cast—again, forgive my theater training—when many of them aspired towards the same thing?

Despite such daunting challenges, I've done my best to limn the journey of Esperidi Mon-Sequana and Colleen Addison and the forgotten art that united them, finally—at least, for long enough to alter the destinies of their respective worlds.

It isn't always comfortable reading. For many beings on both sides of the Partition, existence had grown unmistakably dark. Both worlds were purged in fire, floods, cyclones, and upheavals, whether one might interpret these in psychological or physical terms. And in the depths of their suffering, each world began to long, more and more, for the other.

Sarpienta's fangs! If I persist like this, I'll likely be out of breath before I begin! But perhaps you can better understand my attachment to this story's emotional sweep if you consider—and as you'll discover—that I participated in some of its unfolding events. By which I mean I lived them in a physical body.

Remember, always, that the distance between the worlds is, to awakened eyes, akin to the distance between our twins: no more than the breadth of a thought. Or, as my teacher once said, "Naught but a wisp of gossamer gown."

Soon, it will be time for others to speak. But first, to prove my dramatist's salt, I must paint the opening scene for my audience. Imagine our troupe of actors—participants in the most ambitious stage drama we've yet attempted—not yet born but quite alive. To do this, you must, of course, suspend disbelief. If the very thought conjures up resistance and denial, know you are not alone! All of us have weathered this. How many times have we cried, in the face of physicality's sorrows, "Never again!"? And yet here we are—again. Sitting cross-legged on an ethereal plain of lustrous wheatgrass, caressed by a breeze, facing each other in a circle pow-wow.

Think of this as a mental meeting place. Imagine spiders weaving their homes and then allowing their webs to enmesh. From this commingling of personal realities, a ritual ensues, a kind of opening ceremony wherein each player in the planned drama announces their presence and intention. Love has bound us through countless lifetimes. Now, we gather so that one, the entity known as Sydwyn, can receive counsel from the rest, for she alone must grow to adulthood—without our presence to console her—in a world that will often baffle and terrify her.

With the timbre of a devotional chant, the woman's sister-soul introduces herself. "In the language of my people-to-be, the Shaini of Ophia, 'Erawen' refers to the motions of the spirit. It evokes Raven, a being as wild and capricious as the winds.

"I will share a world with Sydwyn only briefly—and under another name. But when I depart, I will do my utmost to communicate with her across the Partition. My Sophryne training will help me fulfill this promise. May the bond we rekindle prove durable enough to bridge the worlds!"

Erawen-Esperidi is as keen as her namesake bird, and

the knotted hair grazing her shoulders befits Raven's ebony wings. Anticipating a life to come in sun-kissed climes, her ethereal body is swarthy and slight. As with the others—all save Sydwyn-Colleen, the woman who will be our lone ambassador to Earth—Erawen's slightly reptilian eyes and sharp ears identify her as Shaini.

Sajna, whose name signifies fire's essence, is next to speak. She is a scarlet-haired bludgeon of a Shaini maiden with azure eyes. Casting a sly, sidewise glance towards the others present, she says, "I cannot share a world with Sydwyn, nor would I ever want to—not the world that she intends! Where do I even begin reciting its litany of ills? Oh, it's an abode of flesh-eating diseases, a malign place where the human mind and Earth's soul seldom make common cause. Befouling land, air, and sea... These are the most common occupations. The sexes forget their harmony; individuals forget their identities. If and when they resolve such questions, they only find them renewed in mid-life.

"Nay! For madness of the magnitude of Earth's humanity, one's only options, methinks, are debauchery, lechery, and savagery. One must either be numb or drowned in sensation!"

Most of us just smile and exchange knowing looks. Sajna is prone to such displays of mock cynicism when she feels daunted—and she is not easily daunted. At any rate, she soon sobers and surrenders to the solemnity of the occasion. Closing her eyes and inhaling slowly, she declares her fidelity:

"In the being of Ashangtu Lanore, I will ensure that Sydwyn never wholly forgets who she is or where she has come from. Whenever our dream paths cross, leastways."

"I'll remind her that the difficulties of physical life are like a dream where you fall and almost hit the bottom of the chasm before you realize that gravity is just a belief and you can quite easily fly," Erawen adds.

Then, guided by the needs of the moment and our powerful mental rapport, we chorus our support for Sydwyn—"We will never stop trying to reach you!"—and consider this so deeply that the landscape hums to the notes of our inner resolution.

Acturius speaks with my voice and being. "Have you thought of a name?"

"Colleen," Sydwyn says. Then, as if this needs clarifying, she adds: "I'm not ready to jump back into a lifetime as a man."

"And you know your parents?"

"I do." She makes this slow admission with at least a partial awareness of how challenging the road she's chosen may prove. "The Addison family will support me in their way, though they won't understand me or my path. I will use this as an incentive to break away from tradition and all that is sanctified and find my own truth."

"A worthy aspiration!" effuses Sajna, whose heart and feet have trampled upon every holy effigy on Earth and Ophia.

"But if you intend to be a healer," Jormada, the snake handler, says, "you must do more than grow comfortable in your own skin. You must translate your soul's comprehension into symbols and expressions that the people can understand."

"We'll have strong motivations this time," Erawen says on her sister's behalf, "circumstances that will splinter our personal worlds and open us to those other dimensions. These are the ruptures that Sydwyn and I have planned together."

"There are lots of charlatans down there!" Sajna cries. "Be careful who you learn from!"

"And you'll forget so much of what seems clear to you

now," I add. This remark reminds us all of many lifetimes during which we'd truly and <u>deeply</u> forgotten.

"Those lifetimes are difficult to think back on, even now," Sydwyn acknowledges. "But we must embrace all of this. It is like stepping back from a canvas—I was a painter once, you remember? You step back to gauge a portrait's balance. You <u>feel</u> the aesthetic whole and then start to discriminate—maybe a little green coloration for visual interest here; perhaps sharpen the shadows or heighten the light there. Like our various lifetimes, it doesn't evolve in a straight line."

Something in her voice enables us to feel Sydwyn's inner certitude and realize she has received what she needed from us. By silent consent, the formal portion of our pow-wow reaches its end. She and Erawen separate from the group, but all of us remain within the fluid, numinous landscape to lend our emotional support.

And here I shall sign off for now, consigning myself to an "omniscient narrator" role until more personal commentary might bring clarity. Enjoy this tale as it unfolds. Recognize yourself within its tapestry. If you did not partake in the epic described herein, to some extent or another, on Earth or Ophia, you would not be reading these words.

Sanyori Mon-Sequestra
In the Hereness and Nowness
The Sentient Library

Teacher of Fire

"Why hasn't Bocuan joined us?" Sajna demanded. "This is unlike him. Indeed, his is often the loudest voice in our councils."

"Do you mean to say you yet fail to recognize our other guest?" Acturius said. "To be so distracted... Oh, you *must* be frightened at the prospect of what's ahead!"

"Never before has there been so much at stake," Sajna said.

But as if the dramatist's words clarified the perception for her, she was suddenly aware of gentle lapping; her nostrils filled with moisture and the tang of salt. She smelled fish and kelp.

A wet boundary appeared just beyond the edge of her firelight. It kissed that edge and receded in an indolent peristaltic motion, like the exertions of a lazy snake.

The water stretched to the uttermost ends of her northern horizon.

Moved by an obscure impulse, Sajna crept—vaguely aware of the flamboyant man-child following her—and stopped to kneel before the water's edge. When it surged again, she cupped some and let it trickle through her fingers onto the damp sand.

"Maybe we'll find better answers to the seeming contradictions this time, brother," she whispered.

From the corner of her eye, she noticed Acturius

knuckling his forehead in the ostentatious way he often delighted in. "And now you forget the pact! It'll be 'sister' this time."

"Ah—yes." Sajna trailed her fingertips across the water and mused, "I suppose that will simplify some dilemmas and complicate others."

Rising, she glanced towards the twins, who'd ventured beyond the firelight. Her conflicting emotions made her unintentionally brusque. "What's keeping them?"

"Well, now, it isn't easy *planning* joint bereavement, is it? Especially when—one hopes—it'll prove sufficient to alter their life paths. It's easy enough to say, 'This is the adventure my soul craves.' But to step into it..?"

"Yes," Sajna acknowledged. "Sometimes I think they're both braver than I am. Sometimes, I wish we'd all agreed they could shoulder this task alone. I could use some more rest and reflection."

For a moment, they regarded the two retreating forms. Then the red-haired woman added, "I almost wish I could think of some way to dissuade them. Almost," she emphasized, noticing her companion mustering a protest.

"Well," Acturius considered, "what they propose is something their respective worlds sorely need. Somebody has to step in and embody the myth. Who else would you suggest?"

Sajna raised an eyebrow. "You, to begin with."

Acturius waved a dismissive hand. "I'll play a bridge, a living link between past and present. I'll serve more as a chronicler than a participant. Those two will be the future." He slowly shook his head, making even that simple gesture look grandiose, and chuckled. "It is amusing, isn't it—talking about Time in a place like this?"

"Indeed," Sajna said. "Mostly, I'll forget about both of them the moment I'm clothed in flesh. And yet here I stand...

and worry."

"Erawen is going to need your fire," Acturius said. "Both of them will. Does your will suffice"—he teetered on the edge of a taunting grin—"Red Buffalo?"

"They'll both need your flair and seasoning," the other countered, ignoring her friend's baiting. "Spring means little without autumn's contrast."

Erawen thought about her personal stake in her vision of futurity. Or was it the past? She'd seen her likeness graven in stone and carved upon tall wooden poles. Humans called upon her in moments of anguish, confusion, and fear. They marveled at her delicate figure, sharp ears, and long, slim fingers. There were fearful whispers. But many associated her image with mercy and compassion. She was the goddess who heard the entire world's cries and held forth the healing balm with hands of grace.

Such was the myth in store for her. Or the myth that had once been. A myth her sister had also embodied.

"This is a Sophryne journey we're embarking upon," Erawen told Sydwyn when they reached the firelight's edge again. "But for you, it's in a land where there aren't even Shaini, much less Sophryne."

"Yours begins there, too," Sydwyn reminded her. But then she grew wistful. "Teaching inner knowledge to a populace that's in danger of wiping itself out, and it seems the clock is ticking, and the chances of averting disaster are slim..."

"We're about to clothe ourselves in the camouflage once more," Erawen said, "just as we, as practicing Sophrynes, once learned to throw it off."

"How confident are you that we'll prevail this time?"

Erawen's exhalation blew wind across the two worlds. "Only a part of who we are can ever be physically expressed. Whatever personalities we clothe ourselves in, we will sense our greater nature to some extent. But our personal leeway is as unbounded as our imagination. In some lifetimes, we clearly apprehended the source of life. Others passed from birth to death in utter ignorance. Their days were shadowed."

Then, overcome by emotion, she dispensed with all these caveats. Stepping forward and embracing Sydwyn, she vowed, "I *will* find a way to reach you!"

"You always do, sister-soul," the other returned.

Then they laughed in tandem when they heard Sajna call, "Don't forget to dance and get intoxicated—and make love!"

But Erawen's laughter was clipped, and she hugged her heart. Sydwyn was beginning to fade.

Sajna glanced over her shoulder and saw that Acturius was already gone. "It looks like our beloved playwright has woken up."

Erawen pulled away from the space Sydwyn had occupied and faced Sajna. "I'd say it's time we did, too. I want to get deep into my meditations this day. I must soon journey across the Partition and be there for the birth!"

"Hers or yours?" Sajna asked, her laughter dancing like a lick of flame. "Fortune favors you this time: You don't have to choose!"

This remark, however, made Erawen recall the other part of the bargain she and Sydwyn had sealed. *We've already chosen*, she thought. She felt a momentary, frigid gust that made her long for her sister, whom she sometimes called the South Wind.

Without another word, Erawen faded from the dream-moot.

Sajna, dealt a pang by her dissolving form, moved

towards the fire circle to warm herself. She paused to smile fondly at the bearded man still kneeling in the sand: the last remaining participant aside from herself, at least in human form. Bocuan's ocean hair had dampened Jormada's knees.

"Any parting words of inspiration?" Sajna said, with a *timbre* of teasing sparkle.

In all likelihood, the two would not become lovers in their Ophian expressions to come, but they'd consummated their bond many times in the "past." Some of the sweeter memories of those sojourns prompted Sajna to watch the logs feeding the flames—or being consumed by them, depending upon one's point of view.

"Remember Sarpienta," Jormada said. He made a thrusting, "give-and-take" gesture with his hands. It reminded Sajna of the insight she'd received while watching Bocuan lap the shore.

"There's no escaping his rhythm," he said. "If you adopt a body, you learn to dance his dance. Chewing. Swallowing. Digesting. Taking two steps forward and one step back at each stage of your journey. A leap of faith followed by a partial retreat to get your bearings. And let's not forget sex."

"You know I seldom can," Sajna said, flicking her tongue between her teeth, imitating the serpent he described.

"But for you and Erawen, this time around," Jormada said, "that motion is also the secret of your joint power." He repeated the peristaltic hand gesture. "She is the gathering coil. You are the surge, the spring."

Sajna allowed herself some open flirtation: The indulgence blunted some of the edges of her trepidation. "Well, sir," she said, "if we can master the serpentine motion between us, what do we need you for?"

"Well, you'll need something to slither *over*, won't

you?" He repaid her with a lascivious smile and pointed back to where Bocuan still lay in peaceful resplendence. "Unless you want to be a water moccasin. Or unless you're curious how far you might get, wriggling in the void."

He mulled over that image for a moment. "I might enjoy witnessing such a spectacle, actually."

Sajna leered back at him. "I think you enjoy watching me move, whatever the context. Remember how transparent our minds are to one another in this place. Don't embarrass yourself trying to deny it."

"Saucy and ribald to the end," Jormada said. "Or the beginning, I guess we ought to say. Are you certain you'll not consider being born in Helwen Hive? There's still time."

"Their ways have grown too predictable for my blood," Sanja said. "A planned orgy never carries the heat of one that catches its participants unaware."

"And yet, given the circumstances you've chosen, you'll likely be celibate for the greater portion of your life this time around."

"That's a big part of it," she acknowledged, shuddering at the prospect. "My people will know the honey and nectar of Ophia, only to feel it snatched away. And I'll know the depths of my passion but find no outlet or object. All this, in the hopes that once I do find a focus for it..."

The man shook his head. "May the pillars of both worlds tremble upon that day!"

There was nothing suggestive about how Sajna smiled at him this time, only deep fondness cultivated over countless lifetimes. "I am saddened that our paths aren't liable to cross this time."

Jormada shrugged. "Yes... well, there are always dreams."

"Dreams," she mused. "Yes. I intend to become a more proficient Wakeful Dreamer now than ever I achieved before."

Her stare sharpened, suddenly galvanized by comprehension. "That's the root purpose of all this deprivation, isn't it? It'll be an impetus. For the rest of the land as well. Dreams can seem frivolous when you're constantly surrounded by opulence, comfort, and privilege.. But when you're bereft of all that and cannot even know when you might feel the very ground bucking beneath your feet like a herd of maddened horses—or an enraged serpent," she added for her friend's benefit, "well, then you ignore dream guidance at your peril."

The squatting man appraised her in silence and nodded as if he'd surmounted an essential crest of doubt. "I think you'll do well, Sajna. Consider: Bocuan has probably lapped this dream shore three-score times since you and I began talking, and not once have you thought about your fear."

She stiffened and cast him a look of mock exasperation. "And so you see fit to remind me of it, eh?"

Then she glanced back at the space the twins had vacated. "Even more rests upon their shoulders. We're all going to forget so much, but if they cannot recall anything at all..."

"It all unravels," the man acknowledged. "But don't you derive a certain thrill from such gambles?"

"I have," Sajna admitted. "But I long for something different this time. We've all been acquainted with a sense of futility. This time, I want victory—no ambiguity."

She let Jormada see, in her eyes, the fire for which she'd been renowned in other places and ages. "Not just for the survival of both worlds, but so I may know it for myself."

"Clear a space for us, sister," the man said. "For what we intend to build together, many old altars must be razed and a ton of rubble removed."

But he was not blind to her underlying distress, and after a moment, he added, "Be at ease, my friend. Our worst outcome will be to fall short of what we dream to accomplish and then try again in a new body and time. Sarpienta does not bemoan any layer of skin he sheds."

"Only you could make becoming a snake sound more appealing by the moment," Sajna said. "But you're right: I have to focus." She nodded towards the space Erawen had occupied. "She and I will be entering Ophia within a couple years of each other, and she looked much more... prepared than me."

Much more resolved, she added to herself.

Of course, "Time" had no meaning in this dimension. Her use of the concept was a lingering vestige from her last incarnation. However, her and Erawen's joint intention was very crucial, regardless of hours or years.

I do best when I'm thrown into the fray, Sajna reminded herself. *If I can but match her courage for that first leap, the rest I'll rise to when it confronts me.*

"Blessings of Sorsajna go with you, Jormada," she said, suddenly somber. "The family you have agreed to be born into... Ah! You might be the bravest of all of us—or the one most blissfully ignorant of peril."

The man rippled his shoulders in a way that reminded her of shifting mountains. "I see no other way. Someone must erode that foul edifice from the inside. Besides—" He nodded again towards the watermark. "I've agreed to no greater sacrifice than what Bocuan will eventually embrace.

"In fact, none of these comparisons signify. All of us have a difficult road, and none of us would choose otherwise." He laughed. "We've had plenty of opportunities to do so."

Noticing he'd begun relinquishing his hold upon the

dream-moot, Sajna sought to convey her complex affection. "Farewell, my brother... son... mother... lover." Her voice betrayed the emotional ambiguities entwined with some of those remembered lifetimes. "I would embrace you, but I fear that might sap my resolve."

So *let us dance this dance again*, she thought, once he'd departed, though she knew she wouldn't be jumping into the fray immediately. An earthly drama needed to play itself out first. But her inner eyes were fixed upon Erawen, anticipating the leagues and hardships they'd chosen to undertake together in Ophia once the woman's earthly sojourn was complete.

Remember that you'll be learning a few steps from me this time. Try not to judge me overmuch if I occasionally step on your toes. You ought to know by now that fire is seldom a gentle teacher.

Now, Sajna wished Acturius was still there. She longed for the soliloquy he often offered on these occasions. In lieu of his presence, she could only conjure his image, face it towards the space that the twins had vacated, spread her arms wide, and intone the words in his stead:

"Oh, passion, vitality, energy that moves the worlds in their orbits... I go where you call me! I'm ready to be clothed in new flesh and surrounded by unfamiliar hills and valleys. I'm prepared to look upon the stars as if for the first time and rejoice in learning anew what was always known!

"I am ready to live again!"

A Broken Bridge Between Worlds

From Colleen's Journal

Dear Stacie,

These words scampered through my head just as I was drifting off to sleep last night: "I told Starchild, and then Starchild ran off and told the whole universe." These hospital sheets almost pulled me under before I realized this cosmic conversation I'd eavesdropped on might be worth recording.

I feel like I know what Starchild told everything and everyone in Creation, though I doubt any words of mine will do it justice. It's saying, "I am!" with everything within you. It's that moment—maybe you're in love, pausing in the afterglow of a great poem, or you just heard a flower tell you her name—when you <u>know.</u> And you can only give voice to what you know with a yea-saying cry.

She is the divinity within us that allows us to awaken each morning and create the day.

Oh, Stace, if we knew that we participated even in the sun's rising, would we ever hurt one another the way we do?

Before I slipped into unconsciousness, my whole mind was filled with the sun. Maybe I felt my kinship with Starchild. I haven't described her because I assume you're already probably more acquainted with her than I am, considering where you are.

She is the light that can never be extinguished. The

light that burns within everything we have done, are doing, and will ever do. And everything we have, are, or will ever know.

The light that can't be extinguished: not by war, suicide, stupidity, greed, racism, hunger... When we want to know how we create the day, we ask that light. Right there is the place where reason will scoff. But we won't pay it any mind. It's just acting jealous.

Obviously, I'm procrastinating here. I often wonder if you think this morbid, my tradition of writing to you on our birthday. Once you hear how I've celebrated the occasion this year—and why I'm so late in reaching out—it might settle the question once and for all. But I'll stay downwind of that particular wolf until I find the courage to approach it. Or, failing courage, I manage to approach the heart of my confession in a circumspect way.

That's why I inscribe these words with blood-ink. Though I might fantasize that you can somehow see or hear them, I'm really counting on them to sweep <u>my</u> heart of old debris.

You may not understand because I didn't start journaling until years after you left. Words unveil what is real within a forest of self-deception. Words are my tight rope stretched over an abyss, my paddles and tiny kayak across a roiling sea.

How many metaphors can I wrap this up in?

I write to probe my life's inner and outer edges. Where are its boundaries? Or, more to the point, where are the boundaries I accept and thus create? Let me not waste page space—or your time—trying to distinguish fact from fiction. Facts exist within our minds; they change as we do.

We shed facts like a snake sheds its skin. Yeah, I'm still infatuated with reptiles! Snakes and archaeology, baby! But imagine if we could just slough off our past like a skin.

How liberating! And it seems we ought to be able to, somehow.

The words on the page always remind me that the contours of my mind will never fit into any neat package or label. This is me, Colleen Addison, Glorious Misfit. On the page, I can transform into a mythic version of myself. Though I'm still grounded in the world of "facts," I feel the dreamy sunburst of a reality that is too deep, wide, and unfathomable to be contained within any realm of fact.

Of course, the same was always true for you, Stacie Addison. It's true for all of us magical beings, though the world's "sacred cows" may condemn the notion.

And so my luminous conscious mind is a candle. I light it and watch where invisible beliefs cast their shadows. Hopefully, I'll find the strength to laugh when they tell me I'm at the mercy of what I created. I'll watch the distortions dissolve as they're exposed to the light. This is my script. I take the yellow marker in hand and highlight where every doubt resides.

You're probably wondering where I learned to talk like this. And well you should, as I've been too embarrassed to tell you about it until now. It all comes from a therapist I saw for a while in junior high—at Momma and Daddy's insistence. This was a couple of years after you passed over. Apparently, they didn't like me spending gorgeous summer months holed up in my room, not even reading or writing, just staring vaguely at the walls and wondering whether I could pass through them and translate myself somewhere else.

Had you lived to experience it, you'd know what a field of landmines early adolescence can be. Things you've been carrying inside, unsuspecting, suddenly become too explosive to ignore anymore. The psyche's eggshell cracks open, and our senses awaken to hitherto unknown worlds.

Sometimes, that crack even offers a glimpse backward into the magic of childhood, that essence that we adults morbidly grope for. We who are "enlightened" enough to "realize" magic doesn't exist, who are educated enough to "know" that we are naught but cardboard caricatures in a barren universe.

But Saul reminded me of that magic. He held a space for it. I couldn't always comprehend what he was saying—intellectually, at least—but part of me absorbed its nourishment. I recorded our sessions on my phone and transcribed them at home. My dream journal is one of the few surviving relics of my old life.

Saul was honest and transparent in a way my twelve-year-old self could appreciate. Our mother, he told me, was worried that I'd never managed to grow beyond my grief. She described how you and I had indulged in vivid fantasies—her words. Now, she was concerned that I was retreating into that imaginary world. Or that I couldn't distinguish between it and the real.

Saul managed to dispel my anxiety around that question. "This world isn't an illusion," he said, "but it's only a portion of the truth. It's thoroughly real to us while we're immersed in it, but we must remember that it's only a story that our five senses narrate, a work of accepted fiction so dazzling that it's easy to mistake it for the whole truth."

Saul believes our souls are doorways that open onto everything we'll ever require for happiness, wisdom, and fulfillment. He said that it's only because we define human nature so narrowly that we're prone to believe in gods, demons, celebrities, Fate, whatever, and give our power away to these things.

He insisted that we create our own life experiences. Nothing is accidental. As you might imagine, many of his esteemed colleagues in the field thought him a flake. But no doubt those same people believe that the miracle of our consciousness is a crapshoot of chemical chance. So, who's really irrational here?

To the extent that we don't believe in our inner enchantment, we don't get to experience it.

I wanted to recapture what I'd forgotten. I wanted reminders of that world I'd forsaken when I clothed myself in this body. Saul helped me forgive my young self for her protective ignorance. If I had known what this journey would entail, I doubt I would have found the courage to take the first steps. Always existing on the margins of society, I've been obliged to search for my own personally resonant truth in the hopes that that truth could become my gift to humanity.

Happy New Year, Western Civilization. Love, yer girl Colleen, Glorious Misfit.

And a part of me was just tired of the guilt, Stace. Seriously. I was nine when you fell. I was in way over my head. And who could I have turned to? Momma and Daddy thought we were loony enough as it was. It was a game. How did you get so caught up in it? Why didn't I see it coming? My life up until that point had provided me with no reference points for anything that was happening. All I could feel was that icy sensation stealing over me. The icicle in the back of your brain that doesn't let you move when you need to. It only knows one line, which it repeats over and over again: "This can't be happening! This can't be happening!"

And once that ice melts, you plunge into deep waters. The lapping waves of what psychologists call the unconscious are never far from my shores. Sometimes, I feel dream reality dripping through the fabric of my daylight world as if nothing stands between the two realities but a wisp of gossamer veil. How does one live with that day-to-day? I had to forsake all thoughts of a normal life—whatever the hell that even means.

I'm here to change the world, not adapt to it.

This world needs its misfits.

And yet... It's one thing to intellectually believe that other worlds probably exist somewhere "out there." Straying into dream-like dimensions while you're wide awake is another matter.

And it's easy enough to wax philosophical about all this, too, right? When the world is long on pain and short on joy, it can be tempting to imagine swiping all the pieces from the gameboard of our lives and starting over on a clean slate.

I once showed Saul this apocalyptic story I'd written. I stayed up late one night, envisioning the collapse of modern civilization. The pages swarmed with images of people walking over dilapidated highways, vehicles wrecked and stripped, wolves and bears roaming the alleyways of vacated cities...

Saul could tell that the whole scenario excited a part of me. What a relief it would be to wake up and realize that we never had to feed the machine again!

"Sometimes," I said, "it just feels like the only solution. Clean the chalkboard and start over."

"What if humanity could <u>evolve</u>?" he said. "What if it could transform without any kind of apocalyptic scenario needing to play out for us to awaken to our true potential?"

<u>Anything is preferable to the way things are</u>, I thought. There I was, imagining it would be easier to find my place in a post-apocalyptic world than in any school, church, or fraternity. I guess I took our "I'm-creating-a-world" game to a darker place than we ever did, Stace.

But lying on this sterile bed, surrounded by blank white walls, I'm grateful for these memories. I'm glad I had someone in my life early on who warned me against turning to therapists, gurus, or religionists to help me understand my own inner mind.

Teachers of all stripes insist that the answers to our questions are either held under lock and key by the gatekeepers or forever buried. Science is a thief in the house of our minds. Religion doesn't want us to embrace the bloom or the blight, not if either sprouts up from this good Earth.

If our lives expand or shrink according to the stories we cling to about them, we should choose those stories more carefully. May my stories never become like that fallen tree in Aspen Park! A broken bridge between worlds, all wrought from rotted wood.

You can't imagine what I had to go through to say these six words to my therapist here at the hospital: "I-had-to-watch-her-fall." Looking right at me, eyes frozen in that horrified moment before being extinguished. Left me abandoned like an E.T. whose Mothership had flown. Left me to eat, sleep, study, and work while my life spun about the whirlpool of a harrowing truth: that there's this unanswerable pain at the heart of everything.

Muffling the edges of laughter. Casting its shadow on every moment of unguarded joy. Gnawing at my mind, every hour, every day.

But if I'm not going to follow you—and I can't; I can't even contemplate hurting myself like that again—then I have to find an answer to that unanswerable pain. Where do I look? Who do I trust?

Me?

Stace, you're the only one in whom I can confide things like this. Everyone around me... it's like there's this shroud pulled over their eyes. And maybe I'm under its pall, too. Perhaps that's why I've been so convinced there is no answer.

There's got to be some way to cast it off. I have to believe that!

Childhood destroyed in one screaming plunge. No more feeling myself an intimate part of a river, or of the trees, or of an ant crawling over the dry ground to the extent that I could almost see through all those other eyes.

That magic bridge of yours was nothing more than a fallen maple that didn't quite reach the other side of the gorge. Parks and services never actually removed it, even after what happened. They just planted a bunch of other maples and made a beautiful grove around it. Not very tall, of course; it's only been ten years. But they cordoned it off and called it a nature preserve.

If I returned to that exact spot upon which you'd stood on that fallen tree—if I leaped into the same space you did—would it open like a portal? Would my feet land in the same place yours did?

This fantasy reached its mad and cruel culmination on our shared birthday a month ago. I hopped the new fence and walked out there the same way you did ten years ago. Part of me was willing to test my insane theory. Or maybe I was just looking for an excuse. Everything has felt so empty, so devoid of meaning and significance. If I don't suffer from ignorance, I suffer from knowledge.

But the universe, that unfinished universe that Saul said we all take a hand in creating, foiled me. It's almost enough to make one believe in the hand of Fate. A little boy watched me as I swayed on that trunk, trying to muster the courage to jump. He couldn't have been older than six or seven. He must have seen me hop the fence and been so curious that he followed me. And then the boy's father caught up with him.

Obviously, I wasn't going to let a little kid watch a woman fall to her death, no matter how badly I wanted that portal that would take me home. So I stood there paralyzed as his innocent presence cut through all the selfishness and self-deception, and I was forced to stare at the naked fact of what I was actually contemplating.

The father took in everything that was happening at a glance. Mute with grief, I straddled the maple trunk as he fetched his cell phone.

That's why, for the first time in ten years, I'm late with my birthday well wishes, Stacie. This misfit medicine woman has been obliged to shelter beneath the umbrella of meds, talk therapy, and rounds of ECT treatment.

I'd heard that siren call many times before. What made it so difficult to refuse this time? If not for that six-year-old angel...

The point is, that bridge wasn't going to lead me to any portal anyway. I should have known better. The true bridge grows out from our feet, wherever we stand. I'll try not to ever forget that again. And I won't begrudge you for reminding me if I do. But please don't tell me that we don't learn to cherish things without loss, can't know joy without pain, and all that blah f'n blah. I've had more than an earful from the doctors and therapists here.

Not to brag, but I can find the words that lead me to that recognition better than any of them can.

<u>Love</u> is the only word that I need to know right now. My universe has been stripped of its sun and moon. But I love you, Stacie. My love for you is strong enough to bridge the gulf between any worlds.

Happy belated, sweet sis.

Part One

Rupture

Last of the Wakeful Dreamers

Occasionally, Esperidi Mon-Sequana recalled dreams as vivid—and banal—as her conscious hours. Usually, if she could manage it—and the universe typically conspired to make it so—she would try to enact those dreams, retracing her nocturnal steps in her waking life.

Hidden dimensions of the dream's significance would then become apparent, perhaps through a (seemingly) chance encounter with a hummingbird that reminded her of her connection with *Sorsajna*, the fire at the heart of existence. At the very least, it would wrap a numinous afterglow around an otherwise dull morning.

Her last dream before arising this late autumn morning led her to Farsilane's museum and library. Esperidi didn't expect to discover anything significant within its "comprehensive" collection of books and scrolls. After all, they contained no messages the Cordonne did not sanctify, no stories that did not constitute part of the mythos that the City Mothers and Fathers sought to perpetuate.

But that was a moot point. The young Shaini knew that emulating a dream's footsteps could lead her to omens, messages, and unseen nudges the Cordonne was unaware of and could never hope to control. The first of those "footsteps" had brought her here. And so, with twists of sometimes comical and sometimes disconcerting deja-vu, she revisited a cubby filled with parchments inscribed during

Ophia's Sixth Season and positioned herself to mirror her recollected dream body as she grazed her hands across the supple vellum.

Then she was distracted by the rhythmic clip-clap of knobbed wood upon the smooth marble floor. Peering around the corner, she sought its source.

An elderly woman now sat at one oval table, looking uncomfortable in the smooth spoon-shaped seat like it was made for younger bones than hers—a newer generation that disdained her own. She huddled within a thick patchwork cloak of topaz and forest green. A thick, knobbed staff, plumed with peacock feathers, leaned against her chair.

But Esperidi drew back with a stifled hiss as her surroundings jogged a memory that momentarily drove the older woman from her thoughts. *Papa* had been in her dream, too—during the only portion that seemed too fantastical to be an ordinary, sunlit event. They walked along Farsilane's outskirts until they reached the river. Somehow, they parted there, winding up on opposite banks. Esperidi kept shouting to Pallides, but his eyes were fixed and unwavering, much like the obsessions that ruled his waking life.

It didn't occur to the young woman that she had to leave the library—immediately!—until she realized it was too late. Pallides, City Father of the Cordonne, entered at the double doors.

Fortunately, in this material echo of the dream, Esperidi was not the object of his attention. Seizing upon this unexpected brush of serendipity, she darted back to the cubby and stood with her back to the oval chamber. A couple of tall, potted ferns shielded her from *Papa's* primary line of sight.

Esperidi doubted that *Sacred Timbre* could grant anyone invisibility. One couldn't simply exchange a body's fleshy garments for wind or silence. When necessary, though, she could draw from that inner wellspring those notes she required to render herself unobtrusive, easily overlooked. She'd had extensive training in that discipline; so much of her life had taught her the merits of being *unseen*.

She sensed her Papa approaching the older woman; a quick glance revealed his chiseled face and his backbone's stiff righteousness. Pallides had donned a tight leather tunic and skirt of overlapping rawhide leaves, an outfit Farsilane's soldiery favored. His eager strides parted the air like all atmospheres were his natural estate, and he spoke without greeting or preamble.

"If not for the legends that still cling to your name, Shiya-coqui, I would have rejected your request outright. You know what we face in this city—what all of Ophia faces. Frivolity is a luxury no City Father can afford."

"Then it's fortunate for you, Father, that I've come for no frivolous reason," the woman said. Her voice's cool but forceful susurration belied her apparent age. "And maybe you hearken to me now not in homage to a legend but rather because you seek counsel at the behest of a wiser part of you."

"The Sophryne order provided one of the great pillars of our knowledge. No one denies that. We will not fail to—"

"Let's bypass these honoraries, Father Pallides," she said, knocking on the marble three times with her stick for emphasis. "Hear, instead, the urgings of an old woman who has nothing to gain from deceiving you. I know you plan to intercept the Chonnen army at Ardhid with something direr than a host of mercenaries and Shetain steel."

Pallides stiffened as if he'd been struck. "By what means do you *know*? Divination? Spying?" The Lore Masons he'd sent with the host were arrayed like common footsoldiers; surely, no civilian could discern the difference.

"Tut, Tut! Now who's getting us mired in frivolities? We have no time for this! I know well enough what you and your fellow Mothers and Fathers intend. You would utilize *Sacred Timbre* to drown the land bridge as the Chonnens march along its spine.

"For the sake of Ophia—for the sake of Earth entire—you must desist!"

"The decision is not mine alone to make," Pallides said, smoothing over his reaction with practiced poise. "But even if it were, I would not choose otherwise. The Chonnens do not possess our lore and might, but they compensate for those inadequacies with sheer numbers. Ours is the feller hand, regardless. But this way, we can spare countless Ophian lives."

"They could be spared *without* calamity if you led them to the underground refuges: Elmicora," Shiya-coqui said. "Oh, I understand the strategic sense of what you're doing well enough. With one stroke, you could eradicate your enemy with no casualties. Only there *would* be a casualty, Pallides: the integrity of Ophia's balance. You cannot rouse the invisible forces of life on such a scale without dire consequences. Have the storms and upheavals you've already witnessed not taught you this?

"The Cordonne... Well, you seek to *contain* the forces you unleash, which is like trying to contain all the steam from an evaporated lake inside a glass jar. And with the Lore Masons to funnel it, *Sacred Timbre* can turn nature herself into a weapon more devastating than anything we've witnessed, worse than all the Sanjesotas in history.

"Ophia has many agencies to maintain Her balance, but she cares for all Her creatures. If we unleash Her forces, we'll have to contend with the repercussions just as the Chonnens do. Nothing within *Sorsajna* will take sides in a conflict between humans.

"I tell you, there are other ways to meet threats than using *Sacred Timbre* to destroy armies. If you pursue that course, well, that kind of fire burns even the hand of the wielder."

Pallides seemed to hear only the portions of her argument that eroded his sense of rectitude. "Maybe that was true for the old practitioners of *your* order, but we've progressed significantly since those nascent days." He swept a hand to encompass the library shelves. "Perhaps you should delve into the records and make your knowledge contemporary."

"Oh, I doubt that human motivation has changed much since I last researched it, dear Father," Shiya-coqui said. "Know this: To the extent that any beings forget that the world is their mirror, they'll rely increasingly upon tools to manipulate and control that world. *Sacred Timbre* is the ultimate expression of this. It's given you all the keys to life and death. And you think that the Cordonne can arbitrate this, that any City Mother or Father can shoulder that responsibility?

"I certainly don't believe that my old order is beyond reproach. But if there's one thing of which I'm proudest, the Sophrynes—You can scour your histories and verify this." She waved toward the same rows of books he'd indicated a moment before. "We never pitted ourselves *against*. We didn't have enemies. We aimed to embody what we were *for* and did not *oppose*. And that is the message I most want to convey to you now. When you embrace the way of violence, the consequences are never one-sided.

"Rendering Ophia Herself a weapon? Who among us is possibly farsighted enough to guess where the reverberations might end?"

"Too long have we ceded the sunlit lands to the primitives," Pallides argued. "You forget the threats that necessitated the formation of the Cordonne in the first place. You forget Sanjesota and his Horde. We do not have the luxury to choose who our enemies will or won't be. And we are the protectors of the Shaini. *Our* people. We're entrusted with preserving our way of life. To that end, we will bring every available resource to bear."

"Your vulnerability, sir, was never due to a lack of power," Shiya-coqui said. "It is lack of *comprehension* that foils the Cordonne."

"We will bring the storms under control—*and* the invaders—just as we brought this city and the Hives in line," Pallides said. "There is naught in nature that cannot be harnessed, and—as you yourself have admitted—we possess the keys now. We have an advantage that our forefathers and mothers never dreamed of. We've ushered in an era of peace for the first time in Shaini history. Even our children can learn how to manifest their heart's desires.

"My gifts run along administrative rather than prescient lines," he admitted, with a stray note of longing, almost regret. "I would leave the broader vision of Ophia's future to more imaginative minds than mine. But all Shaini, regardless of their position, can be eased now that the Weaving connects nearly all parts of the capital. Soon, it will bind all of Ophia: a ubiquitous, protecting presence."

Esperidi fought down a smile, noticing how Papa swelled with pride, straightening as his mind projected grandeur beyond the library walls. He sought to convey that awe to Shiya-coqui, just as he had often tried to impress it upon his daughter.

And Shiya coqui, hearing him speak with such conviction, said, "Maybe I've mistaken the purpose of my mission today. I'd thought to walk into Farsilane and deliver the Cordonne a message, but perhaps the real lesson here is for me."

Then she braved the Father's probable wrath. "Like most leaders who veered onto destructive paths, Pallides, you do not perceive yourself as evil. I've no doubt of that. Much the opposite. You're driven by *ideals*, just as I am. You pursue your goals, or so you think, in the service of all humanity."

Watching him bristle, she relished a grin. "Perhaps I give you too much credit. I should say, 'for the sake of all *Shaini*-kind.' But my point is this: I suspect that your ambitions originate from good intent."

Pallides seemed to be fighting an urge to spit in the woman's face. "Such *rank* condescension! I should have listened to my first instinct and not bothered with you. I concede that the Sophrynes' legacy must be respected, crone, but your arts are antiquated and redundant." His face twisted with an aquired repugnance towards all things mystical. "What need have we for Wakeful Dreamers? We possess the means to mold the very fabric of reality to the shape of our visions."

Esperidi watched as Papa spun on his heels and strode towards the door. Shiya-coqui's shout halted him before he reached it.

"You need dreams to show you the shape of the precipice you race towards, Father!"

But this appeal only delayed Pallides' departure long enough for the man to shrug as if in response to a ghost of regret.

※※

"Ahh... The sense of something within this moment demanding my attention is more insistent now," Shiya-coqui mused, with the affected air of a stage performer amid a soliloquy. "I chastise myself for not identifying it before. It's the girl lingering in the shadows, trying to be invisible. Pallides' daughter! Am I so distraught and distracted that I forget a half-dozen dreams?"

Then, she called out in a more natural cadence. "All right, girl—he's gone. You can quit hiding in the alcove. You *are* his daughter, aren't you?" she added, implying she already knew the answer.

Emerging almost against her will, Esperidi was heartened—enough to soften her scowl—to see that she and the strange woman were alone in the library now.

"Indeed. I'm the daughter of a City Father," she said. "By which I mean more a father to the city than to me." But it pained her to be so critical, and she couldn't sustain her ire. "Ignore that. I'll not speak ill of a man who's not here to defend himself."

Shiya-coqui smiled at the young woman's spirit. In this age of the Weaving's ever-tightening web, courage was required to speak aloud thus. Did she perhaps trust that her surviving parent's influence could keep her safe where others were not? But no: Her *timbre* implied no sense of protection....

"What is your name, child?"

That question dragged a reply like a bird's beak drags a worm from its muddy refuge. "Esperidi Mon-Sequana."

Once Farsilane became New Ophia's capital, messengers were sent to all the outlying Hives, urging Shaini to forsake their ancestral homes and seek sanctuary in the ruling city. Then came the new edicts: Families would be given new names, divorcing them from their Hives of origin.

But I will not submit to whatever new identity the Cordonne has in mind for me, Esperidi vowed.

Sequana meant more to her heart than any family ties, anyway. Her loyalties were bound to its memory—not the Cordonne's imperial dreams.

"Asperity?" Shiya-coqui quipped, curling an eyebrow.

"Not typically, I like to think," Esperidi said, "unless you get me talking about Papa."

"Oh, you're a sharp one!" The older woman's smile widened in appreciation.

Esperidi probed her with raven eyes. "Sharp enough to guess that you are, indeed, a Sophryne. The one the rhymes mention: the last one left."

This gave Shiya-coqui pause. "What betrayed the fact?"

"You've never been in this city before. That much is obvious. And yet you move and apprehend everything as if testing it against old memories. Your waking eyes soak up the sights as if gauging how closely they resemble what your inner eyes envisioned. And Sophrynes are the only Shaini I've ever heard of or read about who dream so deeply and lucidly."

"You've obviously given the matter a great deal of thought," Shiya-coqui said, again reassessing this interaction. Dream memories were beginning to clarify within her inner mind, exposing its hitherto unseen dimensions.

"They feel like kindred—*my people*," Esperidi said, astonished to hear herself sound so forthright. "I've learned as much as possible, which is not easy, particularly now. But it always seemed to me that if there's any way the shadows of our time could be confronted, the answers lie within the Sophryne lore."

Shiya-coqui waved towards the bookshelves. "You speak of learning. How fared you today? Did you find what you were seeking?"

Esperidi stared back, swaying with ambivalence. Part of her wanted to end this conversation. She could feel bat-winged phantoms beating at its edges.

"I spent most of the last two years here," she said, voice carefully dispassionate. "If I want to read something, I know where to find it."

"You don't sound particularly impressed by the selection."

Almost involuntarily, Esperidi stepped closer, unaware of how her hands began cavorting. "I'm grateful to have read some of these books. Most of the others are self-congratulatory. They laud the achievements of our civilization like it's superior to all that preceded it."

"We've ushered in an era of peace for the first time in recorded history," Shiya-coqui suggested, echoing Pallides' line.

"Please don't patronize me. It's obvious to anyone with eyes and ears that we've unleashed forces that can't be contained or even directed by this *order* of which we are so proud. You spoke the truth, there."

Shiya-coqui, sensing the necessity for a test, swept a hand along one of the library's walls. "I have often visited a storehouse of knowledge wherein all this would scarcely comprise a broom closet."

Esperidi flashed narrow, dubious eyes. "No such place exists. Not on this side of the Partition. Maybe you speak of... oh, but that's just a myth." Yet her certainty teetered. "Isn't it? The Sentient Library?"

"I should *hope* it is a substantial place, as I've spent the better part of my life demarking its boundaries."

Esperidi brightened momentarily but then seemed to recall a protective cynicism. "If I've learned anything from the time I've spent here, there are some questions for which knowledge alone is no answer."

"Oh, I couldn't agree more. But what if it was a *living* record?" Shiya-coqui indicated the books again. "What if you could interact, actually engage in dialogue with the authors of these works? What if you could learn to access whatever knowledge was most pertinent to you in the moment? Would that bring you closer to the answers you sought?"

"Perhaps," Esperidi considered. "But then, I think our challenges now have no precedent. Of what use are the lessons of the past?"

Suddenly, her face darkened as if premonitions eclipsed its inner light.

"Usually, when someone goes into exile voluntarily, like you did, it's a bad sign when they suddenly emerge again."

Shiya-coqui pursed rueful lips. "I wish I could claim to be the exception. You heard me arguing with your father. I do not deliver such warnings blithely. But consider our exchange a mere token protest on my part. I didn't expect to achieve much by speaking with him. Such rectitude is not easily dissuaded."

She rose from the chair and leaned against her staff with a dour grunt. "Leaping to the most salient point, let's say I came here searching for an apprentice—specifically, for *you.*"

Unconsciously, Esperidi made a series of hand signs: "The Cordonne would never allow a Sophryne to teach in this city! I'm amazed they've allowed us to converse like this for as long as we have!"

Shiya-coqui smiled and, employing the same hand language, said, "Do you remember where you learned to sign like that?"

"I don't," Esperidi whispered, astonished by her gulf of ignorance. Indeed, the more she thought about it, the more unattainable the feat seemed. And yet, it was accomplished effortlessly through bodily memory when she paid no attention to the process. "It's as if I learned it in my sleep," she finished partly to herself.

She glanced at her hands like they were trained animals that had performed an unexpected trick.

"What if you're in the midst of another lesson right now?" Shiya-coqui signed.

"What?" Esperidi whipped her head about as if she expected the library's walls to ripple and dissolve, the floor to undulate like tempest waves.

"Remarkable." Shiya-coqui's eyes shone with evident pride. "You skipped past a dozen logical transitions to arrive at the most pertinent question: 'What if this is all a dream?'"

Esperidi, angered by her previous startlement, signed, "That was *not* very courteous! You *knew* how I was going to react!"

"Rather than *knew*, let's say I *hoped*. But was I truly uncourteous, I would glean what I wished to know of you by following your thought stream. You do very little to guard it, you know."

"I wasn't aware there was such a need." Esperidi felt wary now, almost cornered.

"There isn't," Shiya-coqui assured her. "One of the things you will discover about the Sophryne arts is they're difficult to misuse in that way. Usually, when one has acquired the means, one no longer has the desire. Unlike what's contained in these books, Sophryne knowledge changes *you* on the inside."

She clapped her hands together loud enough to create echoes in the alcoves and then let them convey her meaning. "You'll learn much more if you consent to follow me."

"Follow you to where?"

"To my home, of course. You said you've always been curious about the Sophryne art. I will grant you your wish. I will train you." Shiya-coqui glanced about as if sniffing the air. "But we'll need to leave swiftly."

"Leave? What... now? I don't recall saying I intended to go *anywhere* with you!"

"There's no time for this, child. Come now! You're stifled in your life here; you've all but said as much. Your father doesn't support you. I daresay you've few friends. You conceal your true gifts for fear their light will betray you. It doesn't need to be this way."

"I may be frustrated with Papa," Esperidi admitted, "but he *is* my only family." She did not add that, sometimes, his proximity made her uncomfortable for reasons she dared not explore. "As for everyone else here, they are still my people. I can't—"

She stumbled. She'd dreamed of flight so often. But now, as the opportunity opened up, she felt engulfed by a kind of sadness she couldn't account for.

Where does this misplaced sense of loyalty come from?

"This city is doomed, child," Shiya-coqui signed. "I speak with the certainty of Vision. If you really want to liberate your people... I think you have a better chance of convincing them of wonder and possibility on the farther side of the Partition. You have a better chance of convincing them to relinquish the old ways leading them all to destruction. Better *there* than *here*. Here, you can do nothing but wither in desperation."

She emitted a low grumble of repudiation. "I can't imagine how you've endured it here for so long to begin with. Right beneath the Cordonne's nose!"

Esperidi was so absorbed in the content of their exchange that it took her a moment to realize her own astonishment. They'd communicated with hand signs again! How did she understand what all the motions signified?

Shiya-coqui, noting the young woman's startled comprehension, signed: "You've recalled some more of your nightly lessons, I see."

She pursued this vein. "I imagine my first task must be to help you learn to trust yourself again. Oh, it's quite obvious what you've been up to, trying to blend in with every other sleepwalker in the city. Making yourself appear unremarkable, beneath notice, so that your father would pay you no special heed; so he wouldn't try to groom you for *his* path. Nay: I don't criticize, child. Don't scowl at me so! I *participated* in some of those dreams wherein you worked out your methods of secrecy and concealment. Where you chose this hour and place to share your plans with me."

"Plans?" Esperidi visibly paled.

"Oh, yes. To speak after your father met with me and departed with his thoughts in frustrated disarray. To remain in this library while the Cordonne take their mid-day meal in the tower... And such is the moment we meet in waking, communicating in the circumspect way we've long prepared. Do you call this all accidental?"

"I call it *your* planning, not mine."

Shiya-coqui shook her venerable, doleful head. "You see? Much has been lost. If you camouflage your inner knowledge for long enough, it becomes concealed even from yourself.

"Thrice before we've met like this in dreams," she said. She opted not to mention that the recollection was new even for her. "Does some part of you not want to remember? Wherever we were, whatever the circumstances, you beseeched me—forsooth, practically begged me—to teach you. 'Make me a Sophryne!'"

Esperidi gasped—to the extent that such a reaction could be conveyed with her hands. "You must have misunderstood!"

What kind of fey mood could have moved her to ask for such a boon—assuming the woman's assertion was true? She reached for a point of stability and grasped naught but unresponsive silence. She was adrift like a phantom in a city that was foreign to her even after two years of brute toleration—and would likely remain so forever. She felt more estranged from its citizens by the day....

"I was only curious," she muttered in a voice diminished by the weight of these realizations.

Persisting with hand signs, she added: "This is *not* a conversation we want to be witnessed by the Weaving." She already felt agitated enough to send ripples through its web.

Shiya-coqui responded in kind. "For most of your life, I've suspected that you carry the gift. I asked how you've endured this environment, but I *know* where you found solace—on the other side of the Partition."

"Is that the only thing that's important to you in all of this?" Esperidi asked. "Just finding someone to whom you can pass down your knowledge?"

"Child, the Sophryne lore may be the only thing that ensures that *any* of us survive. We can't fight our age's shadows in their surface manifestations. We must confront them in the causal place, wither them at the roots.

"You're appalled by the state to which your people have descended. You abhor the rules that your father has adopted and enforced. But can you not see that he doesn't comprehend any other way? He aches to take a hand in creating a new world as much as you do, but he doesn't possess your *vision*."

"A new world," Esperidi breathed. This provoked an unsettling idea, and she remembered to convey it without speaking aloud. "If what I've read about the Sophryne way is true, and time really is an open ocean on the other side of the Partition, then you must have had some glimpses of our future."

"*Probable* futures," Shiya-coqui clarified.

"All right. But is that something you would share with me?"

"I can do you one better than that. I can help you

glimpse it for yourself. That might even be necessary."

"Necessary for my... training?"

"Aye. It'll likely galvanize your resolve or convince you that this path is not for you."

Esperidi drew breath and realized, in that moment, how resolved she'd already become. "And if I realize I've got nothing to come back to?"

"Then this will help you understand what you've committed yourself to. A fly can't help his brother out of the spider's web if he's caught in it himself. Come, child! You wrestle with a decision that a wiser part of you has already made. I won't make you think like a member of the Cordonne. I haven't appointed myself the custodian of power, believing no one else can be trusted with it. Besides, our universe has a way of humbling Sophrynes who try to curtail another's freedom. Remember what I said about the web. We each spin our own.

"Usher of the Dawn; so my dreams name you. But if you disdain that title, well, you can find your place *here* easily enough. Simply kowtow to all the dictates of the Cordonne. And no one knows them better than you, living under a City Father's roof. But if you did that, you would feel alone as any hermit, though you were surrounded by fifty thousand men and women who aspired to the same goals as you.

"Give old Shiya-coqui this much of a chance. My home is a blind spot in the Weaving's eye—deliberately so! And I've left my horse by the quays. If I've still failed to convince you by the time we reach her, you can turn around and step right back in line, and no one will question you. But if there's anything within you that longs for what I'm offering, this is your one opportunity. It will not stay open much longer.

"I'm offering you a way out of the spider's web."

Shiya-coqui led Esperidi to a grassy court flanked by neat rows of poplars that afforded Farsilane's citizens a pristine view of the city's central pyramid. The monolith's six million tons of granite, latticed with ornate designs in quartz, copper, and gold, culminated in a golden, house-sized apex, its needlepoint sparkling almost five hundred feet above the barren plateau upon which it sat.

The two absorbed its magnitude—in physical immensity and numinous stature—in silence for a while. Then, Shiya-coqui spoke:

"If you allow me to, I will teach you the *internal order* of events. Then, you will find you are not easily deceived by falsehood and charades. One has no masks within the dream environment, and once you've grown acclimated to this, the masks of the waking world are a thin veneer indeed."

Watching the edifice with misting eyes, Esperidi gradually grew aware of how alone she and Shiya-coqui were. The sand at the monument's feet was disturbed by naught but the wind. Behind her, beyond the base of the slope, Farsilane's denizens scurried with furtive backs and downcast eyes. Workers in tough leather garb, traders in tan tunics and turbans, visiting dignitaries and Cordonne functionaries in colorful silken pantaloons and sleeveless shirts and blouses all moved as if they carried secrets to a shadowy tryst.

Shiya-coqui addressed her unspoken thoughts, invoking the pyramid's now-obscure name. "They used to gather at Perzora's feet and feel its subtle chimes. Now, they fear its eye will expose them, that it will condemn them for the uses to which they put it. Beat a dog enough times, and it may become a killer, but you may also find yourself on the receiving end of its fangs.

"You live within a city of contrived illusions, child. But comprehend the internal order I spoke of, and everything becomes clear to your inner eyes. Even questions such as, 'How did our ancestors achieve such a construction as this?' You'll realize that everything in your world on either side of the Partition, waking or dreaming, serves as your mirror. And thus, life is never coercive. You don't look for answers outside yourself because you possess an internal oracle."

Eyes still fixed upon the pyramid, uncluttered by nostalgia for what her ancestors had wrought, Esperidi's voice emerged small and forlorn. "And until I learn to hear this oracle, my place will be just to listen and learn?"

"Why should Sorsajna find my voice less worthy than any other's? The universe can deliver the message you require from myriad mouthpieces," Shiya-coqui allowed. Then, wrenching her eyes from the edifice and noticing her young companion's intimidation, she said, "Close your eyes, child!"

Esperidi was so startled by this sudden demand that she shuddered and glared back at the older woman. But persuasion thrummed within Shiya-coqui's voice. The woman had mentioned coercion. How did this differ? But Esperidi probed deeper and sensed a *timbre* of compassion which, she reasoned, could not be faked. One had to *feel* it to mimic it. Thus reassured—momentarily—she closed out the exterior world behind the veil of her eyelids and did as Shiya-coqui bid.

Once she'd done so, she heard the woman's hypnotic monotone reaching her as if from a distant shore.

"Now... You see yourself in a classroom within Farsilane University. But this is the classroom of your formative years. Lessons that carved your thinking and behavior into predictable furrows were received here. But hearken! You see now that your chair faces the opposite direction. It is turned towards what was once the back of the room. Everything you learn now runs contrary to what you were once taught. Comprehension moves in the opposite direction."

As if responding to unseen and unheard cues, Esperidi opened her eyes and saw the Sophryne woman beaming with satisfaction.

"How quick you are to accept this new orientation!" Shiya-coqui said. "Now, try not to second-guess yourself. Do not try to anticipate what kind of answer you think I'm looking for. Just tell me honestly: What do you see there?"

She waved her peacock-plumed staff towards the towering pyramid.

The answer came to Esperidi at once. "A weapon."

Shiya-coqui nodded as if her head was laden with the sorrows of generations. Swallowing hard through a rising lump, she said, "And yet, how can I reveal its original vision and purpose without rolling back the camouflage of time? This marvel lent the ancient Shaini their sense of identity and cosmic orientation. Such feats require a profound awareness of life's essence. Words are clumsy tools indeed.

"In my grandmother's time, to gaze upon the Hive Heart was to feel one's own heart inflamed. Though it was as magisterial and imposing as you see now, humor and gaiety danced within its light. All who looked upon it felt like they stood at the universe's navel—and that's as close to the truth of our being as any physical construct can ever embody."

The woman's raw emotion pulled at Esperidi more powerfully than any of her previous arguments. Under its spell, the great pyramid suddenly appeared to her like the culmination of all her Papa's mad, imperialistic dreams: a sand castle waiting to be demolished by the waves of Time.

Her response was so visceral that it forced her to

compromise without weighing possible consequences. "All right: You've convinced me—for now. I will give your way a chance."

Construction's *timbre*, subliminally humming throughout Farsilane for the last five years, was only now beginning to subside. The physical composition of the city had begun to mirror its inner stasis. Nearly all living quarters were uniform in size, layout, and beige coloration. Extending at least a mile in every direction from the Hive Heart (the Great Pyramid), streets, houses, and establishments were indistinguishable. And the city's grand design ensured that the shadow of the tall, octagonal tower that housed the Cordonne (to the pyramid's north side) would fall upon every house at some hour or another on any sunlit day.

But Farsilane's grid loosened as Esperidi and Shiya-coqui drew closer to the western quays. It would be some time before the riverside neighborhoods reflected the rigid, efficient spread of the city proper. Esperidi recalled how Papa subconsciously tensed whenever she and he entered this "unsystematic sprawl," as he called it.

Its peculiar architecture and composition reflected its residents' tenuous adherence to the ideals of the Cordonne. Some buildings—closer to shanties than houses—wavered slightly, as structures tended to when transforming *timbres* were at work. The fact that the transformation was incomplete meant that the residents resisted such changes. They raised contrary vibrations.

Such people had been known to simply disappear. Shaini vanished. They were taken without trial or even formal charges. Minor uprisings were swiftly stamped out, leaving no survivors.

"Considering the Cordonne's monstrous hubris," Shiya-coqui commented, as if picking up the trail of Esperidi's thoughts, "I'm surprised your father did not imprison me or merely dismiss me as a crazed old woman. Other Mothers and Fathers might have detained me or driven me forth." She snorted. "But I've grown accustomed to such a pathetic welcome from the civilized world. It was little different in the half-dozen Hives I visited en route to the capital."

Esperidi squinted at her companion and ascertained her words' deeper import. Shiya-coqui's devotion to the Sophryne way had so profoundly shaped her nature that commoners could discern the difference. She was a *stranger*, a disruptor of convention, a breaker of paradigms. Whenever she moved within human-made structures, their foundations shifted uneasily. Even a man like Pallides, insulated by political power, could instinctively sense the threat she represented.

Soon, Farsilane's buildings—even the Cordonne's central spire, which loomed taller than the pyramid—faded behind them. Nitahwe River's scent and sun-speckled gaiety reached Esperidi like a water nymph's chortle. Shiya-coqui led her to a horse tethered near a wide pier. The brown mare had a stripe resembling a streak of whitewash running from forehead to nose. She looked hale and well-fed.

"Stella here will take us into the district by the wharves, where Farsilane's wall is still incomplete," Shiya-coqui remarked.

Then the woman handed Esperidi a stick the length and width of her pointer finger. On closer inspection, it looked like several kinds of dried leaves wrapped and sealed together with brown gum.

"What is this?" Esperidi asked.

"I'll not lie: It is a narcotic. Something to make you

feel like you haven't a care in the world. You go ahead and chew on it slowly, now. It isn't pungent; it tastes like cinnamon and cloves. But it's strong. Don't worry." She retrieved another stick from a pocket stitched in her patchwork cloak. "I'll be joining you."

As Esperidi slowly chewed, trying to settle her misgivings, Shiya-coqui patted her mare. "We'll need only a portion of our wits for the journey. Stella knows how to guide us. You may not have felt it, but there are areas where the Weaving is not as strong, not fully formed and tightened. It's an incomplete mesh. This leaves pathways that those with subtle senses can find. Our girl here will know which way to go, and we'll alert no one with our anticipations of the road ahead. Your father may not even think to look for you until after he gets home."

As they mounted, Esperidi already felt a warm sense of well-being growing within her, like when a pint of mead settles into the belly on a frigid night. But there was no attendant heaviness. A sense of ease and plentitude verging on complacency smoothed all the jarring edges of the horse's gait, making Esperidi feel like she was swept by river currents.

Few Shaini working at the docks—fishers and merchant river crews for whom the Nitahwe and Lanorean goods were life's blood—cast them a glance, though Esperidi could feel their curiosity. If she and Shiya-coqui were there on official business... Well, commoners found trouble when they asked questions. And if they were not, most would silently applaud such an act of defiance even if they entertained little hope for it. And the city's garrison was thinned with so many soldiers marching north to safeguard the mouth of Ardhid in case the Chonnen forces dared a winter crossing. Few were ever spared to patrol the riverside districts where no threat was perceived.

Farsilane's overconfidence is our ally this day, Esperidi thought.

Stella trotted along a packed dirt road concealed by lilies that reached no higher than her knees. Then, at Shiya-coqui's whispered command, she leaped a gap in the stockade wall bordering the river. Plunging chest-high into the Nitahwe's water and foam, she immediately started paddling towards the farther shore, a motion that Esperidi found not unlike her usual trot.

By silent consent, she and Shiya-coqui slid off opposite sides, clutched Stella's flanks, and pumped with their legs to ease their burden upon her. The mare was submerged to her chest now, but she was a strong swimmer, and Esperidi felt how her aversion to the Weaving's compulsion was stronger than her dislike of being wet.

The river spilled into a flat, grassy marsh on the western side, and Stella regained her footing. Shiya-coqui remounted, and as Esperidi followed her example, the mare lifted her head and whinnied.

"Our girl here knows the *timbre* of freedom!" Shiya-coqui shouted.

The banks were gray clay beneath a layer of sand and cushioned with patches of yellow tule grass. Farther south, the water looked deeper; no eddies inhibited the river's course for as far as they could see. Slim clusters of black pine thrived alongside both banks. Here or there, willow or birch luxuriated in the sun, heedless of Cordonnes, Weavings, or Chonnen invaders.

Stella ushered the two Shaini over a creaking, rustic gangway that Farsilane's Mothers and Fathers had obviously taken no hand in constructing. Esperidi was relieved to notice no travelers. Most of Farsilane's traffic came from the bountiful province of Lanore to the north. A few score leagues to the south, one entered the verges of the Kawli

Rainforest. The taciturn folk dwelling beneath that thick canopy, Manitohs and Junsas, had scant reason to love Shaini, particularly now that their domain had fallen under Shetain's jurisdiction. And Jain-Toh, their Shaini governor, sent his messengers to Farsilane via underground routes that few knew about.

The trees grew thickly along the bank, but the wood was not wide. Soon, the companions emerged onto a brown prairie, which, Esperidi knew, became a veritable quagmire when the infrequent but heavy spring and summer rains swelled the river.

As the sedative Shiya-coqui had given her exerted its lulling influence, Esperidi's senses quested beyond their accustomed boundaries, redefining her reality with parameters that seemed divorced from any physical signposts. Even her mind's alliance with her body began to feel like more of a guideline, a suggestion rather than a rock-bed fact. The sensation pushed her thoughts into unfamiliar terrain, provoking questions she'd never considered before.

"Why do we give it that name: *timbre*? For the ancients, was it a kind of music they made?"

"*Sacred Timbre* was based upon our understanding of how matter is the manifestation of *ideas*," Shiya-coqui said. "Leastways, that's how early Sophrynes discovered and explained the concept. Every picture our eyes perceive mirrors a picture painted with the mind."

She groped for a comparison. "In the dreaming dimension, you see the proof at once, the evidence that your thoughts paint your world. It materializes before you. Now, there is what we could call an intermediate stage to this emergence that expresses itself in tones, but as you know, they're not tones you can hear with physical ears. They are *felt*."

Over the hump of a small knoll, a road had been carved wide enough to accommodate a Conestoga. The freshness of the hewn stumps suggested that the route was new. Esperidi recalled her father effusing about opening up trade routes with the southern Oskwai, who could be lured with Shaini gemstones–these were as plentiful as coppers in Farsilane–and, in return, enrich Ophia with their exotic fruits and pelts.

"I'll use the immortal metaphor of the butterfly," Shiya-coqui decided. "The butterfly is a manifestation, as a tree or rock is. Liken it to water in motion and placid water, mountains rising and mountains crumbling.

"The caterpillar would be the *idea* that seeks expression as that wave, placid lake, earthquake or upheaval. *Timbres* are forms that ideas take in a kind of psychic chrysalis. They're transforming; they're being deciphered from their non-physical, mental origins into physical objects and experiences. When I speak of root causes—"

She frowned momentarily. "Do you mind if I change metaphors?"

"Oh, by all means!" Esperidi, descending into an utterly careless mental state thanks to the herbal chew, capped her response with a giggle.

"All right: smelting. Smelting, yes. *Idea* is the ore. Let's say it's gold ore. The manifestation is a gold ring. *Sacred Timbre* is the forge, that inner space wherein we melt down the ore and shape it according to what we envision."

Topping a small rise, they gazed over a hillside scourged by a recent fire whirl: another extreme weather anomaly that the Cordonne tried to pretend—and convince the populace—was commonplace in these parts. Bare, blackened pine trunks thrust upwards like charred pitchforks. However, the sister hill to their left was still lush and green, and a narrow waterway branching from the

Nitahwe River meandered down to a small canoe-shaped valley.

Now Stella pursued the *timbre* of freedom across a sun-dried ocean of grass and sand.

"And who does the shaping?" Esperidi asked. "Who's the blacksmith?"

"Haven't you been listening, child? We are. We plant our seeds there, and then, in the middle space, we tend to the budding crops. Here, we reap our harvest, though we can never *consciously* understand how those seeds grow to flowers."

"You do realize you're on metaphor number three now, right?"

Shiya-coqui grinned in wry appreciation. "And, for the record—not that dreamers ever keep count, as a rule—this is the *fourth* time I've had to give you this lecture. So, yes—tending crops. We do our work in that intermediary space: the garden—also referred to as the cocoon or the hammer and anvil."

Esperidi's mind skipped over the undercurrents there, feeling unready to face their implications. "And how do we accomplish that?" she asked instead.

"Well, the Sophryne... All right: Do you prefer if we call it the kiln, the garden, or the cocoon?"

Esperidi was then visited by a luminous recollection of her childhood in Sequana. "I'm the kind of girl who likes to get her hands in the dirt. Let's stick with the garden."

"Very well. Sophrynes can enter the garden in one of two ways: a waking trance or a dream. Then, they can weed the garden if it hasn't become too overgrown or cultivate it if it isn't already parched and dead. That's the Sophryne art, in essence.

"*Sacred Timbre* specifically pertains to bridging that inner garden and physical life. Therein lies the problem. You see, as a tool, it enabled Shaini to bring forth the forms they desired without understanding or seeing what was happening in the garden. You follow me?

"Only a portion of our being is material. Our bodies are expressions of consciousness, of what we are in spirit. We're the creators of our lives. Nothing happens to us by chance. There's nothing new about this philosophy. But self-knowledge is the key. We must comprehend the forces driving us. We need to know our motivations, beliefs, and fears. They foretell where the currents of our lives are sweeping us. We can use that understanding to alter the flow."

"So now we've moved on to a river," Esperidi muttered, grinning. "Number four."

Shiya-coqui rolled on without hearing her. "And so, each of us directs our lives, regardless of whether we're aware of doing so or not—or whether or not we like the destination. Whenever we blame chieftains, Chonnens, or the Cordonne for our predicaments, we turn a blind eye to our power. We forget to tend the garden."

"And now we're back to number three," Esperidi said with a low, languorous hum. She was set adrift for a while, pondering the implications of concepts that sounded foreign to her ears even as another part of her seemed to absorb them with relish.

As if she'd been waiting for someone to tell her such things her whole life.

Towards evening, Shiya-coqui's eyes brightened as she espied an opening at the foot of a fifty-foot-tall cliff. The bare hill seemed to have been gouged by a giant trowel, leaving a jagged face of gray, topaz, and scarlet.

"I've camped here once before," she remarked, slowing Stella to a trot and steering her onto a sandy scrub pan. "My bones feel a rainstorm coming on, so we'll be grateful for the shelter of this cave tonight, methinks."

Looks more like a burrow than a cave," Esperidi thought, realizing she would have to crawl inside. A rock-chewing worm as big as Stella seemed to have tunneled it.

"Are you sure it's safe?"

Shiya-coqui grinned. "Looks like the perfect place for a bear to curl up, doesn't it? But nay: I've marked the place, and animals avoid it."

She didn't elaborate, and Esperidi was left to speculate about how such a cave could be "marked." She guessed that it was probably by scent, some herbal tincture that had the same effect as an animal's urine, demarking territory.

Crawling in after Shiya-coqui, she found that the oval recess opened up overhead, at least enough for them to sit upright. Esperidi, realizing she'd have to sleep without a pillow on the scree-littered floor, thought of her bed in Farsilane. Her life there may have been devoid of emotional warmth, but it hadn't lacked comfort. The contrast flushed her with the ache of rootlessness, and she suddenly felt that she'd been catapulted into a world that had, thus far, made no space for her.

As if sensing her distress and seeking to ease it in an oblique way, Shiya-coqui approached her as she settled her head against her pack. The older woman handed her a few sheets of paper and a thin stick of charcoal.

"Once we get to my home, I'll give you a proper journal," she said, "but this will do for the next couple of nights. Make it your priority, child. First thing upon arising tomorrow, write down everything you can recall of your dreams."

"Where *is* your home?" Esperidi was startled to realize she hadn't asked this yet. So much had happened in so short a time...

"It's a portion of the Elmicora underworld. Only a handful of Shaini could ever access it, and of those, only I remain. It was a Sophryne refuge. The entrance is near the peak of Mount Veneer. We ought to reach it in a fortnight."

Esperidi absorbed this with a wordless "oohhhh." It at least confirmed Shiya-coqui's stature in her mind, as she knew the portals within Elmicora required a nuanced command of *Sacred Timbre* to open. Being the daughter of a City Father made her privy to such information. Nevertheless, a new dimension of insecurity and doubt opened within her. So *I'm going to be living underground. For how long?*

Records in Farsilane attested that Ophia's crust was honeycombed with tunnel networks, some even passing under the ocean from continent to continent, joining her homeland with Chon and lands farther east.

The Shaini had worked differently during the Season when Elmicora was tunneled. They'd sensed the shifts and movements Ophia leaned towards and then encouraged these, forming their underworld's architecture around the bedrock's "wishes." In the process, they'd discovered that much of the area within Ophia's mantle was already spacious.

Esperidi's ruminations conjured Papa's recent words in the library. "Too long have we ceded the sunlit lands to the primitives." This general sentiment had inspired the Shaini to begin building Hives above ground, beginning in places inaccessible as eagle's eyries and sealed behind doors invisible to those who didn't know what to look for.

Even the inhabitants of the lush province of Lanore, who traded extensively with the Oskwai, lived high in the Conhuera Mountains. Farsilane had been tantamount to an act of aggression, a declaration of dominance. "Here is a Shaini settlement you can assail—if you dare!"

Does anyone's pride justify such risks, Papa?

But Esperidi was asleep before she could imagine his reply.

꒷꒷

Her last dream was so vivid that, even after she opened her eyes, it seemed to superimpose its lambency upon her tiny cave refuge. She was only vaguely aware of the verdant scents of the night's rainfall or of Shiya-coqui cooing affection to her mare. Without once thinking of food or tea, Esperidi set one of the papers her mentor had given her upon a knee, took the charcoal pencil in hand, and began writing.

"The earliest entry point I remember was a sand bar made wet by a creek trickling from a cave mouth. I didn't think to pause, turn around, and see the dream's history unfurl. I was too caught up in wonder, the kind of wonder one seldom knows except in the most rapturous states. There was magic inside that cave, the promise of something miraculous.

"Shiya-coqui stood beside me and seemed to guess my emotion. She smiled. I noticed for the first time that her eyes were the brown of rich loam. They were wide with revelation."

The ache in her back and neck from the night's uncompromising bed was rivaled only by the throb of her saddle-sore inner thighs. But the elation of dream recall swept Esperidi along.

"'Only in dreams will I ever discuss matters of consequence with other Ophians,' Shiya-coqui said. 'The Cordonne has too many ears. Ah, look at you, child! I daresay you've never known the savor of life in a free realm. But we must make do! We're free here, are we not? No Weaving carries our words and deeds to eavesdroppers. Our souls are at liberty to breathe. And so—Focus! Remember where and who you are!'

"'But the bars!' I said. And it's as if saying it made it so because suddenly I could see them: iron bars so thick I could barely get my hands around them. They formed an impenetrable barrier across the cave opening.

"'You see? Even here, where we are free of our bodies, we are conditioned by body consciousness,' my mentor told me. 'We recall our limitations in the physical world and drag those ideas along like shackles. Remember who you are! Remember whose dream this is! Are you to be cowed by what your own mind created?'

"As soon as she said this, I realized I had been wavering and losing self-awareness."

Esperidi paused and allowed herself a moment's satisfaction. However she read the dream's outcome, it felt like a breakthrough for her, a significant step forward.

"When I regained full awareness, I understood the truth of what she told me. The bars were no more real than anything else I could imagine. There could have been a row of ibises or a trail of rocks across that cave mouth.

"So when I reached forward, guided by this knowledge, my hand passed as easily as through a water curtain. I took a step, felt the illusory bars slide through me, and with another step, I was inside.

"I don't know what lay inside that cave because I woke up as soon as I crossed over. But maybe that's the point: I'd seized all the wonder I could hold."

When she read what she'd written down to Shiya-coqui, the old woman merely said, "Sit with it, child, and see what it reveals to you. Our road will give you ample time for such a meditation."

The thirsty ground was already drying as they departed. Stella seemed heartened now by her proximity to home. Growth was sparse and seldom higher than the mare's knees. She needed no trails. With a belly full of morning oats, she dove in and out of gullies and leaped over meadow humps with no muscle-tensing hesitation.

Soon, Esperidi was eyeing the jagged mountain that rose to a bald knob of rock reminiscent of a spiral tower. Mount Veneer was the tallest culmination of the Conhuera Ridgeline, which eventually grazed the head of Ilrhea Province, her homeland.

The following afternoon, they reached the mountain's knees.

A path snaked two-thirds of the way to the naked summit in stairway increments. They were forced to dismount there so Shiya-coqui could guide her mare by hand. The breeze felt poignant, even desolate, pouring from the Conhuera peaks.

Two hours later, they reached the edge of a wall of sagging firs and pine. These trees marked the beginning of an ascent that tolerated no clear paths. The land was preternaturally quiet, the foothills brooding over ancient memories. The two toiled amongst the trees for another hour, Shiya-coqui finding natural routes up and through the silent land. Pines gradually diminished in number and size. Then, the pair rose above the timberline, and the air cooled. They finally stopped atop a rock ledge that commanded a breathtaking view of the land they'd just traversed.

"We should sleep here," Shiya-coqui counseled. "Tomorrow, we negotiate the path to its western face, wherein the entrance lies. At this vantage, we'll know of any pursuit. You go ahead, child. I'll keep the first watch."

※※

At first, Esperidi perceived only flames; then, a molten sphere filled Ophia's heart. Her shell shuddered and split into deep veins; imponderable chasms opened; the sea rushed into every fresh channel; lakes spilled; mountains tumbled over one another...

The whole world was ocean and tempest. Waves stung Esperidi's eyes and filled her mouth with a bite of salt. She witnessed Hives sunk below leagues of murky waters. Fish meandered through their archways and darted when they saw their reflections in Shaini mirrors. Esperidi nearly forgot that she could let this sensation pass through her, that she didn't have to drown.

I'm dreaming!

That was fortunate, for no flesh of the waking world could withstand squalls such as these—or this sea's intimate cruelty and vehemence.

Ophia was sealed over, and the roiling waters left no suggestion that any civilization had ever stood there.

As she was pulled under, Esperidi's sky became twilight aquamarine. Then, she was tossed once more up into the gale. This was the mother of all storms!

My storm, she reminded herself. *I shall claim ownership!*

"Never give your power away to any environment, in waking or in dreaming," Shiya-coqui had cautioned her.
Reminded of her power to direct her dream, Esperidi hovered high above the waves.

A misty raven bore witness to all this beside her. It, too, had sought shelter in the heavens. Esperidi and the ethereal bird hovered together far above the havoc and cacophony.

"Who can say what names will be given to this new land?" the raven mused. "Ophia... She rights herself, seeking balance. Sarpienta, lying coiled in Her heart, turns in his bed."

No more substantial than smoke, it floated like a tadpole in water, occasionally thrashing its wings to stay aloft.

"This is your dream, so you and this seascape are one." Somehow, it tossed approval at her like a beak thrust. "You didn't even need me to help you awaken to the fact."

No actual words were spoken; its communications, like its male *timbre*, were simply known to Esperidi. It never even moved its mouth except to form a slight rictus smile.

"I believe in you. You would not be here if you couldn't master this tempest."

Esperidi clenched her fists, deepening her concentration, and translucent quartz solidified from the howling air, forming an egg-shaped barrier. Its crystal walls shielded them from the gale, and the ensuing silence staggered her.

"Impressive, human!"

The raven sounded proud, yet its expression was dour. "But now you must witness other storms in other places..."

�֍✖

Esperidi awoke with ears ringing, a gulf of unimaginable depth echoing the clamor of a thousand trumpets.

This time, she had no time to write her dream down or even reflect upon it for long. In dawn's scarlet hour, Shiya-coqui alerted her to movement over the grasslands. Squinting eastwards, Esperidi identified at least a score of riders in Farsilane military regalia. They were no farther than a mile from Veneer's feet and pushing their horses hard. Even at that distance, Esperidi sensed Papa's *timbre*.

Pallides rode at the head of the wedge.

Shiya-coqui frowned at the scene below. It was the first time Esperidi had seen her appear truly perplexed.

"He came for you himself," she remarked. "This is startling. I had not anticipated—"

"Why should he *not* come for me himself?" Esperidi asked. "I *am* his daughter!"

Shiya-coqui's glance was piercing, with just a hint of reproach. "Let's not indulge in fantasies about what your life with him has been like for all these years, child. If I were to summarize its character in one word, that word would be *cold*. That may not be the truth of his heart, but it's a fair account of his deeds."

Esperidi's expression was equally sharp. "How long have you been watching me?"

"Long enough to know that you've ached to run away since you moved to Farsilane," Shiya-coqui said. "In the capital, you felt your father's emotional aloofness mirrored by everyone else around you. Only in Sequana did you have friends. And even there, they were few."

She drew closer, and Esperidi tensed, perhaps sensing the coming revelation that would smite her core.

"But you could never bring yourself to run away, could you? Because that would rob you of your chance to *atone*, to keep sacrificing yourself to discharge your essential debt: living on after your mother's death."

Shiya-coqui allowed that to settle, then drew even closer. She tried to invest her voice with compassion, but the anger she felt towards the girl's self-condemnation lent it a steely edge.

"If those bars within your dream, the ones keeping you from the treasure that is your birthright... If they could speak, they'd no doubt say, 'What must I do to justify my existence?'

"Aye, child: I know why you cannot recall your mother's face except from paintings and dreams. She did not survive your birth, and you believe it's your fault."

Fat tears rolled down Esperidi's cheeks. She could scarcely enunciate. "It is not fair that you know... so much!"

"You may be right," Shiya-coqui conceded. "Ophia is in peril, and my fear for Her sometimes makes me rash. But what is even *less* fair—an even greater violation—is the harm you've done yourself trying to expiate for something that was not your doing. To blame an infant for the death of an adult?"

"I have to find a way to make up for what he lost!" the young woman wailed.

Shiya-coqui shook her head. Now, her empathy was plain. "Whichever course you choose, let us hope you never succeed in that ambition. Your father attaining everything he thinks he wants? I doubt any circumstance could hurt him worse."

This, finally, penetrated Esperidi because it so closely echoed what she had long suspected amid her heart's tangle of secrets. Her subservience and practiced acquiescence to a creed and vision not congenial to her diminished her *and* Papa. Her self-sacrifice purchased nothing of value for either of them.

She gazed down at Pallides again as he shouted orders to his men. Ignorant of the trails Shiya-coqui had found, they'd begun to dismount and approach the crag at the mountain's sternum, which was too steep and riddled with loose shale for the animals to negotiate.

Shiya-coqui intertwined her fingers to show how all worlds were bound, one to another. The movement drew Esperidi's attention.

"Ultimately, the power of love and belief drives the

universe. You were right to feel daunted by all this, my dear girl. As a Sophryne, a Wakeful Dreamer—as a *sower* of dreams—you'll be responsible for the welfare of every world. But all beings, if they are honest with themselves, must acknowledge that this is true for them."

She squinted at her apprentice for a moment and then slowly smiled. "I see you have already arrived at one of the most crucial lessons in all of this. To forge these connections requires something more than sensitivity and attunement. You must have *empathy*. And because you cannot know where you will forge your relationships but can only seek and hope, you must hold this empathy for *all* beings."

"Yes, I see that," Esperidi said. "One cannot pursue greed, hate, or dominance with a Sophryne's vision."

"Try to exercise it in the service of such base desires, and you'll reap frustration time and again," Shiya-coqui said. "This is why the Sophrynes have always been marked by their depths of compassion. Who else would ever want to step into this role? This vocation holds out few rewards for the selfish."

"The depths of compassion," Esperidi echoed, and she felt a flutter in the pit of her being, knowing that even now, her thoughts and energy reverberated on the other side of many camouflage Veils...

Once she was seen, it would be too late for choice.

"What would you have me do?" she whispered.

She was so fixated on the approaching soldiers that she didn't notice how Shiya-coqui's eyes sharpened. "What would *you* do?" the woman said. "Where would *your* heart guide you if you heeded *its* voice rather than the voices of doubt and guilt? The voices that say, 'How can I atone for my mother losing her life bringing me into this world?'"

That swung Esperidi about again, but for a moment, she was too outraged and bristling with other, unnamable emotions to speak.

"Aye, child. *That* voice. The voice that lies and tells you that anyone could ever be your victim. You create *your* reality, not your mother's, or your father's, or that of anyone else in Farsilane—or of Ophia entire. If you really want to serve anyone, there's only one way to do it: Fulfill yourself. So I'll ask you again: What do *you* want?"

That penetrated the young woman. Suddenly, she was gripped by the irrational fear that if she could not find a way to speak past the rising lump in her throat, she might never find her voice again.

"Let me give you one last nudge," Shiya-coqui said. "Have you not wondered why it was so easy for us to flee Farsilane?"

This dislodged some of Esperidi's voice. "What do you mean? You had to drug me, and we spoke in signs. You call that easy?"

"We're talking about the *Cordonne*," Shiya-coqui said. "I doubt anyone outside their circle really knows the extent of their powers, but I'll wager your knowledge runs deeper than most. Nay! It would have been a trifling task to catch us, had your father's heart really been in it.

"So this was my great gamble. You see, I believe that, in his heart of hearts, Pallides Mon-Sequana understands that the Order to which he's devoted his life will eventually betray his ideals. He sees that the harm is too steep a price for the slim 'peace and security' they've purchased. I believe he made such a sloppy effort to forbid my presence in the city—and prevent your *leaving* it—because a part of him *wants* the Cordonne to fail."

With a wrench of effort, Esperidi turned and faced the rising shadows that demarked the men's progress. The mouth of darkness yelled her name at times. Other times, it hurled curses at Shiya-coqui, "witch" being the kindest of them. Esperidi focused on the stiff, gesticulating figure at the head of their wedge. Finally, she found a point of stability and conviction on which to stand.

Her teacher's empathetic view, which was so congenial to her heart, swayed her.

"I'm sorry, Papa," she whispered. "You have to serve Ophia in your way. I must now serve it in mine. May we both find our condign paths.

"You can help me escape, even now?" she asked Shiya-coqui.

"I can," the other woman averred. "Is that your wish?"

As if acceding to the weight of the mountain upon which she stood, Esperidi nodded. "Yes."

"Then I will confound their pursuit with the *timbres* of fog."

With that, Shiya-coqui retrieved something Esperidi hadn't noticed before: a grapefruit-sized dried gourd with fire-blackened edges around its stem where its top had been cut. The woman removed this top to reveal a hollow packed with dried herbs. She seemed to coax these contents to life with erratic and barely audible snatches of tune. Suddenly, a finger-wide flame burst from inside. Shiya-coqui, eyes now closed, continued to mutter over this flame as if encouraging a living, responsive being.

Smoke began pouring from the gourd, thickening as it expanded. Something lent it weight, making it sag towards the ground rather than dissipating in the subalpine air.

Now Shiya-coqui cupped a fount of milky froth, which spilled about the two Shaini until Esperidi could no longer see her moccasins. The world relaxed its hold upon her mind. Time grew lethargic, forgetting its strident march toward a nebulous future. Esperidi felt the creeping edges of numbed repose that reminded her of the effect of the herbal chew Shiya-coqui had given her as they fled Farsilane.

The fog poured over the slope below them. Esperidi was so engrossed in this eldritch wonder that she forgot about the approaching men. Her sense of ease deepened into profound insouciance. She wanted to float along the white, spectral fingers to some unknowable destination. The froth filled crevices and ravines, rendering the ground invisible. A veritable cloud descended towards Mount Veneer's knees, though the two women could still peer up at a clear starlit sky.

Esperidi, standing on the fringes of the fog's influence, felt as if she'd strayed into a waking dream. Concepts like surrender and flight lost their meaning. How would it be for the men down there? Yes, she remembered them now. They strode right into the midst of the creeping, milky tendrils. In moments, their cries filled the lower wood. They seemed to call to one another as if a gulf of worlds separated them.

Shiya-coqui's voice grew frenetic as if she argued with latent shadows. Then, as her chant reached its crescendo, her eyes snapped open.

"There! Let them wander like phantoms 'til the moon is high! Hard to follow a mountain trail when you can't recall what a mountain is. Oh, try to pierce this Veil with your foul Weaving! Come, child! Let's not squander the time I've purchased us!"

Swatting a vagrant trail of fog from her face, Esperidi nodded and, taking a few tentative steps, made her first true concession to her life's new calling.

The Silent Revolution

"While we are lucid," Shiya-coqui said, "we must consider how our message might be spread. Now, I'd paint a sign if I wanted to call attention to a *physical* location. Perhaps with gilded lettering. I'd send a crier if I were royalty—not that Ophia has known kings or queens in a hundred generations. Being a plucky revolutionary, I might inscribe a few dozen manifestoes and post them all over Farsilane's streets.

"But here—" She waved to encompass their shared dream environment, amorphous and subtly luminous. "How do we create a sign that will draw other dreamers?"

On this side of the Partition, the woman maintained the image that fleshy eyes would behold in her waking life. She'd entered her twilight years, gray and gnarled, sustained by intransigence that carried *timbres* of ancient roots, the kind that uphold cliff-grown trees seeming to sprout from the very rock.

Her apprentice was a dusky native of Sequana on the cusp of womanhood. She'd veritably wrapped herself in the sky—a blouse of a half-dozen cerulean hues covered all but her face, arms, and bare feet—and she'd bleached some of her dark locks the color of heather or cedar bark. But her adopted form already wavered.

"Esperidi," Shiya-coqui said, "remind me again of our objectives here. Remember: They are threefold."

She said this not to test her student but to give her

something to focus on, tug at her awareness, and hopefully make her more fully manifest.

"Our objectives are threefold," Esperidi echoed, understanding her teacher's intention. "Make visitors aware that they are dreaming. Suggest that they can be just as conscious now as ever they are in waking. And remind them... that this environment reflects their inner life. They are free to shape it however they choose."

Shiya-coqui nodded, pleased to see how the young Shaini's presence became more vivid and vital with each word. "And we understand how crucial such reminders can be, don't we?" She squeezed Esperidi's shoulder reassuringly. "I've needed to remind *myself* that I was dreaming, again and again, during excursions such as these. Had I not done so, I might have drifted out of lucidity before even *beginning* my work."

The essential etchings of this dream city were already established when she'd first discovered the place. Shiya-coqui's chief contribution, thus far, was an internal meeting space and repository she called *The Sentient Library*.

"In bringing you here," she said, "I repeat a favor once done for me by my teacher. Lamann was demanding but kind. He rarely coaxed or encouraged me on this side of the Partition. He left me free to weave whatever dramas I wished. And so, before long—moments are difficult to count in such a realm as this, are they not?—but before long, inspiration seized me. I focused on some of my most cherished visions until they crystallized. These embodied the *timbres* of freedom, community, and love for all humankind. Shaini, Junsa, Sendhi, Manitoh... all peoples are welcome here."

Because they were imbued with the light of consciousness, the Library's contours had grown lambent and warm. Or they would be perceived thus by other awakened dreamers. They were real to *her*, at any rate. And dear. Obviously, what she'd woven—and what she and her apprentice intended to create now—would be invisible to physical eyes. But Shiya-coqui hoped it might shine like a beacon upon this, the Partition's far shore, drawing the curious.

As if her intentions clarified the Sentient Library from an ethereal backdrop, details of the dream environment sharpened. A vast space opened above the two Shaini. They stood in an anteroom from which three floors were visible. A spiral stairway of flesh-hued adobe was suspended in midair in the chamber's center. Most of the spacious levels were filled with shelves housing books—or what the rational mind *interpreted* as books. The living records contained therein were beyond counting.

Esperidi's view of the Library differed slightly from her teacher's. She perceived the same immaculately smooth, glass-polished marble floors, but they were littered with debris. This discrepancy confused her at first until she realized what this place reminded her of: the Farsilane library—a mere shadow of this one, she reflected—where she had first met her teacher.

Yes: The present disarray nudged her consciousness with playful contrast. "Your eagerness for knowledge," it seemed to proclaim, "is one of the few *uncluttered* aspects of your life."

"That was the impetus behind this whole dream city," she whispered as the deeper implications of her teacher's words percolated. "It was always intended as a shrine to our ideals. Here, we give our curiosity free rein without fear of waking repercussions."

Shiya-coqui motioned towards the staircase. "You sound like you're ready. Indeed, you sound more focused than ever I've heard you. Shall we go prepare some messages for our intended visitors, then?"

Esperidi, still daunted by the immensity surrounding her, merely nodded. But she relaxed once they reached the third floor. It was quieter here. Windows encircled the vast oval space, making it brighter than the lower levels, even though—she reminded herself—this was dream light emanating from a dream sun.

For a moment, Esperidi pondered which version of the sun might be more potent. Then she reined herself in, recalling how such questions could whisk her away into other dramas in other dreams.

Occasionally, Shainis meandered into the space, most unaware that they dreamed.

"Few ever venture up here," Shiya-coqui said, "and we seek to remedy that. The more obscure books and scrolls are housed along these walls. You realize I'm speaking figuratively, of course. You could say that this room was designed with... *specialized* studies in mind."

Following her teacher's gaze, Esperidi was drawn to where a heavy, open tome glowed white upon a mahogany dais, a feather quill quivering a few inches above its parchment.

"Is that your journal?" she asked.

"*Our* journal," Shiya-coqui said, eyes narrowing like an eagle espying prey. Esperidi realized this sharp regard was another reminder for her to maintain lucidity.

"Remember what I told you," the older woman went on. "Fully manifesting the Sentient Library requires cooperation. I was only able to concentrate for long enough to sketch its contours. But I have to believe that other visionary architects will come."

Her desire swept her to the space before the dais. There, she took glowing quill in hand, bent towards the tome, and inscribed the opening of the "invitation" she and Esperidi had composed together.

"My fellow Wakeful Dreamers! At long last, we may speak freely! With heart entire, I encourage you to join us in forsaking the Cordonne and uncovering the birthright they have denied us. Yes, I expect you to rejoice at the prospect! I assure you, Shiya-coqui and Esperidi Mon-Sequana are friends of freedom and friends of yours."

Surrounded by rainbow luminosity in a kaleidoscopic display, it was difficult, at first, to even recall the shadow whose name she'd invoked. But at last, recollections of the Cordonne passed through the chamber like a winter wind from the Sendhi steppes, carrying cheer and effervescence away to polar oblivion.

Shiya-coqui felt the Weaving's web, watching every sunlit movement, listening to every word, trembling to every emotion, and recording all this within the Cordonne's mute citadel as if in cynical mockery of this inwardly spacious Library and its trove of knowledge.

Weaving? she thought. *More like a tar pit!* The memory made her heart lurch towards all those awake in Ophia and sinking in its quagmire. She ached for her lost community, and for a while, her empathy had to win past spasms of nausea.

"While you are awake, you can only make the oppression of your sunlit days bearable by anticipating the coming night's freedom," she wrote. "Out of necessity, you've become nocturnal creatures. You come most alive while you sleep. So, old orientations reverse themselves. The day is now 'dead time': somnambulant existence."

Purged of some of her revulsion and satisfied with the beginning she'd made, she handed Esperidi the quill. The younger woman felt less certain of her convictions, and at first, she inscribed words upon the dream parchment more to placate her teacher than to satisfy her own inner need.

"This is the key to escaping our bondage beneath the Cordonne. We must seek to awaken every night within our dreams and fly beyond the Weaving's strands. Here, cripples may cast off their crutches. Runners may elude the hunting dogs."

Then Esperidi paused to freshen her attention. The dream's enchantment had lulled her towards forgetfulness, and she forced herself to recall that her waking self lived on the margins of a civilization threatened from without and rotting from within. Tonight, she had surpassed everything she'd accomplished during the two months of her apprenticeship. She'd prolonged and intensified her lucid state. She didn't want to drift into other dreams without realizing it and be left to bemoan her failure when she awoke.

Lamenting the culture that had cradled her moored her to the pier of her present intent. But she struggled to sustain her concentration. Tome and dais wavered, though neither dissolved like physical objects. Rather, they seemed to pull apart from the dream's continuity, becoming disjointed moments. After countless nights spent practicing lucidity, Esperidi was adept at recognizing the signs of a dream's dissolution. Fearful she might lose her grip entirely, she returned the quill to Shiya-coqui.

The woman accepted it, and the Sentient Library's contours immediately sharpened.

"If you're reading this," Shiya-coqui wrote, "you've already acclimated to self-aware dreaming. I'll assume you're here because, like us, you yearn to escape tyranny. To vanquish it, if possible. Only here can we plot rebellion without fear of reprisal.

"So come! We shall explore new paths to freedom even as our bodies turn in our beds. We'll plan our emancipation. Remember the feeling signature of this

Library, its peculiar <u>timbre</u>, and it will forge an inner pathway for you to return by."

This advice echoed her strategy over the years to track down specific individuals within the infinite dream streams.

"Becoming conscious here, we realize that our awareness is not trapped within our bodies nor bound by our physical senses. We are not hounded by mortality. We are eternal. And thus, realizing that, our fears dissolve within this environment—so long as we remain aware of where we are.

"Now, you may think, 'This is all easy for old Shiya-coqui to say. She was presumed dead for years, and the Weaving is unaware of her.' You may consider me too old to care, and indeed, I work towards a future that, win or lose, will not be mine. But my freedom can be yours. My example can liberate those still in bondage. And, as I said at the onset, we will always be free <u>here</u>."

The Library lurched like a storm-tossed ship before Esperidi's eyes,. Was she outgrowing the chamber, or was the universe shrinking until it could fit entirely within her mind? She seemed to become an immensity that could not be translated into a finite form.

Nevertheless, she was still self-aware enough to realize what was happening. Her training made such deductions almost instinctive. She'd been derailed by an offhand remark that Shiya-coqui had scribbled into the tome.

A *future that will not be mine.*

For the first time, the reality slipped past Esperidi's defenses.

I *won't always have my teacher!*

Shiya-coqui continued to write, but Esperidi could no longer perceive the words on the page. Instead, she heard them emanating from a disembodied voice, sometimes feeling them intimately enough to mistake them for her own thoughts.

How the message is conveyed is not important, she reminded herself as if repeating a mantra. *We merely have to remain conscious of our intent.*

"I know you all live in glass houses, transparent and vulnerable." Shiya-coqui wrote as if she now authored the entire dream, not just a journal page. "Today, you turn within the Cordonne's monstrous Weaving as within a nest of flames, and you ache for liberation. Your soul cannot breathe. You step in time to a beat that moves contrary to your heart. Speaking your mind is perilous.

"It's strange, in a way," the woman speculated, turning towards Esperidi's now diaphanous form and tapping the thick volume. "We dreamers revere this Sentient Library so much, and yet the essence of Sophryne lore cannot be reached through anything one can read in a book."

It was this casual, human moment that finally catapulted Esperidi from the Library. *I won't always have my teacher,* she repeated. *I'll have to find my own wings.* And the environment she shared with Shiya-coqui was effaced by a new dream's dawning.

She stood upon a lip of rock hovering some fifty feet above the crash and foam of waves. She watched the seagulls, envying their spiraling freedom. And Esperidi trembled on the edges of vertigo when she thought about her intention. Her mind swarmed with images of shattering on the rocks. But assuredly, despite these fears, she'd accomplish it today.

I had to say, 'I'll have to find my own wings,' didn't I? Must I always treat my analogies so literally?

Grinning, she made three long strides and then dove

for transcendence.

It wasn't going to work. Esperidi couldn't shake her Ophia-bound belief in gravity. It had her; it pulled her precipitously towards a splattered end.

Within another heartbeat, however, Esperidi *blinked* back to the stone tongue.

Shiya-coqui's core teaching. The key, always, was to remember that this was *her* dream.

Behind her lay the childhood home she'd shared with some five thousand other Shaini: Sequana Hive, honeycombed into a tall cliff whose feet met the Rudowine Ocean. The waters were dark and turbulent, ceaselessly pounding against the Shaini fastness. Some of the Hive's openings faced the rocky lip Esperidi stood upon.

The warmth of childhood memories invigorated her. Yes, she had it now. Her strides were surer; her leap was exultant.

She soared.

The dreams she recalled upon waking were already interpretations. Her morning mind, confronting visions too expansive for its frames of reference, deciphered them according to its storehouse of symbols. But what Esperidi remembered from her night's adventures heartened her. Shiya-coqui's Silent Revolution had been inaugurated. And her apprentice had found her wings.

Shiya-coqui's home was scarcely more decorated than an Oskwai hut. Hanging hides partitioned the single-floor space into three rooms—she'd painted them orange, blue, and green—decorated with two-tone tapestries depicting remote, lofty mountains and deep-plunging waterfalls.

The tunnels fanning out from this nerve center were thousands of years old and, taken together, could wrap around Ophia several times. One hidden approach led directly into an immense underground route that ran from Lanore nearly to Esperidi's old home of Sequana—almost two hundred leagues.

"Most of the branching tunnels and the living quarters connected to them were made much later," Shiya-coqui had said. "Work on them proceeded in earnest after the threat of Sanjesota and his Manitoh Horde. That's why they appear rougher, not as glassy as the originals. Our understanding of *Sacred Timbre* had grown decadent by then."

Upon this morning, the two Shaini descended a staircase into Ophia's deeper bowels. Occasionally, a tunnel would become so narrow that they had to get down on their hands and knees. The passages converged at sharp angles. They were alternately narrow and wide. The walls were immaculately smooth. The convex ceilings appeared, at times, as if painted with a slightly incandescent, verdigris glaze.

Shiya-coqui brought Esperidi into a polished cavern lit by a single glow-sphere. Petroglyphs adorned nearly every surface in vibrant whites, reds, and blacks, every symbol suggesting translation from one mode of existence to another. Though she couldn't translate the inscriptions, Esperidi intuited that they were concerned with entrance—initiation—passage.

Her momentary awe reminded her of the scale of her fragile, mortal existence. Granted, she huddled within a network of caves largely denied the sunlight—except on rare occasions when venturing outside could be risked. But the place was home. The loving *timbres* that had smoothed its granite floors, bulging walls, and domed ceilings hummed welcome and reassurance. "You belong here," they whispered. "You are held in the arms of Sorsajna."

And yet—while she ate, slept, and studied—outside these walls, a nightmare played out across the land of Ophia. Esperidi's heart wailed for her brothers and sisters still in bondage. At times, Ophia's bruised, caged heart spread before her percipience like a gaping wound. Everyone who'd once been close to Esperidi in her former life, her pre-apprenticeship days, enacted their daily charades, pretending to be productive members of the new Shaini regime while awaiting the opportunity to seek better answers when the walls of sleep closed over them. All Shaini—particularly those living within the capital city of Farsilane, the heart of the spider's web—stood naked before the eyes of the Cordonne.

Except when they dreamed.

Esperidi voiced the question at the heart of this perplexing labyrinth. "How did our lore become so corrupted?"

Shiya-coqui's mouth thinned with distaste. "The Cordonne has made it nigh impossible for anyone of your generation to learn Shaini history. But you know that *Sacred Timbre*, upon which our civilization was built, once allowed us to harness the forces of life—Sorsajna—and create undreamed-of luxuries and freedoms. No discovery impacted the very pillars of our society more.

"It's ironic, isn't it, that the keys to our greatest freedom should lead to the severest repression we've suffered in our history?"

"Yes, but *how?*" Esperidi persisted.

Shiya-coqui smiled in appreciation of the young woman's spunk. "All physical phenomena, as I've taught you, are manifestations of consciousness. The art of *Sacred Timbre* illustrates how the secrets of creation are intertwined with destruction.

"Very well: the short answer. We'd unlocked nature's secrets—ostensibly—but had not mastered *ourselves*. We learned to manipulate the physical world but forgot the inner processes that make *Sacred Timbre* possible. A void opened, and the Cordonne stepped into that breach.

"The first Mothers and Fathers probably had noble aspirations," she considered. "Many were even Sophrynes. They embodied the inner knowledge that most Shaini had lost touch with. But as time went on, their descendants corrupted it. Or else they grew ignorant of its true nature. The two go hand-in-hand, really. This we have all witnessed."

Esperidi assimilated this in silence. Her father, Pallides Mon-Sequana, was a member of the Cordonne and high in their councils.

"But we could have found another answer," Shiya-coqui said as if arguing with a ghostly, dissenting voice. "The Weaving embodies the *grasping* tendencies of those who have forgotten how to dream. And being ignorant of dreams, they can't understand real power, only control."

She clapped her hands suddenly. "But why bemoan these circumstances, child, when we can seek solutions? I trust you've got some strong bodily memory of the Sentient Library's *timbre* now?"

"I do," Esperidi assured her.

"Good! Then you must return there as often as possible. Every night, at least once. Be alert to any who may be drawn to the message we left there. And your presence will invigorate its strength and luminosity. Liken this to nursing a cookfire."

Esperidi was unresponsive at first. Her mind roiled like a barely controlled storm. She'd only been learning from Shiya-coqui for two months, but already, she'd begun to reassess her motivation for committing to this path. The terror of the Cordonne, the stifled atmosphere of Farsilane, the mute desperation of her life with Papa, laden with the weight of a thousand things unsaid... all these factors no longer seemed to account for the ceaseless aching in her breast. Something else drove her, something she could not name and doubted that even her teacher could identify for her.

It was as if some essential part of her, which she'd long suspected and mourned the loss of, lay in wait on the other side of the Partition, beckoning. She was homesick for a place she'd never seen, one never even alluded to in all the stories within Farsilane's library.

It was not an "answer" to her life's riddle. Rather, it was a ray of light, an orb of lambent promise, without which her soul could never fully flower. It sparkled on the margins of every dream. It made her ache like the bereft mother of an unborn promise.

She recalled the *timbres* of finality with which Shiya-coqui so often spoke about her old life. Esperidi's mentor would not always be here to help her find that luminescent trail nor lend her the courage to follow it. What if she wound up with no real road, only this truncated longing that she was obliged to drag through her hours and days like a phantom limb?

If she was the heir to two worlds, if this really was her birthright, as Shiya-coqui insisted, why did she feel at home in neither?

"This game is between you and your own mind." A woman in a recent dream had said that: a woman who seemed familiar, as if from accumulated lifetimes beyond counting.

And she looked like me!

It was often that way in dreams. No one felt like a stranger. History seemed to grow up from every conversation, casting roots back into the shadows of antiquity. So, this sense of homesick, rootless wandering was the product of her imagination? If so, what new picture could she paint to remedy it?

Esperidi understood better now why many of the Oskwai and even so many Shaini believed in deities. It seemed easier to follow the dictates of even a demanding god than to try to catch the vagrant trails of one's own heart. Easier to blame that god than to accept that the obstacle was one's own fundamental inability to choose whether to leap or falter, to embrace one road knowing that it entailed turning a blind back to all others. Easier to flagellate one's self before an effigy than embrace the risk that one might never recover what was lost—and forever ache for it.

Simpler, it seemed, and yet ultimately impossible. Esperidi's heart could not tolerate such trite resolutions. How could she believe in remote and implacable overlords of creation when she had so often witnessed her own thoughts giving birth to wonders?

Shiya-coqui can't give me what I'm seeking, she repeated. She felt utterly unprepared for the task opening like a maw of darkness before her.

"But... isn't this all intrusive? Like eavesdropping?" She was groping for a tangent to distract herself. "Is that what you do when you enter into someone's dream? You invade the landscape of their inner mind and then make adjustments where you see fit?"

Shiya-coqui apparently found the very notion repugnant. "That kind of coercion is unthinkable. Don't mimic your father, now! Something like that is not even possible to begin with. Every being's inner terrain is inviolable. No meetings occur except by consent."

She waved to encompass the spread of the unseen, sun-kissed meadows beyond the cavern walls and untold tons of gut rock. "I do not own this land. All Ophia's beings share it. If, however, you came here as a stranger and I had lived here my whole life, then surely I would know things about the lay of the land that might benefit you.

"That's the true spirit of all my dream interactions."

Heartened by this exchange, despite a few questions it left unresolved, Esperidi threw herself into the experiential side of her training. She searched for new allies during her twilight hours, hoping to bring them to lucidity. Some dreamers, she discovered, required only a gentle nudge. Others needed a cathartic shock. Some she could cajole and entice. Her artistry, as Shiya-coqui had taught her, involved discerning which approach a particular personality responded best to.

She lost track of how long it took her to forge relationships with those she met on the other side. Any estimate would be misleading anyway because her Sophryne work demanded manipulations of time as much as space. Esperidi felt that the Sentient Library dominated her attention for weeks. On the other hand, it might only have been a space of heartbeats. After all, she'd experienced epical dreams within a single strike of a clock's minute hand.

It was best not to ponder it all too much. Connections had been achieved, and seeds were planted. Esperidi was certain of that much. Trying to translate her progress into linear terms would be gratuitous and wasteful on both sides of the Partition.

The first of the Library's visitors to draw her attention was a man perhaps a decade older than her. In his surreptitious waking life, Sanyori Mon-Sequestra was a playwright and actor within Farsilane City. He occasionally traveled with his circus to outlying territories. Indeed, he'd been known to perform even for Oskwai. And the majority of productions hosted by Farsilane's Ambrosine had been composed by him.

His *timbre* felt flamboyant to Esperidi's dream senses. That was not surprising, considering his occupation. Even his simplest movements expressed lithe ostentation. He flowed like an athlete who adored the attention of a coliseum. Tucked behind his sharp ears and scarlet headscarf, his crow-black hair hung to his shoulders. His sleeveless, varicolored tunic and hose clung to his wiry physique.

Esperidi flushed when she realized how long she'd allowed her gaze to linger.

"You'd better leave that one to me," Shiya-coqui said, with a coy smile, when Esperidi related the incident to her. "Sounds like he's honey on the eyes, and that's bound to distract you."

"But there must be some reason why Vision pointed him out to me," Esperidi said.

"Oh, doubtless so!" Shiya-coqui said. "Consider: We're embarked upon a most clandestine quest. Now, think of the tools of secrecy that theater has at its disposal: allusion, symbolism, and idioms only the initiated can hope to understand. It's a secret language, much like the hand signs we developed to communicate beneath the Cordonne's nose.

"A theater production is akin to dreams in that respect," she concluded.

Esperidi tried to absorb all this. Modern-day Shaini might not personify the forces of life with images of deities like the ancients had, but those forces still found expression upon the Ambrosine stage. The amphitheater was still Farsilane's philosophical and spiritual center. The Cordonne dared not dismantle it—yet. And so the City Mothers and Fathers carefully monitored the performances it hosted.

Shiya-coqui, sensing the general trend of her apprentice's thoughts, said, "Yes! Consider the possibilities:

our dream-time communications translated through the medium of drama. This Sanyori is already practiced in crafting symbols and vernacular that won't run afoul of the Weaving."

"He's developed *subtler* ways to make his points, too," Esperidi drawled, recalling how the man had moved. "He conveys his intent with pantomime—gestures and dances. Some of the other cast members passed in and out of the Library, too. Something draws them to congregate there. They've learned to recognize—"

"Inner signposts," Shiya-coqui said.

"Yes! There are clues strewn throughout Sanyori's plays. I think he's been acquainted with the place since before you even brought me there."

"I'm certain of it," Shiya-coqui said. "But I wanted to wait and see if you'd discover him for yourself. Since your longings run along similar courses, it seemed probable that your dream paths might intersect."

Esperidi's eyes widened at the implications. "But that signifies more than just chance encounters in dreams! If he writes such things into his plays, allusions that can be heard by waking ears, then some part of him must remember what he has witnessed and read within the Sentient Library!"

Shiya-coqui smiled. "All of us, you see, compose our real-life dramas while we sleep. So take heart from your first success! See if you can become acquainted with other members of his troupe. See who else might be receptive."

Esperidi drew a slow breath, marshaling her courage for this new directive. But Sanyori's image tugged at a memory of another equally vivid dream from months earlier: Ophia baptized in fire and water, while a misty raven with eyes like the wells of time bore witness beside her.

"Why do you leave it up to me to seek the others?" she asked, suddenly suspicious. "You want me to understand that the key to all this is realizing that I'm moving within my own self-woven dream. But any misstep could cost those people their freedom. Why take such a risk?"

Shiya-coqui frowned and kept her head averted. "If you know enough to ask that question, child, then you don't really require an answer, do you? That's earned knowledge. I couldn't have given it to you. You wouldn't have possessed the ears to hear it."

"And now my *earned knowledge* tells me that Ophia races towards the precipice," Esperidi said, "and that you do not believe you will survive what is coming!"

Shiya-coqui appeared reluctant but steeled as if a trial had come upon her sooner than she expected. "We can discuss all that another time, Esperidi," she said. "Why not rejoice in your breakthrough? Celebrate it. There's time enough to mourn when loss has become a reality."

But Esperidi would not be derailed. "You said you believed the Sophryne Way was the only thing that could ensure our survival. And yet you don't believe that you, the last master of the art, will survive to see the new dawn. And so you would invest all of your hopes in me!"

Finally, Shiya-coqui faced her, gray eyes roiling like the presage of a storm. "*None* of this is what I would have chosen. Do you remember our garden analogy? I was obliged to sift through and try to find any seeds that might take root. Well, I found *one*."

"One," Esperidi echoed, feeling like she was now obliged to find some way to transform herself into a full-grown sycamore overnight. She recognized what she was doing now and saw and understood its futility.

She wanted Shiya-coqui to transform into a nurturing mother and offer comforting words that the woman did not possess.

Living on the verges of the coming shadow, what

assurances did *anyone* have?

꽃꽃

Esperidi returned to the Sentient Library over several consecutive nights until she finally managed to engage another member of Sanyori's theater troupe. Rona Mon-Ilrhea was the most vocal and tenacious of the "dream insurgents," as Esperidi and Shiya-coqui had taken to calling those who were learning to awaken. Esperidi recognized Rona, having encountered the young woman casually in her homeland Hive.

Sanyori preferred composing dramas to enacting them. He was reluctant to take an active hand in any kind of mass exodus from Farsilane. He was uncomfortable taking responsibility for other Shaini and feared leading them down a path to ruin. Shiya-coqui had her work cut out with him.

Rona, in contrast, was brash and outspoken, and she nurtured a fiery, personal vendetta against the Cordonne. Her husband, Caius, had been imprisoned by the ruling elite for being "unstable" and "delusional" and had died in his cell after nearly a dozen years of serving an unjust sentence.

Rona's hatred of the Cordonne ran deep, and Esperidi marveled that the Weaving had never detected it. If not for the love of Caius, she might already have taken an irretrievable step across the lines. But what Rona could not do for her own sake—subsume her rage and bitterness beneath an outward veneer of peace—she could do for her husband's memory.

Rona often played the lead heroine in Sanyori's plays, wearing a tan shawl with tapered fringe over a calfskin dress that accentuated her olive skin and amber almond eyes. Playacting was such an all-consuming passion in her waking life that she often indulged in it even while she slept.

Indeed, Esperidi first encountered the woman as she was delivering a soliloquy within the Sentient Library. Something about the performance tugged at her, and her curiosity transformed into wonderment when she finally identified what it was. This character Rona portrayed—the low staccato; the way emotion propelled her at times to spread her arms in a tall V; the peculiar lilt of certain phrases; the gray owl feathers that draped from her shawl; even the way her mouth curled around certain words—these traits powerfully evoked her mentor's presence.

A young Shiya-coqui?

As she struggled to follow the story Rona enacted, Esperidi's intuition seemed to be confirmed. The narrative corroborated a cruel tale that Shiya-coqui had told of her childhood, witnessing the massacre of thousands of Manitohs who'd fought under Sanjesota the Scourge.

Silane Hive had feigned defeat, retreating into the catacombs beneath the mountain. They'd waited until the main part of Sanjesota's Horde was inside the walls. Then, they'd employed *Sacred Timbre*, sealing the doors and awakening latent fires within the gut rock. Thousands of Manitohs had slowly baked like clay in a kiln.

Esperidi shivered. She'd read about that conflict in Farsilane's library. It was a historical account that the Cordonne permitted, as it ostensibly "explained" the harsh measures they'd enacted for peace ever since that day.

Assuming Shaini did not precipitate the conflict, she thought, *by trying to dictate how the Manitohs should live and think!*

She had, by now, grown deeply distrustful of the "official histories."

"We numbered some twenty-thousand," Rona intoned. "Had every one of us been warriors, the Manitoh host would still have overwhelmed us. We will gather and reassemble the pieces of our lives tomorrow, but we will never be the same. Our face as a people will be altered, likely beyond recognition."

The young actress flourished and swayed like a dancing flame.

"If we were ever possessed of innocence, if there is such a thing, it is lost to us now.

"Sometimes, I wonder whether survival is worth what we've lost. Yes, we have sent a message to every potential enemy, but we have also delivered a message to ourselves: that we can utterly destroy those who oppose us.

"What happens if *we* become the aggressors and still possess such powers? Will we trample everyone beneath our wheels? Or will someone develop a direr weapon to meet the threat *we* represent?"

She seemed to perceive herself surrounded by a throng of spectators, responding to their collective *timbre* of hushed expectation.

"Whenever I think of that day and night of carnage, it steels my resolve to find the inner solutions that eluded us then. Riddles in the flesh: such are the lives of humankind, riddles that must discover their own answers by living them.

"If *Sacred Timbre* has enabled us to understand the unseen energies beneath events, then may it teach us how to neuter violence before it erupts! But now, the light in our skies is dimmer, even as we are diminished. The largest mass grave in the land has taken the place of our home, and there is no returning."

Rona was nearly lucid, and with a stream of reminders and prompts, Esperidi finally made her aware of the true nature of her situation.

Grinning when she finally caught the woman's attention, Esperidi said, "I see that the upcoming play weighs on your mind."

Rona's enthusiasm for the drama swept her along. "It's been approved for several performances!" She addressed Esperidi like an intimate friend. "We're calling it Gossamer Veils because one must look behind the curtain to capture its real essence and meaning."

"And let me guess," Esperidi said, with the most disarming smile she could adorn upon her dream face. "Behind that curtain is precisely where Sanyori wants to lead his audience."

"The audience in spirit, the troupe in fact," Rona clarified. But then her voice grew distant; already, her mind pursued a separate thread. "I have to wonder... Even if we attain freedom, how long will it take us to learn to express our souls once again? They have been caged for so long."

"Tell me more about this play," Esperidi urged her, groping for anything that might corral the fragments of Rona's attention.

"Eighteen of us are involved in the production." Rona's image, translucent just a moment before, solidified as she spoke. "Most are receptive to what I have told them about this place. Some have even found their way here and read the words of your teacher and yourself. They are all artists, so of course, they are averse to the kind of conformity the Cordonne imposes."

But here, Rona's dream whimsy took a turn that Esperidi was unprepared for. "I admire your courage," the woman said, "defying your father in this way." Rona had known Pallides from his days in Sequana prior to becoming a member of Farsilane's Cordonne. "It requires a warrior's heart to sever one's past as you have done."

Esperidi tried to quell or at least camouflage her inward tremors, but her version of the Library trembled and convulsed. She now understood why Rona was drawn to her. She could finally piece together the fragments of half-recalled dreams that made the young woman so familiar. But she thought some of Rona's perceptions were misguided.

I haven't severed anything, she thought. *I'm still encumbered by the weight of history.*

But Rona seemed to intuit the source of her distress. "This place would challenge your father's assumptions," she said, in a tone that aspired to lighten the mood and set her younger companion at ease. "He'd have to grope for a new guiding philosophy, as we have done. Let him savor the taste of wonder here! Even members of the Cordonne have the potential to awaken. Do you not think so?"

But then she was distracted by a new arrival and didn't wait for a reply.

A young man in tight-fitting beige clothes moved across the marble floor, marveling at how each square burst into white luminescence beneath his feet. A lit candle hovered above his head, illuminating arches of ruddy brick painted in ornate designs. He had the aura of a man who'd come here to study but couldn't recall the books he sought.

"He is a riverboat captain," Rona whispered. "I had hoped he would find his way here. I kept telling him about this place. We're going to need him and his boat very soon."

"You mean to go through with your plan, then?" Esperidi prodded.

But her attention had splintered so severely that her voice lacked force. She couldn't hold herself within the dream environment long enough to hear Rona's reply. Memories of *Papa* were too strong for her to resist. They launched her along a new trajectory.

A dream began on a blood-drenched meadow littered with corpses beneath a livid sun. Papa Pallides stood near her on the field's highest hump, a small hillock mercifully covered with wheat rather than splashed crimson.

The City Father was a pillar of rectitude in his tight leather tunic and skirt of overlapping rawhide leaves: the uniform of a Farsilane soldier. Though his posture and *timbre* betrayed his awareness of his daughter's presence, he didn't glance at her. He seemed to address the corpses dotting the plain.

"For every Manitoh life we took today," he pronounced, "we no doubt spared ten Shaini whom they would otherwise have butchered."

He may have been trying to reassure her. Esperidi had heard arguments like these before, but the words did nothing to diminish her present horror. Pain, rage, and fire convulsed her dream body, and the landscape mirrored these inner tremors with seasick undulations.

Sensing her reaction, Pallides added, "If ever you'd laid eyes upon a village they'd ravaged, you'd not pity them."

He sounded as devoid of empathy as a stone, but Esperidi's percipience, whetted during the months of her apprenticeship with Shiya-coqui, penetrated his armor. She saw how bitterness had warped the natural course of Pallides' life. It had deepened his conviction that *all* of life must be this way, that its conditions were brutal, and only the heartless could survive its tests.

Such convictions had driven him through the ranks to finally become a City Father and then to urge the Cordonne to harness the power of *Sacred Timbre* to meet the threat of the Chonnens, a gambit that Shiya-coqui believed could utterly destroy Ophia.

As Esperidi pondered these things—and the awareness that allowed her to hold two streams of history simultaneously, one "past" and the other "present"—an entity began to take shape beyond Pallides. She recognized the

Weaving at once. One had to train the eyes to detect the subtle ruby veins running through glossy cobbles, smooth carpets, glass, and even trees and parks. Once you'd noticed it, though, you couldn't un-see it. Suddenly, you were aware of its pervasive presence, like an eye forever hovering just over your shoulder, pulsating, obsessed with your every movement like a love-struck stalker.

Recalling the sensation of flight she'd achieved in previous dreams, Esperidi slowly conquered the fear that had often smothered her voice when she'd tried to argue with Papa in waking.

"Why must these always be the choices we're presented with, to take life or to lose it? Where is the love that ought to fill the spaces between us?"

"Don't overtax your mind," her father said, still avoiding her eyes. "You aim to cure ills that have attended humankind since its infancy. Dreaming so loftily will only raise you for a devastating fall."

Esperidi was too distracted to retort. She gasped as the Ambrosine Theater, which she'd passed countless times during her walks in Farsilane, superimposed itself over her fading visions of the Weaving.

It appeared just as it did to her waking eyes. The Ambrosine's design took advantage of its enclosure's natural terraces, which descended almost to the banks of the Nitahwe River. The walls and steps mirrored the composition of Hive walls: interweaving veins of quartz, copper, and gold latticed the granite.

In non-Shaini hands, such a construction would have offered terrible acoustics. But the seating area, stage, and dome had all been formed with *Sacred Timbre*. The stonework remembered its birth in song, sure as it recalled the rich heritage of plays, many now banned, that it'd borne witness to.

Those banned plays existed now only within the Sentient Library.

The main bulk of the stage described a half-circle some twenty meters at its widest point, which afforded even those spectators in the wings—for the open-air auditorium formed a similar arc—a clearer view of the drama. Granite globes perched on both sides bathed the night performance in a warm lime-yellow glow when fed with the *timbres* of lambency. Fifteen tiers of seats could host five hundred Shaini.

Pillars shimmered like mirages behind the stage, supporting a wooden festoon from which curtains hung, dividing the rear space into two dressing rooms and a storage area for props.

Behind the divisions, a flight of stone steps shaded by olive trees led to a causeway that ran parallel to the river until it reached the quays.

Esperidi marveled at how many details that she hadn't witnessed before now revealed themselves with the certainty of Vision. *First, Rona conjures up images of Sanjesota's wars, and now, fantasies of Sanyori raise the Ambrosine before my eyes.*

But the stage and seats were empty.

"It's been more than a year since a performance was held at the Ambrosine," Pallides remarked as if the theater's appearance was commonplace. "Contemporary writers seem incapable of composing plays that are appropriate for viewing." He dismissed these thoughts with a brusque gesture. "But I never cared much for theater anyway. To my ears, most of it rings of melodrama. Why bemoan suffering when suffering can be eradicated with Truth and the force of law?"

But Esperidi recognized the heart warmth that pulsed beneath Pallides' caustic shell, though she'd seldom witnessed it. She stepped closer, grasped her father's shoulders, and forced him to face her.

Papa was too startled, at first, to resist. "But knowing that my dreams might be unattainable," Esperidi said, "does nothing to diminish their fire. I *know* that it lies within us all, the capacity to make Ophia a wise and loving place."

She appeared to him in a heavy, sky-blue shawl draped over a blouse of comparable color and thickness. Unlike the ones she often wore in waking, this version covered her arms—and she wondered at the vague uneasiness that caused her to adorn an extra protective layer.

But Pallides' incredulous expression only made her voice ring louder. "Why does love burn within us if its fulfillment is forever impossible? How can we say that harmony can't be achieved simply because we haven't done it yet?"

In this way, Esperidi Mon-Sequana uncovered the true passion underlying her decision to learn the Sophryne way. She awoke with eyes and cheeks damp, gasping as if emerging from deep waters.

She and Shiya-coqui often spent their early afternoons sitting on rush-woven chairs in the largest of the network's caverns, sipping jasmine tea. The central space was dominated by a copper orrery the size of a house with two dozen wooden globes representing planets and moons, the largest of which Esperidi couldn't wrap her arms around.

They'd settled into a loose routine of comparing progress on their separate dream fronts during their midday break from study, training, and meditation.

"You do me proud, child," Shiya-coqui said when

Esperidi related her latest experience. "Few, in or out of the Veils, could muster the courage to confront a Cordonne Father, and considering that this one is your own flesh and blood..."

Esperidi winced at this echo of Rona's words in the Sentient Library. "Have you made any progress with Sanyori?" she asked, feeling vaguely disturbed by the trend of the conversation and hoping to divert it.

"I have," Shiya-coqui said, a bit noncommittally. "Initially, I only observed him, never allowing myself to be seen. His first moments of self-aware dreaming happened spontaneously. I didn't prompt him.

"But such incidents occur more frequently and for longer durations now that we've collaborated on his script for Gossamer Veils. It's verily an instructional for self-aware dream adventures when viewed from the far side of the Partition."

She smiled wryly. "It's a relief for me, at least, that his mind isn't so often derailed nowadays."

"Derailed by what?" Esperidi asked.

"Oh, what does any man want when he suddenly realizes he has unhindered freedom? Erotic fantasies, child! Sanyori would become lucid and immediately realize he could fulfill all his desires. That idea would drive out all other concerns.

"Anyhow, I've spent weeks teaching him: first, how to awaken, and secondly, how to keep his *mind* on the task at hand once he's done so.

"As I've said, he and I have been collaborating on his play." Her voice now carried a *timbre* of grudging admiration. "Sanyori wants to make his exodus, but he also wants to leave some parting reminders for those who will remain behind. We've agreed to teach them some of the history the Cordonne has forbidden. It's a cruel subject: Sanjesota's

Manitoh Horde and their awful fate."

"Yes, I know," Esperidi whispered, recalling that crimson acre of corpses, many of them Shaini. And she remembered Rona's soliloquy in the Library. "I dreamed of Manitohs slaughtered."

Shiya-coqui mulled this with a speculative brow. "Interesting that it was Manitohs, and yet your father was there—he being the chief strategist in this new conflict brewing with the Chonnens. Perhaps it's meant to underscore how most of the Shaini have learned nothing from the Manitoh massacre and now must repeat the atrocity.

"But a century ago, we were a complacent nation too smug to realize the threat growing up around it. Calconipur Hive was razed by Sanjesota before the rest of us realized the true extent of our danger. Then we were mastered by fear and rage."

Shiya-coqui's eyes sharpened. Perhaps she sensed her apprentice straying into disconsolate thoughts. "You've achieved a personal victory," she said, "but how have you fared with the others in the troupe? Do you yet pass one another like strangers?"

"Rona is the only one I can communicate with," Esperidi admitted. "She seems to recall what passes between us. As for the others... Some are undisciplined and thus impossible to reach. Some encounter me in the Library without ever realizing that they're dreaming. And then there are those who are lucid throughout their interactions with me, but they wake up with no knowledge of the conversations that we've had."

"This is a process of slow accretion," Shiya-coqui said. "But I think it's time you corralled them. The Ambrosine performance is less than two weeks away."

"How do you propose I 'corral' them?" Esperidi asked.

"Have you got a cowbell stashed in the Sentient Library?"

Shiya-coqui measured her. "You found your wings, didn't you? Surely, now you can find your voice."

And so Esperidi squandered three nights trying to find Rona again. She focused her attention like a white-hot pinhead on the woman's visceral *timbre*. But she awoke each time with only the vaguest impressions of what she'd been involved with across the Partition.

On the third such morning, she opened her eyes to see Shiya-coqui bending over her bed, eyes intent as an eagle's upon a rabbit.

"Would it help if I told you how the performance at the Ambrosine unfolds?" she said.

Esperidi shook dreams from her head like the remnants of disintegrating garments. "But the performance is still more than a week away!"

Shiya-coqui chuckled. "Have you already forgotten all my lectures about Time?"

Esperidi glared at her. "You have told me more than once that you can't know for sure whether Shaini forces will attempt to destroy the Chonnens crossing the land bridge or, if they do, whether Ophia will respond with cataclysms. So you can't *see* an event before it's happened, obviously!"

Over the last few months, she'd learned to recognize Ophia's distinctive *timbre*. She could withdraw her focus and experience independence from her physical body. She was, theoretically, free to travel anywhere so long as she had a firm grasp of her bearings and destination. The key was to feel the essence of a place, the nameless quality that could not be accurately described but only *felt*. But Esperidi had never considered it possible to actually swim against the currents of Time.

"That's true," Shiya-coqui acknowledged. "I can't *see* it. But in this case, it is such a strong probability, nearly crystallized, that I perceive its shadows."

She frowned for a moment, struggling for a way to describe the ineffable. "Think about what it's like when you travel. As you leave Ophia, you pass through layers of actuality. They become less and less substantial as you move. Now, the layer closest to us, where things feel foggy or dreamlike, is an almost manifest dimension.

"If you look at your chair there, it may appear to you just like the one you're sitting on, save for small details—some discoloration, say. It might flicker. This more ethereal place is nearly tangible. The vibrations have formed structures just on the verge of becoming physical. On that level, I witnessed Sanyori's play-to-be. And oh, your Rona does my young self justice!"

She swept a hand across her forehead as if the gesture was high drama and winked. "Always, my objective is to challenge your beliefs about what is and is not possible, dear girl."

Esperidi didn't respond. *She's pushing me hard*, she thought, *and she knows it*. Sometimes, Esperidi felt like a decade's worth of Sophryne training had been packed into the last three months.

Shiya-coqui is relentless because she doesn't believe she has much time.

And the older woman, for her part, was obliged to cease her twirling and swipe her damp cheeks. The cruel memory of a century ago was as insistent as the morning. "As for the story they enact... That was an evil day that Ophia should not have witnessed once. That such an ill could repeat, as if we're all incapable of learning from it... It's appalling.

"But, concluding the play, having reminded us all of the depths to which we might plunge, Sanyori turns and leads his troupe of actors—and even a portion of the audience—down the back stairway towards the river, never to return." Shiya-coqui brightened at her recollected vision. "The remaining spectators watch, believing this is all part of the performance. And the troupe flees in the cargo hold of a riverboat, packed in with its usual crew. Aye: Old Shiya-coqui is not the only one potent in the *timbres* of fog! Sanyori hides the craft, and with tones of mobility, Rona speeds them northward. They will settle the Sendhi steppes, a region where the Weaving's strands do not reach.

"Sanyori and his followers embark onto a place wherein they might govern themselves—with all the risk and reward this implies. What more could a band of eccentric outsiders hope for? We can't even say that they violate Ophia's guiding ideals. After all, their 'revolt' doesn't spill a single drop of blood."

Shiya-coqui bent towards Esperidi, her eyes brimming with sorrow and empathy. "That is one strong probability—an event that still could be. It requires only one thing to focus it into manifestation: for you and Rona to *speak* and thus serve as its catalyst."

When she finally succeeded in tracking Rona down, Esperidi feared she'd trespassed upon sacred ground. The woman stood before a man who Esperidi intuited at once had been her husband in his last physical incarnation: Caius.

Esperidi had often dreamed of the deceased. Here, on the other side of the Partition, they lived on. This place knew no slow decay of time. Mortality was forgotten. And so Rona had found her husband in a meadow where the sun sat low but did not hurt her eyes.

"All is mutuality within the heart of Sorsajna," Esperidi recalled Shiya-coqui saying. "There's no imposition, no assertion." But she couldn't wholly shake the sense that she was intruding.

Everything we see resonates with what we are. Is this what drew Papa to me in my last dream of him? she wondered. *Does some of my idealism still burn inside of him?*

Galvanized by that sting of memory, she cried out.

To Esperidi's astonishment, the man turned towards her and smiled. He seemed to acknowledge not only her presence but also its meaning and purpose. Rona, however, was as oblivious as if she and her former husband were the universe's last remaining dreamers.

Caius' love shone down upon her as he gripped her shoulders. "Stop for a moment," he said, "and realize you can come awake. This is your dream."

At first, the momentum of the narrative she'd already begun swept Rona along. "I scarcely know what to say. This plan began with Sanyori. He— Wait, what was that you said just now?"

"Realize, my love, that you're awake in your dream."

This time, the words reached Rona's core. She paused and became self-aware in that crucial moment of reflection. She recognized the man who stood before her and felt how much he meant to her. And at the same time, she understood the necessity of touching upon this with delicate mental fingers.

"Oh, Caius, my love! There's something I have to do. It tears my insides to say it, but I have to leave you for a while."

"I know you do." His smile never wavered, nor did his grip upon her shoulders. "Don't torment yourself. We have all the time in eternity. Yours will be the first generation to taste true freedom since before your grandfather's time. Remember that. And you will savor its *timbre* like few Shaini ever have."

And so, her heart near to bursting in her chest, her Caius's shade tugging at her like a siren call from some far and mournful shore, Rona passed through several dream transitions to arrive beneath a grand archway that signified—for her—the entrance to the Sentient Library.

Esperidi trailed her like a raven's shadow. *If she can only hold her focus!* she thought. Rona had not yet awakened to the "real world." Therefore, its remaining night hours might not be wasted.

Suddenly, Rona inclined her head and acknowledged Esperidi. Her dream body was more substantial now, as if it had discovered the courage to fully manifest and announce its right to be.

"I know who you are now," she said. "You are no stranger. But I have trouble remembering our errand."

"This is the Sentient Library," Esperidi told her. "The place where we've met before. You and I want to convey a message to the rest of your troupe and even to all of Ophia—to anyone who finds their way here."

"Yes!" Rona's ethereal body brightened with the force of her excitement. "We must declare our purpose!"

For a moment, her *timbre* reached an urgent crescendo. She seemed to forget her companion as they approached the now-visible journal. No books adorned the walls this time, but hundreds of rolled scrolls filled the ceramic vases along their circumference.

When Rona reached the dais and grasped the quill, she recalled her companion again. Esperidi nodded in affirmation and encouragement.

"Inscribe the Declaration of the Free Peoples of Ophia upon the dream tome!"

Rona nodded as she shepherded her thoughts. Then she began setting down the ideas that had percolated within her since she'd first met Esperidi weeks before.

"I am Rona Mon-Ilrhea, actress and agitator. For long years, I've beheld this silent war between the citizenry and the ruling Cordonne in the place we now call New Ophia. But here, within this dream space, the real battle is being fought: a conflict between those who fear freedom more than they long for it and those who long for freedom more than they fear it.

"The time has come to express in our waking lives what we have lived, learned, and dreamed here. Our vision is crying out for utterance. We had to learn how to dream consciously. Now, those dreams find their voices.

"We know that the Weaving diminishes us all. Our continued reliance on it expresses our fundamental distrust of human nature. Surely, we can grow beyond this.

"I am grateful to have spoken with the spirit of my Caius before coming here. He reminded me of something I'd almost forgotten. We cannot serve love with hate nor reach freedom through violence. How potent is it when such a lesson comes from a man who was persecuted unto death by the very forces that we oppose now?

"The Cordonne courts eruptions to beggar any earthquake. Can any sane argument be raised in favor of our ability to usurp the very forces of life? But we who congregate here and are inspired to awaken know that miracles can occur even when the elements needed for their fulfillment seem not at hand. We change our beliefs about what's possible, and new doors open. Our hearts are connected with the soul of Ophia, and so our healing is the world's healing."

There, she faltered. Her initial burst of passion had expended itself, and she was uncertain how to proceed. But Esperidi, inspired by her friend's example, stepped up beside her at the dais and reached for the quill.

Rona proffered it gratefully, and Esperidi took up the narrative.

"I've often been told that I am naive to think that the Sophryne lore can become accessible to everyone and that we can know peace and harmony through knowing ourselves. But Ophia has witnessed epochs when light was prevalent in this way. It is not innate in us, this desire to make war and oppress others. Such circumstances grow out of a misunderstanding of our own nature. Knowing our creative power, we would never covet what others possess. When our minds encounter their source, we recall our reverence for all of life.

"In this moment, the script constantly swims on this paper's surface, and I can't keep it still within my field of vision. No matter how I squint, lines and curves cavort with one another, refusing to settle into stable rows. Is this not how it feels to try and hold to one's desire for peace amid turbulence?

"But I cannot afford self-doubt. None of us can. One needs no surer testament than the creation of the Weaving to know that despair has long been more potent than the forces of optimism and vision within Ophia.

"None of our citizens—veritable prisoners now—have been able to muster the *timbre* of freedom with enough strength to realize it. Under the Cordonne's yoke, many Shaini have forgotten that there is such thing as power of choice.

"The time has come for us all to remember!"

Widowed Soul of Lost Ophia

From Colleen's Journal

The moment I met Dr. Visinski and shook his hand, I read, in his eyes, precisely what he wanted to impress upon me.

The gig was up. Time to admit how out of touch you are, girl. No more games. No more evasions. No more camouflaging your inability to live effectively behind a wall of fantasy. You're nineteen. Time to grow up. You're going to stop pretending that your maladjustment is a gift. And you'll start calling your so-called "fount of inspiration" by its right name: mental illness.

Doctor Visinski was a decent human being, but his opinions epitomized our culture's idiotic assumptions about the nature of life and the universe. This man vacuumed magic out of every corner of Creation.

The sky's blueness? Short-wave light Rayleigh scattering on the backs of tiny air molecules.

My cat Magda nuzzling me when I cried? Pheromones.

Human emotion, passion, aspiration, creativity? Electrical and chemical activity in the brain.

And he explained all these soul-dead mechanics with a smugness that made me want to scream.

But I never did because I sensed that he really believed he was helping people. He wanted to help. And I knew I had also bought into our civilization's blindness to an extent. At times, I didn't believe in life's wonder and mystery any more than Thomas Visinski.

After Stacie died, I gradually learned to trade enchantment for "rationality." I'm talking about that little death that occurs in most of us, the death that prompted Freud to refer to an adult as a degenerated child.

I regret that barter because I know how small it made my world, how it strangled my imagination. It made me feel separate—from nature, other people, and myself. The illusion felt real because my belief made it so.

As my new therapist droned on, I drifted into daydreams. I thought about Stace and me enacting Arthurian legends. Most times, we'd fight over who got to be Morgana. But sometimes, I actually enjoyed playing Arthur just as much. No matter how you play it, though, by the end of the story, Avalon fades. The Fae disappear. And more and more, the Arthurian world resembles our contemporary one.

But see, a "new age" doesn't just roll over the world, any more than an "old age" vanishes. People's minds change. They start believing in different ways, and as their beliefs change, they perceive a different world. Avalon never went anywhere. There were just fewer people left in the land who could see it.

I wondered if anyone ever fully escaped our cultural myth, the one that insists that reason is the one voice of truth and that magic is a fairy tale for children.

But the good doctor hadn't summoned me to talk about Avalon. He wanted to know why I was there. What was going on? I mean, really?

What passed through my head when I walked out over that gorge?

Foresight saved me. I'd stayed up half the night anticipating this question and formulating a response. But I had to write about it all in the whimsical guise of a play. I needed that protective distance. Only by casting the spiraling circumstances that had landed me in the hospital in fictitious form could I bear to look them in the face.

It also allowed me to simply hand the good doctor a sheaf of papers and let him decipher what it all meant for himself.

The Ballad of Colleen and Greg, with special guest Kwan-Yin

A drama in three acts by Colleen Addison

Part One: Museum Philosophizing

Scene: Colleen and Greg viewed from a distance. He's taller than her, with lighter hair. Put a spotlight on that devilish smile as they enter the museum.

Narrator (from the wings): "Ostensibly, this outing is for the purpose of exchanging notes and ideas for a graphic story the two are working on: "Tales within the Veils." Story: Colleen Addison. Illustrations: Greg McLaren.

"By now, though, it's become obvious that both of them realize their increasingly frequent rendezvous are more than just collaborations..."

Colleen: "So... would it be presumptuous of me to consider this our first actual date?"

Spotlight their conjoined hands.

Distant view of the two. We see various exhibits.

Narrator: "The two budding lovebirds browse the museum. Early date jitters make them talk a little too fast and laugh a little too loud. But their minds settle when they reach the room devoted to ancient Oriental mythos.

"They stop in front of a statue, about two feet tall and encased in a square glass box, of the Chinese deity Kwan-Yin, whose name is pronounced in two other ways that our heroes make ludicrous attempts to enunciate. She's sitting in the Lalitasana, or the royal ease. Spectators unfamiliar with the position open their phones and do a word search. One of Kwan-Yin's hands forms the mudra: forefinger and thumb joined in a circle."

Greg: (reading from the plaque and muttering under his breath.) "Comforts those who are afraid... Protects travelers... She hears the cries of the entire human world."

Narrator: "The wide pan shows four other people in the room: two parents, their daughter, and a solitary older man. Colleen hands Greg a bundle of pages."

Colleen (close to him and speaking low): "Sorry I keep changing the story. Please be patient with me. Anytime it flows like this... I can't help but wonder whether I've read it somewhere and subconsciously soaked up the whole thing or if everything I'm writing down is actually happening somewhere. Like, somehow, I've got this pipeline to it, and I'm taking it all down like a reporter. That it's all real, basically."

(Her face is now shy but determined.) "Which do you think more plausible?"

Greg (looking thoughtful): "Define real."

Colleen: "You can see it, touch it and taste it. And anyone else who's around can vouch for it, too. So, basically, as much proof as we ever have."

Greg: "Wouldn't a dream satisfy all of those criteria? I mean, while we're dreaming? We react to everything as if it's actually happening..."

Colleen: "Then I guess maybe dreams count as real, no?"

Narrator: "Lost in thought, they wander the exhibit.

Then Greg turns and points to the statue they'd been looking at earlier."

Greg: "You felt it, too, right? Like she was about to come to life? That's the magic of art. When I sketch a protagonist, I hope people will look at it and feel a little more heroic themselves."

(Closer up on Greg's face.) "But I don't think that Kwan-Yin is 'real' in the sense of her being alive somewhere out there in the universe, being able to answer your prayers, anything like that."

Colleen (facing away and musing): "I wonder what the difference is, exactly."

Greg (trying to be solicitous): "So you think you're really recording something that's—"

Colleen: "I don't think I can record it. The reception isn't that strong. And that's what it feels like: this radio station barely coming through, what with all the static. What I've gotten down on paper is my own best guess.

"Look, Greg... if this is weirding you out, I'd rather drop it. I don't even know what to make of it all myself, and if you're gonna call me crazy..."

Greg: "Whoa, Col, back up! I'm not judging you. Faces have poked right out of the paper in front of me while I'm sketching, all right? I don't rightly understand it all, either, but I've got a sense of where you're coming from."

Colleen: "Forget it. I shouldn't put it on you."

Greg: "Put what, though?"

Colleen: "Look, it's been on my mind... asking if you'll spend the night with me tonight. And I wouldn't put that out there if I didn't get the feeling that you want to as much as I do. But it's just... Something is standing in the way right now, and I'm not sure I even know how to talk about it."

Greg: "Well, shoot from the hip, like you do best."

Colleen: "I think this story is real. Somehow. In some

sense." (She starts pacing.) "Do you ever feel torn in two, Greg? Like there's these urges inside you, both really powerful, but they're each going off in totally different directions?"

Greg: "Well, there was a point where I had to choose between music and illustration. There weren't enough hours in a day to pursue both—not as serious career paths, anyway. But you know all about that."

Colleen: "Yeah, it's like that with me, too. I experience something that just burns in the pit of me, and then I want to capture it in a poem or story. I want to make a movie about it. I want to express what I'm feeling in so many ways that a lot of times, I don't end up doing a damned thing!

"See, this is why I think we keep being reborn. There's so much to know and experience, and we all have so many inclinations... Our souls are just enormous, with all these different potentials... See, it's like, we <u>can</u> explore all those avenues. There <u>is</u> enough time. We have forever. We just can't do it all in one lifetime.

"I doubt any of us will ever feel totally contented. We sense infinity inside ourselves, but there's no way we can ever embody it fully. That's why I believe we have limitless other lives to live aside from the one we know right now. But each time you experience the world, you've got to focus, which means being this separate little self—or <u>believing</u> yourself to be no more than that. This little self encased in a body. A prisoner of time. So you always ache to dissolve your boundaries and become part of everything because you sense that you <u>are</u> a part of everything."

Narrator: "Embarrassed by her emotional display, Colleen squeezes Greg's hand."

Colleen: "They're closing up at five. Let's see as much of the exhibition as we can."

Part Two: Let's Spend the Night Together

Narrator: "A variation of their discussion at the museum now ensues when our heroine confides in Greg that she's had to settle for being an 'amateur' archaeologist after being rejected by all the schools she applied to."

Colleen: "I just can't approach it their way. I can't be that methodical. It frustrates me; it feels unnecessarily slow. And even after all their work... I don't agree with the conclusions they draw about the evidence in front of their eyes. They seem so invested in the official explanations.

"Me, I just take these leaps in the dark. Sometimes, I'll know I've landed on something..."

Greg (shrugging): "You're psychic. I've seen the evidence enough times to vouch."

Colleen (offering him a sly smile): "Is that why you brought me home tonight? You think I can give you some winning lottery numbers?"

(But her smile is difficult to sustain because she feels more vulnerable than she's letting on.)

Greg: "It doesn't look like you get to pick and choose how it happens. But I've noticed that you speak in this particular way when you're really certain of something. And when you say things in that tone of voice, you're usually right."

Colleen (nodding but sounding distracted): "It's like that statue of Kwan-Yin that we looked at. She doesn't <u>tell</u> you that you're forgiven. She has this way of making you <u>feel</u> that the universe is merciful and doesn't judge you. That's the difference. The feeling."

Narrator: "She rolls the word over in her mind, allowing her enrapt audience to do the same."

Colleen: "It's like dousing for water. I douse for pasts and futures."

Greg: "Yeah? Huh! The future part, I can see. The world can always use another bona fide fortune-teller. But the past... ?"

Narrator: "He makes peacekeeping gestures to head off the retort on the lips of his dear and hopeful lover-to-be."

Greg: "Archaeology is fascinating, O.K.? But that lasts as long as it takes me to watch a two-hour documentary. After that... it's fossils, Colleen. It's dead."

Colleen (speaking with sudden conviction): "Not to me, it isn't. I think if we could find the right keys to unlock some of those mysteries, it would tell us as much about ourselves as it would about ancient peoples."

Narrator: "Greg has obviously had enough gravity for one night."

Greg: "Tell you what: We'll go trip mushrooms out on the sand dunes one of these nights. Then I bet you'll have a better chance of convincing me."

Narrator: "Colleen laughs. Suddenly, she realizes she is as much in need of levity as him now."

Colleen: "Oh, if you trip with me, Mister McLaren, I'm liable to lead you places you'll never find your way back from!"

Part Three: Abort on All Fronts

Narrator: "She leaves early the next morning, knowing she will never return to his apartment. For all their glib banter, she's aware of some truth underlying all those coy words. Colleen really is drifting somewhere where Greg can't follow.

"A few weeks later, Colleen discovers she's pregnant. She knows Greg is the father. She has not been with anyone else in the interim. And this is absolutely the only aspect of the situation that she feels certain of.

"In a crisis like this, those close to you, people you can confide in, often urge you to take your time. Think it through. What could you stand to lose by the decision you're about to make? Colleen does the exact opposite. She resolves not to think about it. She intends to act before other voices can intrude, force her to either reconsider or agonize over her choice and wallow in doubt and guilt."

Colleen: (with hands held high towards the heavens and a voice of unbearable pathos!) "My life is spiraling out of control, and that's not a situation I'm willing to bring a child into! It's as simple as that!"

The End

Doctor Visinski lingered on the last page, half-curled between his hands, his expression suggestive of someone trying to swallow a pouch of sand.

"Well, you <u>have</u> stepped in over your head, haven't you?" he said at last.

I guess it's fortunate, then, that I omitted the parts of the story that thread a narrow path between mystical experience and madness.

"No: There's no threading here, girl! It's either one or the other!" So insists my vicious logical mind. But I don't imagine this entry will settle the question of lunacy vs. illumination once and for all. If this be insanity... well, it tastes like the nectar of the gods compared to this sterile hospital with its austere walls and soulless lights.

Anyway, I'd been insulated from the natural disasters occurring in Sadenport, which might have provoked the dreams. I wasn't aware of the flooding until family members contacted me to assure me they were all right.

The Willamette River overflowed its banks to such an extent that western portions of Sadenport were virtually underwater, and when business as almost usual finally resumed, tentatively, on Tuesday—with many still lacking power—the wreckage was strewn all over. Nearly every yard was piled high with the salvaged remains of basement and ground floors, all covered with thick silt and scarcely recognizable for whatever it had been originally.

Before long, the sun dried out all that silt, and then the dust forced people to wear masks while they worked outside.

The part of me that had once written a treatise on the collapse of Western Civilization felt vindicated. Modern life, here in its waning days, has a way of keeping our energies consumed in petty frustrations and toils, blinding us to life's more epical sweep. When faced with nature's unbridled fury, we can feel this primal kinship with her and bond more profoundly with each other.

Barriers fall away when it's life or death. We humans face the primordial spirit that birthed us and can yet consume us. It cuts through the pettiness, slackness, and complacency of civilized life. It can draw out the best in people and lift ordinary men and women into a more heroic sphere.

I was apprised of this disaster just before I completed the slightly cathartic exercise that was my "play" revolving around Greg and me.

Then, I went to bed and dreamed of the Great Pyramid at Giza.

There's little I can add to what other people have already said about the sensation they experienced inside the King's Chamber. I'd always weighed towards envisioning the Great Pyramid as a kind of machine rather than a tomb. I thought of it as a giant Tesla coil and imagined it might work as well for us as it had for the ancients if we ever figured out how to activate it.

This dream forced me to refine my conception. The immensity surrounding me was closer to an instrument than a machine, just waiting to be winded by some titan's breath. A line from an Arthur Rimbaud poem floated through my thoughts: "One tap of yours on the drum releases all sounds and begins the new harmony." The right note or set of notes—the proper frequency—would unleash the pyramid's power.

The scene shifted to an aerial view of an island I associated with Atlantis. It was a sprawling continent characterized mainly by rolling green meadows, their length and breadth bathed in sunlight. The great temple lay in the east (where I somehow expected it to be), so gigantic that it could be clearly glimpsed from that height—like China's Great Wall from a satellite.

And though the waves that lapped her shores were gentle and kind as the sun, I thought of the ones that would one day wash over her, swallowing Atalanta into the depths along with her people and all their overreaching inventions.

Her people were probably my people of old. That was my first thought upon waking. How else could I explain the vision's familiarity?

From Sanyori Mon-Sequestra
In the Here-ness and Now-ness
The Sentient Library

The Motherland. Why did we call it that? It had not mothered us or planted the seeds that sprouted into the fruit of Shaini

Hives. But the Chonnen armies, hailing from the so-called Motherland, finally made their move as summer thawed Ardhid, the land bridge.

And then our Cordonne made *their* move, intending to employ a form of might that should never have been used as a weapon. We Shaini had grown increasingly intimate with the lore of *Sacred Timbre*. But we'd largely remained strangers to ourselves. And power without self-awareness is a dreadful thing.

Shiya-coqui had tried to warn us.

As we have seen, Esperidi's dreams also warned of the consequences of that ignorance. While she tossed and sweated on a bed of furs, magma spilled to the knees of distant hills and limned prairies in baleful red. Once lush meadows were choked with ash. Fires scorched sand to the hardness and hue of obsidian. Ophia's body convulsed, lashing angry retorts from the ocean that cradled her.

Her skin was torn, and flames as tall as trees licked forked tongues through the cracks. Rivers were reduced to sandy washes beneath a merciless sun.

And so our beloved sister-souls—who scarcely suspected the bonds of love that bound them across the Partition—echoed one another's bereavement.

Once upon a time, their visions for the future had felt like simple forecasts. They would pursue their vocations: a dream spelunker and a seeker of ancient Earthly mysteries. They would find love, though both often debated whether children figured into that portrait. And they would fulfill their lives in ways that would lift others from the muck and mire.

But Esperidi suspected that a young woman's frivolous dreams weighed little upon the scales of coming storms, and Colleen had seldom dared to dream with a full heart since being forced to watch her sister fall.

Because of these emotional resonances—and the twins' aforementioned bond—we may speak of their journeys at this juncture as if they were congruent. "Time" is part of any physical world's camouflage, and even if we accept that camouflage's surface significance, it moves differently on Ophia than on Earth. And Esperidi had already learned to lean against time; she'd witnessed it wobbling. She'd begun to suspect that it was just as navigable as space in some respects.

Here in Ophia, where I would soon count myself among the few surviving Shaini, Esperidi Mon-Sequana was sent on an errand one morning by her mentor, Shiya-coqui. Nothing momentous: She merely needed to gather castor seeds and wild marjoram.

Now, the network of passages that Shiya-coqui had claimed beneath Mount Veneer was a portion of old Elmicora, the Shaini underworld. All such places were only ever accessible through concealed portals, usually consisting of an iron archway and double doors embellished according to the builders' tastes—lilac and honeysuckle, in this instance—rendered in thin lines of jade. And so one with the proper knowledge of the *timbres* utilized to construct the door simply pressed two fingers against a spot above the flowers, held that frequency or vibration or emotional tone (however you prefer to describe it), and the stone would rumble like the grinding of Ophia's bones to admit them.

We Shaini had long dwelt in places like this, where we could observe Outer Ophia without its Oskwai—our name for all the comparatively more primitive peoples—observing us. Though wrought of steel, the doorways were transparent as glass and appeared from the outward-facing side like a part of whatever natural feature they were set within: grassy hillside, rock wall, waterfall, and so on. They were, in short, invisible to non-Shaini eyes. Nevertheless, each was emblazoned with the same words of welcome: "May the light of Sorsajna illuminate love's path for you. A Way has been prepared."

But returning from her errand that morning, Esperidi couldn't find the inscription above the doorway. She couldn't see the portal at all. The space it occupied was now indistinguishable from the rest of the mountain's face. Shiya-coqui, you see, had unstitched the old pattern of *timbres* across that threshold and woven a new one. Knowing that Esperidi would never willingly forsake her, she'd taken these brutal measures to push her apprentice out of the nest.

Esperidi could not have opened the doorway even if it'd been visible. And the horse, tethered to a nearby tree, had already warned her that something was amiss. Exhausted from crying, howling denials, and pounding on the unapologetic granite face until her palms were swollen red, Esperidi finally stumbled over to Stella, her mentor's gentle mare. She held the animal and begged for comfort. And as she did so, she saw a note attached to a bulging sack.

That note is preserved here, available to anyone who knows what to look for, as is anything with enough emotional force behind it to etch its presence into the Sentient Library. And so we may read the last words that Shiya-coqui wrote to the young woman in whom she had invested so many of her hopes.

"My dearest Esperidi,

"I'll not apologize for what I've done. There are realities more urgent than your willingness or unwillingness to forgive me. And I'll offer you no soft sentiments. Though I know that Sorsajna is eternal, I weather my own seasons of grief and surrender. Yes, life will continue, but it will not continue in this way, and my heart aches with that recognition. Pain is the memory of love, after all.

"We only truly learn to cherish our moments when they seem ephemeral. But we can trust the love that birthed us and know that this source infuses all things. Thus, we can search for light within the heart of any loss.

"This isn't mere wish-fulfilling fantasy, but something I have viscerally felt and witnessed. And as I write these words to you now, I possess unshakable faith.

"I have told you that Savwain Desert will be mostly untouched by the coming Rupture. I've packed a map and provisions sufficient to keep you alive for a few weeks—if you're frugal. Once settled, you can devote your abilities to growing and nurturing what you need to sustain yourself.

"You know I'm in no condition to journey alongside you. And so I must repeat what I've said before. The Sophryne Lore must not die with me. I must trust that what I've imparted will sustain you until you find your own way.

"I know it is not an easy choice, but there is no kind of existence that does not involve sacrifice. None of us only pour the fullness of our hearts in one direction. In every decision, there is loss, but the recognition of that can make us more fully cherish those choices that we do make.

"Death waits for us all, child, with or without a cataclysm.

"If ever you feel lost, remember the Sentient Library. It is not merely a repository of knowledge, though it has become a formidable storehouse. It is like a child performing a new trick and hoping its parents will notice. Its knowledge wants to be discovered. It attracts the curious. It is also a platform from which one can leap into other realities. Think of it as an ocean that laps against all shores on all possible worlds. If I meet my end in the cataclysms, know that my existence will continue within one of those worlds, and if there is a need, I trust you will know how to find me.

"Please set poor Stella free before you cross the

Arjena Hills. The Vandrene covet horses and will doubtless try to steal her if you bring her into the Savwain.

"Whatever befalls us now, I feel blessed to have found you. May my pride in you and your promise, slim consolation though it might be in these dark days, go with you as you ride into the coming whirlwinds.

"Yours eternally,

Shiya-coqui"

Meanwhile, on the Earth plane, Colleen emerged from a dream, a momentous journey to a monument of a (seemingly) vanished age.

She lingered in that languid threshold between waking and dreaming for a while. I sensed how she floated within an unfamiliar mind. She weighed Earth's bones, the immensity of Her oceans and currents as if an infinite recess inside Colleen's skull gave them utterance. There was no exterior world; it was all inside her, and she could touch any part she chose or even all of it at once.

A natural mystic, I thought. But at the same time, I knew she was frightened. The myths of her age often described one's inner mind as a dark sea of choppy waves riddled with monsters in its dark depths. Such stories make sailors want to stay close to the shoreline, where they can still see the lighthouses.

Colleen had never ventured out this far before. Her emotional extremity, lashed by losses she scarcely knew how to weigh the cost of, had driven her far past the old landmarks, banishing safe bounds and familiar voices.

Part of the catalyst had been a play she'd recently composed, a somewhat satirical account of recent trials and bereavements—an attempt to feel their fire from a distance. It was this activity, indeed, that first drew me to her. I am, after all, a dramatist. Even among my own troupe, I'd seldom encountered another person who so thoroughly believed in the power of story as I did—that it is perhaps our most potent tool for understanding ourselves and our universe, forever posing the essential question: "What does it mean to be human?"

It warmed me to this particular human being on the other side of the Partition, even though I was aware of Colleen's great pain and how she sometimes used stories to distance herself from her own life.

I took advantage of her openness. I interpreted it as an invitation. Does this sound presumptuous, even manipulative? I told myself that such communications are never possible without inner acquiescence on both sides, even if the people involved are not <u>consciously</u> aware of their agreements. There's no coercion. Colleen called, and I answered.

I slipped into the gap she had created within her consciousness. On that subliminal level, we were both aware that we were taking a gamble, given her fragmented state. A communication from "beyond" may have proved enlightening and consoling. It may also have deepened her conviction that she was losing her mind. But I had to believe in our girl. Was that not the promise that those of us who were closest to her had made before her birth? To trust in the course her soul had set upon?

So I experienced alongside her that prickling sensation in her fingertips as a creative outcry rippled through her tendons and joints and moved into her extremities. I chuckled alongside her as she muttered, "Restless Hand Syndrome," naming the sensation according to the parlance of her culture. This wasn't Colleen's first experience with spontaneous composition. Thus far, though, it had only occurred at unexpected moments. This was the first time she attempted to <u>consciously</u> cooperate with the process.

I experienced her wonderment as words began to take shape in her notebook, as if her fingers were speaking through the pencil. She stared, bewildered at times, at the tell-tale signs her muse left on the page. As I conveyed the story that I've related here of Esperidi's unwilling exile, and Colleen managed to capture it in snatches and fragments, a part of her was astonished by this echo of her own fears. And when those fears threatened to overwhelm her, she tried to latch on to this correspondence. I heard her say, "That's all it is. This is about Sadenport and the flood and me worrying about my family. It's like how I processed the situation with Greg and me and my abortion. I'm creating a fantastical account to distance myself from the whole thing."

Then, she would falter when this bargaining voice felt remote and unpersuasive.

I persisted through the medium of Colleen's hand while often feeling like a canoe obstructed by the boulders and eddies clogging its waterway. She kept trying to anticipate her destination and take control of her pencil. Then, she'd admonish herself to let go. Barriers between her vulnerable self and this direct apprehension of the universe began melting away, but the process occurred in fits and starts.

Her mind swarmed with questions. <u>Where are my contours now?</u> <u>What are boundaries anyway?</u> Meanwhile, she floated along, her hand guided by my intent, crawling across the page like an enraptured spider. We passed together through Esperidi's bereavement, venturing into the days that followed, when she was sent into the desert, a place where the lash of Sarpienta's tail was felt only in slight convulsions, and two mountain ranges buttressed that land from the gale winds raging without.

Esperidi could sense the hard stamp of time, the slow

bake of eons, most profoundly amid those graveled washes, bands of cacti, and white sands like powdered pearls. Topaz, russet, burnt umber... These are colors not usually associated with life. They made Savwain Desert fertile for thought, urging her to imagine forms she'd not yet glimpsed, relationships she'd not yet pondered.

And so she was sitting cross-legged on a dune the moment her beloved Ophia was rent, and impenetrable ash blanketed the sky, devouring the stars. For weeks, Esperidi waited in vain for the moon to show its face until she could only conjure that comforting silvery visage in her dreams. She wove effigies of the sun from dry yellow rushes to remind herself of its fidelity. As Ophia's verdure withered in the absence of that great globe of fire, she wandered beyond the familiar boundaries of her mind at times—like Colleen.

In the wake of the Rupture, both strayed towards the margins of madness. The edges of reality blurred. The warmth of Esperidi's life in Sequana as an only child had given way to loveless ice and distant tumult. And Colleen dreaded being catapulted back into a world she'd tried to forsake.

Almost the two women seemed to become a singular being as Esperidi cried out, "Who am I?" and Colleen glared at her hand: "Who are you?" What was this unfathomable world that engulfed them? Both tottered as if beneath the weight of their own foreordained myths.

This is how Esperidi Mon-Sequana became a Wakeful Dreamer and Colleen Addison became a medium: out of necessity. Well, perhaps it was not necessary, but inner needs compelled them.

Hoping to bridge the gulf of loneliness that estranged them, I conveyed the last words I heard Esperidi say before my connection with Colleen dissipated.

"I have only dreams. No single vision can paint a

certain future. Dreams reflect naught but probabilities, the shadows cast by futurity. For now, I am merely Esperidi Mon-Sequana, widowed soul of lost Ophia. I bear the seeds of renewal. O powers of life, grant me fertile ground wherein I may sow them!"

Then Esperidi wept, Colleen hurled her notebook across her room in the convalescent home, and I awoke from my life's most profound and riveting dream.

Dreams in the Crystal Citadel

Kanchi beheld the vision for three consecutive nights before she finally mustered the courage to seek counsel. For a while, she vacillated between the two people who'd been (in spirit, at least, if not formally) her guardians since her parents' deaths.

Chief Okonkwa would likely be frightened by such portents. When confronted with forces he could not name, superstition tended to fill the gaps in his knowledge. Mother Inolda, the Narwhal tribe's Singing Chieftess, found the invisible world more congenial. The older woman may have even beheld the green, luminescent globes herself upon a time.

Kanchi had often gone to Inolda's wigwam seeking companionship when her peers lost patience with her signing and gesturing. The same illness that had orphaned Kanchi had bereft her of speech. It seemed implacable in its hunger for her vitality and happiness. The young woman shared this vulnerability with the Singing Chieftess. Inoldas' fragile health kept her mostly consigned to her tent beneath a heap of furs. Scents of chamomile, garlic, and sage, which Kanchi had come to associate with healing, permeated the space.

That night—the fourth since the visions began—Mother Inolda was awake, thankfully, humming snatches of broken tune as she stared at the gray, domed ceiling.

"You come to me in secret; that was wise," she remarked. Apparently, she'd not only anticipated Kanchi's visit but also intuited the reason for it. The smile within her face's weathered folds was disarming. She lifted herself slightly from the bed, the effort costing a labored groan. "I won't begrudge losing sleep if it means we can speak unhindered."

Then she squinted as her weak eyesight sought and gauged her young visitor's wavering presence. "You've come to me with your dreams since before your first braiding," Inolda observed finally, "but never with such a look of urgency as now."

"I wasn't asleep this time," Kanchi signed. She'd stopped within a couple of paces of the mounded fur bed. "When Vision came, I was walking outside the circle of tents."

"You're in the habit of that, aren't you—walking alone while others sleep? Inolda is not blind—yet!" The woman's voice, hoarse after eight decades in the Sendhi steppes, was still surprisingly buoyant. "Indeed, as eyesight dims, other faculties sharpen. I'll wager I know what you saw: luminous globes bearing lime-yellow fires?"

Kanchi recalled their pulsing hearts flaring beneath translucent skins: a deep verdure like the essence of growing things. Though she was relieved by the Singing Chieftess' confirmation, she hung her head as her hands furiously disseminated.

"I feared I'd gone mad. I knew that if there were other Sendhi with me, they'd not have seen."

Inolda frowned. It pained her to see the young chastise themselves so. "But there's gaiety in their light, yes? They etched your path in green moon glow; they made your soul feel inflamed."

Stunned by the acuity of this description, Kanchi

could only nod. Though constantly flickering with their accustomed self-doubt, her almond eyes were now alight with curiosity and cautious hope.

Mother Inolda studied the girl for a moment with dim, rheumy detachment. Kanchi's black hair hung to her waist in two braids, each banded every couple of inches with twined fish designs dyed in sky-blue hues. For the Sendhi, such a style signified the cusp of womanhood.

What an eager apprentice she might have made, Inolda thought. *But now there is no time—leastways, not for me. Perhaps San...?*

"It'd be unwise to describe what you saw to anyone else," she decided. "The Narwhal tribe may praise heroes of ages past who followed those emerald will-o-wisps, but that doesn't mean they want to see those legends spring to life."

Kanchi, still transported by a sense of wonder, couldn't repress her eager gesticulation. "They hovered. They illuminated the ground but never touched it. And they seemed as alive as you or me."

"The Rudowine," Inolda whispered, brightening at her recollections. "Thus they name themselves. Sometimes, we say Sophryne lights."

Kanchi conveyed her marvel with her hands. "Their shape always changed. They beat like hearts; they shrank and swelled. Even though I felt the Vision was only for me, I wished someone was beside me to agree on it—"

"Few eyes are prepared for such astonishment," Mother Inolda said. "If you seek confirmation, only one decision silences doubt: Follow their lighted trail to its destination."

"Do you think that's what I should do?"

The Singing Chieftess shook her head. "This affair is between you and the powers, girl. Inolda cannot have any personal stake. The motivation to undertake such a journey must come from within yourself. No one else can give it to you.

"These spirits straddle the Partition. Whether you believe in Sarpienta, Halama, Toh, or a score of nameless gods, Kanchi, I assure you, none of them could speak plainer. You've beheld the Rudowine with your waking eyes! Do you not understand the significance of this? It means the realm beyond the Partition recognizes you and calls you home."

"If they wanted to lead *you*, would you go?" Kanchi persisted.

Inolda responded with a toothless grin. "Ah, now, you know I'm too old for a journey of that sort. Besides, the invitation was intended for you alone." A leathery hand emerged from the coverings and poked at Kanchi's chest. "No, Mother Inolda will do her questing while she sleeps."

Then, perhaps sensing the young woman's internal conflict, she added, "This is a gift! Without the warmth of the Luminous Realm, this world feels barren and unforgiving. Our days are burdensome when they could be filled with joyous songs!

"And it is not enough that we should contemplate the Sophryne lights or make room for them in our philosophies. We must feel their presence even within our most mundane tasks. Such a path beckons you now. Their side of existence can be your sanctuary when shadows terrify you or aggrieve your heart! Their luminescence is a flame that can never be extinguished."

"But that sounds like they want me to forsake this world for another." Feeling herself faced with an unanswerable dilemma, Kanchi began to slip into despondency.

"Tut! Those lights *illuminate* this world—even as they convey visions and knowledge across the river between life and death."

Kanchi's lips curled around those two words: life and death—the poles of human experience, as the Singing Chieftess had taught her. "What would I do with such knowledge?" she wondered.

Though scarcely moving, Inolda seemed to shrug. "Narwhal tribe's Singing Chieftesses were once chosen in this way. Beholding the Rudowine was proof of Vision. I work the medicine now, but I'm aged; I'll relinquish my house of flesh before many more seasons pass."

Frightened by the portents of that statement, Kanchi pursued a peripheral idea. "From whence come these guiding lights? What is their purpose? Why do they show us this kindness... if kindness it is?"

"Ask where laughter comes from; ask the purpose of the sun's warmth. Some things are just *known* from within."

Inolda lifted a hand to forestall any more questions or demands. "But now you should get your sleep, child. We have a big day tomorrow—all of us. In the morning, I shall warn Chief Okonkwa of the Manitoh embassy. They'll arrive by evening."

"Embassy?" Kanchi's gesture was quick and agitated—a sure sign of fear.

"A small one," Inolda assured her. "The priest Konatep comes—aye, he and his four assassin guards, those Inooks. Only five, though I dare say they'd suffice to destroy every warrior we could fit into the longhouse.

"But we needn't fear their violence, methinks—if we cooperate."

"What do they want?" Kanchi signed.

"Oh, what do these priests of Toh *ever* want? Your pledged faith in a world you cannot see, and they cannot show you. That we accept their tales about this invisible world rather than taste it for ourselves. That we look contrite and repentant, ready to make sacrifices to placate their Toh's disgust."

Inolda shook her head, dispelling distaste. "We have one advantage, though. My premonitions have bought us time. Konatep and his killers are wont to visit villages in secret. The priest knows people are more vulnerable to his mesmerism when caught unprepared.

"Do not fret, Kanchi dear. You may feel your life turned upside down on the morrow; your curses become blessings, and your blessings, curses. But this needn't be cause for fear. Inolda wishes wondrous dreams for you!"

Some sixty men and women—roughly a quarter of the surviving Narwhal tribe—gathered in the central lodge the following evening. Ceremony and diplomacy demanded that a handful be present. The rest were too curious to stay away.

The longhouse was constructed of wood planks and bark cover. Its roof curved like an arbor. The inner space was thirty feet wide, with a central aisle running between the lines of beds and storage chests. Hearths were spaced twenty feet apart down this aisle, and smoke holes had been cut in the roof above each. Three smoking braziers—one in the lodge's center and one at each entry flap—further warmed the space.

Always averse to drawing attention to herself, Kanchi stood—mostly on tiptoe—at the outer edge of the press of bodies, peering over the shoulders of two tall warriors. Chief Okonkwa sat on a tall ermine chair on a dais at the rear. Like most Sendhi, Okonkwa had a smooth face and an olive complexion paled by the long snows, although only the space between his forehead and chin was typically visible behind his tufted hood.

He rose and bowed when the five strangers entered.

Kanchi had never seen Manitohs before, but in stories, they usually adorned headdresses made of fiery-hued feathers. The man at the head of this solemn cortege was even more extravagant. He wore a strange, wooden conical helmet from which beads in every conceivable color dangled over his brow. His skin was bronze and dashed with scarlet, but his eyes were gray and bleak as the Sendhi wasteland.

The four cloaked figures flanking this man made Kanchi shiver in a way that had nothing to do with the frigid winds. She felt lethal promises in their sleek strides and insolent silence. Their cowls mostly concealed their faces; what little was visible appeared gaunt and vulturine.

The leader—Mother Inolda had named him Konatep—clapped his hands, swept his imperious eyes across the lodge, and then addressed the spectators. Kanchi supposed that he did this deliberately to minimize Chief Okonkwa's importance.

"My children, you need not look so fearful, so chastised! The faithful have no cause to shun the judgment of Toh—and the unfaithful cannot hide. So, seek not to rally defenses and excuses. His Will shall be made plain to all."

Listening for duplicity, Kanchi realized that Konatep's sometimes stumbling speech was a ruse. She guessed that he was probably quite fluent in the dialect of her people, though she could not imagine where he'd acquainted himself with it. But the way he seemed to grope for words to convey his meaning caused everyone to hush, lean in, and carefully attend.

Kanchi recalled Mother Inolda's warning: "People are more vulnerable to his mesmerism when caught unprepared."

Chief Okonkwa cleared his throat. "We welcome your embassy, Konatep, and we would honor you. But remember that we do not worship the same as the people of the Kawli jungles. We are not followers of Toh."

Konatep pointedly ignored the chief even as he repudiated his words. Spreading his arms wide, he cried, "And look at what your willfulness and disobedience have wrought! Behold the misfortunes brought upon all of Ophia: whirlwinds... waves to drown forests and mountains... gouts of fire from cracks in Sarpienta's great bed. Do some of you here believe you are blameless in this, that you are above reproach?"

Many Sendhi, even some warriors, hung their heads in shame.

"To appease the Rupture's hunger," Konatep pronounced, "all must make sacrifices. We must join in common purpose. We cannot afford division."

Okonkwa could no longer suppress his outrage. He leaped from his seat. "All Ophia's children must decide how they will devote themselves to Her healing! It is not a decision for one man to make!"

Konatep, squandering no energy on anger or even irritation, merely nodded in the chief's direction. One of the cloaked figures, swift as a piranha, reached the dais and dealt Okonkwa an openhanded blow behind his right knee. To Kanchi's eyes, it seemed only a slap—and one cushioned by heavy leggings—but it sapped the chief of all his strength. As a collective hush smothered the longhouse, Okonkwa clutched one side of his ermine seat as if only his arm's exertion kept him upright. His face paled. His body, though quivering, appeared torpid, robbed of volition.

"That was needless!" Konatep had the crowd's attention now. "This is not the way Toh would choose! He wants to unite, not divide us: one law, one Sacred Writ. We must be ever-vigilant against false prophets and unworthy mouthpieces!"

"Are any of you the Creator? Do you presume to speak in His stead?"

The priest continued with this general sermon as he meandered through the space, occasionally stopping before a mother, warrior, or child, sometimes clapping his hands or snapping his fingers to punctuate his speech. Twice, he turned his eyes to the roof of the longhouse and sang snatches of song in a language none could understand.

"By Toh's fire, we die away from who we were and weather the pain of new birth," he remarked as the tune dissipated. "We unravel from the world's lie. Our masks taste flame. Burn us! Consume these illusions of willfulness and self-worship!

"We can rely on no one save for our fellow brothers and sisters in the Way. Our devotion reveals the destiny Toh means us to fulfill."

Then he stopped before Anoke, a youth of fourteen winters. "What say you, boy? Speak you on your own authority, deeming it greater than His?"

Clearly terrified, the lad shook his head.

"You have witnessed the folly of man," Konatep said. "You have seen the face of Toh's displeasure. Are you repentant?"

Anoke nodded avidly. Konatep held the longhouse in rapt attention.

"Our sacrifices, however grievous, can never measure up to His." The priest sounded rapturous. "Oh, how he bleeds for the sorrows of Ophia! His tears, they burn! Do you not feel them? They strike your forehead. They scald you. There—behold!"

Murmurs of shock and awe rippled through the longhouse, all eyes fixed on Anoke's face. The skin above his eyes reddened like a cooked lobster's shell; blisters clustered on his tender flesh. The lad stood aghast, on the verge of unconsciousness, groping vaguely towards the newly-formed blights but obviously afraid to touch them.

"Now, that's a grave omen, to be sure!"

That voice made the collective Sendhi body shudder as if snapping out of a trance. No one knew this stranger; thereafter, none could recall how he had come to stand in the center of the lodge. But there he was, fanning his hands before the central brazier, warming both sides and appearing only casually interested in the proceedings.

Chief Okonkwa gasped and lurched as mobility returned to him. He stared at his afflicted leg like an unfamiliar, betraying appendage. As he reseated himself, he eyed the new stranger as warily as Konatep and the Sendhi.

Kanchi couldn't guess what people the newcomer belonged to. His skin was darker than a Sendhi's but lighter than a Manitoh's. He was dressed like a Vandrene fortune teller. His silken leggings—until now, Kanchi had only ever seen such pantaloons on women—matched the clear azure of his eyes as they were reflected in the light of the coals. A crimson scarf around his head concealed his hair but accentuated his sharp ears.

A Shaini, here?

At first, the man seemed to confer with himself. "The more we deny our souls, the bigger we must make our gods. And the farther from Ophia they will dwell. A sky god who rules alone always heralds judgment."

Then he raised his voice to address the crowd. "Toh's displeasure is made plain, the priest says. We bear guilt for the Rupture and must placate it with sacrifice, say the frightened herd. Aye: we've all read the signs."

He turned to Konatep. "Is it not true that in more savage lands, they kill their strongest or their most beloved to appease the gods? Do you think, O Mouth of Toh, that in this instance, perhaps, He will be merciful and accept the life of one whom the Narwhal tribe can bear to lose?"

Konatep eyed the newcomer with utter bemusement, but Kanchi marked how his mind hastened to maneuver. "He may indeed," he said after a cautious pause. "But tell me, friend, do all the Sendhi grant that you make this appeal on their behalf?"

"Well, perhaps Toh Himself will speak for us again!" The silken-clad stranger sounded solicitous. Three strides brought him close to Toh's priest, who gave way in surprise. The shadowy Inooks flanked Konatep but made no other move.

The newcomer stopped in front of Anoke. "What say you, lad? Are you ready to feel loving grace, to let the touch of divine favor soothe you?"

Without waiting for a reply, he moved his hand over the boy's forehead, and again, the lodge gasped. The blisters shrunk and then dwindled entirely. The redness faded.

This second transformation was quite beyond what Anoke could endure. He collapsed into his father's arms.

The stranger lifted his hands, almost mimicking Konatep in his priestly rapture, and twirled. "Toh has spoken! What worthy, devout people you must be to warrant two signs from the godhead in a single evening!"

Konatep, seething, nevertheless made a gesture that stilled his minions. Perhaps he feared he would lose credibility if his desperation showed.

Okonkwa took this opportunity to reassert his chiefly formality.

"Ours are lands of the long ice," he pronounced. "They test us even when meat is plentiful. Narwhal tribe has always known struggle, and at the worst of times, we've gone hungry.

"Many things changed with the great spirits' wrath, even after most eruptions and storms subsided. Herds disappear or are impossible to predict. Animals find new places to sleep in the winter, shelters our hunters do not discover. Old, familiar trails are swallowed by the ground. All of these circumstances have forged a kind of life that demands difficult decisions."

Shen, the fiercest warrior among the Sendhi, stood and broke the onlookers' collective stasis. "Has the required price not already been named? We must appease the storms with a sacrifice, and this sacrifice can be someone who costs our tribe the least.

"We all know who is the least of us, who burdens us on every expedition: Kanchi! She can't hold pace with any of us on a run. The clothing she sews cannot forbid the wind. And she cannot even speak!"

As if in echo or affirmation, Kanchi coughed. She often had this reaction during moments of fright or insecurity. She pressed her face into her parka, trying to muffle the sound.

"No one is denied a place in the Narwhal tribe unless they violate sacred law," Okonkwa said. Kanchi could hear the effort the chief made to keep his voice steady and dispassionate. "If they are of sickly body, this is a burden that all tribespeople shoulder."

"Maybe it has become too big a burden to share!" Shen shouted. "Even the strong among us struggle in these times! And would you even argue as you do if the gangi was not an orphan?"

Gangi was a derogatory label for someone who was not merely a girl but too timid to be a woman. But that was not what made Kanchi shudder; it was not what caused her heart to lurch. In her memory, no one had ever challenged Chief Okonkwa like Shen was doing now. The strange visitors had disrupted the tribe's equilibrium, casting forms and traditions into chaos.

She couldn't unravel the mystery. Surely, Shen's belligerence had been stirred up by Konatep and his demands. But it was also abetted by the nameless newcomer dressed in silks, who didn't *feel* as nefarious to her as the priest and the four Inooks.

Throughout the debate, no one—not even Konatep and his assassins—noticed this stranger steadily retreating, backing out of the longhouse while Shen argued his case. When the man finally raised his voice, he was already at the front entrance.

"It seems the Narwhal tribe has matters well in hand now! And so my work is done!"

He bowed low and passed between the flaps without ruffling them. Konatep, suddenly alarmed, made a sign, and his four Inooks darted to the entryway, swiping aside those Sendhi too slow to make way. The trained assassins peered out... and froze in bewilderment. A scouring gust tore through the longhouse as they struggled to credit what their senses reported.

The man had simply vanished.

Meanwhile, other voices, from those oblivious to this strange disturbance, rose in protest. Shen had made no secret of his dislike of Kanchi, some shouted, and so, of course, he would plea for her sacrifice. Others sided with Shen in his judgment, punctuating his arguments with cries of assent. Others hesitated. They cared for Kanchi and yet had to acknowledge the merit of Shen's verdict. These were brutal times.

Kanchi's heart sank as she cast her gaze around the lodge, like a drowning swimmer frantic for shore, and realized that her detractors far outnumbered her defenders.

Then, a new arrival to the lodge shattered the general clamor. The stillness became so profound that the thump of her gnarled cane on the packed dirt floor resounded to the far wall. Hunched over and mostly concealed within a mound of winter garb—caribou, seal, and seabird hide—Mother Inolda hobbled across the lodge's center space.

Everyone within the Narwhal tribe understood and accepted that they would not have Inolda's guidance for much longer. She, who'd served as their Singing Chieftess for decades, mostly kept to her bed now. She had little energy to spare and spoke openly about her departure from "this side of the Partition." The Narwhals (aside Kanchi) no longer sought her out for counsel; she participated in the tribe's affairs when she chose to.

They had to cradle their baited questions until the woman stood beside Okonkwa and turned. Mother Inolda was a full head shorter than the chief yet somehow radiated weightier authority. She lifted an orange gourd rattle high above her head and shook it several times, filling the longhouse with the sibilance of snakes.

"Some argue Kanchi is unfit to take her place with the Narwhal. Inolda hears. The storms persist; the omens are rightly read. Kanchi must prove herself. Survive until the shortest day of winter: a full moon cycle on the steppes, alone."

For the first time since this council had commenced, Kanchi experienced true horror and disbelief. No one could survive such a trial! The accusations brought by Shen and his allies were not new. For much of her life, Kanchi had witnessed how her weakness could prove a liability for the tribe. But she'd always assumed Inolda was her ally; she'd trusted the Singing Chieftess.

As friends and detractors digested the woman's proclamation with low murmurs, Kanchi searched her memories for warning signs, precursors to Inolda's disturbing turnaround.

"Banishment is the usual test." Now, Mother Inolda

addressed Konatep. "Anyone who can survive a turning of the moon alone on the steppes must surely have Sorsajna's favor. And if Kanchi fails, would this not constitute a sacrifice? Either way, it is indeed a delicate walk across a slender limb." Suddenly, she seemed to be speaking to someone else in the lodge. "One must feel without knowing, know without proof, and act without consolation.

"Such is the test. Inolda has spoken."

Most of the Sendhi within the lodge appeared perplexed, groping after matters far beyond their ken. But Kanchi watched Konatep reassessing the collective sentiment. He'd discovered where the true power within the Narwhal tribe resided.

"Good lady—" He bore a small, indulgent smile that patronized the old woman in her senility.

Inolda shook her gourd rattle again. "The Sendhi hear the voice of Sorsajna in the wind, feel it in water's flow and the movements of herds. We need no priest to interpret it for us!"

All present were startled by her tone. Though often irreverent and sparkling with impish humor, the Singing Chieftess was always diplomatic when dealing with outsiders. Rarely did she show open anger—especially in a situation as rife with tension and danger as this one.

For the first time since he'd arrived, Konatep's eyes spilled venom. Before he could retort, though, Inolda addressed him again.

"Surely, great priest, you did not come here only to preach the Sacred Writ. Perhaps you have medicines in your wagons? The Manitoh priests are renowned for their cures. Anything to ease an old woman's aching joints? And my head pounds at night like the flailing winds!"

Konatep's rage faded, replaced by a look of cruel cunning. "Indeed, I have remedies to remove *all* your pains, wise woman. Come—let us see what we can find!"

※ ※

At dawn, Kanchi made her way through the village with a bleak heart and downcast eyes. She shuffled past her people like a sleepwalker. At that moment, a single look of commiseration might have shattered the frail resolve that she clung to.

Over generations, close to a dozen men and women had been forced to leave the tribe, but their violations had been extreme: murdering, ravishing, and offering violence to children. Kanchi was the first to ever earn banishment for being a burden on the tribe itself—even if she had been offered a "chance" to redeem herself.

She harbored no illusions about her prospects of surviving this ordeal. She had been weak for so long... It would be a mercy if the spirits took her. She sought only to spare her fellow Sendhi further shame on her behalf.

Mother Inolda had devoted weeks to sewing her current outfit after Kanchi herself had failed, a fact that now seemed like a cruel irony. Her parka included a built-in hood—the distinctive sunburst ruff around the face fashioned from long wolf fur—making a separate head covering unnecessary. Its blue-dyed fringe draped over her chest. The large pouch sewn at her midriff, usually intended for infants, housed dried rations. Trousers, mittens, inner footwear, and outer boots made from caribou skin completed Kanchi's ensemble. Snowshoes were forbidden during the trial.

While she trudged, squinting in the glare of the sun off snow, she mentally reviewed her pouch's inventory: a wrap of salt (derived from boiled seawater), venison, Stone Pine nuts, dried strawberries and currants from the summer stores, flint and steel, and a rough map of the region.

Kanchi coughed, sweating in her exertions despite the cold. The slopes on the north side were too steep; she was obliged to give up trying to follow a familiar direction and go among the weeping pines to her right. Within a few hours, she emerged from the last of the trees and descended a minor slope to reach new flatlands.

Nothing lay on her horizon for the next three days to brighten her spirits; the homogenous white expanse was as featureless and desolate as her heart.

She'd begun walking parallel to a northern ridgeline—one of the few landmarks to disrupt the monotony of the steppe in that region—when the snow started. The wind swelled in the peculiar way that presaged a storm. Anticipating a dire trial, Kanchi stopped to consume some of her rations, washing the dried fare down with handfuls of snow. She'd endured four days of exile, and already her food was dwindling.

Her landscape was drenched in a beige-gray curtain.

Part of her was grateful for the engulfing wash. Within its swirling blindness, she could easily convince herself that this was a dreamland wherein nothing was real, including her futile choices. Therefore, there could be no consequences. During those moments when the surrounding whiteness would coalesce into strange and repulsive visions, Kanchi entered into them as unquestioningly as a dreamer.

If only the storm could whisk her out of the clutches of her memory.

So much could be resolved for her if she simply languished. She would sleep, the snow would seal her over... and she would not awaken again to the never-ending struggle through pain and incapacity that comprised her life. Why should she not simply relinquish the fight?

I will lie down, and then there will be no more

pain—either from my body or from my shame.

Yet somehow, she loved this body that housed her, and she knew that shame was not the sum of her being.

Very well, another part of her conceded. *If I will die out here, it'll not be because I surrender.* Her body's frailties had prevented her from living a warrior's life, but she could still die a warrior's death.

Since the wrath of the great spirits, the wind seldom committed to one direction for long. The air's commotion was erratic, like a riot of angry bees. Kanchi witnessed this in areas where the snow, caught in conflicting currents, swirled in eddying disarray.

She cursed herself for not heading towards the northern ridges while they were still visible. She might've traveled along their flanks, where the snow would be shallower, and the jagged rock wall could foil the wind.

Now, the snowfall was so thick that the afternoon resembled twilight. But a dim verdigris glow occasionally penetrated the blizzard's fanfare. It drew Kanchi's gaze, made her forget her myriad inward curses and fears. Lights appeared on the horizon: globes, seemingly no larger than her head, bobbing some four or five feet above the ground, enticing her onward. Kanchi's heart leaped as if she beheld the face of a loved one. Unlike the landscape and storm in constant flux, the lights retreated steadily, their fixed shape and luminescence impervious to the tumult.

The Rudowine had returned to her! Even after consulting Inolda, Kanchi had not resolved the question of whether or not to trust them. Nevertheless, she aimed towards their glow because it was her only visible guide. Following that vivid trail would ensure she didn't walk in circles.

She wandered as if somnambulant. Her extremities—ears, fingers, nose, and toes—were numb, but she was like a child following a procession of enchantments. To a large extent, she forgot the cold, the ache of thigh muscles that'd spent days contesting high snow drifts. A sense of wonder subsumed the long loneliness of her life.

Though the rigors of the steppes and the storm wore down her body and will, they brought clarity in other ways. The green globes reminded Kanchi that there were forces at work within her world that surpassed her comprehension. She accounted herself neither knowledgeable nor wise, but she knew what loving regard was. Mother Inolda held her in such regard. The Singing Chieftess must have had some hidden motive for arguing for her banishment.

To spare Kanchi—or the tribe—an even more dire fate? To grant her an appointment with these Sophryne lights?

But this faint, wild hope fled as Kanchi realized *where* the verdant lights were leading her. On her horizon rose a structure whose visible radius was too smooth to be a natural formation. With sharp lacerations of ancestral dread, Kanchi identified it: the ruins of a Hive built by that ancient, lofty race known as the Shaini.

She'd been aware of the Crystal Citadel, as her people called it, her whole life. By all accounts, it had been abandoned more than once before the cataclysms. According to Inolda, the original builders were Lanoreans, dwellers in the Conhuera Mountains whose descendants had grown vast orchards and vineyards.

These ruins were taboo.

But it was too late to consider changing course. Out in the open, the blizzard would conquer her. And there was no other refuge. Kanchi felt her body aching to succumb, eager to forsake this battle against elementals that it couldn't possibly prevail over. Her only hope was this "sanctuary" that her people equated with madness and death.

And the floating verdigris lights, which pulsed in affirmation of life and warmth amid the desolate, howling waste, were insistent.

As she drew closer, Kanchi saw that the Hive was bathed in the same luminescence that characterized those lights—hence its visibility. Vaguely, she wondered whether that glow also exuded warmth. Was that why no snow or ice concealed the structure? It was bored with so many recesses that it appeared like a piece of volcanic rock, except that its shell was immaculate, a crenelated swirl a hundred feet tall consisting of granite polished to the smoothness of glass and glittering with flawless quartz, jade, and copper veins.

It evinced no signs of life.

Now, even the wind seemed to abet her progress, pushing at her back. Finally, Kanchi reached a window at the Crystal Citadel's feet that she could clamber through.

It was warmer within the chamber than the mere cessation of wind accounted for. An organic quality to the enclosure made Kanchi imagine she was inside the body of a living thing.

The spectacle was so dazzling that minutes passed before she became conscious of another wonder: that she could see at all. Some kind of yellow-lime phosphorescence, the commingling of sunlight and verdure, kept the Hive bathed in light so unobtrusive as to almost go unnoticed even as it illuminated every corner and crevasse. It aided Kanchi but also compounded her sense of alien menace.

This sensation was heightened by a barely perceptible hum within the stone, a vibration she felt rather than heard.

The floor was smooth as a placid pond on a windless day. In every direction, the walls were pockmarked with perfectly cylindrical holes. Kanchi followed the floating lights to an opening at the far wall, entered a circular tunnel slightly higher than her head, and began exploring her new and altogether foreign surroundings.

The tunnels resembled burrowing holes for giant worms more closely than anything carved by human hands. Like the outer wall, everything within the enclosure was composed of polished granite intertwined with glittering veins: jade, quartz, copper, and occasionally gold. How had these minerals been rendered so glassy? Several walls even bore arcane symbols rendered in thin platinum lines.

The seven green globes—the Rudowine—seemed to shrink or swell in relation to their surroundings. They'd appeared like lime-colored moon jellies out on the steppes. Inside the tunnels, they more closely resembled fireflies. They were always out of reach; they maintained the same proximity to Kanchi regardless of how fast she moved, making her question their essential nature. Did they even occupy physical space?

Whatever their form, the Rudowine soon proved their benevolent intent. They led her to a chamber full of food and provisions. Considering the time that had passed since this place was last inhabited—two years, according to rumor—Kanchi marveled that the space didn't reek of rot. But she discovered that every item in the Shainis' age-old stores was encased within durable, smooth, and completely transparent wrapping.

The contents looked edible. For the moment, that sufficed. Kanchi would wonder at their baffling state of preservation later. Made courageous or foolhardy by hunger and fatigue, she began nibbling at the provender and then bit in avidly when it proved agreeable.

The dried meat tasted like it had just come off a fire. The fruit burst with exotic flavor. These were sensory delights hitherto unknown to her.

Eventually, however, her returning strength brought

renewed caution. Although the interior of the Hive was as warm as a wigwam spread about a hearth fire, and she longed to shed her parka, this was a concession to the strange sanctuary that she was not ready to commit.

And something about the place's ambiance made Kanchi contemplative. If this repast didn't poison her, she could endure her trial in this refuge, given its unaccountable comfort. She could triumphantly return to her tribe at the end of the moon's cycle on the year's shortest day.

But some members of the Narwhal tribe had never viewed her as anything other than a burden. No doubt, many hoped she wouldn't survive this ordeal. Was she so eager to be in their company again, to win their approval? Even Inolda had betrayed her in the end. Unless...

Kanchi resumed the line of inquiry that she'd begun out on the steppes when privation and suffering had pushed her mind beyond its accustomed boundaries. Mother Inolda possessed uncanny foresight. She'd guided the Narwhal tribe to herds and shelters countless times. Was it possible that she'd somehow foreseen Kanchi's discovery of this place? Had she *intended* it?

For what purpose?

Lost in such ruminations and aimlessly wandering, Kanchi stumbled upon a cache of bound scrolls within a bowl-shaped recess. She untied one and purveyed it. It didn't surprise her that she could decipher the script. Legend maintained that Shaini had originally taught her people to speak and read, and in honor of that legacy, writing comprised part of every Sendhi child's education.

"Though we were relieved to discover Kublai Hive–a foray into the aboveground world that perhaps Lanore made prematurely–neither I nor my troupe could abide the long, dark winters. By Sarpienta's forked tongue and all the other lofty invocations I can think of! Did this land even <u>have</u> any other season? But we knew that the cataclysms also caused this severity. Ophia's tremendous gut-belches had expelled ash sufficient to blot out the sun, ushering winter even into places like the Kawli Rainforest, whose people had never before beheld snow.

"So we ventured south to warmer climes and (hopefully) larger audiences. I intended to create a new theater to rival Old Ophia's Ambrosine someday."

In her loneliness and bereavement, Kanchi was drawn to the confiding undertow of these journals. Bereft of her tribe, she'd found someone willing to trust her with secrets.

"But as you can see oh traveler, I made some preparations beforehand, leaving lore and clues that may serve the seeker after knowledge and, more importantly, wisdom."

Something about the cadence of the words reminded Kanchi of the silk-clad stranger who'd appeared so suddenly in the longhouse and intervened in her fate. Intrigued, she opened another scroll.

"Look about you as you sleep! When you are deep in dreams, no physical eyes can watch your movements or dictate your experience. This is how we met and planned our bid for freedom—beyond the Veils.

"It's true that time and effort are required to learn how to move purposefully there. But consider how long it took to master walking in the waking world. For a large group of Shaini to learn the art of lucidity, coordinate their nightly meetings, and create dream sanctuaries... That was the work of generations. Hail the Sophryne, I say! And maybe someday one of them will teach us how to access such abilities without all this damnable discipline!

"But you, oh reader of these transcriptions, don't need to learn all this with a fresh mind. I share my knowledge just as my ancestors once taught your people language and tool-making. I can impart knowledge that might take you a lifetime to attain on your own—assuming you ever attained it.

"Many fears bind us when we believe we're trapped within our bodies, bound to our physical senses, and hounded by mortality. Those fears dissolve within the dream environment—if we become conscious!"

Kanchi was startled by how a thread of continuity seemed to run through everything she read, even as she picked parchments at random.

"When you find yourself within a dream, ask what brought you to that moment. What is its history? Watch it unfold behind you. When awake, ask yourself, 'Am I dreaming?' While dreaming, ask yourself, 'Am I awake?' Are there really such sharp divisions between the two worlds?"

In essence, the idea of a dream's innate wisdom was not strange to Kanchi. Her people often made crucial decisions based on information obtained in the dreaming state. For uncounted generations, dreams had illuminated the movements of herds, the locations of water and tubers and fruits; they had warned the Sendhi of coming storms and diseases. When members of two clans decided to mate for life, they had often already consummated their bond in dreams. Mother Inolda had attained the title of Singing Chieftess partly because she was known to be a proficient dreamer.

Some passages meandered across the pages like naked appeals. The last one Kanchi read seemed directed at her personally.

"Is your heart still unresolved? Nay, I think you long for this sacred experience as much as I do. We Sophrynes always recognize our own. Take a moment to look—not with your meaty eyes but with your delicate senses—and see that there's no longer any path behind you. Do you understand? You feared the Sophryne lights would lead you astray. But sometimes, we must lose ourselves to find ourselves."

Despite the curiosity and excitement the words awoke in her, Kanchi faltered there. Her long weariness—engendered by exertion, frost, and fear—wholly overcame her. She lay on her side, pillowed by three layers of thick clothing, and surrendered to darkness, never noticing how the lights overhead respectfully dimmed.

She stood near the shoreline of a star-dancing ocean. It was evening. People gathered. An island was visible—a magical refuge. Like the Rudowine, Kanchi recalled, it constantly morphed, never appearing the same size and shape from one heartbeat to the next.

Thirteen glowing green globes floated amongst its trees, rambunctious in their numinous pageantry.

People looked at her askance when Kanchi tried to draw their attention to the globes. They couldn't corroborate what she saw. She nearly succumbed to despair before merry jingles brought her around, and she met the eyes of a dark-skinned man dressed in lavish, gaudy silks. He knelt before her. His black hair was bound in several long braids;

the chiming was produced when his movements shook the tiny blue beads tied to each of their ends.

"Do you want to walk out to the island?"

His soothing tenor dispelled her tension. Kanchi realized at once that he, too, witnessed the lights.

"I'm Sanyori." His eyes waited for signs of recognition.

"Hello, Sanyori. I'm Kanchi, of the Narwhal tribe." *I am too shy to speak this confidently!* Kanchi thought. Then, she recalled her waking identity; she beheld it in a wash of shame-gray light. *I don't normally* speak *at all!*

But she found herself doing so now, quite spontaneously. "I'd love to go with you!"

Kanchi remembered that low tide—now nearly peaking—formed a path to the island. And so the two of them, hand in hand, descended to the sand and waves. Ophia's heartbeat reverberated through the ground. The water divided its vast body to reveal a path, uncovering stones that had known the ocean's floor and the sun's caress. All Kanchi's senses tingled as if in concert with the bells on Sanyori's braids.

"I'm sure that was a terrifying ordeal," the man said. Somehow, Kanchi knew that he referred to her experience in the longhouse the night before her exile began. "I sorely apologize." Indeed, he *looked* contrite. "We could see no other way. We had to appease Konatep somehow—and in a way that would put his mind at ease so he'd leave the Narwhal tribe alone thereafter. You bore the worst brunt of the plan, all the more so because you could not know of it beforehand.

"Please understand that your sacrifice likely spared your people unspeakable suffering. The priesthood of Toh might've orphaned every child there before placing them in bondage if they failed to convert your village."

"Who else are you referring to?" Kanchi asked. "You said 'we'."

"Mother Inolda," Sanyori said. "She and I have been dream companions for many adventures. She comes awake at will, more often than not. Although... the nature of her reality is quite different now."

"What do you mean?" But Kanchi's heart admitted the shadow even as she spoke. "She's gone, isn't she?"

"Gone, no. Dead to the world of the one-eyed, yes." Sanyori made an abject gesture. "I am sorry."

Kanchi circled in a whirlpool of sorrow for a time, but then, at an obscure thought, she brightened. "Can I speak with her again? I mean, when I'm here?"

"There's nothing stopping you." The man stared at her curiously as if seeking more and then shrugged. "I'll repeat what my teacher, Shiya-coqui, once made a kind of Sophryne credo. My intentions tonight are three-fold: make you aware that you are dreaming, suggest that you can be just as conscious now as you ever are in waking, and remind you that this environment reflects your inner world. You're free to shape it however you choose."

His words tugged at the strands of Kanchi's awareness until she suddenly alighted with comprehension. In the middle of the ocean, she stopped.

"It's you—the stranger who came to the longhouse that night!" Guided by sudden intuition, she asked, "Are you the one who wrote those journals?"

Sanyori smiled. "Mother Inolda was right about you—bright as a Sophryne light and quick as a lash of Sarpienta's tail!" He spread his arms wide. "Well, here you are. Awake and dreaming."

He flexed his hands. "It was exhilarating the first time I learned to do this. I hope you enjoy it as much." He bowed with a flourish. "Now, learn to dream while *awake*, and you'll be able to speak on *that* side of the Partition as well!"

Following his example, Kanchi studied her hands. No

longer covered with thick mittens, they swelled and contracted, never remaining the same size or shape from moment to moment. She seemed to constantly discover them for the first time.

"That's right—pause and renew your focus," Sanyori said. "Dream currents can sweep you into other oceans before you even realize you're wet. Lose your grip, and it's bound to be the closest I'll ever come to seeing a sweet girl like you curse.

"Anyway, I'd rue the lost opportunity. I've always cherished the moments we've carved out on this side of the Partition."

Once the boundaries of the dream sharpened, Kanchi returned her attention to him. "What was it you and the priest did? I mean, with Anoke? Was that Sorsajna?"

Sanyori noticed her wavering again and spoke sternly. "The dream state is rife with distractions. It's a realm where countless doors open simultaneously, each vying for our attention. Perhaps you should hold your questions..."

But Kanchi leaned against one of those inner doors and, with no presentiment of her destination, passed into a different environment. Like a powerful undertow, her curiosity carried her away.

⚜⚜

The edges of a woodland engulfed her. Every branch, bramble, and weed acknowledged her presence in a wordless welcome, inviting her deeper into the forest's mysteries.

She sighed with relief, noticing Sanyori walking beside her. "There is memory and history here," Kanchi said, voicing sudden comprehension. Then she paused to study him. "We've shared many dreams at many other times, haven't we?"

Sanyori's eyes beamed. "No Sophryne was ever prouder of an apprentice! Yes, you are right, indeed!

"Perhaps now you grow aware of the continuity within this environment. We've never met in the waking world, but we can speak familiarly because of our many interactions on *this* side. It is not singular and isolated. This terrain"—he swept a hand—"can melt, erupt, crystallize, disintegrate... and yet, amid all that fluidity..."

Kanchi smiled. "There are people we can meet again and conversations we can resume."

Sanyori spread his arms. "You travel through the landscape of yourself. You are eternal and whole. What is there to fear?

"But in another time, in another dream, you mentioned Sorsajna. That name refers to the aware and responsive spark of life within every part of Creation—you, me, a whale, a shooting star...

"But as for that priest, Konatep, I'd sooner call him a second-rate hypnotist—speaking as a first-rate one, myself!"

He laughed in a way that made Kanchi feel that he was amused by his own hubris and also utterly serious.

She was vaguely familiar with mesmerism. Mother Inolda had once confided in her that her "cures" often involved nothing more than convincing ill people they were well.

"So what we all saw within the longhouse... that wasn't real?" she asked.

"You mean the burn marks and blisters on the young man—"

"Anoke."

"Anoke's head. Yes. You and all the other witnesses saw rightly. It was Anoke who was hypnotized. Konatep convinced him he'd been burned; I convinced him he'd been soothed."

Discussing the Narwhal tribe's longhouse sent Kanchi's ruminations down another avenue. "I don't want to return there, but I have nowhere else to go."

"Who could blame you?" Sanyori's eyes watered with empathy. "Though you survived, you were still a sacrifice—*their* sacrifice."

Kanchi hung her head, unconsciously slipping into her accustomed depression. "Maybe it was for the best. I only slow my people down, and they can't afford that burden, particularly in winter."

Sanyori cupped her chin and lifted it until their eyes met.

"There was a gift wrapped up within all the ravages of the Rupture. Do you know what it was?"

Confused, Kanchi shook her head.

"Those with Vision were more likely to survive and lead others to safety. And so the survivors were reminded of the preciousness—in the most pragmatic sense, mind you—of the inner light. An individual can live without a tribe. A tribe cannot exist without individuals. And the Narwhal tribe ignores *your* gifts at its peril!

"Do you think *anyone* could have followed the Sophryne lights, understood the ciphers I left, or found me here on this side of the Partition? You did all this because you can *see*. And because you can see, you're the only one who can warn your people."

Sanyori nodded to his left; suddenly, they stood on the Sendhi steppes, Kanchi's homeland, overlooking a precipice facing black gulfs.

"There's something here you ought to see," he said.

Then, Kanchi's dream plunged into ominous chasms, accompanied by the deep roar of thunder. The ground lurched and swept the companions' feet out from under them. Kanchi's dream shins crashed against the rock; her imagination embellished the pain. Ophia tilted and rumbled; great Sarpienta stirred in its bowels, and foundations fell into fathomless pits. Ocean waters poured into the cracks, effacing the ground.

Tremors turned Kanchi to and fro; her dream mind groped for their source. Fissures opened all around; hills collapsed. Soon, she and Sanyori were forsaken on a sea-devoured finger of land.

At last, waves engulfed them, washing away all memory of land, Sendhi woman, and Shaini trickster.

🌿🌿

Though he wasn't entirely satisfied with the outcome of his missionary expedition, Konatep could no longer justify lingering in the Sendhi steppes.

He disliked departing before receiving confirmation of the Narwhal girl's death. But here, unfortunately, the superstitions his order had cultivated did their work too well. None of the natives could be persuaded, coerced, or threatened into going to the Lanorean Hive. The Inooks, who'd surmised that this was the girl's sanctuary, shunned it for their own reasons. The energy of such places served as mirrors for their profound darkness and thus became abodes of nightmares and lunacy.

At least the old woman is out of the way. One contrary voice had been stilled. His Master would be pleased with that much. Thus consoled, Konatep offered the Sendhi some parting platitudes and rode on.

The Narwhal tribe sighed heavily like a black cloud had passed overhead, withholding its lightning. Though they mourned Mother Inolda and Kanchi, they knew they had been spared a much blacker fate.

Kanchi awoke too shaken to unpack the previous night's revelations. Days passed before she could approach her dream memories and assimilate their lessons. And she cradled her loneliness to her bosom, for the Sophryne lights had vanished.

She'd always considered dreams phenomena that "came to her," like a caravan of Vandrene traders arriving to barter for Sendhi clothes. Never before had she experienced such a sense of participation, of self-awareness.

She was Sanyori's apprentice? For how long had this been going on?

If she could be just as awake "there" as "here," which side of the Partition was real? Was the distinction even important?

Those last images warned of a peril on this side, though.

Like most of the Sendhi, Kanchi had often dreamed of the great spirits' wrath. But these particular visions had felt more precise and insistent, more prophetic.

She spent a few weeks aimlessly wandering through the Crystal Citadel's myriad tunnels, halls, and stairwells. She revisited Sanyori's journals, seeking clues to unravel the mysteries of her experiences.

Some entries described the dwelling that sheltered her—Kublai Hive. They shed light upon its ancient builders, who'd understood how to generate energy, move water, and even uplift their community's mood in ways that utterly baffled her. As best she could understand it, the process involved manipulating a kind of sound that physical ears couldn't hear.

Those vibrations still lived within these walls. That explained the subtle hum Kanchi had felt since first entering this sanctuary. If only she knew how to rouse them to full wakefulness...

The text explained how extensive tunnels connected this Hive to a southerly dwelling named Mangoyen. Sanyori had even provided a rough sketch of the route. But Kanchi could see that it involved a journey of many leagues, so she was not about to attempt such an expedition on her own.

Before long, she began to awaken with a feeling like springtime in her flesh. She'd not known such vigor since childhood. Circulation warmed places in her joints and extremities as if reaching them for the first time. Kanchi knew that the nourishment she'd discovered in the Hive, and the beneficent properties of the structure itself, had contributed to her convalescence. But equally significant were her internal changes.

She walked with an unfamiliar spring in her stride.

This, in turn, galvanized the sense of inner purpose steadily growing in her since her lucid dreams. She better understood what was happening to her in this Shaini sanctuary. What she'd once considered a curse—her difference, her apartness—Kanchi now recognized as a gift. She was different because her mind and senses were meant to venture down twilight paths that others could not tread and return with treasures others could not find. Her dream auguries were a natural part of her heritage.

Nothing in Kanchi's world looked quite as familiar as it had before her dreams in the Crystal Citadel. Everything she saw carried suggestions of an unseen dimension, of significance that escaped her in waking but was illuminated while she slept. Every face the world showed her concealed another: one as significant and condign in its native place as the prosaic ground she walked upon. Her very thought processes evinced signs of this profound shift. She'd never been so introspective before, never reflected so deeply upon her inner mind.

꒐꒐

By the time she reached the outskirts of the Narwhal settlement, a score of curious eyes had gathered by the outermost wigwams to follow Kanchi's approach. She didn't stop until she found Chief Okonkwa, who also watched her from a place closer to the village's heart. Murmurs followed Kanchi as she wove past the dwellings of her old home. But no one spoke up. Few—if any—had expected to ever see her again.

But Okonkwa's eyes burned with pride. He lifted his arms high and addressed every Sendhi within earshot. "Behold, she has returned!" His rapture was deaf to any voices of dissent. "We remember Inolda's words. 'Let no one doubt her again,' our Singing Chieftess said. If Kanchi has survived, the great spirits have willed it so."

Then he lowered his gaze to Kanchi; his eyes encompassed the marvel of her newly-manifested health. "You look well, near-daughter! The great spirits have made you strong, and there is a light within you...."

Kanchi met the chief's eyes and bowed low. She momentarily shrank before the task she'd committed to, an ambition grown out of evanescent visions that could be harder to believe under the light of day. Her trust in her inner guidance had grown, but she was still cowed by the eyes of the tribe, most of whom were her elders.

Then, galvanized by the severity of her visions and recalling the rituals in which Mother Inolda had delivered her prophecies, she signed: "Bid the Narwhals bring drums and rattles."

Startled by her request but almost compelled by the conviction in his near-daughter's eyes, Okonkwa complied.

When the instruments were brought, he bade those Sendhi who seemed most eager to participate to strike up a rhythm such as they employed when Mother Inolda, back in more virile days, had delivered in-trance prophecies.

Kanchi's percipience sharpened at once. Much of the Sophryne training had been imparted to her during dream time. Hence, as she drew closer to its characteristic state of consciousness, that interior terrain was both startling and familiar.

She knew not to struggle or make logical sense of what she perceived and intuited. Sanyori had taught her to surrender to this flow and trust that this mode of perception was as natural, as much a part of her birthright, as the external world her five senses reported.

Closing her eyes, she was scarcely aware of her body's response to the urgent rhythms. She couldn't feel the snow, sand, and stones beneath her. Breezes seemed to pass through her as if they encountered no obstacle. She felt earth, air, and sunlight as energies—possessed of vibrant, exuberant personalities of their own—in constant flux.

No one, not even Shen and his sympathizers, dared disrupt this performance. All sensed *Incora*, the arrival of spirits into an earthly vessel. From the Sendhi steppes to the Kawli jungles and beyond, no Oskwai of any denomination would interrupt *Incora* when faced with evidence of this sacred visitation. At all costs, space for Vision must be made.

Kanchi began dancing in an abrupt, jerky rhythm reminiscent of the contractions and thrusts of peristaltic motion. She emoted in a foreign tongue, its origins lost in antiquity. The melody and rhythm filled her head, banishing thought. The sensory impressions of life—heat and cold, pleasure and pain—lost impact and meaning. Kanchi drifted, along vast, concentric rings of light, into a fathomless tunnel. Nurturing a newfound sense of boundless freedom, she passed from terror to exhilaration.

She belonged in the Luminous Realm. This place was Home.

"A dread in my heart reechoes in my dreams," she intoned. "Of what it portends, there can be no doubt. Forsake this place! It is fit to be no one's shelter hereafter!"

This declaration—both the urgency behind it and the shock of its origin, a young woman they'd long considered a mute—drew listeners closer.

"I speak with the sureness of *Incora*. These steppes, all along the pine forest"—She waved a hand vaguely west—"open like a deep gash in flesh. Sarpienta coils and unspools. Hillsides fall into fires as wide as Lake Pahloka. Only the Crystal Citadel provides sanctuary!"

This would have been a frightful proclamation even if she hadn't mentioned that place of taboo and fear. As it was, all Sendhi within earshot, including their chief, were too astonished to speak.

"It is safe, Chief Okonkwa," Kanchi insisted, speaking from her dim awareness of her conscious self. In lieu of eyesight, she could yet *feel* the man's reaction. "I've lived there. I sheltered from three blizzards. I found food, healing herbs, and even much counsel."

Okonkwa squinted as if her newfound voice and manifest health, causes for wonder just moments before, had become mysterious and sinister.

"Even the beasts will not approach that place," he whispered. "It was birthed from a brand of magic perilous to us!"

Kanchi opened her eyes and regarded the chief with a loving regard that daunted him. "It is a place of healing. There is warmth. There are stores that could sustain us all through the winter snows. I beg you—There is plenty for all. I wish not to have to return alone!"

"Do not persist in these fancies, girl," Okonkwa urged her—though he wasn't entirely certain who he was addressing anymore. "Doubtless, your trials have put too much strain on your heart and mind. Remain with your people. *Your people.* You have proven yourself. No one will doubt your worth again."

"Join me! This land will be devoured and smothered! I have seen it."

"Seen?"

"In dreams and waking omens," Kanchi said. "Were she here, Mother Inolda would echo them."

She paused to give the pain of that revelation its due. Whispers rippled through the onlookers. How did she know Inolda had crossed the Partition?

Kanchi tolled on as if their question clamored to her ears. "She drifted on the wings of Konatep's poisons. But she was eager to relinquish Ophia and availed herself of this opportunity. This she bid me tell you. She hoped her passing would distract the priest and spare the Narwhal tribe."

Kanchi felt it urgently now, the sense that the old woman had somehow passed her legacy onto her. But she could not afford to revisit her grief. It would grow into a much more monstrous thing should she fail to convince the tribe...

And so, throughout their meals and the time spent around the evening fire, Kanchi persevered with her arguments—with hand signs, now, as her throat closed with the folding of the trance. She related the full tale of her trials and revelations in the Hive.

But the Narwhal tribe would not be swayed.

Most of the Sendhi cast their eyes to the ground when she searched them for any glimmers of assent. Some even closed their eyes and pressed the flaps of their caps against their faces as if to insulate themselves from some sorcery evoked by her gestures.

"She has walked with ghosts, and now she signs like one of them."

"She doesn't *appear* mad."—But these voices were few.

Kanchi found no receptive hearts. Her people looked away as if they no longer knew, or wished to know, who she was.

Some, like Shen, laughed and openly mocked her.

"We will be safe, she says, in some ruins abandoned even by its builders! Truly, we must go!" Those gathered around him chuckled and sipped their fermented gruel. "We will spend our days crawling through worm tunnels and carving rocks!"

Kanchi found no allies. Exhausted and dispirited, she left at first morning's light after spending the night in the longhouse that had been her home. Though some of the Narwhal tribe argued and tried to restrain her, and Chief Okonkwa repeated his appeals, she set her mind eastwards.

In her profound grief, one inner voice insisted that the village was her place; if she could not sway the Narwhal, she should still stay and die as one of them. She wasn't sure what propelled her forward when she could only foresee a profound emptiness within the solitary life she pursued.

On the first night of her return journey, Kanchi could still hear the Sendhi drums, though the beat had an apathetic air as if no one knew or cared what it signified anymore.

One morning in early spring, in a still hour before dawn, Kanchi was roused by powerful vibrations that shook her haven. The smooth stone floors swayed as if intoxicated. The woman rubbed sleep from her eyes as a distant cacophony filled her ears.

She knew the threat was not imminent; these were only the echoes of a cataclysm ten leagues distant. Nevertheless, she clambered down to the Hive's knees. From there, she descried how the dip of the northwestern horizon, usually demarked by a tree line, now plunged like a precipice.

Kanchi was startled but otherwise calm. Her dream premonitions of this cataclysm had been vivid and explicit. She knew that a serpentine canyon devoured leagues where the Narwhal tribe had once hunted, feasted, loved, mourned, and sang.

Eyes moistened with grief, she mouthed a devotional chant on behalf of those now dead, those who had remained behind. It was a kind of prayer or invocation that the Shaini had taught her people long ago and which Mother Inolda had taught Kanchi in turn.

"No one belonged here more than you.

"Sorsajna's fire lives within you still. Whose support do you require when you are upheld by the very forces of life? No gods or chieftains need to carry your destiny. You require no idols against which to measure yourself.

"When every memory throbs with the pain of what might have or could have been, you are held in the arms of Sorsajna. Neither of you can ever leave the other.

"Follow the voice that fills your heart and mind with the flame of life, illuminating its possibilities, scattering its sparks in countless dreams and passions.

"Sorsajna—all that exists—forever discovers and expresses itself as you. It dances within every portion of your being, every step you make, even as it spurs the seasons and their turnings. To discount your own divinity is to belittle divinity itself.

"You are held in the arms of Sorsajna."

Kanchi even included Shen in her appeal. The brash warrior had not been her friend, but Kanchi had never wished for him to meet such an end as this.

She spent the remainder of the day huddled in her pain, wishing she knew of some way to contact the Rudowine or Sanyori to ease her bereavement.

The following morning, however, a strange noise roused her. While its *timbre* (somewhat akin to birdsong) still reverberated within her mind, she wondered if an animal had wandered into the Hive. But beasts had always shied away from this place...

It came again. "Ai - Hee - Ah! Ai - Hee - Ah!" This was a call that the Sendhi used to communicate their location over long distances when they dared not use talking drums. But before she even interpreted the call, Kanchi recognized the voice.

She hastened to the Hive's front entrance.

The air below was misty with the breath of fifty or sixty Sendhi milling about on the still-snowy ground.

How..? She tried to shake off remnants of sleep and encompass it all.

Okonkwa, the author of the calls, stood at the head of the wedge and spoke for the gathering. "Some of us dreamed as you did following your departure. Inolda's death and your loss... that grief pulled the Veils from my eyes. I beheld the lighted, floating globes. They insisted I follow. Not knowing if I went to my doom, I asked no one to accompany me. But these others chose to.

"For all our lives and the lives of our forefathers, this has been a place of dread. This you know. But if we deny vision when it manifests, and even the counsel of our dreams, we cease to be who we are."

Kanchi was moved to keen relief and joy—a joy tempered, however, by her awareness that these folk didn't comprise the entirety of the Narwhal tribe but only a portion.

The chief guessed the source of her unease. "Some listened to Shen's counsel and not Okonkwa's. He became chief of all those who remained behind."

He gazed to the west with rueful eyes. "As we've seen, he did not relish his new authority for long."

Then he raised his arms high; thrice, he clapped his hands together until the hills re-echoed. "But we would share this abode with you if you unroll the rug of welcome."

"Yes!" Kanchi's hands conveyed how her heart soared at this unlooked-for reprieve. Her family had returned!

But the mute appeal in their bereft faces demanded more from her. "I was a poor sewer or tracker of caribou," she signed, "but now I hunt within the land of dreams. In this time of need, I will work medicine for the Narwhal, as Inolda did. I will mediate between the dreaming and the waking worlds. I will speak to the realm of the spirits on behalf of all Sendhi who ask it."

That night, she dreamed she stood in the middle of a circle while a ceremony was in progress. "Kanchi has gone where no others may follow," a robed figure proclaimed. "She is guided by lights no one else can see. But she will return—Aye, and when she does, she will teach the Sendhi to dream new dreams!"

With that, the figure threw back its cowl, and Kanchi stared into Sanyori's smiling azure eyes.

"What an adventure, eh?" he beamed. "Learning to recognize where your consciousness was poised, awake or asleep... This is what you learned in the ruins of Kublai Hive." He smiled somewhat sheepishly. "I hope you will excuse my stumble of pride over what my people achieved. But verily, it startles me that, so long after those walls were wrought, the loving vibrations that informed them still have the power to instruct.

"But the choice to open to them—that was yours, dear Kanchi. And it is quests such as yours upon which our future hangs!"

He rubbed his hands together with fierce satisfaction. "Such a relief to see you finally awaken; you have no idea how many attempts I've made. Oh, don't look morose! You were a great deal quicker to learn than I was.

"I have to admit, too... It pleased me mightily to dress that Konatep in clown garb. He's pilfered so many of my trade secrets; his hypnotic tricks ape my inventions, and badly, at that! A blow to his smug pride was the least I owed him."

Kanchi allowed Sanyori his moment of self-congratulatory mirth. But his mention of Konatep stirred up her memories of the Narwhal longhouse and certain unanswered questions.

"There's something I'm still aching to know," she said. "That night in the lodge, the night I was banished... How did you do it? You just... disappeared. Even the Inooks couldn't find you. And there were no prints."

"Ah, yes—that. Perhaps a fuller lesson is due—another day." Sanyori bowed with a single-handed flourish. "It will be a piercing pleasure, dear Kanchi, if someday I can visit and instruct you in person. But thus far, I have never been inside a Sendhi longhouse—leastways, not in my body!"

Savwain Desert

Virgoda Plains

D'yangi's Mines

Conhuera Mtns

Shetain Ruins

Arjena Hills

Ruptured Hills

Magda's Oasis

Tunzao Trail

Na-Viltaj

Mantanya Pass

Sajna of the Savwain Desert

I can't hide away anymore! I've given grief its due. It's time for me to step into the currents of life again. I need to be of service. I need an image of the mountain towards which I'll move.

But first, Esperidi needed to know whether that mountain still existed. What kind of world surrounded her now; what was Ophia's true condition? What had the Rupture actually wrought?

Her dreams had offered her plentiful glimpses—enough, perhaps, to piece together a consistent picture. But the storms and upheavals had not wholly subsided. Ophia's face continued to contort and writhe. Still, people had begun to emerge, wander, and settle over the last couple of years. Many had weathered the worst part of the crisis huddled in portions of the subterranean network that Esperidi's ancestors had once prepared for such exigencies.

The region she studied now housed a stray nest of such survivors. And one dream omen spoke succinctly. She would meet a woman there, the one for whom the Oasis was named: an elderly Vandrene who had spontaneously learned some of the fundamental uses of *Sacred Timbre*.

No doubt that was what had earned the woman's authority. She could sense water in the desert as easily as shifting weather patterns—the movements of the Rupture. Those twin gifts were more valuable in the Savwain Desert than a cartload of gold. Such a person might be attuned not only to physical phenomena but also to movements within the human community. Esperidi would wager that Mother Magda was a lodestone for news and rumors: the desert's centrifugal heart.

The young Shaini slowly panned her line of sight along the full length of the wide, sandy wash slithering towards Magda's Oasis. Squinting lent Esperidi a look of reproach that she couldn't wholly suppress. Even after a score of months in exile, nurturing her Rupture-dealt wounds and bereavement, she glared in the direction of the Oasis with defiance that proclaimed, "Nothing you offer can possibly compensate for what has been lost!"

But she drew a few dry, measured breaths and schooled herself to compassion. *That very reaction,* she thought, *proves the necessity of this pilgrimage.*

Her solitude, fruitful in the months following the cataclysmic eruption, had grown stultifying. Moving forward required hope, which, in her mind, was always conjoined with a sense of purpose, a guiding vision. And any vision necessitated educating herself about what resources she had to work with.

Like many journeys towards a mountaintop, hers began that morning with a descent. Sensing how loose the gravel and coppery topsoil was, Esperidi squatted until her fingers grazed the ground and allowed herself to skid down the ridge's sun-warmed side until she reached the soft, sandy wash.

The weight of her pack, bulging with dry foodstuffs, reminded her that she would not be returning.

It's time to rejoin Ophia, though her face be unrecognizable.

Within the ravine, her view was constricted, affording just a small glimpse of a handful of buttes a few miles distant. Magda's Oasis was usually only visible at night:

a thin, flickering chain on the western horizon.

Esperidi ascertained that the wash was a gradual creation resulting from intermittent flood waters from the Conhuera Mountains behind her, not something wrought by the Rupture. She would have been aware of any flooding on such a scale. Indeed, the Savwain Desert felt largely untouched, ignorant of the deluges that had reshaped both shorelines, the dust devils scouring the southern prairies, or the gouts of magma that burst from the heart of Ophia.

Of course this region was untouched, she thought, with now-familiar bitterness. *That's why Shiya-coqui sent me here to "commune with the desert." She knew.*

Esperidi, too, had known. This constituted a portion of her grief, being forced to acknowledge that this outcome had been the only acceptable one under the circumstances. Her mentor could not have made this journey. Esperidi could.

"And the Sophryne lore must not die with me," Shiya-coqui had insisted.

Esperidi thought, for easily the thousandth time during` her exile, *Is that what I am now, the last Sophryne?*

That internal query made her quail again at the prospect of the road ahead. Traveling to an unknown settlement in these times was frightening enough without a pervasive sense of alienation. But she had educated herself, as thoroughly as possible during her sojourns across the Partition, about the Savwain Desert and its Vandrene inhabitants. It was time to test those visions against the dense field of time.

After a few miles, the wash opened into a broad dust plain. Here, one could hike all day, and the flat-topped rock buttes on the horizon would appear no taller than they had at the journey's onset. Esperidi was grateful for the cloud cover on the second day; it spared her some of the sun's glare. By the time she reached the outskirts of Magda's Oasis on the third afternoon, she'd emptied her waterskin.

Peace, or at least its facade, graced the Oasis. A few milky cumulus clouds lurched across the sky. The land's instability was difficult to conceive while the honey mesquite trees swayed and the cactus wrens chirped contentedly.

Esperidi noticed that most of the settlement's labor was done in the main thoroughfare. Buffalo roaming the Virgoda Plains and cattle from the more verdant pastures in the Savwain—like the land surrounding the Oasis—provided most Vandrene necessities: clothing (down to moccasins), meat, shelter, and bone and tooth ornaments.

Hides were smoked, stretched, and soaked in oily water to keep skins from hardening into rawhide. Other items were crafted with flax, such as the rush mats laid before the cavern-like adobe homes and the backrests for repose, woven of willow shoots and held up with wooden posts. Children labored as diligently as their elders, stirring pots, fleshing hides, weaving, and carving. They wore tunics and leggings of buffalo or buckskin. Many of the adult males, skin bronzed from the desert sun, were bare to the torso.

The Oasis tensed with apprehension as Esperidi crossed its threshold. A sandy-haired boy clutched what looked like a wooden blowpipe as he peered at her through an upper-story window. A dour-faced woman stood in a doorway, oblivious to the two children tugging at her dress as she studied the Shaini. The gathered Vandrenes hushed, waiting with hoarded breath for some indication of this newcomer's intentions.

Perhaps some perceived in Esperidi those telltale signs of Shaini *lightness*, as if her fleshy being could float away with the slightest provocation or transubstantiate into the stuff of wind and dreams.

But we all emerged from the great dream, Esperidi reminded herself. In many respects, Shaini were long-lived simply because they hadn't entirely forgotten this.

Thrusting such fanciful flights aside, she approached an adobe hut whose image mirrored her recent dream. Esperidi recognized that azure symbol emblazoned on a silken banner of purest sendaline: a crab carrying a glowing, diamond-shaped amethyst into deep ocean waters. That banner had sprung to vivid life in her dream, enfolding her in a world of tempest waves and fathomless depths. But the crab's descent had not wavered. And it had spoken to her...

I doubt I could've mustered the courage to meet those depths otherwise.

Passing through a curtain of violet and purple beads, Esperidi paused a moment, swaying uncertainly, and Mother Magda glanced up and squinted as if her eyes were just coming back into focus.

Magda's smooth face and slim, upward-slanting eyes evinced her kinship with the Sendhi who roamed the northern steppes. The "Mother" appellation reinforced this sense of lineage. Sendhi often used the term to denote respect, even for a woman without children. When uttered in tones of reverence, "Mother" was synonymous with Vision.

"A newcomer," the woman remarked.

Esperidi, even with her unusually attuned senses, couldn't discern what conclusions Magda drew from her appraising glance.

"You'll be wanting your fortune, then?"

A faint, rueful chuckle escaped Esperidi's lips. Then, noticing the rising indignation in the Sendhi woman's eyes, she forestalled her with an apologetic wave. "Your pardon, please. It's just that... I wonder who'd desire a foretelling when Ophia lies already devastated. Fortunes," she mused. "People still come seeking them?"

"Was fortunes *built* this town," Magda said with a sour twist of her lip. "And faith in it lets us to sleep at night, no worrying our homes be swept away before we rise."

Esperidi reminded herself that the Vandrene were a secretive people: spiritual exiles. Best not to presume a sense of humor or any consensus on what, exactly, constituted a joke. These roamers of the Savwain Desert were alternately shunned, feared, or sought out by desperate people. They were outcasts who'd gradually gathered in the Savwain Desert simply because other people avoided it. And now, in an Ophia remade by the Rupture, they had become a culture of consequence. Their land had been preserved while other regions were decimated.

They were a law (and morality) unto themselves.

Reaching for reparation, Esperidi voiced the fullest depth of honesty she was capable of. "I think that is the way for all of us now—trust. Trust in the unseen. Trust in what we know inside, even when our senses cannot confirm it.

"I recognize that that's what you and your people have done here, Magda. Oh, yes," she said in response to the woman's widening eyes. "I know your name—and a few other things about you—from dreams we've shared. Dreams that you, perhaps, do not recall.

"Again, forgive me. That was partly why I laughed: You referred to me as a newcomer. We've actually shared a horizon since before the worst storms and upheavals." Esperidi waved vaguely east towards the Arjena Hills. "And we've shared half a dozen adventures on the other side of the Partition, besides."

And I'll swear by the heart of Shai-win and Sarpienta's sore tooth, she was a talking cat in a couple of those dreams!

Mother Magda scrutinized the young woman again. "The Shaini part, I surmised as you walked through the curtain. But a Wakeful Dreamer? A Sophryne?"

Esperidi bowed her head in acknowledgment. Where was the merit in hiding her identity now when order was vanquished and the land roiled like an agitated anthill?

"I *was* one—in training. That training was cut short, at least on this side of the Partition." Her voice sank almost to a private sermon. "Now I have only the dreams themselves to guide me."

"No doubt your mentor, were he or she still walking the sands, would say you no need other guidance."

Magda grinned as Esperidi's mouth fell open. The Sendhi's first flush of indignation was forgotten, and her voice softened. "But I'll no claim to share your inward eyes. Of Shaini, I speak familiarly because you're the second I've been acquainted with.

"Aye: she lent her hands to mine, building this town from a well and a cluster of palms. I feel when there's water about. It tugs at me like the ground tugs at a bird's wings. But Ashangtu... Oh, she predicts how deep a well must be dug—to the foot—and tastes precious metals littered in sand and stone: iron, copper, gold..."

Magda frowned. "Though such knowledge buys more woe than fortune these days."

Esperidi pursed her lips in thought. Why had no dreams warned her of another Shaini's presence? Doubtless, the answer lay within her own fears and places of resistance. Given the choice, she would not encounter others of her kind until she had something other than her pain to share with them. Unfortunately, if it ever truly arrived, such a moment would not be announced with drums and bells.

That's the conviction that brought me here, she reminded herself. *I am never ready ahead of time. I make myself ready by leaping into the fray.*

"I would very much like to meet Ashangtu," she said, hoping her tremulous thoughts wouldn't make her sound false.

"Most nights, we gather in the saguaro circle. Out

past the southern wall." Magda pointed towards an edge of the thoroughfare opposite where Esperidi entered. "As for Ashangtu... I dare no promise, yea or nay. Impulse guides her comings and goings, and none can predict it. I doubt even the cards can tell me what occupies her when she goes off alone."

Her eyes sparkled with mischief. "Some come to Savwain Desert to find forgetfulness. They like Vandrenes because we are the people with no past. Nowadays, there's peace even outside our rickety defenses, though we pay dearly for it."

"How so?" Esperidi asked.

Magda waved a hand. "No doubt Ashangtu will tell you all you want to know—if she joins us tonight. Seldom does she miss an opportunity to flail her temper. But I've no heart for more tales of woe today." She pressed her palms together and bowed slightly. "Glad am I to make your acquaintance, Olen-sa!"

Esperidi flushed, startled to be addressed with the honorific reserved for a female Shaini. "Please, call me Esperidi, Mother."

"Very well, Esperidi. And you call me Magda. I will see you tonight?"

"I will be there," Esperidi assured her.

※※

Beyond the wall, the cobbled road cut between two mesquites and opened onto a broad flat. Esperidi approached a cluster of at least two dozen fires. She estimated that at least a hundred Vandrene were gathered.

She shook her head, considering the absurdity of using such a name even in the privacy of her thoughts. For such an eclectic mix of people, "Vandrene" did not denote a race but a lifestyle. They were bound by their lack of ties, rooted in rootlessness.

For centuries before the Rupture, the Savwain Desert had become a haven for those ostracized by their native societies. Some came as the result of banishment, either cruel or condign. Others came voluntarily, feeling choked by the superstitions or physical constraints surrounding them. Some brought families. Others forsook their families and wandered alone.

Several of those by the fires resembled Magda: smooth-faced, olive-skinned Sendhi. Paler men and women, their hair fair or firebrand, hailed from a race from across the sea—the Jona-chon. The Jona-chon were generally more boisterous and animated than the Sendhi. But they, too, had been outcasts and refugees, making their precarious way across Ardhid, a land bridge that sometimes formed in Ophia's northeastern corner during particularly long and brutal winters.

The same land bridge that the Shaini of Farsilane, under the direction of Esperidi's father, had drowned in the sea, foiling an invasion and provoking the Rupture in consequence.

Scarcest of all the racial types represented here was the swarthy folk whose ancestors hailed from the southern tribes. Manitoh or Oskwai, they moved with a natural swagger that reminded Esperidi of someone wading through waist-high, forceful waters.

Magda, noticing Esperidi, trotted over and joined her near the saguaro circle. She took the young woman's hand and, bustling with surprising urgency, escorted her to various fires to introduce her to the gathering.

Most of their names and faces slipped through the sieve of her overwrought mind. But one taut, muscular youth in a sleeveless tunic and breeches, drawn by her nameless mystique, tugged at her sleeve and asked for her full name in a stumbling dialect she didn't recognize. Though he was nearly as dark as a Manitoh, Esperidi surmised he was one of the pale-skinned new settlers. His complexion was the work of the desert sun.

She obliged him. "I am Esperidi Mon-Sequana."

Her response elicited the youth's fond, abashed smile, but he seemed struck speechless.

"Ilatan doesn't talk much. But he remembers his tongue in songs fit to wring your heart from your breast. Perhaps you can persuade the starry-eyed lad to demonstrate."

This challenge was uttered by a woman squatting nearby: a Shaini whom Esperidi assumed at once must be Ashangtu. The woman was slightly shorter than her and hardier, with a blunt face that seemed to demand explanations from the cosmos at every turn. She wore a thick cream-colored shirt trimmed with red horse hair, a white bone clasp around her neck, and wide leggings and moccasins made of calfskin. At first glance, Esperidi thought of *fire*, and not only because of the woman's waist-length drape of lush, if bedraggled, scarlet hair. Her *timbre* felt vehement. But it was vehemence aimed at something nebulous and abstract—an existential crux more than any clear and present adversities.

"A mug or two of mead would probably loosen me up enough!" Ilatan said. "But that's a luxury that Magda's Oasis can no longer afford, apparently."

"Would you rather we paid tribute in mead or blood, sir?" the woman said.

When the lad merely blinked at her, seeming amused by her mild reproof, she returned her attention to Esperidi with an exasperated huff.

"My family had dealings with Sequana," she remarked.

"They praised your 'fine aesthetic sensibilities, second only to our own.'" She scoffed, but at the memory, not Esperidi. "I am Ashangtu Lanore."

Hearing the woman's surname, Esperidi momentarily gawked. It was akin to discovering that a scullery maid was, in fact, a queen. Lanore had birthed Ophia's finest artisans, renowned across the land (and even the Elmicoran underworld) for their honey, wines, cheeses, and breads. And their fabled orchards and majestic crenelated Hives had been as gorgeous and extravagant as the goods that had earned their fame.

It was an appalling height for her to fall from, Esperidi thought.

"Magda told me you helped bring this community together," she said, her voice carefully neutral.

"Sometimes, I think the woman would have fared better had she never met me," Ashangtu said, glancing at Magda, who was now bustling towards another fire. Her jaws bunched in a way that suggested she was accustomed to grinding her teeth. "She had matters well enough in hand. She knew how to find water. What more should anyone ask for out here?"

Even before meeting Shiya-coqui, dreams had been Esperidi's predilection. With water's *timbre*, she possessed only the rudimentary, working understanding that any Shaini in her Hive possessed. It didn't suffice to cure thirst in a pinch. She could merely sense moisture's presence, whereas someone intimately familiar with its essence could coax forth a geyser under the right conditions.

"But I did," Ashangtu went on. "I asked for more. I sensed ore in the D'yangi foothills and the mountains and thought about everything that could be wrought with it."

Esperidi studied her, trying to pierce the woman's ire. "Is it wrong to make use of the abilities that are given to you?"

"You have to ask?" Ashangtu glared. "You're a survivor, too. If the Rupture has taught us anything—and I'm not convinced it has, even now—it should have taught us that power isn't the real issue. It's the uses we make of it that create or break our world."

"Magda did intimate that your discoveries have brought... troubles."

Ashangtu spat her words at some obscene target on her horizon. "At first, it was just a loose band of thugs who disdained honest work in favor of pillaging farmers' harvests. But they've become much more... methodical of late, more organized. I mentioned my sensitivity to ores. These brigands are keenly interested in iron, copper, and gold."

"It sounds like other Shaini have survived aside from ourselves," Esperidi ventured, feeling certain this was the cue the other woman hoped she'd pick up on. "Who else understands smelting?"

"The Manitohs learned what they know from *Shetain*," Ashangtu said, her voice spilling venom.

Esperidi mouthed the word—"Shetain"—in mingled confusion and dread. She recalled her history—and what she'd seen enacted on the Ambrosine stage during trance journeys. A century ago, when a vast Manitoh horde had tried to conquer the Hives, the victorious Shaini had punished the survivors by placing them under the governorship of Jain-Toh, Shetain's high priest. Their indoctrination into a world of guilt, atonement, and sacrifice had begun there—with dire consequences for those who would not accept the new creed.

"*New* Shetain," Ashangtu clarified, noting Esperidi's unspoken inquiry. "The old Hive was swept away—a series of quakes tore a sinkhole a hundred miles long. Shattered hills. Looks like a pile of shale tilled with a giant hoe. Scarcely anything of that mountain stretch endured. But some of Shetain's priests anticipated the Rupture somehow. They built ships and preserved what they could—the Hive's lore, and those Shaini whom they handpicked for salvation."

Then, startled by sudden revelation, the woman said, "Why am I so forthcoming with you, like you're someone I already know?" Her eyes sharpened with suspicion but then relaxed just as quickly. "Wait! We *have* met before, haven't we? I mean, I've dreamed of you. At least twice, as far as I remember. The woman was always in shadows, shrouded in a cloak, and she spoke in all these cryptic phrases that I had to puzzle out afterward. But sitting with you now, the *timbre* is unmistakable. It *was* you!"

Esperidi gasped as similar recollections flooded her. "I remember now! Leastways, *some* memory stirs. I wish I could recall more. But there was one encounter... You said that fire is never a gentle teacher. You were trying to warn me of something, though you seemed to realize that nothing you said could alter my course."

She didn't have the opportunity to explore her wonderment further. Mother Magda paused in making her rounds, returned to their fire, and bent beside Ashangtu. "I began telling the Olen-sa about the price our town pays for peace," she said.

Ashangtu's eyes never left Esperidi. "It seems Mother Magda didn't want to scare away our new Shaini guest by saying too much. But it's true. For months after the Oasis was first established, we were raided for our crops every turn of the moon."

"And for our *women*," Ilatan cut in.

Ashangtu stiffened and scowled. She apparently hadn't wanted to venture there. "Sometimes they raided for women," she conceded. "Girls, even." For a moment, portents of murder flared in her eyes. "Then we made a pact with that batch of human scum, offering no more lives but rather food and whatever we can wring from our hands."

"Enough to beggar us," Magda said, rising. "But they had sense enough to realize there be no more easy crops if all the farmers be slaughtered."

Ashangtu seemed to have reached a crucial point that she wanted to stress. "Thus far," she told Esperidi, "they've been punctual, and so, in all likelihood, you'll get your chance to see the embassy. Much as I hate to give that rabble such a dignified title. But they ought to arrive tomorrow."

Ashangtu invited Esperidi back to her quarters to sleep. She lived in one of the few two-story adobe buildings in the Oasis, though the interior was as sparse and austere as any others. For all her abrasiveness, Ashangtu seemed comforted by Esperidi's presence and eager to keep her close by.

A circular table took up most of the kitchen space, but it was covered with maps and papers. It seemed utilized more for communal planning than for meals. Indeed, Esperidi noticed no food at all, a circumstance for which Ashangtu immediately apologized.

"I take my meals in the bazaar when I can't ignore my stomach anymore," she explained. "Folks here are unwilling to charge me for anything or even let me barter. I try not to take advantage. But Mother Magda promised us a big breakfast tomorrow after the embassy leaves."

Perhaps not wanting to alienate her guest, the woman forsook her feather bed that night. Thus, the two Shaini shared her fur-padded bedroom floor.

"There's one thing I'd like you to help me understand straight away," Ashangtu said. She kept her eyes studiously fixed on the ceiling. "I've been thinking about our couple of dream encounters. You see, right now, I don't question who I am and the reality of this world that surrounds me."

She extended her hands and fluttered them as if tasting the air with her fingertips.

"I take it for granted that this is real. And I respond accordingly. There isn't a moment where I start wondering, say, whether you're an apparition."

"I appreciate that declaration of faith," Esperidi said.

Ashangtu seemed to hear neither the wryness nor the humor. "But from what I remember from all my dreams, I do the same thing there. When I wake up and think about it, or if I write it down, much of what happened seems absurd, impossible. But when I was experiencing it, I accepted it all as real, just like I now accept the air and floorboards.

"It's almost as if there are two different mes, one at home in this world, the other at home in that world, and I can change between them like they're different costumes. But it involves more than just transforming my body. It's a whole different personality. It's a creature at home in another environment."

"I'd say that is accurate," Esperidi said, concerned lest her limited knowledge lead the other woman astray. "It conforms to what I have experienced—and everything I learned about the Sophryne lore.

"But I wonder—and this is a part of the lore, too—I wonder if it isn't the tendency we have to try to define ourselves so strictly and narrowly that creates the appearance that we are bouncing between two worlds or that they are utterly foreign to each other.

"Consider: Today, I may speak with a sweet-natured child, and you'll hear nothing but honey dripping from my tongue. Tomorrow, someone could disrespect me, and I might rant. Does the one reaction negate the other? Both are real in the moment; Esperidi from yesterday doesn't unravel

Esperidi today. But to some stranger observing me, I may seem to be two quite different people.

"A big part of the Sophryne art involves learning to weave the two worlds together. So, while dreaming, you can be aware of your waking life and personality. Just as right now, having this conversation, we open our minds to understanding our dreaming selves and the worlds that they inhabit.

"And all of this barely scratches the surface. Shiya-coqui taught me that there are infinite worlds. Or, you could think of it this way: There are limitless ways in which we can turn our senses, and each way we turn, a different world presents itself."

Here, Ashangtu made an abrupt turnaround—something Esperidi would grow familiar with in the coming days.

"I know you've traveled some," the woman said, "and no doubt you've roamed farther in your dreams. Why have we encountered so few Shaini, do you think?"

Esperidi, having spent considerable time weighing this question, offered an immediate—if partial—response. "Perhaps because we were the catalysts of the Rupture and thus stood at the epicenter of its destruction. That would explain why some areas of Ophia have been virtually untouched while others were completely defaced."

All right, she decided, *I've been forthcoming enough for the present. She owes me some transparency in return.*

"I sense it is an adopted name you carry. 'Ashangtu'—'Red Buffalo?'"

"It isn't my birth name," Ashangtu admitted. "It's—" She crushed that moment of budding candor. "I don't want to talk about it! Didn't Magda tell you that the Vandrene are the people with no past?"

"She did," Esperidi said. "And yet, knowing a little

about your past might help me to decide whether I should trust you with my future."

Ashangtu scrutinized her. "Are you always so cryptic? Well, you can guess part of it from my surname, can't you?"

"Yes. And you do not say 'Mon-Lanore' but 'Lanore,' which indicates that you were part of an actual ruling house. Your family—"

"There are no 'houses' anymore! And when there were... no one who bent the knee to Shetain could claim to 'rule' anything, their own lives least of all. Now, if your curiosity is still unappeased, do what my family could not: Unlock the Kublai vaults. Everything you could ever want to know lies there—sealed away forever."

With that, the woman turned on her side and feigned sleep.

For a long time, Esperidi's mind was awhirl. She couldn't surrender to sleep. For nearly two years, she'd scarcely seen another human being (on this side of the Partition) and never interacted with one. Only her dreams had kept her mind facile enough for conversation. Now, she lay in the house of one of her kindred—and they were off to a rocky start. There had to be portents wrapped within this meeting that she lacked the skill to read. Or maybe she was just too tired to disentangle the threads.

After a while, Ashangtu ceased even pretending to sleep and stumbled off to the kitchen, grunting her agitation. She paced for hours into the night.

※ ※

Ashangtu was silent as the two awoke and dressed. She guided her Shaini companion down the Oasis' main street, replying tersely to any greetings or questions.

The long adobe court evoked little cheer aside from

its olfactory delights. Curry, olive oil, garlic, onion, and honey dominated its aromatic swirl. Every dish the Vandrene created here contained cornmeal, cracked wheat, or both. Such staples thickened paltry soups and made crusts for pies and tortillas for wrapping.

But otherwise, Magda's bazaar was quiet and somber. The gaming tables were unoccupied. Citizens had little of value to gamble with anymore. Colorful tapestries, once adorning the walls, had been looted, and no one had the heart to weave new ones.

Once the central bazaar was in sight, Ashangtu finally broke the silence.

"There's no time for me to explain it to you," she said. "I've been up all night trying to shepherd my threads of courage, get myself to stand behind this mad scheme. I'd apologize... but there's no time for that either. Will you help me? Can I count on you? I'm going to have to speak on your behalf."

Esperidi surveyed the poverty and desperation surrounding her, and it tugged at her native compassion. Thanks to her knowledge of Sacred Timbre, she'd been spared some of these people's sufferings. She'd spent the last two years grieving, questioning, and feeling lost, but she'd never truly had to fear dying of starvation or thirst—or at the end of a bandit's cutlass. These folk had no such assurances.

"What are you roping me into?" she whispered.

"No time now!"

Commotion rippling through the gathering and the clap of a dozen hooves warned them that the delegation drew near.

Her sense of Ashangtu's empathy, the woman's devotion to Ophia's dispossessed—whose timbres affected her acutely—persuaded Esperidi to make a tentative concession. But since Ashangtu committed to so little, she felt justified in repaying her in kind.

"I will watch and wait. And if your cause is something I can condone, I'll help you to whatever extent I can."

Despite the surrounding squalor, the embassy's cortege surged into the adobe court as if it were a palace anteroom eager to receive them. The men were olive-skinned and hook-nosed, with bluish-black beards. All were dressed in turbans and silks, with rapiers or broader cutlasses at their sides.

Their leader's boisterous smile capsized, however, when he surveyed the plaza and saw no worthy entourage there to greet his arrival, no baskets laden with goods. Struck momentarily speechless, he glared at Ashangtu.

"We will pay no more tribute, sir," the woman explained. "But I trust that you will leave here satisfied with the reasons I give you. This is as much to your advantage as it is ours."

"Explain, woman!" he snapped.

"I'll demonstrate, rather." Ashangtu withdrew a slim knife the length of her arm from elbow to wrist. Two men knocked arrows, but the captain forestalled them with a raised hand, as it was obvious Ashangtu was not threatening them.

Instead, she approached a nearby table and shoved the blade into the stone clear to its hilt guard. It passed through as if the rock was a slab of buffalo fat. Once she was assured that all eyes had witnessed the demonstration, Ashangtu withdrew the knife with grim satisfaction.

"This is why your prospective buyers are interested in iron. Their masters know how to craft weapons such as these. There are a couple of vital things for you to take from this, Captain. First, be aware that when you trade, you may be empowering those who can come back and overrun you without expending a drop of sweat or blood. Secondly—"

She raised the blade in front of her forehead so its lethal promise seemed to partition her eyes. "If you intend to harm another member of our village, you'll have to step over my corpse to do so. And my death means all that precious iron stays in the hills, though you brainless louts spend a decade puttering around with your spades."

With scores of eyes watching him, waiting for a display of authority or wrath, the captain seized his composure with visible effort. Mustering a sly grin, he gestured back the way he and his party had come. "D'yangi's mines—"

"Will soon be depleted," Ashangtu said. "That's but a pisspot vein. You think I'd trust the location of a great hoard to the likes of you? What you extract from there may suffice for two more trips south, no more. And then you can explain to your masters in New Shetain why you come empty-handed. Unless you follow my conditions to *my* satisfaction."

Now, an uneasy susurration—a collective tremor—rippled through the waiting horsemen. The captain, confronted with too many factors beyond his ken, was sufficiently humbled enough to say, "What are your terms?"

"The merchant among you: Tohbin. I will deal with him directly. He and his son, no one else. He will drive the wagon with me and the Olen-sa beside me." She inclined her chin towards Esperidi. "We'll help guide it. And we will trade for goods, not coins. They'll be evenly distributed amongst *all* our peoples upon Tohbin's return.

"And if ever I detect a worker consigned to your mines against their will, I'll consider you in violation of our pact, and you can go comb the beaches for pearls for all I care."

Concerned that the bowmen might loose their arrows this time before their leader could restrain them,

Ashangtu tossed rather than hurled the knife, so it landed by the foremost hooves of the man's black horse. Despite the gentleness of the gesture, something in her eyes made him draw the reins tight as the blade was in flight.

"Kiss it before your cronies to seal our pact," Ashangtu said. "Or drive it through my breast, as you choose."

Slowly, the captain dismounted and, never taking his eyes off her, found the dagger with his hand and gingerly lifted it.

""Kiss it with *love*, great leader—if there's aught left in your shriveled heart."

The man, no doubt sensing the fatalistic *timbre* that fairly screamed to Esperidi's inner senses, raised a placating hand. "Peace, woman! Our bargain is sealed."

"Yesterday, I thought you were wantonly reckless," Esperidi remarked. "Now, it occurs to me that the more apt word is *suicidal*. Some hundred leagues across a ravaged wilderness, bearing a cart full of precious ore, guarded only by a man, his son, and two Olen-sa...?"

Ashangtu responded with the fragment of attention she could spare from the dusty yellow horizon upon which her eyes were fixed. "No one possessed of any wits would dare attack us along this trade route. Though the priests claim that Toh has no images and can't be rendered—even symbolically—because he's 'so far beyond our ken,' they've still settled on their own rendition. No doubt it even made its way as far south as Sequana on occasion: a bearded man with a headdress of beads and a rectangular headpiece? Not surprisingly, it's a fair likeness of Jain-Toh himself."

"I've seen it," Esperidi said.

But she answered absently because something in that

image stirred a recollection. Her anticipation of this day's events and all its attendant anxiety had made her neglect her morning practice. She usually carved time to reflect on her dreams before she arose. Now, an image surfaced: a bearded man, much like Ashangtu described. But in her dream, his visage had been almost a caricature, a scarecrow rendition in straw. A raven had alighted beside the head and pulled some golden strands from its beard.

Then it had pecked out both the man's eyes.

"I suppose the Rupture can be thanked for one thing," Ashangtu commented, still scowling at the horizon. "There's less to bid farewell to before embarking on a perilous journey."

"If you say so," Esperidi said. "I promised nothing more than to *support* you this morning. I've not committed to any journey. It doesn't sound like you've planned very far in advance yourself, anyway."

"Did I mention having less than half a night to think this all through? Calculating the distance between here and New Shetain, I'll wager that gives me another month to worry over the finer details."

"Do you trust this Tohbin?" Esperidi asked.

"Trust him?" Ashangtu sounded distracted, adrift in cruel tangents. "He's the least repulsive of that lot. He shows some glimmer of integrity. I'll take my chances. But Tohbin doesn't trust Shaini," she added.

A wagon emerged at the edge of the shimmering tan flat and began to solidify from a translucent mirage. As it angled slightly towards the rising sun, Esperidi saw that Ashangtu had spoken truly. An image that was not Toh and yet was meant to be associated with Toh covered most of the tarp on its visible side. The imposing face was articulated in black except for the beads draping from its headdress, which encompassed all the colors of the rainbow.

"Tohbin looks stout," Esperidi remarked once the man had drawn close enough for her to examine him. When Ashangtu's eyes widened—part startled, part amused—she clarified: "One does not build muscles like that driving a wagon all day."

"That's from the hammer and anvil. That's what he's in this game for: He trades with Shetain for smelting and blacksmithing secrets. He's Manitoh, native not to the Savwain but to Kawli Rainforest."

As if this fact might aid Esperidi's comprehension, Ashangtu added: "He keeps a pet tarantula in a jar." Then, she pointed to the driver's shorter companion. "Tohbin's son, Kunsei. He loves to fish." The hefty lad wore nothing but a loincloth. His long, black locks were bound back and wrapped in a way that resembled a beehive. "In Na-Viltaj, he checked his traps first thing every morning. I'll wager he's chewing on snapper jerky right now."

The wagon was drawn by two tall, rangy horses with white coats spotted black in so many places that they reminded Esperidi of paintings she'd seen of leopards in the Chonnen jungles and steppes. Drawing within five paces of her, they were reined in with a whistle they must have been trained to obey. But whistling scarcely shifted Tohbin's stoic, unyielding face. One might have thought he'd halted for some reason other than the two Shaini standing in his path. The lad beside him betrayed subtle signs of curiosity, but he suppressed them, striving to mirror his father's dispassionate mask.

But Esperidi scarcely noticed their reactions—or lack thereof. Her eyes fixated upon a dark image covering most of Tohbin's bare chest.

Skin embroidery, Shiya-coqui had called it. It was a tattoo of a bird perched on a slender limb, erect in its magisterial profile, facing Tohbin's left shoulder. In the sideswipe of the desert's late dawn, Esperidi descried the work of needle and thread rendering the black lines, even the creature's stripes. The work was so detailed, in fact, that by the shape and posture, she could guess its name.

Not a raven, then, but a sparrow.

Almost unconsciously, she reached out and grazed Ashangtu's arm. Trembling in wonderment, her voice scarcely rose above a whisper.

"It looks like I *will* be joining you after all."

Esperidi had seen Manitohs even before coming to the Savwain Desert. In Farsilane, she'd witnessed small embassies from Khempsa and Khampalu—deep in the rainforest—arriving at the behest of Shetain's priesthood. Though merely messengers, they'd been treated like visiting dignitaries. Nevertheless, those lean bodies and severe faces bespoke extravagant self-denial.

Tohbin proved no exception. He was taciturn to the point of obliviousness, giving every appearance that he was scarcely aware that Esperidi and Ashangtu rode with him. He studiously avoided her imploring glances as if he feared her words and eye contact might bewitch him.

This accorded with what she'd heard about Manitohs generally. History always painted them either as aggressors or as persecuted people. Thus, they were furtive and reticent when dealing with other races. They strove to live according to the Sacred Writ, the alleged word of Toh, as the priests of Shetain preached it. But Shiya-coqui had told Esperidi that many Manitohs still secretly paid homage to Great Grandfather Serpent, Sarpienta, who lay coiled within Ophia's heart.

Esperidi's dreams had offered her glimpses into these

matters, but their symbols were shadowy and elusive. It seemed that many natives attributed the Rupture to Sarpienta's discontent. After all, it was Ophia itself that had convulsed and shattered. Many believed in their secret heart that Sarpienta's tail had crumbled the mountains, churned up the seas, and whipped the air into a malevolent frenzy.

Nevertheless, they were taught to abase themselves before Toh and seek atonement for whatever transgressions had supposedly provoked the cataclysms.

And those with the audacity to believe, or even hope, that they deserved consolation during these dark and turbulent times, rather than punishment and repentance, called out to Shai-win, their patron of love and forgiveness, in their dreams. Esperidi had been taught one of Shai-win's poems, and its lines directly contradicted the Sacred Writ.

There's no greater Divinity than where it
fumbles forward with your fingers
in the fertile dark
Gropes ahead with your light as its verdant sun
Peers out of your eyes at its
immaculately muddied reflection

But she doubted that her two Manitoh companions would deepen her understanding of these matters. Tohbin was only responsive when Esperidi asked about his life among the Vandrene. Apparently, this portion of his past was not as laden with taboos and prohibitions as the subject of his native country.

"They say we prowl with coyotes and wolves," Tohbin said. His voice was steady as a boulder being rolled across a flat plain. "We're the bilge waters, the dregs of the land." He sounded like he was quoting from a sacred text. "Some hunt us like wild animals. Some will not give a dying Vandrene water from their well. They brand us thieves, but we've only ever *been* thieves to survive."

Esperidi could hear how his phrasing had been strongly influenced by the Shetain priests and their incendiary sermons.

"Chieftains in some southern lands force the Vandrene to cook their food outside, in the open, to prove we're not cannibals. 'Vandrene' and 'Wains' are words that frighten children into obedience."

But despite the man's simmering ire, Esperidi felt a growing kinship with Tohbin and his adopted people. She, too, was an outcast who had been sheltered by the Savwain Desert.

There was scarcely sufficient room for her and Ashangtu to sit in the wagon amid the burlap sacks of ore stacked to its hood, so they'd often trot after the rear wheels, occasionally making way for cattle drives and lavishly painted wagons carrying Vandrene families. Tunzao Trail was only packed to the width of a footpath anyway, and the yielding sand and patches of brush that plagued the still-forming double-track slowed the horses enough so the two women could easily keep pace.

Esperidi recalled her trek with Shiya-coqui from Farsilane to Mount Veneer. The older woman had always taken the most circumspect possible routes and camped in secluded places. Tohbin did the opposite. He usually stopped his wagon at the highest promontory he could reach before sunset. If Shetain's banner was his only defense against marauders, he would display it from the most visible vantage point. Much of Tunzao Trail ran along the ridge's spines anyhow, as the sand of the soft ravines was too yielding to make passage viable.

During their less guarded moments at camp, Esperidi could distinctly feel how the Manitohs' aloofness was a mask they expended tremendous energy to sustain. Tohbin sometimes shot Esperidi furtive glances with an intensity that startled her. She tried to adopt the imperious poise that Shiya-coqui had taught her. Still, she could not escape the thought that she was a woman alone—save for another female companion—in the wilderness, in the company of two strange men who could physically dominate her with ease.

But the *timbre* of Tohbin's scrutiny did not feel desirous. Rather, he grappled with some riddle written upon her face. His furrowed brow would get no rest until he unraveled the mystery of it. To his mind, some aspect of her could not or should not exist, yet he was reminded of its reality every time he glanced at her.

"'I'm going to run away and join the Vandrene' has been a mantra for anyone marginalized by their tribe or nation," Ashangtu said. The two women experienced the semblance of privacy even as their silent companions sat naught but three paces away. "It's the credo of every undesirable in the land—which includes, unfortunately, those with little or no regard for the rights of others.

"No one is too strange to join the Savwain community. All are welcome, provided they drag their own carcass."

Then, the woman shifted so swiftly that it seemed almost a natural segue. "Why did you suddenly commit yourself? You were undecided, or at least you gave every appearance of it. And then—" She snapped her fingers. "Entirely invested in this journey. Not even a backward glance. Explain that!"

Knowing that no words would thoroughly satisfy her companion, Esperidi opted for brevity. "It was Tohbin's tattoo," she whispered. "The sparrow on his chest. It's an image that has meaning for me. I took it as a sign."

Ashangtu's eyebrows arched and joined like a bridge

between two storms. "A sign? You do this often, do you?"

Esperidi shrugged. "I can't say it's *never* failed me, but oftentimes, it has served me very well. In my dreams, I often notice that certain people, animals even, represent paths for me. One may lead into the past, into a quagmire of stagnation—a stuck place where I cannot move until I remember that I am more than I think I am. But then, there may be a coyote bounding for the horizon—" *Or a raven*, she added to herself. "And if I chase after it, my world opens up."

Her eyes widened as unfamiliar implications penetrated her awareness. "It's almost as if freedom itself has a *timbre*!"

"Why should freedom not have its *timbre*?" Ashangtu said. "Sure, it can seem like an abstract concept to Farsilane scholars sitting in their armchairs. But try telling a prisoner in shackles that freedom isn't a concrete reality."

Esperidi mulled this, feeling thrown again into tempest waters. "There's so much I still don't know," she muttered.

Ashangtu's look of incredulity was almost comical. "I should hope so, for the rest of our sakes! You've seen all of, what, twenty summers? And you expect to have unraveled all the mysteries of the cosmos?"

Esperidi made an abject gesture, feeling utterly inadequate to articulate her need in the moment. "I can't afford my weakness or ignorance anymore. *Ophia* can't afford it."

Ashangtu barked a laugh. "Now you're a one-woman crusade, are you?" She swept her hand across the horizon. "This catastrophe is yours to clean up?"

Her eyes narrowed. "I don't like preaching, but I've got to say something now, and I hope you're in a place to hear it. You possess abilities that make your survival a likelier prospect than it is for most people, Shaini or Oskwai.

Remember that."

Esperidi *was* in a position to hear this assertion—and also to understand its flaw.

"I am grateful," she admitted, "both for my native abilities and for what I was able to learn in the course of my training, short though it was. But mere survival is not enough for any of us." She glanced across the fire at their two Manitoh companions, marking the vestiges of strife, fear, and privation that scored the faces of both father and son.

She finished more to herself than Ashangtu. "We need hope and vision."

That night, the fifth since leaving Magda's Oasis, they camped on a red rock and sand butte made maze-like with its patches of prickly pear and squat Jumping Cholla trees.

Esperidi was grateful for how the day's exertions had wearied her. She hadn't the energy to question the possible madness of what she'd undertaken. The rigors of the trail pulled that acquiescence out of her. She traveled with a wagon that could carry a lot more water than she could fit on her back or in her skin. Facts like those weighed more than any amount of philosophical speculation in the desert.

Once Kunsei set up a lean-to for her, she scarcely noticed or remembered the transition between sprawling onto her buffalo fur pad and sinking down into the world below...

... until she gasped as if she'd suddenly broken water. A moment of still mind elapsed before she realized she'd been roused from dreamless sleep. Still acclimating to life outside the Arjena hill cave that had sheltered her for almost two years, she groped at her unfamiliar surroundings, uncomprehending.

Then she stiffened when she noticed a humanlike shadow hovering over her.

"Come quick!" The voice belonged to Ashangtu. "It's Tohbin. He's collapsed by the fire pit. Snake bite. I did what I could, but—"

Esperidi beat the sleep dust from her mind with a violent head shake and rose unsteadily. Feeling utterly unprepared for this crisis, she let Ashangtu lead her to where Tohbin's recumbent form sprawled beside the ashes of their dinner fire. His supine body was so placid it seemed the vehicle of a soul at peace, but his breathing was shallow and labored. He twitched at times as if his limbs rebelled against his torpid state.

Ashangtu had knifed a hole in his tight leggings and tore the hide enough to expose a sluggishly seeping wound. The woman knelt and grazed her fingers over the dark, mottled splotch on his right shin. She'd removed the dark bandana from his head and tied it above that red affliction.

"A war rages inside him," she hissed, "and the man has not chosen a side!"

Esperidi perceived at once what Ashangtu meant. Tohbin's spirit had forsaken his ravaged body. His *timbre* was barely audible to her inner senses. She and Ashangtu faced his existential trial alone.

"I gave him some of Magda's antivenin," Ashangtu said. "I always bring some along when I have to travel the desert." When Esperidi stared at her, alerted by a trembling *timbre* of deception, she added, as if the confession had been wrenched from her: "I burned most of it first, all right? I cut, sucked, and burned. I can manipulate the *timbres* of fire with some delicacy at times, you know."

Esperidi nodded absently. Extending her percipience, she perceived that Ashangtu had indeed stemmed the blood flow and cleared the infection. A scab was already beginning to form over the two punctures.

But Tohbin did not appear convalescent. The skin around his clenched jaw and wrinkled brow was slack. His breathing was weak and erratic.

"Convince him his life is worth reclaiming," Ashangtu said, "and he's got a chance."

Esperidi's attention was wrenched away from Tohbin as the weight of Ashangtu's *expectation* hit her. She gaped at the other woman. "I'm not a Singing Chieftess!"

"The body is the creation of the spirit, right? Isn't that what the Sophrynes say?"

Esperidi trembled, but the force of her companion's personality worked on her like coercion. And she could not deny the raw appeal of Tohbin's suffering.

As if she needed to convince herself that she'd done everything she could, Ashangtu began to ramble. "I felt warm energies working there. It tickled my fingertips like a hundred tiny ants were moving over his skin or little spiders were weaving webs over it."

Esperidi made another noncommittal nod. She had experienced healing energies in this way—an ethereal tickle akin to tiny spiders scrambling across her flesh.

For the love of all Sorsajna! A test was upon her, and she was so unready...

He needs Shiya-coqui, not me!

But Esperidi's mentor was not here, and Tohbin would not survive her inadequacies and self-doubt. Her training was all that stood between him and the void.

She had traveled in dreams and waking trances. Towards the end of her short apprenticeship, she'd divided her practice, more or less equally, between the two environments. Her facility for entering the Sophryne state was not what intimidated her.

The fundamental question was *how*. How would she

appeal to Tohbin, even granting that she could find him? Should she let compassion guide her? Should she strive for aloofness and not let her efforts to save the man become derailed by emotional investment?

Recalling a stray remark that Ashangtu had made about that young man at the Oasis, Illatan, and his singing, she said, "Tamborly can be helpful, even without instruments. Will you sing something for me? It might help me to surrender. At any rate... it would be a comfort."

Ashangtu straightened and balked. "I've not much of a voice, particularly for soothing. Nothing like Ilatan." But, almost without transition, she added, "Oh, very well! But I never claimed to be a Tamborlin, so no complaints!"

Esperidi closed her eyes with a slight smile. "None!" Then, she stretched herself out beside Tohbin as Ashangtu began a low croon.

> If I am the one who must
> be the wind's bride
> The one in whom Sun and Moon
> both confide

The woman's singing *was* rough. It poured through channels paved with the gravel and grit of stoic endurance. But Esperidi found her voice utterly appropriate for a night of old fragile hopes broken and new ones scarcely finding their feet.

> Will they call me their savior,
> or will they greet me with scorn?
> Will I fulfill the great promise
> for which I was born?

Esperidi's inner being slowly unwound. It was a

physical, tangible thing. Suddenly, she was more in touch with herself, more attuned to her internal movements: the longings and necessities that had brought her to this time and place.

I love the fire that hides in the heart of the camouflage. But I love the camouflage, too.

> The road is uncertain
> No maps have been drawn
> The fire in my eyes can be
> frightful to look upon

Esperidi's inner doubts began to dissolve. She could focus on the source of her power and forget the personal attachments that bound her to the man she sought to save.

> And who's there to meet me in
> those most-secret places?
> What bodies can abide
> all those high, airy spaces?

Nearing a state of consciousness akin to the gates of slumber, Esperidi suddenly stirred. "That's not from Old Ophia! That's a Sophryne song written to evoke the voice of Shai-win! They called her Bride of the Winds. How did you—?"

Ashangtu thrust the woman's head back down. "You're not the only one who's delved into the mysteries, you know. What else did I have to occupy myself with, anyway? Now, do you want your lullaby or not?"

She's right: I cannot afford delays, Esperidi thought, and she nodded tightly.

For a while, she mouthed some of the melody Ashangtu sang. Its *timbre* evoked a seed borne on the wind.

Her subtle body began to rise, but her fear was only temporary. Soon, mortal concerns were left behind in the body's domain. Esperidi felt a loving presence, a beautiful echo of music from beyond the farthest horizon. Compassion and fierce love tangibly manifested like cupped hands supporting her.

It occurred to her that, in a certain sense, she was meeting her soul for the first time. It was strong, certain, invincible as child's laughter.

Her exhilaration, however, made it harder to focus. The thought of enclosing herself in her surroundings, losing herself within them, was seductive. That fantasy plunged her into the inner heart of Ophia, and for a moment, she stared through a screen of warm topaz towards a remote sun, feeling its caress.

The poem attributed to Shai-win echoed in her inner mind. She was, indeed, groping forward with her hands in the fertile dark. Her essence and the light she sought were indistinguishable. The one could not exist without the other. Sorsajna needed her, depended on her, as much as she needed it. Breathing and focusing on how she'd been taught to enter the Sophryne state while awake, Esperidi slipped by gradual degrees across the Veils and beyond Ophia's surface veneer, where loss and woe relentlessly wailed.

The melody now echoed within her consciousness as if seashells were pressed against her ethereal ears. Though she no longer had any sense of where the song originated, aside from the distant, wounded *timbre* of the woman who sang it, Esperidi encompassed the gentle breeze around her in a mental rather than physical gestalt, neither warm nor cool.

Finally, her Vision clarified as a grey-tan wasteland, one that her inner eyes could not penetrate more than a few strides in any direction. She stood upon its shimmering ground.

Before her, Tohbin wandered alone, friendless in an interminable sandstorm. He was unaware of her. In the transcendent grip of the Sophryne state, however, Esperidi did not see a lost, feeble man. She saw a being of soulful grace.

She had to meet him on that plane. The transparency afforded by this less-than-physical realm and the urgency that had brought her here allowed her to peer into the man's inner being, unraveling layers as if from a psychic onion.

Prior to the Rupture, Tohbin had a life-mate, the woman who'd brought Kunsei into the world. They'd bound themselves to one another according to the rituals set out in the Sacred Writ, but Tohbin had wed his Lamya for love.

Esperidi witnessed Lamya's death in the jungles, and she intuited that the gravest darkness in Tohbin's present life was not comprised of any defined threats but rather of *absence*.

He rarely indulged in hope. Perhaps he had forgotten it was possible. He did not remember how to nurture it. It had, seemingly, betrayed him too often in the past. After all, his life-mate's illness and death had been rendered more cruelly tormenting by his hopes for their shared life.

Yes, the trails he feared were the ones he'd already traveled. Tohbin didn't know how to disentangle his consciousness from the webs of the past. But maybe, experiencing his freedom from his body—with all its attendant fears—here, he could sever those cords, claiming an oasis for his soul.

For a while, Esperidi hovered close by him. Perhaps because he sensed her presence and kind regard, Tohbin's surroundings softened somewhat. The desert was still as featureless and uncompromising, but the winds tapered. The horizon brightened; pink and orange washes crept across its edges.

But what assurance did Tohbin have that that sun would not crash onto Ophia and set it aflame? He had seen such things. Rarely did he travel to a place without hearing how wind, fire, flood, or earth convulsions ravaged humankind. He had no assurances, no points of stability amid that Rupture-wrought chaos. But wait—

There *was* one point of warm affirmation, though Esperidi couldn't identify it at first. She tried to recall her teachings. Shiya-coqui had told her: "Your natural thoughts will lead you, like a trail of crumbs, one by one, towards the destination you seek. Just remember your *intention*."

What *was* her intention here? Healing. Yes: That insight made her realize that the barrier she experienced did not originate within Tohbin but within herself. And so she plunged into that place of resistance within her to identify the burning *timbres* of pride and love singing within Tohbin's heart.

Esperidi had to venture back into her childhood to when her Papa had not yet been beset by overwhelming grief and loss, burdened by his duties as a member of the Cordonne, plagued by fears of the coming invasion. When all these things had not dovetailed to divert the course of his life from a young idealist to a man obsessed with control and order.

But when she traveled back far enough—Oh! It smote her heart to feel how far back she had to go!—She was a child, no more than nine years old. But there, she could identify it, the light that sustained Tohbin.

It was a father's pride in and love for his child.

For the love of his son, Tohbin had been willing to leave their home and tribe in the Kawli Rainforest and drive caravan runs for the Masters in Shetain. That provided the two of them with stability and hope for the future. Tohbin could not afford to consider the ethics of what he did beyond that. Life was cheap and raw in post-Rupture Ophia, whether in the jungle or the desert.

And the constant travel afforded him another kind of freedom. He often couldn't treat his son with integrity without fearing mockery when they were among the various villages and settlements. Many believed he should "toughen" his boy, teach him self-reliance, and not "weaken" him with affection, encouragement, and praise. But once on the trail again, Tohbin could express his love without restriction—the one free avenue to joy left to him. And his son flourished under its glow like a flower in sunlight.

Esperidi now understood the fundamental *timbres* of quiet contentment and confidence that characterized the younger man.

"Tohbin," she whispered, "your son needs you. Ophia needs fathers like you. Ophia needs *men* like you."

Tohbin, registering that whisper in the sandstorm, halted his aimless wandering. Reassured by his recognition, Esperidi repeated her appeal several times.

Then, she reached the uttermost limit of her exertions and had to release Vision.

The exhilaration, the urge to dissolve into Sorsajna, was almost impossible to refuse. Esperidi returned her focus to her physical body, resurrecting the sensation of inhabiting flesh, the feel of the ground beneath her, and the bonds of gravity. She opened her eyes to the night's moonbeam. And a rush of earthbound feelings assailed her: her fresh heartbreak, loss... and cautious hope.

The Seduction of Ildriss Lanore

Jain-Toh's quarters were sparse: all polished marble and quartz with small patches of floor softened by white fur carpets. A copper bed with a thick feather mattress leaned against one wall beneath a slanted ceiling. The central space was dominated by an obsidian obelisk, the thickness of a stool, that nearly reached the tower's roof. The uppermost foot of it was half as thick as the base and steepled.

New Shetain's Canted Citadel had been fashioned utilizing *timbres* to amplify its acoustics. The black obelisk, when awakened, enhanced this effect, projecting Jain's voice to every corner of the Citadel when he wished to convey a sermon or make a demonstration.

The stone was quiescent now, meaning the lady Ildriss enjoyed as much privacy as anyone living here—besides Jain himself--could hope for. Now, Shetain's Master circled the obelisk to more closely appreciate the woman's sea-green eyes, rounded nose, high cheekbones, and peach-white skin. He even let her witness some of the light of admiration in his eyes this time.

But he made no greeting. Too much familiarity might overwhelm her with feelings of unworthiness or set her too much at ease. Neither suited his purpose. Thus, Jain had masked a smile when the lady was brought to his quarters, projecting only the rigid stoicism with which every acolyte was familiar. Sometimes, silence was more powerful than any words.

The young woman appeared awed in his presence, nearly trembling but not cowed. He marveled at this rare—perhaps even unique—combination and felt suddenly certain he'd made the right choice with her. Her *timbre* sang with peculiar eagerness.

To learn? To implement his ideas?

Jain suspected that if he had never lived, Ildriss herself might have tried to achieve what he had and establish her own belief system with new idols and doctrines. She was a young woman who required spiritual certainty. Though silent and rigid, her slightest movements betrayed an air of devotion, a perpetual awareness of the transcendent.

Jain studied her with growing appreciation. At five and a half feet tall, Ildriss could stare a devotee in the eye without intimidating them. Her twenty-four-year-old body retained the freshness of spring, though her favorite time of year was autumn. Her hair was the color of white prairie grass laced with gold. Jain knew her complexion was pale year-round because she'd spent a couple of years in New Shetain, and the first few months had convinced him to pay her special attention, at least from afar. What he'd gleaned had earned her this private audience.

Ildriss was not merely beautiful but someone one would intensely desire to know, to unravel the mystery of.

Flocks of penitents would feed right out of her hands.

"Tell me, child," he said at last, "did you ever imagine a moment such as this, alone with me in my chambers?"

There were a few possible ways to interpret that question, all of which could lead her mind down avenues conducive to his aims. When she hesitated, Jain added, "The herald of Toh bids you speak your mind."

"My mind has worth only as wood for Toh's fire," Ildriss recited. "It will be pleasing in His eyes only when it has been burned empty."

Jain drew a long breath to still his irritation. How could he fault her for becoming his creature so completely? "For most devotees... Yes. The mind is an impediment. Truth is not to be questioned, much less disputed. But when one reaches elevated levels of understanding, it can be used as a tool or entirely discarded, as it serves Toh."

Poison for the babes is nourishment for the Masters, he thought. But how could he impress the difference upon an acolyte? How could he lead Ildriss to understand that the Sacred Writ that had guided her steps, keeping her on the condign path all her life, could impede her progress now if she didn't reinterpret it?

"I say that your thoughts are pertinent, perhaps even valuable. Do you question my wisdom?"

Ildriss bowed low, bending slightly at the knees.

"Toh speaks through you, Lord. A pure vessel cannot lead us astray."

"Then speak!" Jain's patience sometimes frayed when the obedience he so carefully inculcated into his flock became an obstacle. He felt snagged by his own machinations. "Not even your most secret or trivial thoughts are hidden from Toh. He is omnipotent and omniscient. Therefore, your humility is inappropriate."

Thus chastened by Toh's mouthpiece, Ildriss conquered her timidity. "I know so little... and yet I have always wondered what lies beyond the limits of my knowledge."

"I see. You think of this as a kind of initiation. You came expecting revelation."

She bowed even lower. "I can hide nothing from your eyes."

"I am pleased," Jain said, allowing a small smile as he saw how she trembled at this brief affirmation. "What I would teach you would be much more difficult to master if you lacked desire and curiosity."

"Curiosity leads me astray, Lord," she intoned.

Again, that snag! During the decades of his rule from the shadows, Jain had never developed a methodology free of such pitfalls.

"Ildriss, do you grant that I am mortal?"

He watched her wince at this two-pronged attack against all her preconceptions. This was the first time he'd ever used her name, ever called her anything other than "child." And in that same breath, he'd asked her to comment on his immaculate person.

"You are a clear vessel." Ildriss' distress quickened her cadence and pitch.

"Yes, the Word of Toh!" Jain snapped. "But am I not one man of flesh?" He placed his bare forearm within her reach. "Is this not skin? Touch it!"

Trembling, she did as he bid.

"And you were right," he said. "This *is* an initiation, and you've surmounted the first trial. Henceforth, you will cease referring to me as Lord. Now, how many bodies have I?"

"One." Ildriss caught herself and refrained from adding, Lord.

"Aye: one man in one body. And how many evils are there in this broken Ophia for the will of Toh to redress?"

Perhaps sensing he wanted alacrity, Ildriss allowed herself no hesitation. "They are myriad... countless."

Jain-Toh nodded slowly, giving her time to mull over her revelation. "So now you see what odds beset me. Thousands of needs cry out to my ears: a host of wails from this fallen world. And I with only my two hands.

"But you, Ildriss, intuited the meaning of your presence here. That pleases me."

Jain had learned long ago that trying to smother intuition entirely was counterproductive. It was more fruitful to utilize it and bend it to his purposes.

"I can manifest only a portion of Toh's great vision alone," he said. "Others must be willing to serve—not just obey, but serve. There must be those to whom I can entrust knowledge and wisdom that would be disastrous for the uninitiated."

Ildriss seemed to hear only the portions of his message that carried personal implications. "I... am... overwhelmed."

"That's obvious! I need you to be *attentive*. These matters are difficult to explain even to those who possess discernment. To be a servant of Toh in this fallen world means one must be prepared to do whatever is necessary to see His word fulfilled."

At long last, Jain-Toh witnessed comprehension dawning on Ildriss' pristine face. He exploited that opening. "Aye, even if it means speaking or acting in ways that seem contrary to the Sacred Writ itself."

He stroked the dangling roots of his beard, considering. "Can you understand why I would forbid children still unsteady on their feet to ride one of the Jona-chons' horses?"

Ildriss nodded. "They would be killed... or paralyzed."

"And yet, when those children are grown to adulthood, does such a prohibition still make sense?"

The woman considered this and shook her head.

"No indeed," Jain concurred, "because horses can be emissaries of Toh. They hasten the spread of His Writ. There must be those among us who can ride. So, we get to the meat of it now. When you were a child, Ildriss, the Sacred Writ was necessary. It *had* to be obeyed. But now, I say you are no longer a child and must put it aside. Are you ready to do this?"

"If my Lord asks it." In her startlement, she forgot his previous admonishment.

Jain straightened and held her eyes until he felt she was sufficiently cowed. "Recall what I said earlier about the importance of desire. Is this what *you* want?"

It was a momentous question to pose to a woman whose entire education had railed against her desires, calling them, at best, distractions and, at worse, abominations—spite and willfulness hurled in the face of her god.

"I... I want to serve Toh," she managed.

"Right and wrong are mortal strictures," Jain persisted. "For Toh, there is only creation and necessary destruction. Will you do His bidding even if it means acting in ways that violate the Sacred Writ?"

Ildriss hesitated, perhaps wondering if this was a snare. "I trust *you* to interpret His word as circumstances necessitate," she said at last.

Jain smiled; he didn't mind if the woman saw it this time. He could not have hoped for a better response. He maneuvered behind her willowy figure and laid his hands on her bare shoulders—an avuncular gesture, at first, until he traced a couple of fingers around the curve of her ear.

Leaning down, he whispered, "What have you learned of the pleasures of the flesh, Ildriss?"

He felt her rapid *timbres*—unfamiliar strands of arousal beating against a wall of blankness. Ildriss' thoughts were in turmoil. To be invited into Jain-Toh's private chambers represented her imagination's uttermost bounds. That her Lord should now deign to touch her..!

"Speak, woman!" Jain knew her primary urge—to obey and please him—would prove stronger than her confusion.

"If the older generation cannot fulfill the Writ of Toh," Ildriss recited, "we place our faith in the younger. Our race must propagate itself, that Toh may never want for worshippers."

"Aye." With both hands, Jain cupped her neck and cheeks. He began stroking in a hypnotic, spiraling pattern. "Our taint is abhorrent to the light of Toh. He cannot abide our presence. But He is a just and forgiving deity. He understands the weakness of the flesh. Though He does not love it, He makes allowances. What is the allowance He makes in this instance?"

Ildriss echoed another fundamental article of faith. "We may explore our bodies' cravings within the confines of a marriage you have sanctified."

A hissed intake of breath punctuated this. Jain-Toh had kissed her neck and slid to the furtive area behind her ear. Momentarily, he gave the other side of her head the same treatment. His eager beard bristled against her soft flesh, reddening her cheeks.

"That, too, is part of the Writ given to children," he whispered. "But I have said that, as of this day, you are no longer a child but a woman. Ildriss of the Chosen, are you ready to be initiated into the deeper mysteries?"

His hands slid into the gap between calfskin blouse and skin and cupped her breasts. Each time he squeezed, Ildriss' world reeled and lurched.

"For us," Jain pronounced, "the only prohibition is that our desires shall never interfere with or seek to supplant our devotion and obedience to Him.

"Also," he added, as if in afterthought, "you must not dance for anyone other than me—Toh's humble servant—henceforth. The sight of you is too arousing for the acolytes. They're too weak for such a test. Now that you are an initiate, you must devote your gifts and charms to only the most sacred purposes."

"I understand."

Jain doubted she truly did. He decided to press the lesson, just in case. "Your suitor, Jandha—he must be tested. He will transcribe texts in my tower study."

New Shetain's design, ventilation, and deliberate acoustics carried every sound from this bed chamber down to the lower floors as if one stood right outside the door.

"All the rapture of our lovemaking will be for his ears to relish. Do you think this an overly harsh lesson?"

"Cruel," Ildriss whispered. She shuddered. "But I doubt not that it's only my ignorance that makes it seem so."

"Indeed, it is. Attachments and possessiveness are human weaknesses that no acolytes can afford. Jandha *must* be broken in this way. He needs to understand the limits of his power and choice. Ultimately, each of us belongs to Toh, not to each other.

"He must accept that his hoped-for wife has advanced beyond him into a rarified sphere that he cannot share with her. He must not fault her for progressing faster than himself. Only Jain-Toh can meet her in this place. Ildriss has become a priestess of Toh, and thus her treasure becomes the prerogative of the Master."

꾩

Jain admitted that it whetted his pleasure to even greater heights, thinking of Jandha's agony during those moments when he was forced to hear his beloved and Jain in conjoined ecstasy. But what did that signify? Toh's perfection was something Jain could never attain. He was not *meant* to reach it. Therefore, these moments of human weakness were inconsequential; he may as well enjoy what pleasure he could wring from them.

Within that rapture, he would occasionally whisper to Ildriss, "We are not bodies, but two flames spawned from the breath of Toh, united in our devotion to Him. In this place, you are permitted to call me by name."

He knew she would treat the suggestion as a veritable command, and her compliance would complete the agony of the man on the floor below.

I merely hammer home the lesson, he thought. *One must not place the pleasures of marriage before one's devotion to Toh. If ever they are in conflict, devotion takes precedence.*

Besides, what greater cause could there be than to still the waves and, at long last, bring Bocuan to heel?

The moaning and grinding, the smack of caresses, the whispered confidences... these things had scoured Jandha's insides so severely that madness gaped and gibbered just over the lip of a precipice. But he no longer felt like a man bound to a raging pyre. His extremity had taught him to stare his bare predicament in the face. Having done so, he realized there were only two narrow roads available.

Acknowledging and accepting the limits of his freedom and choice lent him a kind of fatalistic calm.

He had to escape New Shetain or die in the attempt—even if that death was accomplished by his hand. He would not spend another night excoriated by the heights of Jain-Toh's rapture and release with the woman Jandha (had once?) loved.

Nevertheless, despite the searing focus and resolve that drove him—that of a man pushed to his last throw—he despaired how to accomplish the thing. Toh's flock were still regaining their footing in a world that'd buckled beneath the Rupture. But they grew more fully welded to Jain-Toh's will by the day.

The Inooks alone—those preternaturally powerful

assassins trained in ancient Shetain arts—sufficed to quell any opposition.

Then Jandha recalled an adventure he and Ildriss had thrown themselves into in the early days of their courtship when he'd still imagined that a shared life beckoned them. It had seemed extraneous at the time: the thrill of sharing forbidden knowledge, almost a game that children would play. But now, it loomed with significance.

Ildriss had shown him the entrance to a passageway behind a small statuette in Jain-Toh's anteroom. Jain often met with chieftains and other dignitaries from the surrounding territories there. Sometimes, it was whispered, he even conferred with emissaries from the Underworld. The passage wound down a narrow stairwell into the catacombs. Hence, these visitors could arrive and depart in secret.

At the time, Jandha had not questioned why Jain-Toh would confide this secret in Ildriss. He'd been blind to the intimate implications. But that no longer mattered. It was part of the dead, ashen past. All that signified now was that the passage still existed—and Ildriss had taught Jandha how to open it.

He closed his eyes and saw Ildriss disappearing into the abyss of his previous life, a life he hoped to seal over like a tomb, suffocating it into extinction.

He needed to move, to *go*!

The Serpent Trail

The pink and scarlet figure dominated Wakeen's opening vision. It—she—regarded him from across a stone chamber. The torch a couple of feet to the right of her head seemed sluggish, even muted as if the very wall sought to suppress the firelight. But he could see that the color, which reminded him of Azaleas and momentarily warmed his heart, came from her robe.

Tracing it upwards, he met chestnut eyes whose emerald formed a beautiful contrast. Wakeen hadn't been awake long enough to rally defenses or dredge up any past into this pristine space. So, when he met those eyes in that unguarded moment, he felt that the universe he'd been hurled into could be a comforting and nurturing thing after all.

Then, he began to grapple with his surroundings.

Identifying the other four figures in the room, he realized—or perhaps recalled—that he was a prisoner. He had not come here voluntarily. The snatches of memory that began to emerge felt like fragments of a fever dream.

A slave camp seen through slits in a burlap face covering that made him nearly blind with sweat. Tight around his neck. Bound by thick rope, like a perpetual noose.

Relentless toil endured only to earn him another day of it.

The fences penning him and the Manitoh laborers

like pigs cooped for slaughter.

The twists of razor-sharp wire shredding the hands of one man foolish enough to try clambering over the stockade wall. And the hounds on the other side of that wall: giant Shetain-bred dogs that could breakfast on wolves.

"He awakens," a voice tolled. "You cannot justify further delay."

Wakeen didn't need to look up to ascertain the nature of the speaker. No other human *timbre* ever rang as cold as an Inook's. The laborers had been too weary and famished for empathy in the work camp. The Inooks *possessed* no empathy. The same drugs and disciplines that inured them to pain made them oblivious to the suffering of others.

That icy *timbre* reminded Wakeen that he didn't want to fully awaken to his environment.

He latched onto the one comforting memory that had bubbled up into his consciousness. *Water* had been necessary to wash the dirt and rocks from the crates, leaving behind only the precious substance, the fine golden ore deposited in the bottom slots...

Some of it would be made into jewelry, more gilt lettering on the arches of New Shetain or utensils in Jain-Toh's banquet hall, but the greater portion would be used for something much more precious: Power. Power only the surviving Shaini knew how to generate.

But Wakeen recalled the only reprieve he ever found from the heat during those months of slavery: when his work had set him elbow-deep in the creek. That's what this woman's sympathetic glance reminded him of. Her eyes were like an unforeseen fount in a parched desert.

"Bring him."

This time, Wakeen's gaze was wrenched up despite himself. He vaguely recognized the speaker. He'd seen that long, angular, and stoic face several times when he'd lived in

New Shetain—always looking ill at ease and eager to depart on other errands. Senoa had been demoted (or elevated, depending on one's point of view) from warrior to priest of Toh.

Tumoset had established himself as the mightiest warrior among the Manitohs. In little over a year, he had brought most of the scattered Kawli tribes under his dominion. The mere whisper of his name sent shudders through the outlying settlements. Chief Senoa, whose prestige had once swelled during the months the Masters had left these shores, and Ophia had trembled beneath Sarpienta's lashes, as their folklore described it, was now a mere shadow beside the Chief of Chiefs. Rather than lead his fellow Manitohs in the field, he'd been relegated to performing clandestine sacrifices and other secretive practices within the bowels of Khempsa.

Tonight that duty requires him to shed my blood, Wakeen realized, *and probably the woman's as well.*

He groaned as two Manitoh acolytes bent to either side of him, got their hands beneath his armpits, and hauled him to his feet. These devotees wore leather neckbands studded with iron spikes half the length of his thumbs. They were Toh's collared hounds, and this perception made Wakeen marvel that he was not bound in any way. But the reason was made plain when he tried to struggle. He understood why his mind was still sluggish, dragging its feet through a silted river bottom. His limbs were leaden; his tongue was too numb to locate; his strength scantly sufficed to part his lips, much less howl.

I'm drugged!

He didn't want to think about it, but he knew only Karia possessed the lore and skill to brew concoctions with such specifically debilitating effects. *Poisoned by my own sister!* Perhaps his father had hoped that his labor in the

Kawli work camp would kill him as it had so many others. He could never fathom the source of resilience his son had discovered. Now, more drastic measures needed to be taken to silence this voice of dissent.

Wakeen scarcely felt the acolytes grasping his arms. His flesh was dead, inert, but his mind had begun to connect fragments of insight, and he gaped at the picture he slowly pieced together.

He began to comprehend why this gathering evinced little of the ceremony that usually attended sacrifices, why the inner sanctum echoed with no drums or chants.

The surface of the sacrificial slab was nowhere flat. Its center was depressed a few inches to form a vaguely humanoid shape as if a slave had been pounded into the wet clay before it was baked into stone, incinerating the living being that had molded it. On either side, grooves the thickness of Wakeen's arms ran at a gradual decline so that blood could collect in a stone basin at its feet.

Senoa regarded Wakeen momentarily with an imperious expression that betrayed nothing of his inner estate. His *timbre* rang like cold steel, but Wakeen felt how much that facade cost the chief. He loathed performing the function that had been entrusted to him.

As Senoa turned to watch the woman being hauled to the opposite side of the altar, Wakeen looked for the Inook. Shetain's master assassin felt like a lurking jaguar. And that *timbre* of coiled lethality led Wakeen's eyes to a pillar some ten paces from the bottom of a stairwell. Apparently, the Inook had positioned himself where he could keep an eye on both the entrance and the priests.

Senoa's gaze flickered between the two captives. He held himself erect against a thick wooden stave whose branched head cupped a ball of quartz carved in the likeness of an infant's skull, which glowed pale in the chamber. After deliberating, however, Senoa leaned this staff against the altar to retrieve a clear cylindrical tube from a fold in his robe. He extracted a rolled parchment, unfurled it, and held it before the woman's eyes.

"These two have already been sentenced," the Inook called. "This is needless."

Senoa stiffened and glared, an expression that Wakeen had never seen a Manitoh level at one of Shetain's henchmen. "She will know that this order did not come from me!"

The woman appeared no more cowed than Senoa, nor did she spare a glance at the Inook. After the merest cursory look at the parchment, her wide emerald eyes shot defiance at the priest.

"This is written in Khempsite script," she said. Her voice sounded cool as a well bottom. "Doubtless only the priests of Toh can decipher it—and your Master, who forced the Sacred Writ upon the Manitohs."

Senoa stared back like the blankness of the void, then turned to his right. "This one I know can read it," he said, pressing the paper against Wakeen's chest.

Wakeen's hands felt heavy as if still laden with slave labor. He marveled that his legs could uphold him and then realized that the two acolytes still bore most of his weight. His jaw felt torpid, but he discovered that this effect, at least, he could slough off with an effort of will.

As he started reading, his voice recovered some of its native surety.

"It's of small account that Tumoset disgraced himself, allowing the unvirtuous woman to enter his bed without resisting her. Toh perceives the weakness of all flesh. He understands that we, being thus made, can never aspire to his state of purity."

Wakeen discovered he could not only decipher the

script but could verily deliver the message without the parchment. His ears had been full of such sermons his entire life.

"But Toh desires that the fact of this indiscretion remains secret. All men shall deem Tumoset indomitable. Thus, what recourse have we? The woman is educated. Should you remove her tongue, she could still convey what transpired with her hands. She could write an account of what occurred between herself and the Chief of Chiefs. There is but one way left to silence her."

Wakeen couldn't bear to lift his eyes and see how the woman met these accusations, but her *timbre* felt more outraged than afraid.

"As for the other—" Wakeen almost choked on the word–"he has been chastised for his defiance. He has been punished with privation, fear, and the most grueling labor the Kawli masters could devise. And yet he remains unrepentant. Any further mercy shown will be interpreted as a symptom of weakness, and his life will be a constant reminder that some men are too willful for even Toh to bring to heel."

Now Shetain's estranged son, reading his own indictment, finally understood why his punishment would be enacted in this secret temple below Khempsa, far from the eyes of the other Manitoh penitents in the city. Usually, sacrifices were publicly exhibited in the plaza. There—so the propagated myth proclaimed—mighty Sarpienta slithered to the top of the ziggurat to devour the smoking hearts of altar victims.

"Consume their bodies in the sacred fire," the condemning parchment tolled. "Smear their ashes upon yourself, and upon the faces and hands of your acolytes, as signs of your covenant. Then, when thunder and rains come again, Toh will cleanse the taint upon your people as those ashes are washed away. He will favor the Manitohs in the wars to come."

As Wakeen finished reading, the Inook ignored Senoa and spoke directly to the two acolytes. "This can brook no more delay!"

Senoa snatched the paper from Wakeen's hands and, crumpling it in a fist, stamped the heel of his staff against the polished marble floor three times, producing a sound as hollow as the tap of a spoon against a dry skull. But he wavered....

"It is as Tumoset has claimed," the Inook called. "You aren't ruthless enough when ruthlessness is required."

Senoa spat a wordless curse and waved the quartz head of his staff so the skull-eyes seemed to stare down at the indentation in the altar's center. Wakeen was hoisted and turned until, after some tossing and manhandling, one acolyte had him by the arms and the other by the moccasins.

He could not have fought, even if the toxin hammering in his veins like venom had permitted him to. The cords that held his defiance together had been cut. He sagged in the grip of the two priests like a sack of useless meat.

So he would be burned after his heart was set on the altar. His mind numbly registered this fact. Usually, the priests removed and preserved all portions of a sacrificial victim's body—brain, heart, organs, even bones and teeth. Perhaps only Wakeen's sister, High Alchemist Karia, knew the full uses to which these body parts were put.

Senoa bent so low his nose nearly grazed Wakeen's ear. "A gift from your sister," the man whispered. "A leaf she gave me. I have crumpled it in my hand; it is powder. Inhale it swiftly, and you will fall into blackness. You'll feel nothing of your body's ordeal."

"Give it to the woman!"

"I cannot. I have my orders."

"He didn't even name me in the letter." Wakeen's voice was nearly hoarse with disbelief.

After all that he'd been through, his shock was irrational, but somehow, he could not bring his emotion in accord with what his logical mind had long known.

"Soon, you will forget he was ever your father. Be at–"

Senoa straightened and whipped his head around, and the two acolytes gasped simultaneously. Wakeen noticed the woman's widening eyes even as he recognized the scent suddenly permeating the space: an ophidian odor so intense that his eyes watered momentarily.

Beneath where the man-sized stone carving of Sarpienta's head glared from the far wall with one jade eye and one ruby eye, a circular opening about a meter wide gaped where his belly might have been. The priesthood had not dared to carve the official effigy of New Shetain, that of bearded Toh with his heel set upon the serpent's head. Not in this place, not yet. Old beliefs persisted. What could not be stamped out must be assimilated.

The Inook, his senses whetted by years of brutal training in the Kawli Rainforest, was the first to hear the disturbance within that tunnel. Like a cat sneaking up on prey at the edge of the savannah, he stalked to the opening and sought to pierce its black maw. It protruded somewhat like a spout, one he could not have reached from where he stood, so he stepped back a pace and listened as the stone seemed to groan.

Then the woman cried out, almost wailing, and Wakeen, startled to hear such a sound after all the other cruel turns of this night had left her undaunted, forced himself to sit up partway and follow her line of sight.

He moved his head in time to behold the statue, which seemed to spawn its counterpart in flesh. The torches set beneath the giant idol to either side caught the green-yellow glare of reptilian eyes the size of fists peering down from the hole. For a moment, that tableau—primordial menace and six humans paralyzed by a sight their minds could not assimilate—held.

Then Wakeen sighed and almost smiled.

The Inook, long trained to face every situation with a still mind free from preconceptions, broke his stasis and leaped clear as the giant serpent dropped from the mouth of the wall to a damp smack upon the marble. Then the snake unspooled its tremendous length, some twenty meters, and lashed out at the Inook in the same motion.

The ferocity of that attack surpassed even the instincts and sinews of one of Shetain's most deadly assassins, and the man uttered the first cry of shock and agony in his life as fangs the length of daggers buried themselves to the hilt in his chest. His body began twitching even before he hit the ground, and in a few seconds, even this last feeble protest stilled.

The two disciples screamed and, apparently realizing that the snake could mow them down long before they reached the exit tunnel, tumbled together off the altar stairs and curled in its shadow, gibbering.

Senoa stood transfixed, forgetful even of his own mortality. But Wakeen was on his feet now, and as if he shared some of the serpent's vitality, he felt life reaching its fingers into his limbs. Nevertheless, he moved cautiously. He could never be certain that the history he had established with this creature would preserve him from the whims of its nature. Only when Sarpi lowered his great head to the floor, reminding Wakeen—absurdly—of a horse waiting to be mounted, did he quicken.

Stopping within a few paces of the enormous creature, he muttered, "It was dangerous for you to have come, but with all my heart, I am grateful."

Then he turned and beseeched the woman who had nearly shared the ill fate prepared for him. Wonderment and horror waged an indecisive battle within her. For an interval of five heartbeats, she could neither move toward nor look away from the uncanny spectacle. Those feral eyes demanded some response from her elemental being, but she couldn't find it.

"Climb on!" Wakeen said. "I'll be right behind you. It'll be alright."

Finally, her desire to flee this place of nihilism and death won out. Grabbing the hem of her skirt with both hands, she began to walk, though her trembling limbs betrayed her fear that she might be moving towards a fate no better than the one that had awaited her at the altar.

The creature's ophidian odor now completely permeated the dank chamber, which typically smelled of naught but attar, charnel, and torch smoke.

Reassured by the woman's newfound resolve, tenuous as it was, Wakeen turned to the priest. "Sarpienta deigns to enter the temple of Khempsa, blessing its floors with his twisting passage!"

Senoa swallowed hard and gathered enough fragments of his shattered consciousness to utter one word: "Aye."

As her steps brought her within the light of the torches on the far wall, the woman could see that the serpent's body was mostly a deep viridian, blackened in places as if some of its scales had been scorched, though a line of yellow and gold diamonds ran along its spine. Its head, nearly thrice the size of hers, regarded her with the kind of patience only the predatory animal comprehends.

"The serpent's wishes are preeminent," Wakeen told Senoa. He'd been schooled long enough in such rhetoric to understand what the priestly mind responded to. "Aye, even if they contradict your master's commands. You must attend and not interfere. Await the serpent's will."

Senoa's eyes were wide and entranced as if they beheld the uttermost source of their being. He managed only a half nod. The acolytes had ceased even to gibber. Wakeen didn't know if they were conscious.

"This is a test of our faith," he said. "A sacred drama in which we've all been chosen to play a part."

Senoa let out a long breath as if his insides had unwound now that he seemed to grasp the nature of the great game he was involved in. He held his staff out at arm's length and deeply bowed towards the serpent. The woman had nearly reached it, but she cried out when the creature made a slight movement in her direction.

"Sarpi's bidding you to make haste," Wakeen said. "He's anxious to be gone from this place."

Then he moved to her side and gently helped her onto the scaly back. She drew a deep breath and held it as if preparing for a plunge. Her hands found purchase on rough scales on either side of the tremendous body. She straddled the great bulk between her legs as if it were a primeval saddle. Once Wakeen was nestled behind her, the creature began to move, reaching the stairwell and negotiating the steps with deft lunges. Then, it darted along the passageway leading out from the sacrificial chamber as if it knew it had been wrought to honor it.

Not until its ponderous tail disappeared into the shadows—or the outer void—did Senoa finally find his voice and wail, though he could not have said if it was in agony or rapture.

༜༜

The tunnel was unwavering for a long, dreamy interval that the two companions scarcely bothered to measure. Their thoroughfare was wide enough for four wagons to ride abreast, and the portions of its floor that hadn't been crusted by drippings from the domed ceiling or the slow accumulation of rubbish were smooth as a mirror.

The woman gasped. For the first time, her attention was drawn by something other than the fright of her predicament. Wakeen guessed that she'd begun to ascertain what he already knew about this place. The broad avenue had been wrought with *Sacred Timbre*. It was meant to instill an overpowering religious awe in visitors, reminding them that they were insignificant motes in Toh's eye. A faint trail of moonglow awoke in the stone in response to Sarpi's belly warmth as he glided, reinforcing this sense of the transcendent.

"Before the Rupture," Wakeen said, "Shetain's Sovereign Priest had been governor of Khempsa during the decades of its occupation."

His companion had noticed the latent light keyed to respond to organic warmth. She saw, too, that it was dashed with scarlet, suggesting ichor.

"Toh's blood, shed by the willful and disobedient," she rasped. "People like you," she called back, her voice more deeply seated in its center now. "That's why you were sentenced, was it not? And yes, I know my history. My people had dealings with Shetain before the Rupture, though it galled the priests to have to treat with us."

"Fortunately," Wakeen said, "we have not Toh but Sarpienta to thank for our salvation."

The woman half-turned, lured by this jesting note. It was the first time she'd heard the man chuckle. "Is that who you take this creature to be?"

"That's who the worshippers, and even many of the

priests, are meant to *think* he is," Wakeen returned.

"Meant?"

But the man made no further response. His companion felt the slim *timbre* of their connection dissolve as quickly as it had flickered to life. In the dim light awakened by their passage, she noticed that the tunnel walls were ribbed in a way that evoked a snake's underbelly. This seemed to lend further credence to the man's assertion. The very stone seemed to proclaim, "Abase yourself! You are within the Presence!"

Aching for reminders of humanity amid all this austere grandeur—and the force of nature moving beneath her belly like Ophia's urgent pulse—she tried to engage her companion again.

"We almost shared death in the sanctum, friend. And for all I know, we race to no better fate now. Can you at least tell me your name?"

More silence.

"I am Jemcay," she offered.

No doubt he noticed her omission of a surname and wondered at it. But what she *had* said elicited another chuckle, which sounded involuntary.

"Like the old stories," Wakeen said.

"Oh, so you've heard. I wasn't aware that the Shetain priesthood permitted its populace to read."

According to Shaini myth, Jemcay had always managed to unwittingly hurt those who got close to her. Only after she'd been transformed into a rosebush could she bear her blood-colored flowers, thus offering the world something beautiful—a gift to any bold enough to risk her thorns.

"I hope I don't sound ungrateful," Jemcay said. "I owe you and this creature both my life and freedom. But if we aim to get beyond Khempsa's grasp, then we have leagues to go before we can truly call ourselves free, and they would pass much more enjoyably if I knew something about my companion."

"I'm Wakeen. If you want to know more, ask."

Jemcay shook her head, regretting it when her chin scraped along an abrasive scale. For the moment, her consternation made her forget her fear and discomfiture. "A terser response I could not have hoped for! I'm pleased to see that I warrant such investiture on your part. But you interest me. You're obviously Shaini, for one thing, and I thought that the small remnant of my Hive were the only ones to survive the Rupture."

"Our *people* survived," Wakeen said. "Not our Hive. We fled because we were forewarned. I am from Shetain."

"And... Shetain Hive?"

Wakeen grunted. "That whole region of the Nahalia Mountains now looks like ten leagues of shattered pottery. The six rivers have dried or found new courses. That's what the Vandrene traders say, anyway." Then–Jemcay could hear the obvious effort he made to sound cordial–"And what Hive do you hail from?"

Her voice brimmed with playful derision. "You waste yourself with this feigned ignorance. You've no other audience out here aside from myself. And I am not fooled. You know how I earned my sentence of death. You were the one who read the writ. So... Who else would come on behalf of her people and try to placate the Manitoh warlord with sex?"

Wakeen nodded slowly. "I see. Helwen Hive. You are a priestess, then?"

Jemcay snorted. "That would be the Shetain interpretation. No, my friend. Every Shaini's body is their temple. You can call it a temple of worship if you must."

The tapestry of scales beneath her lurched as the passage dipped and spilled onto another flight of stairs.

Gasping, Jemcay faced forward again and clutched harder at her precarious handholds. Already, her palms were being rubbed raw. She knew she was probably exerting herself more than necessary, and the ache in her inner thighs was likely needless too, but she couldn't help herself.

She sought to master her fear by sustaining the conversation. "It's strange you say that your people survived because they were forewarned. Isn't Vision considered heresy among the folk of Shetain—trusting one's own revelations over the word of Toh?"

"It wasn't Vision but *lore*," Wakeen said. "My sister... she masterminded the creation of Cundras sensitive to disruptions within Ophia's body. They'd detect unrest in the oceans and skies. She did this at our father's behest because he suspected what was coming. As well he should. It was largely by his grasping hands that the Rupture was wrought."

"Father." Jemcay mouthed the word in stunned wonder as obscure references made in the inner sanctum dovetailed with what Wakeen said now. "But then... you must refer to the Sovereign Priest. You're Jain-Toh's son?"

Though it frightened her to take her eyes off the tunnel ahead, she felt compelled to turn and watch his response. Wakeen's eyes simmered, threatening to erupt. "Pray don't make me regret the admission."

"You seem to regret it sufficiently on your own," Jemcay said, nestling her head back onto the scaly bed.

The two Shaini didn't realize how dependent they'd grown on the floor's subtle luminescence until they were expelled into a night so blackened by the jungle canopy that only the animal calls and the humid breath of trees informed them that they were no longer enclosed in stone.

Wakeen, attuned to what the serpent perceived, shouted, "Hold on!" And as she did so, Jemcay felt buffeted as if she was tumbling down a broken hillside. But she soon realized that the gaps and jolts occurred with a certain regularity. *Another flight of steps*, she guessed, *though these feel steeper than the last.*

She risked loosening her hold enough to pat the serpent's side. "He's familiar to you," she called. "It begins to make more sense now—why you weren't surprised by his sudden appearance."

"I felt him coming, yes," Wakeen said. "That opening in the chamber, under the big snakehead statue, it's meant to instill fear. It serves as a constant reminder that Sarpienta *could* arrive. But those who wrought it long ago were believers. I'm not sure how far back that tunnel goes, but like the one we escaped through, it lets out somewhere in the jungle."

Jemcay faltered in her stream of thought, forgetting what she'd intended to ask next. The adrenaline surge provoked by her confrontation with death and subsequent miraculous salvation was beginning to subside. The weariness growing within her throughout the whole slow ordeal since the Manitohs first came for her suddenly pounced. And that noxious concoction still thrummed in her veins, making her sluggish.

Wakeen seemed to sense her struggle. "Hold on just a little longer," he urged her. "We haven't gotten far enough away from Khempsa yet to stop. If there are more Inooks in the city, they at least will give chase when they discover what happened. And any warrior will obey their commands. If we hear drums tonight, be assured they're beating every bush for leagues around."

He mustered this bravado for her sake as he fought his own bone-deep weariness.

No wonder the kindness in this woman's eyes makes the whole world seem even more unreal, he thought.

"All right," Jemcay said, rallying. "Then tell me: How

does Jain-Toh's son come to slave in a Manitoh work camp and then get brought to an underground sanctuary to be sacrificed?"

Wakeen groaned. *Eyes brimming with compassion, the woman might have, but she also possesses an uncanny instinct for prying in the most unwelcome places!*

"When the storm subsided enough to allow our ships to sail," he said, "we returned to these shores. I fled the Shetain order shortly after that. I'd always feared the darkness that seemed to follow my father like a shroud. But now, the Rupture left me with questions I couldn't answer. There were certain things I could no longer ignore. So I left, or tried to."

"You were caught?"

"Eventually, yes. Before I left, I tried to convince my sisters to join me. But Karia is still loyal to Father. Shireen, my elder, came with me, and she found sanctuary with the bandits that roam the Conhuera Mountains. There are easily a hundred places to hide in those rock piles and a dozen ways of getting out of each one. But I was caught—sold out by some of those cutthroats.

"And so I was... disciplined. But when the first punishment failed to break me, I was sent to the slave camp. After that... I really don't know. I can only suppose Father was afraid somebody would eventually discover who I was."

"As for the other..."

"They made me wear a mask while I was slaving there. But apparently, I'd become a constant reminder of his failure. I was too much of a liability to be left alive."

"Maybe that's why he sent you here," Jemcay considered. "It was the last little shred of humanity within him. Maybe he'd already made up his mind. But this way, he wouldn't have to actually witness the consequences of his decision."

Wakeen glanced out at the boughs, leaves, and vines passing like a waving mass of black phantasmagoria. His eyes were beginning to adjust to the darkness, and what he saw brought dim relief. Sarpi, reading the ground's natural inclinations with his belly, found passage in ways that would be very difficult for even the sleekest human hunters to follow.

"You give him too much credit with that supposed shred of humanity," he said at last.

But Jemcay gave no indication that she'd even heard him.

※ ※

As Jemcay awoke, her gaze slowly slid along a tangled bundle of vines until she realized she was supine beneath the umbrella of a broad banyan tree. The vines had claimed a dense circle of trees, exuberantly filling the gaps so that the space resembled a wooden hut tall enough for two floors. The woman saw that the interior had been cleared, the work of hatchets and flame, but there were no signs of more recent human activity.

A monkey sounded a shrill alarm. Glancing to her right, Jemcay saw a whole troop of the creatures, a dozen or more, huddling together for security, shaking the summit of a nearby tree with their frantic weight.

Wakeen peeked in through the one significant gap in the banyan's weave, which resembled an egg-shaped doorway.

"You fell off Sarpi's back not far from here," he said, "so I thought maybe we both needed to stop and rest." He gazed about the dome with a glint of approval. "This was the best shelter I could find."

Jemcay sat up, groping for something to hold her

reticent companion, whom she already felt pulling away. "And our savior?" she asked,

"He needed to feed," Wakeen said. "That ought to be easy for him in a place like this. Besides, he knows the ways of the Kawli. This is where they bred him, after all.

"I wish I could offer *you* something to eat. I don't know if you recall... We mostly followed a waterway coming here, and that whole area was stagnant and rank."

Unconsciously, Wakeen ground his teeth. The woman's proximity, exotic beauty, and the whiteness of her shapely legs revealed by her divided riding skirt were distractions he intended to resist.

Trying to redirect his thoughts, he said, "My father bred and raised Sarpi in the dungeons beneath Shetain. Can you guess why?"

Jemcay shrugged. "Likely, the thing was done in tribute to Sarpienta the Sage Serpent. You suggested as much last night."

"I might have agreed with you," Wakeen said, "had I not had the dubious fortune of being son to Jain-Toh. He gives nothing in tribute. When priests talk about Sarpienta today, when they pay homage through rites and rituals, most of what they're repeating comes from my father. His Sacred Writ; his Toh.

"He's old even by the reckoning of our people. He has been an inventor and a manipulator of myth and religion for over a century. And he twisted the pre-existing myths that he couldn't abolish or rewrite, like the ancient worship of the Sage Serpents, to manipulate the minds of Ophia's believers."

Jemcay's eyes shone with eager light. "I'll risk prying further," she said, "since I sense that a part of you appreciates it. What was the first punishment you spoke of? The one that failed?"

Wakeen gestured vaguely towards the jungle

denseness, and she knew he indicated their missing companion.

"Yes, him. Explain. How was it he came to you? How did you earn this strange loyalty he shows you?"

Suddenly earnest, she rose and strode to within arm's length of him. "My friend, how is it that we rode on a giant serpent, and it did not harm us?"

Wakeen considered and discarded a half-dozen offhand replies.

"It *began* as a punishment," he admitted finally. "The first that I mentioned. I told you that my father deliberately bred serpents. He was trying to produce one that could masquerade as the deity Sarpienta. Well, he achieved it with Sarpi. That's why I gave him that name.

"When I was younger, I was sometimes thrown into Sarpi's pit when I was disobedient."

He paused to weather the chill conjured up by that ill memory.

"I was too young to understand that he had a full belly and, therefore, no interest in eating me. So I'd squat in that cave all night, trembling, waiting to be swallowed. But that terror awakened something in me, and because I had nowhere else to direct it, it latched onto Sarpi.

"I heard his thoughts. Not as words, of course. But some part of me could sense and decipher the drift of his mind. And then I discovered that I could send him my thoughts in return. After a while, this warmth grew between us—what you could call creature camaraderie and loyalty, I suppose."

Wakeen's attempted smile plunged into a grimace. "No doubt you think you've taken up with a madman now," he finished.

"Hardly."

Encouraged by his wavering resistance, Jemcay lifted

a palm and pressed it against his chest. "I not only believe that such bonds are possible, but I could teach you how to deepen them. Though I doubt you would approve of the method."

Wakeen turned from her as if he'd been struck.

Undeterred, Jemcay addressed his rigid side. "And why shouldn't I? Why shouldn't I reward the brave man who's rescued me?"

"I would have done the same for anyone unfortunate enough to have shared that fate with me," he said. "It was the right thing to do, that's all."

"You're very concerned with doing the right thing, I see," Jemcay said. "Perhaps you haven't escaped the influence of Shetain's philosophy so much as you think. But I dare say I prefer the way you interpret it."

Wakeen slowly turned, pretending he found the ground by the woman's feet infinitely more interesting than her face. "I can't comprehend how you've made it this far," he said at last. "You wandered alone into the heart of Tumoset's camp and offered yourself..."

He began to pace, face contorted, alternately clenching and relaxing his hands as if wrestling with an apparition. "What was your thought? You really believed you could placate a man like that with your body?"

"I thought perhaps I could open a little window into his soul," Jemcay said. "Remind him of his humanity."

Wakeen, suddenly vehement, grasped her shoulders, provoking a startled cry. "That beast *has* no soul! There's no love *in* him!"

"He is a fanatic," Jemcay allowed. She made no effort to retreat or remove his hands. "You and I may see that as monstrous, and rightly so. But every fanatic begins as an idealist. That means they want for all humanity in their heart of hearts. They rail against their fellows because they fall short of that vision. They cause atrocities; there's no denying that. But the original seed of tyranny is rooted in love."

"You can't possibly believe that!" Wakeen spat. But he released her as if his conviction had dissolved.

"I have to. I have to believe that the capacity for love is innate in all of us and never wholly quenched."

"You're mad."

"Oh, yes? And would you prefer I go mad with belief or with despair? The latter, you seem to say, would be more realistic. But whom would it serve?"

Wakeen sagged, his sustaining passion spent. He lumbered outside the banyan dome to a nearby log and fell upon it, clutching his head between his knees.

Jemcay circled behind him. Her voice sounded cautious but determined. "You have to find someone or something to trust, Wakeen," she said, "else this nihilism you carry will destroy you."

"Maybe it already has."

Her snort lifted his head involuntarily. "You convince neither of us. Now, it is you who sound hopelessly naive."

Alerted by subtle sensations, Wakeen looked over his left shoulder and saw that Sarpi had returned to the edge of the banyan cluster, absorbing the heat of rocks lying momentarily in the sun. The man nodded towards his companion while addressing Jemcay.

"Do you suppose that, given enough love, Sarpi will eschew slaughtering animals for his sustenance?"

"You're closer to him than I am," Jemcay said. "You tell me. Does he kill with hate?"

"No," Wakeen said as if the admission pained him. "No, he does not." Then, with a long sigh, he relinquished the argument. "And you and I aren't liable to solve the mysteries of the universe whilst our own bellies are empty.

"Whatever his motivations, Sarpi does seem to

participate in human passions at times. He hasn't forgotten his old captors; I'll tell you that. Particularly, he hates one of the priests. Konatep. Though he wasn't there when I was sent to camp, Konatep lives in New Shetain when he's not abroad spreading his foul doctrine of guilt and sacrifice."

As he said the priest's name, Wakeen revisited sensations he'd received from Sarpi during the snake's moments of agitation. "Yes, that's the one. My sister, Karia, was tasked with feeding this creature. She nurtured his growth, making him exceed the limitations of his predecessors. In Shetain, they'd been breeding towards this goal for generations. But Konatep would take over Sarpi's 'training,' as he called it, whenever he was within the citadel. It seemed to amuse him."

The hefty man shook his head as if the weight of human futility tolled through his skull. "Killing for survival... It's an ugly business, but I can at least understand it. Same for killing in the heat of passion. But to torment a living creature for fun? Where does such a sick predilection come from?"

"It comes from a heart that's been hurt so badly it no longer knows how to reach for love," Jemcay said. "And so it finds relief only in making others feel as tormented as it does."

"Well, such a person may deserve *our* compassion," Wakeen said. "But I would not cast my lot with Konatep if he were ever again in Sarpi's line of sight."

Disembarking upon Sarpi's back, they were soon soaked in a vehement downpour that turned the serpent's trail into a veritable marsh. Wet, muddy, and miserable, Jemcay rummaged through scraps of her memories for consolation.

She envisioned Helwen hearth fires that consumed no fuel, incandescent spheres warming body and soul, and *timbres* that could shelter vulnerable flesh from the fiercest storms.

Meanwhile, her serpent savior negotiated mud pits that pulled at his underside and torpid streams that latticed the swelling swamp. His brilliant hues vanished beneath a dark brown coating.

"But this at least feels like a natural storm—rainfall that nature intended!" Wakeen called. "I sense no force of amok within it."

Jemcay's grunt might have been intended to mean, "That's a small consolation!" But she took his meaning and was consoled. Amok was a term the surviving Shaini used to describe the Rupture's lingering effects, its perversion of natural patterns.

Nevertheless, they toiled for six days beneath relentless rains, feeding upon what jungle bounty they could snatch at a run, consoled only by the thought that the storm obscured their passage. Then, as the rains finally tapered, they reached a waterway that ran fresh—with little reek of rot.

They dismounted to drink their fill. Wakeen, despite himself, stole a moment to soak up the sight of his companion. Jemcay was deeply attractive. His indoctrination did nothing to obscure his perceptions, and they were scant defense against the feelings that her beauty stirred up in him. Her hair, the color of ripe raspberries, was long and straight, and her skin appeared almost lambent as if it'd absorbed a portion of the sun and never given it back. He'd callously thought of her as a Pale Face the previous night. Now, her skin's color reminded him more of yellow corn. Her high cheekbones, piercing green eyes, and bold nose bespoke stern purpose and indomitable will, but her full lips softened this effect. They seemed to savor life's simpler, kinder pleasures.

She was bold and delicate in pleasing proportion. He decided he would stop fighting this perception of her.

She even smelled good: an aroma reminiscent of honeysuckle.

Feeling his regard, Jemcay straightened, but she seemed to misinterpret its cause. "Was I cupping the water properly, oh chief? I fear to make mistakes in your august presence." Her eyes narrowed. "But then, doesn't your Toh say that I cannot do otherwise, being mortal and tainted?"

Wakeen was certain the woman was deliberately provoking him this time, but he opted to resist the bait. "You spent so much time down there, I thought perhaps you were communing with the stream," he said.

"Indeed, I was," she said with a taunting smile. "It told me you are divided within yourself... conflicted. You resolved not to trust me, but now you're not so sure."

Her voice shifted into something more solicitous. "I think you should trust me. But of course, I *would* say that, wouldn't I?"

Before he could respond, she closed the gap between them and grasped his arms. He hissed at her impertinence and stiffened... but did not withdraw.

"Wakeen, I could be the one friend you've got left—if you gave me a chance." When this failed to elicit a response, she returned to provocation. "You know, this kind of spiritual rigidity brought on the Rupture. It may never have happened had we all esteemed pleasure a little higher. How long do you think you can sustain that rigidity with me?" Her smile teetered on the edge of a leer. "How about after sharing a bottle of Lanorean wine?"

When the man merely seethed in silence, she tried a surprising tactic. "Do you dance, Wakeen?"

"Every child of the priesthood learned the sacred

dances. I was made to memorize the steps and songs for rain and war—to celebrate birth and honor the dead."

"I don't doubt it," Jemcay said. "And I'm sure your movements were impeccable." Damn that sarcasm! "But do you *enjoy* it?"

Caught off guard, Wakeen answered with the ancient, deeply ingrained litany. "I enjoy it as much as Toh permits."

"Do you think you'd enjoy seeing *me* dance?"

Fortunately, Wakeen was spared this time by a happy discovery: a nearby patch of acai trees that his furtive eyes descried. The purple berries were plump and ripe, and the two Shaini gorged themselves before climbing onto Sarpi again.

The rain relented, and they found it easier to focus in the ensuing quiet. They attuned themselves to a new face of the land, to the auras of its features and the resonances of its spaces. In the steamy late winter dawn, they emerged from the depths of the Kawli Rainforest into towering elephant grass nearly twice their height. They had to bury their heads against their savior's scales to avoid being lacerated. And Sarpi sped faster as the ground beneath his belly began sloping downwards.

Slowly, as they descended, the elephant grass tapered and diminished, finally giving way to a broad, gravelly wash that appeared like a desiccated riverbed to the traveler's grieving eyes. Treetops and jagged rocks punctured the soft topaz. This ravaged body plunged precipitously towards a destination shrouded in fog. Feeling its pull, Sarpi began to sidewind to keep his head above the sand.

"This was once an arm of Sequestra Forest," Wakeen surmised, "filling that big gap in the Conhuera range. This is what's left of it, buried under muck tossed up from the sea bottom, which dried from the fires that blackened those foothills."

As he said this, Jemcay realized that the slope, which had seemed so smooth from a distance, descended in rapid rivulets that reminded her of low tide bands. Its darker striations had absorbed the hues of seaweed and kelp. Glancing to her right, she sensed the stark drop-off beyond a rock wall in that direction and feared they raced towards a precipice.

But soon, the dry silt slope spewed them out of a gap fifty paces wide between two cliff faces several hundred feet tall, whose texture and color reminded her of burnt logs. Now, the muted salt tang of an estuary filled their nostrils, and to Wakeen's inner senses, Sarpi seemed to grin in anticipation of water and easy hunting.

Jemcay cried out as the snake skidded across a flatter band of pebbles and uprooted chapparal to plunge into a roiling, bubbling brown belly of water. But the splashes that soaked her were no cooler than the air, which felt like an amphibious exhalation. The water's surface seemed scarcely deep enough for Sarpi to submerge himself had he chosen to.

Patches of young mangroves thrived along the banks. Amid a maze of dead cedars and floating forest debris, the terrain offered no consistency to comfort the travelers' weary minds. One thrust of Sarpi's would launch them onto a patch of tule grass the length of a wagon. The next would pitch them back into tepid mire.

A roughly pyramidal structure gradually coalesced out of the eldritch mist. Even at a distance, they could see it was man-made and crude, a house-sized version of a child's clay mound. The ziggurat seemed to mock the pyramids of old Farsilane and Sequana. It had been piled onto this region's longest stretch of drained, sturdy ground: a canoe-shaped island a half-mile long, around which a river, sluggish and gray, divided itself.

Weak, forlorn wails issued at odd intervals from its summit.

"An old woman and a boy child," Wakeen muttered, most of his attention focused on groping towards the sounds and trying to puzzle out their meaning. "Perhaps they climbed those steps to escape predators."

"But what were they doing out in a place like this, alone, in the first place?'" Jemcay asked.

"'Indeed," Wakeen considered. "'I can think of only three possibilities. Any humans who find themselves here are either lost or seeking to die–or disappear."

Then the man, attuned to Sarpi as to a primordial undercurrent of consciousness upon which his own rode, was alerted to a sudden shift. "Roll off!" he shouted. And when Jemcay was slow to respond, he clutched her hips and pulled even as he dismounted. The snake suddenly bolted from between her legs, nearly sending her tumbling.

Wakeen, bearing the brunt of her unbalanced weight, stumbled back a few feet into the muck. The two sought each other momentarily, Jemcay turning and groping for him as if he were a retreating shadow. Then, distracted by splashing, she turned to see Sarpi's tail disappearing into the mist.

After assuring himself that she was okay, Wakeen released his grip. "'He spotted something, maybe a beaver or otter,' he said.

A high-pitched mammalian squeal rose as if in response.

The big man seemed to scent the air momentarily and then shrugged. "Probably for the best. I mean to find out who's up there on that pyramid, and they'd likely be terrified if they saw Sarpi.

"Can you swim?"

But even as he risked a few steps towards the structure, bidding her to follow, he realized the question was moot. The water was only knee-deep, merely enough to create the illusion that they stood within a sizable lake body. It was discolored in places; bands of copper and orange evoked the ruddy blood of Ophia running over saturated loam.

The cries came again, with a beseeching *timbre*, a plea for mercy–or at least for someone to acknowledge their desolation.

"Come on," Wakeen urged Jemcay. "It's closer than it appears. That mound's not very tall."

They tramped through the mire, quickening as they realized the waters were not deepening. At times, they even broke onto spongy grass, and these patches grew more frequent as they drew closer to the mound. To Wakeen, they seemed to be approaching the heart of the swamp's stagnation. Even in the most torpid pools, he felt *flow*. Too slow for human perception, perhaps, but still vital. But all flow seemed to cease at the ziggurat.

There, the quagmire became a vortex into a realm of unlife. At the structure's flat summit, the two figures' *timbres* reminded him of a candle nearly guttered, its last flickering instants thrown up in a futile hope for renewal. And alongside this, Wakeen sensed the repudiation that had consigned the two to this place.

With the instinctive identification and fury he felt on behalf of the ostracized, he began to outpace Jemcay. She called after him as his boots met springy ground, and he broke into a sprint. The ziggurat steps were uneven and high, sometimes three feet from terrace to terrace, but Wakeen took each with a single bound, glaring at the summit like a wolf at a snare.

He was so fixated on the climb that he didn't notice the ziggurat's peculiar design at first. There were no actual terraces. Rather, a crude walkway a couple of paces wide rose from the base and gradually wound around the structure to the top.

Almost like it was made for Sarpi, he thought, noting its unmistakable serpentine suggestion. Grim memories and new perceptions converged, painting a picture of this place's purpose and whetting his fury.

From the center of the summit plateau rose a rectangular stone tapered in crude imitation of a Shaini Cundra. Wakeen thought of the obelisk within his father's chambers, which dominated the space like a phallic emblem. The two humans chained to this stone possessed barely enough life and hope to acknowledge his arrival with more than a faint stir and flicker. He could have portended salvation, judgment, or doom. It made little difference. They sat with their backs against the black stone, legs spread flat and arms bound overhead in thick metal clasps.

One was a lad who appeared no older than ten. The woman was the most aged Oskwai Wakeen had ever seen. The perils of scarcity, predators, disease, and tribal warfare usually claimed them much younger. The woman moaned softly but seemed to be speaking more to herself. Wakeen was but another hallucinatory swirl before her rheumy eyes.

"Sacrifices," Jemcay whispered. In his shock and rage, Wakeen hadn't heard her reach the summit. Now her breath steamed beside him, and her *timbre* felt appalled as if she'd discovered a hitherto unknown form of cruelty.

"And look at those shackles," Wakeen spat. "No Oskwai ever forged such things."

"Brinsteaders?" Jemcay suggested, but she didn't wait for a reply. Compassion for the bound humans overcame her, and though she saw them tense as she approached, she squatted before them, undeterred, and began mumbling reassurances.

Wakeen reached over her head and felt the metal.

"It's possible," he said. "But the Brinsteaders make little of it themselves. Most of their ironworks are acquired from trading with Shetain, and the priesthood is stingy with its supply. They hoard as much as they can to make conduits of power."

Fuming, he began to pace. "As if one Rupture wasn't enough! In this—" He indicated the heavy chains. "They could have fed and clothed a village with the same expenditure."

He stopped, gripped the chains again, and drew a slow breath. "Jemcay," he said, "I've some skill with the *timbres* of fire, but I don't trust myself right now. Too much rage courses through me. I'm liable to scald these two before the chains break."

She rose and gripped his shoulder. "We'll do it together then. All right? I'll help steady and focus you. We'll need our combined strength anyway. Even with that, I doubt we can do more than weaken the links."

"They were crafted with scarcely any more care than this ziggurat," Wakeen observed. "Had they been wrought with *Sacred Timbre*, our cause would be hopeless. As it is, these people will have to bear the manacles. But unless this is the only time these bonds have ever been employed, someone must possess a key."

"We have no time to look for that someone," Jemcay said. "We've got to offer what aid we can at once."

"Aye," Wakeen concurred. "Else, these two will not survive the night."

Hands conjoined, the two Shaini probed the chain, searching for natural flaws or weaknesses to exploit, places where the joins longed to separate. Jemcay would not have thought there could be any weaknesses within such thick iron, but after a few minutes, trickly fire veins formed, growing like webbing within the links, reminding her of cracks in porcelain—only these glowed red like magma. Once the webwork was complete, she and Wakeen were able to crush the chain at its eroded point with a single concerted squeeze.

Wakeen removed his hand and swiped rust from his palm, feeling reluctance surge through him like the sting of defeat. Though it brimmed with pain and incomprehension, his companion's presence was stabilizing. Jemcay, he realized, had never fundamentally doubted her rightness in the universe—in herself—as he had. She was, in her way, as accepting of the natural motions of her being as Sarpi was. Touching *Sacred Timbre* had cost him much more.

What I would not give, he grated. His brooding thoughts intensified as he gazed down at the two captives, who were scarcely cognizant that they'd been freed. Perhaps they were too famished to rise. Wakeen needed to do something for them, at least conceive a plan.

But for the moment, his outrage ruled him, and he strode to the lip of the roof and hurled defiance into the darkness and fog. "What manner of people are you, abandoning your own like this? Tiny, craven souls!"

His challenge was answered almost immediately by the swish of oars. A cedar bark canoe glided into view to his right, cutting a path along a sluggish stream clogged with lilies. Six lean, coppery-skinned men, bearded with square-cropped black hair, alternated at the oars. Bone necklaces and piercings accentuated their bizarre and (to Wakeen's mind, sick with civilization as it was) alluring barbarism.

In low basso voices, they hummed a sonorous tune with long vowels.

"It looks like you've gotten your answer," Jemcay remarked.

"What folk are these?" Wakeen studied the men in the boat a moment longer. Though they were clearly aiming for the island and no doubt came in response to his call, they never lifted their eyes from the water.

"Junsa," he muttered. "Maybe they've mingled with other tribes since, but those offspring would be but children. These are Junsa, certainly. My father was the governor of Khempsa during the decades when they were held in captivity there. I can't be mistaken."

"They probably hold little love for the two of us, then," Jemcay said, "even if we hadn't committed the blasphemy of freeing their intended sacrifices."

"No," Wakeen whispered. Then he stiffened with sudden decision. "When they draw close, try to talk to them. Use that diplomacy you folk of Helwen are renowned for. I've got to get still. Try to quiet my mind."

"What are you going to do?"

"Jemcay, please!"

The rowers reached an inlet on the island's northern side, still lofting their low chant like a somber malediction. Wakeen assumed a cross-legged position on the uneven clay floor as if forming a human barrier between himself and the freed captives, forcing everyone out of his thoughts. He had to attempt something he'd never done and was not sure was even possible to do on the level of conscious will.

Gradually, he grew attuned to the life of the swamp, as if his tactile senses extended into the lilies and moss, the sycamores and lichen, the worms and the very loam and water—until it became a singular soup, an interdependent gestalt sustained by the fire of his mind. There was no separation—leastways, none but what his fears and inhibitions might conjure.

Until now, he'd been able to tacitly accept Sarpi's aid, though it seemed he anthropomorphized the creature by even giving him that name. But actually calling out to him, beseeching him for help, seemed like a final concession to madness. Would it erode the last vestiges of his sense of humanity? What *was* humanity? The Shetain priesthood proclaimed that the Oskwai were savages. But he, Wakeen, had witnessed things in Shetain that would make any Oskwai shudder to his marrow.

And even as he thought this, Wakeen felt Jemcay with an acuteness that surpassed all of his previous sensations and impressions. With naked love and vulnerability, she pleaded with the Junsa below for mercy towards their two abandoned kin. The rawness of her appeal nearly overwhelmed the man, and he intuited how her promiscuity, which had so revolted him, the idea of it, was in its way her expression of the same thing that he was experiencing now: the beauty, grace, and interconnectedness of all things.

How could such passion arise unless nature herself possessed a heart? And how could Toh, the judger and condemner of humanity—granted that he even existed—how could he ever have created such a thing when it obviously did not sing within his own soul?

With a pitch to rival Jemcay's appeal, Wakeen called out to the cavernous depths: *Come back to me, brother! I need you!*

He felt the snatch of the serpent's attention, the primal tug which, scarcely an hour gone, had launched the creature into the mist in pursuit of prey. Perhaps instinct *was* love's child, after all. Through the lens of that love, Wakeen felt the rippling of water, the mild abrasion of swamp mud and tough grass as it scratched and massaged a belly formed for such terrain; that was, in a sense, a moving extension of it.

He was scarcely aware of the panicked and awestruck cries wafting up from the sodden, unstable base of the ziggurat, of the gibbering of the two captives, who feared that the maw of their god's judgment drew near to devour them, or of Jemcay's urgent reassurances.

For the moment, all Wakeen felt was the overwhelming joy of reunion. Then, the appalling weight of his privations finally overcame him, and he drifted into painless black.

POST-RUPTURE OPHIA

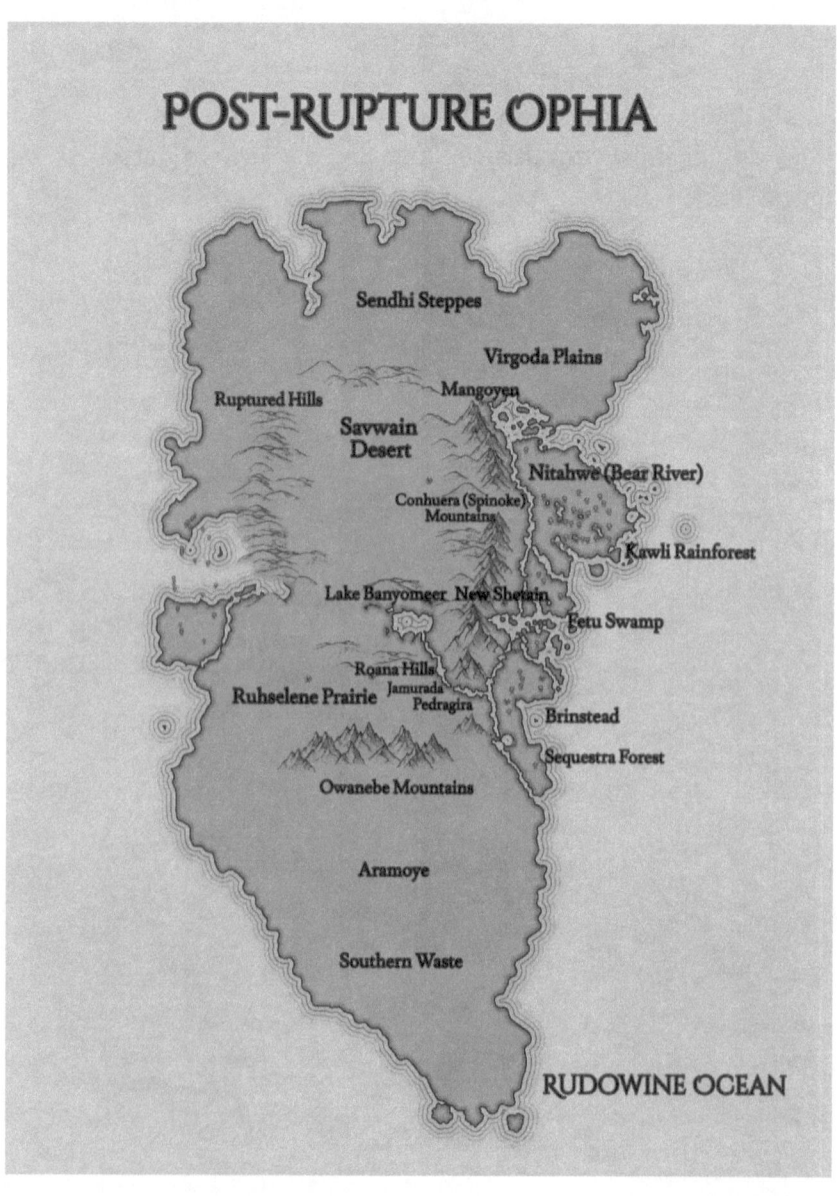

Sendhi Steppes

Virgoda Plains

Mangoyen

Ruptured Hills

Savwain Desert

Nitahwe (Bear River)

Conhuera (Spinoke) Mountains

Kawli Rainforest

Lake Banyomeer   New Shetain

Fetu Swamp

Roana Hills

Ruhselene Prairie   Jamurada   Pedragira

Brinstead

Sequestra Forest

Owanebe Mountains

Aramoye

Southern Waste

RUDOWINE OCEAN

Part Two

The First
Conjunction

Shifting Winds in Two Worlds

From Colleen's Journal

Dear Stacie,

If my life has a purpose—if I dare to proclaim that it does—it's to embody as much of my soul as possible, even though I know the soul is limitless and so can never be fully expressed here. This is the paradox that every artist—every human being, really—faces.

Every uncovered truth is only a portion of the truth.

That longing for infinity within a finite world, the tension inherent in this entire game... That tension has driven some of the truly great creators mad. Or maybe they just forgot how to play.

It's the promise of great music that still leaves you craving. All of reality in a grain of sand.

I live in a state of confusion partly because I've tasted it already: timelessness, immortality within the seconds and hours. Can we ignore the root assumptions of this world so that they can't hold us anymore? Is this not everyone's birthright, the capacity to do this? To outgrow the playpen?

And yet... we want the limitations, too, because certain kinds of expression are only possible in an incomplete world. A world where, oftentimes, love seems absent. That's why so many prohibitions cropped up in those fairy tales we loved as kids. Back then, we accepted the fright when the witches appeared because we knew they also heralded magic.

Certain forms of beauty are only possible in a realm wherein everything must perish.

So death teaches us to appreciate the moments, and eternity reminds us to take this adventure more lightly. To remember to play.

Will I remember my promise to myself, the one I made before birth?

Forget to remember to forget to remember to forget to remember...

I recently ranted at Doctor Visinky, the hospital therapist I've been assigned to. "Life as we know it in this culture," I told him, "is soul-dead."

I suppose it was a justification to spare myself humiliation and remorse. The logic goes like this: Existing where the soul is dead lends the idea of suicide a kind of simple inevitability. If there's no place here for what I feel and dream and long for, then I must be meant for some other world. I didn't want to hurt my body to get there, but I didn't see any other way.

But if I was meant for another world, why was I born into this one? Your typical preacher or minister would tell me it was a punishment. Your typical scientist would tell me it was an accident. But what "chemical chance" accounts for these hot tears streaming down my face and this burning in my chest? Which compounds churn up the thought, "How am I going to endure this all another day?"

It's a small wonder that there are so many alcoholics and drug addicts here, you know? I don't think I've told you this before, but Daddy got a monkey on his back—painkillers—after Momma died. It was easy for him to get ahold of them through his work. Nowadays, he doesn't even want to pop those pills anymore. They don't make him feel any better. But he can't stop.

Misguided beliefs create these prison walls around us. Children rail against them. Many adults see no way out of the cell except for the temporary relief offered by Artificial Paradise.

To feel alive and vital, we need ideas that vibrate our souls. We need beliefs that nourish expansion, freedom, possibility, hope, and love.

You're the only person I can write things like that to without fearing ridicule. That's why I sit hunched over my journal into the small hours tonight.

The world you left behind, the one I am still caught in the soup of, is riddled with war, tyranny, poverty, and disease. It's lorded over by media that focuses on the tragedies and failings of our race, ignoring our valor. The last thing they want is for any of us to become heroes.

But when you were still here, did you ever awaken from a magical dream and almost feel like the world was made new? As if there was so much more to life, so many more avenues open for you to express and fulfill yourself than you'd ever imagined? Those sensations are not fantasies, whatever my dear Dr. Visinsky may tell me.

Oh, Stace, this little voice inside me will not leave me alone. It cannot and will not give up on the promise of life. My soul insists, "Just give me one more moment, and maybe I can show you how different it can be. There's no such thing as a hopeless life."

But everyone around me insists that my soul doesn't even exist, so how can I believe anything it tells me? This very conversation might be proof that I've cracked.

I don't mean to disparage the hospital staff here. I was pretty cynical when I first arrived, but I've seen how many choose this line of work because they want to help people. And yet, the mind-body relationship is something they're just beginning to explore and understand. Even what we call alternative medicine often gets off track, perceiving everything as a battle outside the mind. It just uses more exotic terminology to describe that mock battle. But mind and body are entwined, and if our minds perceive existence as a sterile and hostile landscape, it takes a toll on our tissues.

Anyway, I don't know if it's a testament to his skill or my depth of self-doubt, but it was easy for Dr. Visinsky to set me at war with myself. Stepping into his office, my mind split into two camps. One side immediately resolved to prove him and everyone else here wrong. My spiritual quest, henceforth, would be to unravel this confused knot of erroneous belief and experience again what I knew as a child, the magic that underlies everything.

The other part of me, frightened and cowed by his words and the way they echoed my internal doubts, resolved to stow away all those childish illusions before they tore my life and sanity to shreds.

Stace, the scariest episodes rear up when I can't identify with either side. When that happens, I can scarcely trust the ground I'm standing on. I'm a stranger to myself. I can hardly recognize my reflection in the mirror or the sound of my voice when I speak.

I've even got a name for this particular panic attack. I took inspiration from something that came through during one of my (scary) spells of automatic writing.

I call it The Rupture.

Sometimes, I bring it on myself by being an overly trusting fool. Like the other day. I confided everything in the dear doctor: my confusion, breaking up with Greg, my abortion... I just couldn't hold it anymore, and there was no one else around.

He blamed the whole fiasco on biology and chemistry

if you can believe that. "Any human emotion can be reduced to chemicals," he insisted. He must have noticed the fury flushing my face because he waved his hands and said, "Hey, don't kill the messenger here. I don't invent the facts. But ultimately, everything has an underlying physical cause. We're all just the sum of our body's chemical reactions, and the brain is a part of the body. It's no different."

Oh, Stace, they say the term delusional refers to someone's inability to discriminate between reality and illusion. That describes my whole goddamn civilization! Human consciousness, the root of our lives, is supposed to be an accident, a byproduct of atoms colliding. Our thoughts and emotions are chemical secretions. Mr. Visinsky has given lip service to these insane ideas his entire career. Why hasn't he been labeled delusional and put on medications?

Ignore that last part. I don't wish medications on anybody.

"Colleen," he said, "your fundamental problem is simply your inability to accept life and face the world as it really is. You keep holding onto these philosophies and justifications, insisting that reality conform to your fantasy, and look where it's gotten you!"

You see what I'm up against? Millions of people on Earth—hell, it might be billions now—subscribe to beliefs that bring them nothing but misery and hopelessness. And some of these same people are responsible for putting we, the "maladjusted," on psychoactive drugs, or in padded rooms, under surveillance, into enforced counseling and evaluation...

I gave Mr. Visinsky a rather less eloquent version of that argument. A dose of my "potty mouth," as Momma would have said.

"So you're suggesting that people who want to jump from bridges because they believe they can fly should be given the chance to try?" he said.

For your sake, I'll omit the expletives from my response.

"If you all didn't expend so much energy convincing them that their lives were meaningless, maybe they wouldn't <u>want</u> to jump from bridges! Maybe, instead of constantly asking, 'What's the ideal medication to put this patient on?' How 'bout you ask, 'Why have we created a society that everyone needs to be medicated to endure?'"

Sometimes, I feel guilty for my outbursts. The doctor has been decent and respectful. I don't want to make him feel ineffectual or like he's devoted his whole adult life to chasing chimeras. But in a world populated by individuals, normalcy is a myth. The cookie cutter cuts everyone. Not a one of us fits into any social average if we just think and behave in the ways that are natural to us. Why is this so hard to wrap our heads around?

At one point, he just lifted his hands in a gesture that looked like humorous abjection. "We just do our best with the hardware nature gave us, Colleen."

"Nature in her mindless, soulless wisdom?" I cracked. I couldn't help myself. "Love has a chemical basis, but somehow, an impersonal nature manages to populate a planet with thinking, feeling, dreaming, intuitive, conscious beings."

Who love, long, ache, strive, and mourn.

I fed his patented shrug back to him. "I don't know... You probably think of yourself as an atheist, Mr. Visinsky. But it seems to me your Gods are just chemically produced."

He was growing more frustrated by the moment. "They all have a chemical basis, Colleen. Infatuation, lust, even what we call love."

I waved towards the lobby, where a television was vaguely audible. "And you wonder why the idiot tube spouts little else besides war, murder, and suicide? Gee, why can't humanity learn to revere life as much as it reveres its chemistry sets?"

But he did something really unexpected here. It changed my whole idea of our good doctor. For a moment, that professional mask slipped from his face. His eyes shone with real compassion.

"Have you ever thought about getting a dog?" He scrutinized me in a way that looked surprisingly kind. "I think you could really benefit from having some living creature around that you could give your love to. It'd help you retrain your brain. You're not all that different from people I've worked with who have social anxiety disorder or high-functioning autism, you know. You need to find a way to connect with the world, and you suffer when you don't. I think the need for connection is really strong in you."

I couldn't do anything but stare at him, probably for a full minute after hearing that. Then I blurted, "I'm sorry I pigeonholed you."

"Occupational hazard," he said, shrugging it off. "When you make a good living doing something that the wider community generally respects, some assume you do it for the basest of motives."

"Please don't lump me in with that," I said. "You speak of humanity like we're all soulless machines with one breath and then pontificate about love the next. It's confusing."

All the while, I just wanted to be home, buried in a pile of books about Nikola Tesla, ancient Egypt, and Ley Lines. I just wanted to be surrounded by _my_ people, whoever in the hell they may be.

It's so strange, Stace... Whenever I think of you, I often see stage curtains closing. Here I am, still enacting this drama on Earth, but you've gone backstage, behind the curtain. And I keep imagining that the play you're enacting back there is at least as interesting as the one I'm enwrapped in.

Does that play revolve around some of the same myths as ours, that the universe is empty or hostile, that our human nature is flawed and sinful?

How is it that I know I've dreamed of you so many times, and yet I can't recall the details of a single one? Just to see your face, write a single sentence down in this journal of something you've said...

I'll tell you about a recent dream I do remember, even though it hurts to think about it. It took place right here in this hospital.

They'd had to restrain me several times. Then, apparently, they were satisfied that I'd learned my lesson, so the hospital staff started teaching me how to do those restraints. I was set to supervise one of the patients here, a teenage boy. He was being disruptive, so I kept holding him the way the staff here taught me. At one point, a nurse asked me where he was, and I realized I had no idea. "He disappears like this." I found him in the waiting room. He'd taken all the toys and blocks and strung them out in a line across the floor. I told him he had to "repair" the situation.

Where in the world do we learn to talk like this?

Anyway, it seemed to work at first. Then he rebelled, and I had to hold him again. But this time, I'd forgotten how to do the restraints properly, and I worried my supervisor would chastise me.

I don't think that kid participates in our dear consensus reality. He's where you are, Stace: behind that curtain, following the lines of a completely different script.

Ah, religion and science: They both train us to be "supervisors," don't they? Consensus reality is a big deal to the ego. How else can it superimpose a sense of order upon a world in constant flux?

Did I dream about my most natural self? That boy

understood magic. He knew he created his reality from within himself; thus, he could dispense with rules and structures. I wish I could go back and release him, say piss off to the staff who were trying to train (indoctrinate) me, just release my hold—and pass through the fear. I don't want the straitjacket of reason to have the last word.

I can still see you there in the park, that time when your voice all of a sudden sounded grown-up and distant. "Someday soon, one of us will have to go to Cora. If it's me, do you promise to find me?"

I so often wish I had been the one to go. But then, I don't know this Cora. It hasn't been real to me since you left. So how can I say for sure? There are just times when it seems like anywhere would be preferable to this soul-deadening place.

I woke up from that dream, realizing that I had to get out of here. The medical profession's cookie-cutter definition of sanity is a charade I can't play along with anymore. I don't have the heart to fake it well enough to please them.

But in the end, I think Dr. Visinsky didn't enjoy feeling out of his depth dealing with me, either. He was probably ready to wash his hands of this "therapeutic relationship." I can't account for it any other way because, honestly, I didn't think I was "making the grade" here, and the staff haven't exactly been overwhelmed by empathy.

Nevertheless, he pronounced me fit to leave. Provided I don't do anything to sabotage myself beforehand, I'm going to walk out of these doors at the end of the month.

You're probably the only one who can understand how I'm equally exhilarated and terrified. I don't even know what the pieces of my life are anymore. But somehow, I've got to pick them all up and fit them back together, at least enough to get on with.

Any hope, support, and love you can send me while I

go through this would make all the difference in the world, dear Sis.

      Love,

      Colleen.

"A Time without Measure"

Returning to the familiar house of his body, Tohbin first perceived Ashangtu's soothing, dulcet croon cooling to a whisper and then fading. Heartbeats passed; he was forced to recognize the hot throbbing in his leg with greater and greater acuity.

Then he noticed Esperidi beside him. His eyes flared with his awareness of what had passed between them.

Reassured by her glimpse of the nascent vitality growing within him, the Shaini woman began to rise, but Tohbin grasped her sleeve.

"Please!" His gasp was so weak that she was forced to squat again to hear him. "I had orders. I was to take you to the Masters in Shetain. The Savwain raiders believed the Masters would know how to force the woman to reveal what she knows." He nodded towards Ashangtu.

Then, overcome by weariness and regret, he settled his head against the sand. "But I cannot do this thing. Not now."

Carefully, Esperidi said: "Will it endanger you if you disobey?"

Tohbin considered this. "Only those thieves in the Savwain know of it," he said. "Those few who conceived the plan. They hope to curry favor with the Masters thus."

"You ought to at least fulfill your engagement," Ashangtu said. "You'd arouse too much suspicion otherwise."

She glanced at Esperidi. "But obviously, we can't accompany him any farther. If they aren't aware of it already, those in Shetain will soon know that two Shaini wander this region."

"We can't hope to outrun other possible messengers," Esperidi agreed, looking thoughtful. A moment later, though, her attention was snatched by a *timbre* of cruel self-laceration. It drew her eyes back to Tohbin.

Moved by compassion, she grazed a hand along his furrowed brow. "Do not punish yourself for your part in this, Tohbin. When you agreed to it, we were strangers to you, and you had a gang of ruthless men to worry about. You chose to protect yourself and your son."

"You called me back from the misty gulfs where it is said that only Grandfather Serpent may travel with eyes open," Tohbin insisted. "You did this for a man who'd betrayed your trust."

"In return," Ashangtu pointed out, "you changed your mind."

"Even knowing the cost," Esperidi added.

Then, she was gifted with inspiration. "Do your people preserve tales of Shai-win?"

The lightening of Tohbin's being answered her before he spoke.

"Every Manitoh remembers Shai-win's love for us and our love for her," he said. "We have not forgotten. It was this way for all our ancestors. Every Manitoh knew his or her place and was honored for it. They were happy to serve their Singing Chieftess. The warlord who rises now... He cannot command the love once given to the Wind's Bride. He must hold us by law and the force of his Horde.

"Shai-win is gone now. In her wisdom and completion, legend says, she returned to the winds while still in her body. She forsook Ophia without dying."

Esperidi chose not to contradict this assertion,

though her visions and Shiya-coqui's teachings had taught her that it was a deliberate distortion of the truth, a story perpetrated by the Shetain priesthood to encourage their flock to disdain the Earth beneath their feet.

"Have you ever watched a colony of ants?" Tohbin went on. "Thousands perform their tasks with energy that seems inexhaustible, no? With a single purpose. One must wonder how they all came from the same mother. Without their queen, they are lost, without direction. The life of Sorsajna withdraws from them.

"Shai-win did not birth every Manitoh. But she knew and loved each of them as their own mothers did. She embraced the Manitoh tribes like a mother duck warms her young. No people ever loved their leader more than the Manitohs loved Shai-win. And she did not wish for us even to call her our leader.

"But after her death, Manitohs became ruthless again. And their numbers swelled."

Esperidi laid a palm against Tohbin's chest, beseeching his heart. "My mentor taught me one of her prayers. It speaks to this moment. Shall I invoke it for us?"

Eyes moistening and brimming with gratitude, Tohbin nodded.

Still kneeling, Esperidi straightened and closed her eyes. "It's said that she made this speech when she came to understand how the Manitohs are wont to punish themselves for their missteps. This pained her. She understood how such a thing creates needless suffering, closing the doors to learning and growth.

"Who can say how she delivered her sermon in that vanished age? I can only repeat what was taught to me."

Drawing a deep breath for clarity and courage, she began.

"Natural guilt uses a moment of reflection to close

the gap between love and its seeming absence. It fills that gap with a deeper sense of life's sacredness. Its purpose is to teach. It never seeks to punish. In nature's realm, punishment itself is a violation.

"Natural guilt educates human beings as they journey without animal senses to guide them. It teaches compassion. It speaks in a moment of self-awareness, following a regretted decision, in a voice that reverberates forever thereafter.

"You know the touch of its hand in such moments. Always, the message reads thus: 'Here is the boundary. Remember it next time.'

"That, and naught else.

"You make peace with every portion of your life as it manifests. You open to every moment as it presents itself. You're perfect as you are, perfect in your eternal Becoming. Perfectly poised for the next step. Everything unfolds from where you stand—limitless possibilities for creation and everything in its right place. With naught to justify or explain."

After a moment of reverential silence, Esperidi opened her eyes and said: "This revelation releases Sorsajna's flow from the places where it has been trapped. It tears an opaque veil from our eyes. New organizations of meaning and significance are created, new roads to expansion and joy.

"Understand from whence this flow originates, Tohbin. Only the ignorant try to claim ownership of the wellspring. This is where the Masters of Shetain lose themselves. And I see how you are learning to disentangle yourself from their webs."

But while she spoke, Esperidi strove to disentangle *herself* enough from the emotional bond she'd formed with the man to consider the implications of his words.

The marauders could not possibly have anticipated

Ashangtu's gambit in the bazaar. The people of Shetain can't know the particulars of Tohbin's secret orders. Not yet.

"What happens when the trail ahead appears insurmountable," she said—for all their sakes, now—"and nothing from the sweep of our pasts can offer guidance or hope? We must remember that the hurdle only seems insurmountable in the eyes of who we were. Those eyes don't gaze upon this moment of Now. The odds they recall are meaningless to the people we're becoming. Thus, our salvation lies in uncovering a new conception of ourselves."

There, Esperidi trembled. Bringing Tohbin back from the edge of the void had exhausted her and left her susceptible to fear.

"But it must be more dangerous for you to travel now," she told the Manitoh, her voice betraying its new, unsteady footing. "This new warlord you spoke of...."

"They leave us alone—for a price!"

Kunsei, drawn by the commotion, emerged from his tent. The young man hissed when he noticed his father and raced to his side.

"I am alright," Tohbin assured him, taking his son's hand and squeezing it. He mustered a wan smile.

Kunsei swept his glare across the two Shaini, his eyes hot with demands and appeals.

"His crisis has passed," Ashangtu said. "He battled rattlesnake venom, but now there's naught left to conquer him."

Kunsei lowered his head and, perhaps averse to seeing his father so vulnerable, stared at the base of the waning fire.

"What is the price?" Ashangtu quietly prodded him.

"They take a tribe's food," Kunsei said. His eyes were a smoldering reflection of the dying coals. "What the bandits of this land do, they to imitate Tumoset and his Horde. Each turn of the moon, the Horde comes, and they fill their saddlebags with what the women labored so long to grow and pick. We remember what the Shaini taught us about the uses of plants. But the men stand back and allow the theft of that bounty. None fight."

Tohbin, responding to the note of anger in his son's voice, lifted his head and glared. "We would be fools to do so! All would die–and for naught."

"Many die anyway," Kunsei muttered, his sullen outrage outweighing the respect that usually restrained him in his father's presence.

Then, as if seeking support, he turned to the Shaini women. "The older ones—and even some children—are starved and sickly. I hear you recite the Shai-win prayer. In her time, stories say, Manitohs no need to make war. They called no one enemy.

"Now... How can we fill our bellies while children starve? Before this privation began, at least six-score Manitohs ate, sang, and danced in every village. Then the...."

He groped for a way to describe a phenomenon his mind had no categories for. Esperidi, guided by Vision and faint telepathy, followed the drift of his imagination.

"Snows," she suggested.

"Yes," Tohbin said, his voice more hale than mere minutes before. "The sky ice fell and brought famine. Tribes grew thin and were easily conquered. Now, those who will not fight in Tumoset's wars are spared only if they offer peace bribes. Chiefs from both sides meet, and the bounty is proffered."

"Tumoset's Horde will continue to accept these bribes?" Ashangtu said. "You're certain of this?"

"It is wise of them to do so," Tohbin said. "If they crush a tribe utterly, they make ripples of fear that could unite the other Oskwai. This they can't afford. Not yet.

Besides, who will work the fields if all are slain?

"But soon, I doubt not that Tumoset will realize it serves him if other races show strength. The Scourge—" He knit his fingers together. "It is easier to keep tribes united when he gives them an enemy to kill."

"The Scourge?" Ashangtu asked.

Tohbin scowled. "Thus we call him, though we dare say it in naught but a whisper. Not a chief, not a Valchi. Just a name drenched in blood. But he is Tumoset, a Manitoh chief trained in Shetain, weaned on the same unspeakable trials that forge the Inooks.

"What choice is least ill? Villages resist him and refuse the bribes, they lie a smoking ruin. Those that submit... They pile sickly cairns: the bodies of their kin claimed by hunger and sickness. Victims of the famine his raids spread. We hear cries and wails burst from every thatched hut."

With a groan, he lifted himself to his feet, spurning the aid that the others offered. "I give no words of comfort that may deceive. The road ahead is perilous for all of us, and there is little hope for it. Manitohs blaze trails of blood or live in terror. Other Oskwai migrate, unsure of where safety lies. Brinstead, land of the Pale Faces, arms itself. Voices whisper that their people make bargains with the Scaled Brotherhood. They rebuilt their trading post as a stockaded fort."

Esperidi suddenly turned to Ashangtu. "You have your promise to those Savwain bandits to consider."

Ashangtu shot her a furtive glance and slowly swallowed. It was the first time Esperidi had seen her look shy. "Well, how I deal with that depends on you, I suppose," she said.

Then, the woman dodged her vulnerability with exposition. "My gut tells me the priesthood of Shetain is involved in the same thing we've been doing here in the Savwain. They're gathering their strength, rebuilding. Once that's done, I doubt they'll have the patience to treat with traders anyway. They're liable to send a force up here, strip the hills, just like what happened during the Manitoh Wars. Magda and her people have got to be prepared to flee somewhere safe if it comes to it.

"I know more than just the location of lodes. I found the entrance to a Shaini mine that connects to the old underworld, Elmicora. Lanoreans fashioned it. I know how to open the gate.

"It's cool down there year-round. Magda's folk could find water. But they'd need food and light."

Esperidi curled an eyebrow. "And all of this depends upon me how?"

Ashangtu drew a long breath to garner her resolve. She was only partially successful. "That's the Sophryne creed, isn't it? Be sure to pass on what you know so that inner knowledge is never lost to Ophia? If I learn to do what you do, I could reach Magda and tell her where to find these places. I doubt even those thugs are depraved enough to try torturing information out of an old woman.

"So that's the meat of it. I want to learn from you."

"You *did* do a fair amount of studying in Lanore, didn't you?"

"Likely for the same reason *you* studied," Ashangtu said. "I wanted to understand what was burning inside of me. What you said earlier... it's true for me, too. We can't survive if that's all there is on our horizon: survival.

"I want to be of *use*."

"You know, I was only partially trained," Esperidi said. "Inevitably, dreams will have to serve as mentors for both of us. But what you say is true. If you were a Wakeful Dreamer and desired to see Magda, the leagues between you would be of no consequence. You could share your knowledge, and none within the length and breadth of Ophia could intercept it. I did something similar when I helped a theater troupe escape from Farsilane during its last days."

"So what'll it be then?" Ashangtu persisted.

Esperidi laughed. As pink dawn outlined the contours of Conhuera, her night's trials seemed to lift from her shoulders. "Do you remember asking me what swayed my decision to join you? I only confided half of the truth. The other impetus was the way your spirit impacted me. It didn't begin with our meeting in the Oasis. Since then, I've recalled dream interactions from long before that.

"You see, Ashangtu, we're not nearly as different as I think the two of us assumed. I believe our wounds have made us kindred. I see now that you, too, possess a healer's heart.

"For the first couple years after the storms, I was a woman who ached to repay Ophia for the hurt it caused her. Eventually, I learned to name my true longing: to devote myself to Ophia's healing.

"You see? The Rupture had nearly withered my heart. The Sophryne lore nurtured it back to life. It can be this way for the Oskwai, too. The Manitohs and Sendhi, all people. I foresee a rapid flowering. When they become conscious creators, they'll run where they have hitherto crawled. They will civilize without massacring each other.

"I have seen so much. I have witnessed new pyramids in hot sands and old ones reawakening. I see the birth of new, guiding myths. Will we live in the probability where this evolves, or will we not? Some expressions of Esperidi and Ashangtu will witness that flowering. Why should it not be us?"

Ashangtu frowned, but the expression also served to hide a sly smirk. "So... is this how folks say 'yes' in Sequana?"

The desert's lowermost ribs persisted for a score of miles as Tunzao Trail veered southeastward. Then the few clouds dispersed, and the sun baked shale all day. Everything in the boulder-strewn broken lands bordering the mountains—rock, scree, and sand—was rusty-hued.

Assaulted by the oppressive heat, Esperidi evoked the tonality of winters as she'd known them in Farsilane. This brought some relief. She wished she could share this surcease with her companions, but they did not seem to suffer overmuch. Ashangtu had lived in the Savwain for a handful of years, prior even to the Rupture, and the two Manitohs, when not traversing the desert, spent most of their time beneath the steamy trees of the Kawli.

Partly to ground her sore heart in a fond memory, Esperidi insisted on continuing the tradition she and Shiya-coqui had inaugurated. "We should devote the first part of every morning to our dream recollections," she told Ashangtu, "and discuss our reactions to everything we can remember. Shiya-coqui said that one of the biggest challenges Sophrynes face is overcoming our long tradition of separating the states of being: waking and dreaming.

"If you wait until you're fully roused and your mind is aimed at the challenges of the day, you'll likely regard your dream in the same light, the bright light of logic, and thus forget its emotional *timbre*."

She chuckled softly at a recollection. "'Not the words, girl, the *tune*.' That's what my teacher always used to tell me when I would do that."

Despite her beginner's enthusiasm, Ashangtu's first morning session was rife with so many disruptions and false starts that it seemed to mimic the wagon's torturous jolts as it contested the roughest stretch of Tunzao Trail.

This hardly surprised Esperidi. Ashangtu was reticent about everything that touched her most deeply, and she abhorred talking about her past, even casually. The naked reality that her dreams presented terrified her. Esperidi watched her sift through her memories with the furtive and desperate expression of a cornered animal. What did she dare reveal? What did she fear *inadvertently* revealing by sharing a dream detail that was obscure to her but perhaps plain to Esperidi?

It was an agonizingly slow process that Ashangtu felt just as acutely. During the third or fourth hour of their session, she suddenly erupted. "By the serpent's fangs! Is this *necessary*?"

"It *is* necessary," Esperidi said. Her training, short though it had been, left no room for ambiguity. "If you fear encountering something within yourself, you'll carry that fear when you travel among the Veils. When you become lucid in your dreams, there'll be regions that you avoid, though treasures may lie in wait there."

Recalling a dream early in her apprenticeship, she added: "And bars will form cages around your waking life as well.

"This requires *trust*, Ashangtu. No other tactic will avail you. You'll have to find some way to let me get close to you. Otherwise, you'll always keep your own revelations an arm's length away."

She felt a flush of heat in her face as she said this, realizing how much she ached for closeness with someone. *Why must I drag this longing around with me like a phantom limb, only to have the fates mock me by pairing me with one of the most abrasive of Ophia's survivors?*

"There's no such thing as fate, child," she heard Shiya-coqui lecture, "only your own self-woven dream."

So why did I attract it then? Why did I ask for this?

Esperidi found no answer beyond the aching in her breast.

And Ashangtu's inner turmoil littered her sentences with unintentional barbs.

"None of your outpouring idealism—none of these visions—alter the reality that you and I are headed towards swift death or a slow boil. We'll soon leave the one man who could have at least made our presence in the Kawli appear legitimate. We had to do it. I grant you that. But now we've got to navigate the jungle as swiftly as possible and hope we stay invisible. After what Tohbin said, it's clear we can't go back to the Savwain. See, we don't need visions. We need a plan—and very quick-like."

"You make it sound like the two contradict each other," Esperidi said. "For me, visions and plans almost always go hand-in-hand."

She rose, groaning a little at the protest of her stiff legs, and made a half-hearted attempt to swipe dust from her skirt before realizing the futility. They'd paused in a copse of prickly pear and blue shrubbery to take their midday meal.

"All right, so what vision have you had that's clear enough to build a plan around?" Ashangtu asked.

"None," Esperidi admitted. "Mostly, I've been leaning on two little fragments. There was this voice in my dream... As she talked to me, she also inscribed her words in a journal. So strange! She sounded... like the way my voice sounds to my own ears. And she said, "The Shaini migrated south, imitating the geese."

"Sounds like she's got not only your voice but also some of your cryptic habits," Ashangtu said. She clutched her arms and began to pace. "First off, you and your birds! Sparrows, ravens, and now geese. And secondly–" She stopped and faced Esperidi so the other woman could read her frustration. "This is why I have such a hard time trusting dreams sometimes. So often, they sound like jokes."

286

"Perhaps they point out that we are wont to take ourselves too seriously. They remind us that the universe has a sense of humor."

"Maybe it just means you wish you could turn yourself into a bird and fly far away from here," Ashangtu said. "And who can blame you? But all right, south. That's what we've got. Liken thyself to the geese and fly south! So what's the other fragment that you've got?"

Esperidi closed her eyes and mustered the memory of deep ocean currents and the crab that had guided her, the same crab emblazoned on a banner in Magda's Oasis, carrying a shining amethyst into the depths.

"Nitahwe River still flows through the Kawli and even into lands further south, like Brinstead. That's a new settlement formed after the storms. After we part from Tohbin and Kunsei, we must let the river take us—somehow."

The following afternoon, Esperidi stumbled upon a topic that seemed to excite Ashangtu enough to make her forget her resistance.

"Do you know...I often feel that every world I glimpse is a possible history of our own people—a road that we might have taken or might still take. It's an appealing idea, is it not? And treacherous, perhaps. If the past could be reordered, then much could be undone. We could erase our painful mistakes and our regrets. And, just maybe, much greater events could be altered—say, the destruction of our homeland."

"How would you tell the difference?" Ashangtu asked. "How would you know when it is our time and not some other version of history?"

"It is like how you distinguish between a conversation you remember and a conversation you imagined," Esperidi told her. "The images in your mind may be equally vivid if your imagination is strong. But you know the difference. It is the *feeling* that you trust. It is silent knowing."

Ashangtu cradled her chest and probed the other woman. "Well?"

"Well, what?"

"You suggest that time itself could be... malleable. What's *your* conviction?"

Esperidi shook her head, dispelling chimeras. "Do you not think I would do anything for the hope of Ophia restored if an avenue were open to me? But I think you must ask yourself, Ashangtu... Assuming that such a power did exist, and you *could* alter the past, what else would you be willing to wipe clean from the life you know, alongside the destruction of the Hives?"

And so, like Sarpienta's thrusts and contractions, their budding partnership made jerky progress as their wagon labored across ten or twelve miles of broken land until it gave way to the last sandy washes lapping the Conhuera Ridgeline's feet.

Atop the lifeless dunes, the sun felt like immolation. Esperidi could hardly swallow. Her mouth and throat were choked with dust, and the ribbed striations seemed to smoke beneath their wheels. Had the two Shaini been traveling alone, they might have died of thirst had they not been able to feel water's *timbre* and follow the scent to its source.

Here, that *timbre* was faint indeed.

Finally, they were obliged to cut through the mountains via Sonseema Pass. That morning, they sweltered beneath the Savwain sun; by the afternoon, they were shivering within the tall shadows cast by two stark and broken faces of the range, sundered like a giant stone door pushed ajar. The zig-zagging rift funneled the wind, abetting it until even internal thoughts were thrust from their seats of privacy by eternal howling.

Ashangtu was particularly morose, reflecting upon a haunted landmark not far to the north: lost Mangoyen, one of her people's proudest achievements. A durable fastness within a split mountain, the heart of Lanorean commerce and its bastion of ritual, it had been abandoned in a frenzy of confusion as the seas drank the eastern shore, sweeping over the two lakes that once mirrored the mountain home: Espermeer and Pahloka. Most of those frantic refugees had been buried beneath avalanches as the serpent's tail rattled Conhuera's crowns.

But Ashangtu had never lived in Mangoyen. It had become the heart of Lanore partly because of her big sister's star, and her family hadn't wanted her around to sully its shine.

The horses made swifter progress over Sonseema's floor, which retained the ancient polish that Lanore had bequeathed it when it'd served as a vital trade artery of Old Ophia. The sting of Ashangtu's memories made her gasp in relief as they prepared to plunge a few hundred feet into a river-fed rainforest—the Kawli. Shaini (outside of traders and Shetain's shadow government) had seldom ventured into the jungles, but in times passed, they'd taken advantage of the natural barrier it formed between themselves and various Oskwai tribes. Ashangtu sensed a dense population of Manitohs roaming beneath that leafy canopy and shivered. Would even Shetain's banner shield them in this savage land? Or—an even more unsettling question that neither she nor Esperidi could resolve—did they *want* to herald the priesthood's insignia now, after all that had been revealed?

Tunzao Trail wove its serpentine way to a place where the descent to the Kawli Rainforest was gentlest. Although she'd anticipated it, Esperidi gasped when she first beheld that ocean of verdure in every conceivable hue, dashed with vibrant crimson and purple. She glimpsed an arm of Nitahwe River, shadowed in the sunset before disappearing beneath the jungle canopy.

The trail's relative ease made it well-trafficked in the lower land and thus hazardous to the two Shaini. And so, with pain and loss wringing their hearts, they parted from their Manitoh companions the following morning, being obliged now to find a more circumspect route through the jungle.

Esperidi stood before Tohbin and bowed, her open palm laid over her left fist in the ancient Shaini gesture of peace. Then she drew closer and, surprised to see that he did not flinch, dared further, reaching out her pointer finger to trace the outlines of his tattoo. His *timbre* felt both comforted and honored; he acknowledged the affection behind the gesture.

"When I sought for you in the in-between place," Esperidi said, "I used your love for your son to find you. But to find that place in myself, I had to look into my past—to a time when I was very young."

She withdrew her finger momentarily to study the bird emblazoned on his chest.

"I have discovered that my soul's name is Erawen, which refers to the raven. But I've also been called Sparrow."

The Manitoh beamed back at her as she suddenly giggled. "But this holds no sacred connotations—or perhaps I should say it holds no sacred connotations outside of my own heart. It was a joke my Papa made during one of his rare, playful moments. He kept calling me Esparrowdi. Over and over again, he did this. In time, it shortened to Sparrow, and it stuck."

She laughed again. "I was not overly pleased by that

as a child. But now I look back and remember it fondly. I think he was trying to express his love for me in this way. So now, Tohbin, I feel like you're taking a part of me with you when you go."

The man radiated gratitude. He fumbled at the pouch at his side. "Then it would honor me greatly if you would bring a piece of me with *you* as you go."

He withdrew what looked at first like a small skull. Then Esperidi discerned that this was indeed its shape but that it was wrought from an amethyst with a purple heart.

Tohbin cupped it. "My life would be imperiled if the Shetain priests knew I had acquired this. I bought it from a Vandrene trader who was eager to be rid of it. But something about it drew me enough to risk the danger. He said that a Shaini would know how to draw forth its light—a light to beggar a dozen campfires."

Then he proffered it, and Esperidi received it gingerly as if she feared to inadvertently unleash some latent power within it.

"This is a great gift, Tohbin. Indeed, I do carry a part of you with me now." And she bowed again, cupping the crystal skull between her hands.

Ashangtu drew forward and bowed in the same way Esperidi had done. Then she straightened and leveled the Manitoh a stony stare rife with warnings.

"I have no parting gifts for you, Tohbin," she said, "aside from a piece of advice. Finish what business you have with Shetain, then return to the Savwain. I will teach Mother Magda how to manipulate the *timbres* that open the gateway into the mountains and the sanctuaries below it. She already knows how to find the entrance. I fear her people will need to use that refuge soon. You should join them."

Tohbin responded with a noncommittal nod. It was much to absorb at once, and he was unsure how to commit himself.

But Esperidi spread her arms wide and seemed to savor the air with her fingertips. "We dream right now!" she proclaimed.

Tohbin cast his head about, expecting the encampment and the banks to swirl and transmogrify. Ashangtu's eyes sharpened on Esperidi in an expression that fairly shouted, *What is it with you?*

"Forgive me," Esperidi said. She sounded somewhat embarrassed, but it in no way dampened her *timbre* of awe. "We are awake in Ophia, in the land we call the real."

Ashangtu's eyebrow curled. "Thank you for clarifying that!"

Esperidi grinned as if her friend had just delivered the payoff line of a clever jest. "And yet we are also dreaming," she insisted. "Don't you see? I never realized this before. Our dreaming lives and our waking lives do not preclude each other. The one does not stop when the other begins. Both realities are continuous."

She returned her attention to Tohbin. "I say this because it reminds me that I don't really have to say goodbye to you and Kunsei. Beyond the Veils, the heart of you was made known to me. Now, I will always know how to find you.

"I walk dreams, sure as a bird builds a nest or a spider spins a web. They bring me in *timbre* with the rest of Ophia. And dreams will always connect us, my friends."

❧❧

Esperidi tried to revolve her inner universe around this center of optimism she'd discovered. But she felt dark wings of emptiness and futility beating along its margins, eroding its surety.

A few days ago, I practically mocked Ashangtu for

posing the question, and now I am obsessed with it. Can the past be altered?

Early in her apprenticeship, Shiya-coqui had lectured her on the nature of Ophia's root assumptions—physical reality's most rudimentary foundations. "The nature of Time has evolved over the ages. During Ophia's earliest Seasons, it was not yet 'fixed' but elastic. Travel was as swift as thought; visiting a place was as easy as envisioning it. Our world was not bounded—not the self-contained sphere we presently experience."

Esperidi sensed that this question of Time only grazed the surface of her predicament, that it circled around a core of pain that she felt thoroughly unready to approach. As she and Ashangtu descended into the Kawli Rainforest, she struggled to keep it at arm's length.

Part of her problem was uncomplicated: She was afraid. *I didn't survive this long and through such perils to offer myself up as food for panthers!* She'd managed mountains and desert—and not easily, at that—but to wander into a jungle with naught but her slim knowledge of *Sacred Timbre* to protect her?

Nevertheless, she plunged alongside Ashangtu into those scents of vegetation, soil, and decay. The sounds enfolding her were cacophony compared to the silence of the desert she'd left behind. The birds were clamorous: parrots and toucans that occasionally streaked vibrant colors across the airy way. Always in her ears was the low thrum of distant falls. The chattering of bonobos resounded across the jungle's roof, though she never spotted the creatures. Several times, big-eared wild dogs darted across her line of sight. She also felt the presence of a jaguar somewhere near—its feral *timbre* a dim ember in her consciousness. But thankfully, it never showed itself.

On their second morning beneath the Kawli's sultry

roof, she and Ashangtu reached a place where the reeds and rushes grew thick along the riverbank. Esperidi asked her companion to help her gather buoyant wood, stalks, and flax to weave them into a bundle.

"A dream forewarned me," she explained, lightening a little at the recollection. Her voice had to compete with the rush of the water, abetted now by a warm downpour. In this region, all of the Kawli Rainforest drained into the watercourse.

"I saw myself creating a bundle, just as we do now. Upon waking, I thought it symbolized solidarity—the strength of Ophia's people joining together. But as we drew closer to the jungle, I realized it gave me much more practical advice."

"It'll spur our pace beyond anything we could have accomplished on our feet," Ashangtu allowed, nodding in satisfaction. The bundle they'd created was too thick for her to reach her arms around.

The river swelled until it veritably boiled, slipping between dead trees and gurgling through torn shrubbery. By silent consent—and with a shared look of commiseration—the two women tossed their makeshift raft into the torrent and raced after it.

And Esperidi carried all that lay still unresolved within her along the swift rush of the Nitahwe.

Soon, she and her companion were deaf to everything but the current and the tumult of rain, like the sky collapsing. Their speed felt perilous. At times, despite the river's rising waterline, they encountered sandy shoals and were obliged to carry their craft further downriver, dripping and cursing.

Esperidi recalled the song that Shiya-coqui had sung on Mount Veneer to conjure the *timbre* of fog, and she imitated its sounds, draping her and Ashangtu in a shroud that would make them appear like wisps of mist carried along the river. She was grateful for this decision when she noticed signs of cultivation: cornstalks, beanstalks, and squash patches. Once, she and Ashangtu saw a few swarthy Manitoh women in their middle years kneeling by the water. One, undeterred by the downpour, was dowsing and wringing out garments. The other two fetched water in wicker baskets woven tight enough to hold it. All wore wide-brimmed straw hats.

Only the woman washing clothes lifted her head as they passed, and then she shook it as if she could not credit her senses.

After four days of intermittent rains and rapids, Esperidi and Ashangtu finally parted from the Nitahwe River to seek Sonoma Pass. Now, only the land bordering the watercourse was fertile. Each southward mile drew them farther from verdure and deeper into rock and ruin. A portion of the landscape—its belly, from their high vantage point—was ribbed with serpentine bands of sand. Half-buried trees protruded from the otherwise featureless flat. The region reminded Esperidi of a sandbar's striations at low tide. *More devastation from torrential floods*, she thought.

"Our post-Rupture world has a new face," she whispered. "Torn, burned, and disfigured beyond recognition."

Ashangtu's waterlogged thoughts raced along other lines. "Fire! Must... have... fire!"

They decided to make camp.

꽃꽃

Esperidi, caught in the tempest of her unresolved conflicts, could sleep only sporadically. Finally, she relinquished the fight and arose in a predawn hour.

I have to walk, she thought. *I need movement.*

Inspiration tended to visit her when she was on the move, when the sounds of life stretched out around her, and fresh sights unveiled themselves to her eyes. Few things lubricated the flow of creative solutions as well as motion. It reminded her of the greater conversation occurring around her; it encouraged her to *join* that conversation.

She clambered up a knoll that resembled a giant anthill: a splatter of soft loam piled like the rough approximation of a ziggurat. Patches of new grass held portions of it, with even a foot-tall sapling thrust defiantly here or there. But most of the ground gave way beneath her feet like sand.

Nevertheless, its pinnacle was the highest in the region. The forces that had reared it up from Ophia's belly, not unlike the internal pressures that had thrust Esperidi into this crisis, found focus here. The hill appeared like an organic release valve, a giant earthen spout.

For a fleeting moment, this knoll that was too new to bear a name filled Esperidi's heart with a small, fragile hope for spring and renewal. The breeze ushered fertile scents from the Nitahwe basin: life's resilience condensed into verdant promises that any upheaval, conflagration, or wind-whipped scythe could not dissuade.

But when those scents led her on to their source, she recoiled in shock and revulsion, though everything she'd sensed, all the clamor that had lingered from her dreams into her daylit hours, should have warned her.

During her trip south with Ashangtu, she'd encountered enough shoals, bald eddies, overturned trees, and stagnant backwater channels to know that the Nitahwe's course had been profoundly disrupted. From this vantage, though, it did not appear like a river at all but rather like a burst of varicose veins, a gash across Ophia's flesh that boulders and sandbars and ravished forests had turned into sprawling latticework of blue-gray ruin.

Bear River—the Nitahwe—floundered at the farthest extent of her gaze, where it was drunk by the parched ground. Beyond that, Esperidi could only discern a brown-yellow haze beneath the rising sun and lingering gibbous moon. This was not fading light but *obstruction*, as if the sun was always weaker there or the land itself resisted it.

Esperidi had seen a similar haze on the Savwain horizon when a sandstorm was brewing. This wall seemed denser and quieter, like a pall of dust intent on smothering the southern continent and stripping it of its life, color, and hope.

"Where Sequana used to be, it's all as arid as the desert we left behind."

Esperidi nearly jumped. Her percipience was so overwrought by the raw wounds laid out before her that she hadn't heard her friend approach. In a moment, Ashangtu stood shoulder to shoulder with her.

"The waters eventually receded, but all that salt destroyed the soil. The plants died, and then, with nothing to hold the dirt down, it was whipped up to clog the air like a forest fire haze. Leastways, that's what I heard. Few people ever venture so far south. There's no reason to go now. It may as well have stayed submerged."

Esperidi's voice was frail with welling grief. "This is my *home* you're talking about!"

Ashangtu repositioned herself so she could face the other woman. "You *were* aware of what the Rupture had done, right? I mean, you've glimpsed it before."

"It's different through the naked eye," Esperidi whispered.

"Well, this is what it's done!" Ashangtu had the unsettling sense that her companion was slipping away. It roused a feeling of futility that she sought to vanquish in her usual manner—with ire. "Almost nothing is like it once was, and vast stretches are completely unlivable. Nothing can grow there unless the knowledgeable hand of *Sacred Timbre* could coax it back to health."

"I sense some people established a settlement here," Esperidi muttered, flailing for a distraction, "but it feels like its life was brief."

"Maybe another lash of the Rupture—flooding, probably," Ashangtu said. "This whole plain bears the muck and debris of it. And remember that there was snow in the Kawli for a while. Think of all that melt coupled with heavy rainfall, pouring into the river basin. I'll wager that's what happened. Some of these trees might have been carried from the jungle."

She waved towards the ravaged basin of the Nitahwe. "Imagine something like this without the water, and you'll get a picture of what the southern lands look like now."

Ashangtu intended to stumble on and grope for more words to bridge the chasm of her inadequacy. But Esperidi had fallen to her knees. The woman convulsed with silent sobbing, but Ashangtu could feel the energy mounting, and she braced herself for the moment when all that anguish would finally announce itself in an audible howl.

When it came, she winced and clutched her arms as if buffeting herself against a storm. It sounded like a child's death wail.

Esperidi clawed the sodden earth with her fingernails. She felt that some insubstantial entity, devoid of mercy for all human suffering, had flayed her. No buttresses stood between herself and Ophia's raw wound. It screamed on the edges of her frayed nerves. It wracked her until she convulsed like someone about to vomit.

Ashangtu's voice was but one note in an

overwhelming symphony of pain. "What is it? Are you ill?"

Her eyes on the horizon, Esperidi waved an outstretched arm in a long half-circle as if she sought to smooth a balm across all of Ophia. "I have to heal it!" she gasped. "Make it whole!"

"Make sense!" Ashangtu shouted. "How can I help if I don't know what ails you?"

"Shai-win's mercy, Ashangtu! Must you always act so *impervious*?"

That penetrated the other woman's armor. With a grunt of supreme effort, as if she was relinquishing something for which she bore no love and yet had never wanted to surrender, Ashangtu knelt in front of Esperidi, leaned close, and grasped her hands.

"I'm here," she said. "Let me help you."

Esperidi's voice was distorted almost beyond recognition by shudders and tears. Suddenly, she sounded a decade older. "It's too much! Shiya-coqui... She never taught me how to protect myself, only how to *open*."

Then, as if an unseen embassy of mercy heard the woman's plight and raced across the waste to her side, Esperidi's moment of keenest agony passed. Her surroundings sharpened. She was a singular being again, kneeling on her own patch of ground, contained within fleshy walls woven of her idea of herself.

Ashangtu leaned forward and, as gently as her abrasive nature would allow, slowly swiped a tear from under Esperidi's eye.

"You're going through your own little Rupture right now," she said. "Your personal deluge. It could have festered and destroyed you if you'd held it inside. But now there's a chance that it can be washed away."

Esperidi gazed up with eyes both shell-shocked and dubious. "All right..?"

"All right, so there *is* such a thing as necessary destruction, E! Ophia had a lot to release, so it comes out in a field of sinkholes here and a tidal wave there and a huge volcanic eruption someplace else, but then she's relieved. Don't you feel her settling?"

"So much death," Esperidi whispered. "So much *ruin*."

Beginning to feel like she was once again making a futile appeal, Ashangtu grew agitated. "So much throwing off of parasites that were sucking the life out of her; throwing off these towers and monuments that were breaking her spine! Don't you see that it's a sign of her health and her wisdom that she vomits after she's been poisoned rather than holding it in her bowels until it kills her?"

Esperidi lifted herself to her feet and glared at her companion. A few possible retorts half-formed and then died stillborn before she finally said, "You're good at giving advice that you can't take, aren't you?"

She tried to stalk away, but her anger didn't carry her far. In a moment, the other Shaini was at her side again.

"All right, so maybe I can't help you right now," Ashangtu conceded. "But I have an idea that there's somebody who can. You're searching for something. That much is obvious. You've mentioned your old teacher, Shiya-coqui. Is she...? Could you somehow...? I mean, you've said that death only *seems* permanent on this side of the Partition."

Startled by Ashangtu's suggestion, Esperidi stiffened. "You're asking why I don't try and contact her. Well... I suppose I have been afraid to know the truth for certain. What if she does not answer? What if I arrive at nothing but cold darkness?"

What if I don't want to stop believing she might still be alive?

"And yet... if anyone could help you, it would be her,"

Ashangtu said. "I don't think there's any evading it. You won't know peace until you've resolved the mystery of Shiya-coqui, for good or ill."

"Yes, I must," Esperidi acknowledged finally. Now that she was resolved, she was restless to begin. *I can't let the matter rest, not even another night.*

Ashangtu cleared her throat. "I have this song... It began in a dream; then, I composed the rest the next day while we were carried by the rapids. Anyway, I wrote it for you. If you think it'll help... I'll sing it."

Esperidi's eyes widened; for the first time that night, she forgot her bereavement. She swallowed slowly, trying to compose herself. "I would like that very much," she finally managed.

No more words were exchanged. Esperidi settled onto her muddy bed and closed her eyes. A moment later, her friend's rough but strangely soothing voice washed over her, carrying her fears and anguishes somewhere far downstream where they could be met with love and then released.

> Teach me your airy pathways, Raven.
> Lend me your eyes.
> Every night, I come home
> under a different sky.
>
> Coyotes howl from all corners at dawn.
> Manitohs warpath the sun.
> But I fear no blisters
> on your natural contours.
> Your winds and I are one.
>
> We soared a thousand lifetimes today.
> We were born to wander all shores.
> From the salt-tang breezes of Sequana

to the lost treasure caves of Lanore.

Serpentine traveler in whose skin I'm born
I can never bear to linger.
There's no safe port save for where
the cagey Sophryne
gives a wink and points a finger.

Bird of prey, you smell me.
You hover for scraps of skin.
Who taught me that I trespass
upon this ground I was born within?

Wind wails history too old for my mind
but my bones recall all the names.
Blessings on arroyos that foot this land.
Blessings on the shadow that remains.

My mind seizes wonder
And Raven takes flight
over water-rich dreams
and desert climes
'til there's no more shoreline in sight.

When she slipped into dreams, Esperidi initially
thought that she'd merely opened her eyes again. Her body
occupied the same space, though after a moment of
reflection, she realized that she was standing, not lying, and
the hill of upthrust sod and mud that she'd surmounted was
built of bone, mostly interlocking femurs that allowed just
enough crawl space for the myriad black beetles swarming
within and without.

I *wonder if they live off the marrow*, she thought, as
she realized many of the creatures were cracking the bones

open in an organic rhythm that reminded her of a cackling fire.

But what solidified her recognition of this dream environment was her awareness that the singer standing a few paces from her was not Ashangtu but Shiya-coqui, her *timbre* pulsing with something inexplicable that Esperidi had long ached for and could only equate with *home*.

"Do you recognize the tune now?" Shiya-coqui said.

Esperidi nodded, but mostly in growing wonder at the other's presence, not her question.

"I used it once to conjure fog on Mount Veneer," Shiya-coqui said. "Tonight, I sing it backward to *dispel* all fogs and bring us clarity." She offered a smile both warm and challenging. "That is what you came here for, isn't it, child?"

"I came here because I've missed you," Esperidi said. The immediacy of her emotion left no room for subterfuge. Then, as if she feared her old mentor would dissipate like mist if she didn't find some way to interest her, she rushed on. "Shortly before I went to sleep, I sensed there had been a settlement here."

"Aye," Shiya-coqui said. She nodded to the creaking pearl-colored floor they stood upon. "But you're not likely to find many bones when you awaken. Most of the bodies were washed far from here. The Ancient Children gathered what they could find."

Shift.

Esperidi attended rites for the dead and witnessed people, Shaini and Oskwai, in mourning. Their murmurs and occasional sobs lapped against her awareness like sullen waves. Esperidi tried to fence off the mental barrage, the unrelenting cries of "Why?" She knew she was susceptible to such appeals. She'd lived as an outcast for so long that it was easy to imagine that the universe itself was an adversary—a *taker*.

"They don't realize that their ancestors grow and undertake journeys in other places after shedding their earthly clothes," an old peacock-plumed woman said. "And so, when those spirits now speak, it's in voices the tribespeople do not remember or recognize."

Shift.

Esperidi caught her reflection upon the surface of a placid pond and noted the sympathetic marks on her time-worn flesh. Suddenly, the water reflected an elderly woman beside her. "Follow the geese," she said. "Seek the ancient children."

Unsure whether she rightly understood, Esperidi said, "I still have to walk beneath the sun and bear the cost of living."

Shift.

Ashes blew across the Savwain Desert. "It's easier for me to speak to dust than to address you," Esperidi insisted.

Shift.

A woman with emerald eyes and the *timbre* of ice stared into a glass beaker set over a small burner, musing, "How much death and rebirth has occurred within this crucible?"

Shiya-coqui stood on the other side of the laboratory, staring at Esperidi. "Every journey has its own integrity," she said. "There's no such thing as mischance. Sorsajna is so rich—for someone who's awakened to it—that there is no room for any sad nostalgia for experiences that have come and gone."

Then, she seemed to cross the room in a single stride. "Wake up, child!"

And Esperidi became self-aware again. Shiya-coqui stood beside her, appearing much as her old apprentice remembered her: rotund, diminutive, her eyes fixed in a permanent expression of scrutiny. Esperidi ached to embrace her, to pour out her sorrow and gratitude and love. But her forays into self-aware dreaming had taught her how easy it was for powerful emotions to sweep her away. She didn't want to find herself on a promontory somewhere with sea spray and albatross but no dearly departed mentor.

Shiya-coqui twisted her mouth into an expression of mock-sourness "So... the tale of the past... You and your friend were right about one thing, child. That is still being written. People seldom catch its movements, though—at least, few on the side of the Partition where you're standing."

Esperidi shuddered. Inner reservoirs of grief, loss, need, and uncertainty stirred and then whipped as if caught in a whirlpool.

"Where I'm standing?"

Feeling tremors beneath the ground of her being and recalling the predominant theme of her sequence of dreams, she ventured further. "You seem to understand a lot about the dead."

Shiya-coqui favored her with a crooked smile, one eye raised askew. "I thought I was acting livelier than all that. Do I look and sound so dead to you, child?"

Esperidi swallowed hard. "Nevertheless, I will miss you."

With a portion of her awareness, she already anticipated the pain of waking, bearing this revelation, though her heart had long ascertained the truth. *I always say that my heart aches*, she thought, *but my mind creates far more suffering.*

"In case I never get another chance to tell you," she said, "I want you to know that you played your part impeccably. You gave me everything I needed to set me on the path. Thank you. It's just that... I thought that if there could be any compensation for all that's happened, any gift wrapped up in this, it's that the field would be level again. No powers, no tyranny. Just people who are trying to survive. People who could be educated. But now we know that amid all that destruction, one power did survive. And it's the one none of us wanted."

"Any power structure, any paradigm, can only frighten us to the extent that we believe it is them or it and not us that creates our lives," Shiya-coqui said. "The deities that the Shetain priesthood have promoted throughout history have changed. Their names and images were altered depending on what the priests were trying to achieve."

Suddenly, they stood beneath a burning orb that warmed them like a hearth fire. "But if you want to read Ophia's secret history and unveil the manipulation," Shiya-coqui said, "there are clues to look for. For one thing, they always posit some version of a god in the sky. They always portray that. And they remove any remnants of belief in a god or goddess of the Earth. Can you guess why?"

"I imagine they do that for a lot of reasons," Esperidi said. "Imagining such a diety displaces our sense of allegiance to Ophia. We forget that we're meant to be Her caretakers and that this is where our primary loyalty should lie."

"And because we are Ophia's children," Shiya-coqui added, "born and clothed in the materials of her body—the part of Ophia that reasons—when we lose our sense of allegiance to Her, it also erodes our belief in ourselves. It prevents us from owning our power. Then we're much more willing to give that power away to an idea of some authority 'on high.'

"Some of the Shetain priests were very adept at placing a sunny face on tyranny. They would, for example, encourage people to worship the sun." She pointed her peacock-plumed staff towards the fiery orb. "How could one not want to worship the sun, this great beaming ball of light in the sky, the source of all warmth and cheer? But it was still a sky god, and that image served the same purpose as all the others: to disempower."

"Jain-Toh never seemed to put a smiling face on anything," Esperidi said.

"He didn't need to," Shiya-coqui said. "By the time he came into power, that religious order, his lineage, had become so powerful, so pervasive, that he could dispense with subtlety."

Unable to look at Shiya-coqui anymore, Esperidi returned her attention to her fluctuating surroundings. Her eyes were burning now. The fabric of the dream-ravine wavered, seeming stretched and, at times, evanescent.

Don't lose it! Not yet!

"I've borne tremendous loneliness in this lifetime as Esperidi, Shaini of Ophia. It's like what people often said of you. 'But you can access myriad worlds. You are never truly alone.' But I cannot appear in these worlds in my fleshy being. While I live in a physical realm, I abide by its hours and seasons. And so I may feel... enjoy visions and songs from other places, but I cannot... touch or be touched.

"Always I am the Sophryne, the awakener, the comforter. Who is the Sophryne for *me*? Who gives *me* comfort?

"But I have not abandoned hope even there. I cannot."

"I'm not one to offer trifling consolations," Shiya-coqui said after a pause, "but if nothing else, you got to learn what compassion truly is thanks to the Rupture. Now, you must answer that compassion, not flee it in another version of history or bury it with your past. Or mourn for it in a future yet unwritten."

Esperidi's psyche weathered the equivalent of a long sigh. "I think my mind was made up before I came here. I will remain Esperidi Mon-Sequana, widowed soul of lost Ophia, though maybe it means grief and loneliness for a time beyond measure."

Shiya-coqui scoffed. "As if you know already where this all must lead! You are a *Sophryne*, child! The threads of time and space are yours to follow as far as you dare. You could not land upon a dead-end road if you sought it with every fiber of your being!"

Awaking to Ashangtu's voice still crooning over the devastated knoll and not pausing to question the impulse, Esperidi said, "Not the words, girl, the *tune*!"

Ashangtu, relieved to hear her friend's voice sounding so hale, smiled for the first time in days. "By now, I'm too hoarse for words *or* tunes," she said.

After a moment, peace settled over Esperidi—enough to allow her to articulate her new insight. "I can't do it alone," she said. "If we're going to prevail, we'll need help."

"Well, of course we will!" Ashangtu said. "You and I are no hunters. We may have a little success foraging here or there. But then we've got to worry about fanatical Manitohs swarming the jungles, and Sarpienta knows what manner of savages scattered everywhere else. And no idea when the ground might buckle under our feet!"

"That's not what I mean. Or at least, that isn't my *main* concern. I'm not talking about mere survival. I'm talking about healing. Recovering our hearts and our world. Finding hope again." Rising, she gripped Ashangtu's shoulders. "Hope and purpose. I can't live otherwise. I can't bear this—" She swept a hand across ravished Ophia— "without them."

"I can't either," Ashangtu admitted, but her tone suggested that the fact signified little upon the scales of fate. "Allies, you say? You and I know that few Shaini survived this, so I can only assume you're talking about Oskwai."

Esperidi nodded. "But not the Manitohs. Not yet.

Shetain got to them first, even before the Rupture. They've been indoctrinated too long." Inhaling slowly to quell her racing thoughts, she groped for the ineffable. "We need children, souls fresh to experience, ready to receive."

"Where do you propose we find these children?" Ashangtu said.

"South, then west. Unless you propose we swim the Rudowine Ocean, this is the one path left to us."

Ophia's Ancient Children

A gentle breeze caressed the dark, damp butte. Before it subsided, the two Shaini slipped through the gates of sleep and into the dreaming dimension, with which they were more deeply acquainted than most sentient beings in Ophia.

They met in a thick wood that illuminated the faint outlines of bent, brooding trees.

Ashangtu was grasped by mossy vines as soon as she became self-aware. With a cry, she grabbed the two closest to her. White fire rippled through the wooden tentacles, vaporizing them. The smoke quickly dissolved in the still air.

The woman glared at Esperidi, her eyes demanding an explanation. Esperidi rubbed her chin thoughtfully.

"I met a similar challenge here once," she remarked. "I made myself airy and insubstantial to pass through my bonds. Your instinct was to alter your environment rather than yourself."

"Well, it worked, didn't it?"

"Indeed."

"Is that the wrong approach?"

"Walls and moats, banners and insignia can divide Ophia and separate its people," Esperidi said. "But the barriers in our minds create more powerful divisions. The surest way to dissolve limiting beliefs is to trust your instincts."

Ashangtu frowned. The shadows of the trees deepened, mirroring her inner doubt. "Wait! Are you saying there's no right or wrong way of doing this?"

"I'm saying that there are no authorities. This is about creation, not rules. We're all equal; we all bathe in Sorsajna. Let humanity focus on what we all experience together through the Sophryne state, not who the Sophrynes are." She cushioned her words with a smile. "This is our shared dream, and we are free to experiment and find what approaches feel most natural for us."

"I wasn't thinking that those vines were a part of me when I dissolved them," Ashangtu admitted.

Esperidi empathized. "There's no separation between self and environment. Knowing this, we can come to understand that the same principle applies when we are awake. I truly believe that. But I occasionally *disbelieve*. There are *layers* to my belief. So I understand what you're struggling with."

She sighed, and the evanescent owl shade of Shiya-coqui momentarily hovered at the edge of the wood.

I still compare myself to her, Esperidi thought, *and not at all favorably. I'm one to preach about trust in self!*

She thrust the thought aside. Ashangtu couldn't afford her inadequacies. Neither could Ophia.

"In either environment," she said, "we have to be convinced of whatever's happening to us, lest we lose the lesson. Is this not the tale of the human experience? Pretending not to know what a deeper part of us indeed knows?"

But the question of belief versus unbelief so perplexed her that she could no longer hold herself within the dream's bounds. Esperidi voiced her last question in semi-wakefulness, and she felt herself mouthing the final words as she opened her eyes.

While she waited for Ashangtu to awaken, she gazed at the unclouded, starry sky, whose beauty soothed her eyes yet racked her soul with loneliness. She felt pale and missed her dream body, which, though no brighter than moonlight through a gossamer scarf, was luminescent and strong—diaphanous yet commanding.

Recalling her internal conflict, Esperidi wondered whether it might have benefited her to learn more about Shiya-coqui's foibles and shortcomings.

The more I subscribe to the idea of perfection, she considered, *the more I'll fear making mistakes along this path. And that, in turn, can prevent me from taking risks that might expand my knowledge and powers.*

That idea reminded her of Shai-win's prayer, the one she'd shared with Tohbin. It was easy enough to berate herself for the mistakes—or perceived mistakes—of the past. But she could only do so with the benefit of a perspective that she might not have attained without those mistakes.

I can't renounce the "error" without denying the lesson it brought me.

Ashangtu began cursing as soon as she opened her eyes. "That dream of you in the forest, that was the only time I managed to become lucid! All those other dreams... I was just bouncing around, willy-nilly, like a tugboat in a tempest."

"A few days ago," Esperidi reminded her, "you had no idea how to awaken inside a dream at all."

Though she couldn't see her apprentice's face, she felt her *timbres* of frustration counterbalanced by wry humor. "You're not about to laud the virtues of baby steps, are you?" Ashangtu asked.

Esperidi grinned at her dour companion. "You can ask the Cordonne about the wisdom of making *giant* steps, if you like."

Returning her attention to the heavens lent her

inspiration. "Have you ever counted stars, Ashangtu? The stars began speaking to me during my couple of years of solitude in the Arjena Hills. In my dreams, I've encountered beings so spiritually luminous that I couldn't bring myself to speak to them because all the words I could muster felt so paltry in comparison to their light. Beholding them, I could only cackle with delight.

"I've lost myself in the wild moods of a beast on the hunt or the frolic of amphibious children playing chase across a lake bottom."

Indeed, Ophia had become a land one would ache to escape from. Perhaps Ashangtu's ambition to learn ran no deeper than that. The Shaini had been the most privileged of Ophia's peoples, and Esperidi and Ashangtu had grown up during its halcyon days. They'd lived in Hives of surpassing beauty. The opulence of their antediluvian lives never prepared them for their present destitution.

"Not all environments are cause for wonder, though," Esperidi said. "Some are painful or frightening. There are deep chasms in Creation, regions where love and light seem absent. Sophryne knowledge cannot illuminate every void. Even venturing into the thoughts of buttercups can be perilous for anyone unprepared."

"Then prepare me!" Ashangtu grated. "It has not destroyed you!"

Esperidi allowed the other woman to hear the echoes of some of her travails. "It has not always been a source of joy, either."

"All right. I hadn't meant for that to sound like criticism. But tell me this, at least: Why is it so hard for me to move? My dreams whisk me this way and that, but when I *want* to get somewhere—"

"Traveling across the Partition... You cannot look with your eyes as you do when traversing a physical landscape, just as you cannot hear *Sacred Timbre* with your physical ears. You make *inner* movements. When I first attempted ventures like these, it seemed I could lose myself in that immensity. A Sophryne must learn to travel with intention.

"Patience, Ashangtu!" Already, Esperidi was wearying. Their shared dream had consumed little of the night. "If anything, you are progressing faster than I did. You're learning to disentangle yourself from the reality you've been enmeshed in all these years."

I just discovered that the faint hope I clung to, that my teacher yet lived, was a fallacy! Give me some peace, woman!

"A thousand suggestions, delivered by ourselves to ourselves every day, keep us ensconced in this seeming rock-bed environment. You cannot free yourself from such limitations until you learn what suggestions keep you attuned to them. Then you relinquish them one by one."

Approach Vision with a light touch, Shiya-coqui had taught her. *Graze the fingers of your awareness across it as you would a fragile flower. The very intensity of your response can bend it away from its purpose.*

Esperidi carried this sermon with her back into the world of dreams.

꽃꽃

During their nightly forays, the two Shaini had seen many faces of the Rupture. They'd witnessed ocean waves as tall as mountains washing away Hives and forests. They'd seen fissures torn into Ophia's body and rivers of fire filling the cracks.

Oftentimes, what the fires failed to consume, the oceans drank.

Now, their surroundings confounded them. The face

of the land was profoundly altered. Where they anticipated a prairie climbing gradually towards the feet of mountains, they found instead a cliff face overlooking an arm of the sea. Where once hills rolled towards a desert's verges, marshlands now sprawled, latticed with streams. Little conformed to what they'd gleaned from old Shaini maps.

And it was pointless to draw *new* maps, as the land's unrest still diverted rivers, swallowed grasslands, and split mountains.

Even with her expanded senses, Esperidi struggled to navigate. She relied upon dreams and moments of daylight clairvoyance to fill the many gaps in her knowledge. That's how she knew that the coastline was severely eroded further south. She and Ashangtu had to cross through Sonoma Pass before the knees of the mountains met the sea.

The Pass could now be more aptly called a Gap. It was much wider than Sonseema, so much so that the sun was scarcely obscured as they moved through it. Thereafter, the land grew hot beneath a brown, hazy sky. They occasionally sheltered within the shade of pinon pines, cottonwoods, and junipers. Blue grama grass concealed clusters of golden aster, sand sagebrush, and wind-whipped creosotes. Pink spiny star cacti and jointfir grew out of hillocks resembling shattered red bricks.

Golden bands of light broke through a wall of trees on their southern side, and Esperidi gravitated toward their source. Beyond the edge, an awesome sight stole her breath and made her forget her despondency. The trees abruptly ended as if they'd reached a magical forbidding. Below, all was tan or reddish rock. The two Shaini stood upon a promontory demarcated with a crown of stone splinters.

The lower terrain was baked dry, a mesa-spotted landscape where rocks thrust from the ground in fantastically smoothed formations, as if their edges had been softened over ages by dripping waters. The land was not completely arid, however. Hardy scrub and mesquite clung to life in the niches between rocks. Further south, the flatlands stretched on, cracked and broken. Ravines and canyons beyond counting riddled the plain unto the furthermost horizon. Seeing so much dust, they were grateful to still smell the rich, earthy breath of the trees.

Feeling reluctant to venture into that inhospitable wasteland, they stopped on the promontory to eat and share dreams.

"I saw a sleek, full-bellied raven," Esperidi said. "Yes, me and my birds again! It stood erect atop a post twice my height, a tree stripped of all its bark. Somehow, I knew the bark had been used for clothing by those who'd fashioned the pole. After carving it, they'd drilled it into the hard ground so no wind could topple it.

"Around this crude Cundra spread a field of corn, lush and nourishing. But occasionally, blights would form: green or sickly grey blemishes that infected a score of kernels. Whenever this happened, the raven would perch on a stalk and scoop up all the spoiled kernels in its beak. Then, it would fly off to spew them into a nearby river, which carried them to the sea."

Ashangtu listened with a look of growing wonder. "I taught some Oskwai how to plant corn and care for it," she said at last.

When Esperidi didn't respond, she added, "Surely that's no coincidence!"

Esperidi sighed. "Shiya-coqui and I always enjoyed tea while we did this," she lamented. "I think that ritual has made me superstitious. I don't recall as much if I can't sip my jasmine and honey. Do you know if we shared that dream?"

"I don't. But I can think of an easy way to warm what's left in our canteens if you so desire," Ashangtu said, scowling at the flat below.

They didn't dare pause for long. They were still anxious to distance themselves from Manitoh territory as much as possible.

When they reached the flatlands, they discovered that low-lying, tough plants carpeted much of it. The scrub seemed to grasp their ankles at every stride.

"It's like they're lonely and don't want us to leave," Esperidi remarked.

"That's a generous way of describing it," Ashangtu said, lashing a foot. "It feels to me more like they wish to see us dead before we reach the next spring. And the best way to accomplish that is to slow us down.

"My other dream," she added, with a characteristic lack of segue or warning. "I've poured over it backward and forward, but maybe you can read some sense in it that I cannot.

"I was sitting someplace flat with tall grass—elephant grass—but it had been flattened out where I was kneeling. I was next to a sleeping jaguar. I had my hand on his head. I was stroking it, but not because I wanted to, not like you would stroke a pet. It was just the only thing that could lull it to sleep. Somehow, I knew that. And so I was stuck there. The moment I removed my hand, it was going to awaken and devour me. But as long as I kept petting its head, it dozed happily, and I was safe."

Suddenly frustrated, she beat the ground beneath her feet so swiftly that Esperidi had to nearly jog to keep up with her.

"Always trust a dream to illustrate your stalemate but never show you how to break it. Ah, serpent's fangs! What is the point of knowledge if it doesn't liberate you?"

Esperidi was silent for a long time, wandering in meditations so deep that Ashangtu's irritation couldn't reach her. Finally, she said, "Once again, our minds seem to share the same song. I dreamed something very similar, only in my case, it wasn't a jaguar, but a giant snake."

She lapsed again into a more private rumination. "I wonder what would happen if we were to lift our hands."

Ashangtu huffed. "Well, that's no deep matter. We'd be devoured."

"Yes, but if we're aware in our dreams, we realize we're not *there* in our bodies. We're the body of our thoughts. So, considering that, what would it mean to be devoured? It might just be a gateway from one world to another. What is death?"

"The answer I give to that," Ashangtu rasped, "depends greatly on the day. Some days, I might tell you that it means relief."

Esperidi made sour acknowledgment. "I've not forgotten the look in your eyes that day in Magda's Oasis. You were almost begging those brigands to destroy you."

Wishing to dispel her friend's discomfort, she hastened to add: "But I've also dreamed of the land ahead, and I saw my own jaguar. I approached a ravine on foot. Two sentinels stood on the summits of opposite cliffsides: a jaguar and a raven, facing each other. And the voice said, 'This valley is always in shadow. Here, the land speaks and remembers, and nothing is ever lost.'

"When I heard that, I thought about the Sentient Library. And I also knew that the place had significance to nearby Oskwai tribes."

"Is this someplace sacred to them, do you think?" Ashangtu asked.

"Sacred or taboo. I couldn't discern which. There's power in that place and the sense that no one who enters will emerge on the other side unchanged."

"Do you remember anything else about it?" Ashangtu

asked as if groping for an escape route.

"Only a full moon directly overhead," Esperidi said, trailing off again. She was too embarrassed to add that the ravine's opening had strongly reminded her of two inner thighs slightly parted to reveal a vulva.

All these omens left Esperidi with so much to ponder that she was relieved to awaken with a fresh mind clear of visions the following morning. She basked in this unfamiliar sensation of peace momentarily. Then she realized that Ashangtu was calling to her.

She sighed. The curly mesquite, so frustrating to hike through all day, actually made a comfortable bed once her body battened it down. But a *timbre* of urgency yanked her out of this sweet repose. She rose and trotted to her friend's side.

A rush-woven platter laden with dried venison, roots, and fruit lay on a bed of sand that appeared to have been smoothed by hand.

"None of it's spoiled," Ashangtu marveled, "and I don't sense any poison. But my percipience isn't particularly strong in that area. We never had to worry about such things in Lanore."

"Nor did we in Sequana," Esperidi said. She gazed about for tracks but realized at once that the wind would have effaced them. "Under the circumstances, though, I'll take my chances."

Both companions were nearly famished and fell to this unexpected repast with relish. Ashangtu assured Esperidi that there was a creek less than a league's distance from where they sat, so they washed the dried fare down with what water remained in their skins. Then, the scarlet woman asked Esperidi why she looked so preoccupied.

"Your folk in Lanore had extensive dealings with the Sendhi tribes, did they not?"

"We educated them," Ashangtu said. "We encouraged their chiefs to share authority with Singing Chieftesses. And we shared the universal language with them. Taught them to write it, too."

Esperidi nodded. "And by that time, Oskwai living in the Kawli had already developed a strong common identity. They named themselves Manitoh."

"Yes... And then they were schooled in Shetain philosophy when their capital came under the governorship of Jain-Toh," Ashangtu said with a hint of inquiry. She wondered where this was leading.

"But Shaini influence on the southern Oskwai was scarce," Esperidi said. "We kept ourselves aloof in Sequana, and the same was true of Sequestra Forest and its Hives. The primitives had myths about us but rarely interacted—at least in waking. Centuries ago, they scarcely understood the uses of fire. They hunted and foraged because they didn't understand how to cultivate crops.

"But I foresee them developing a much more sophisticated culture. Complex forms and rituals will be observed. They'll behave like a Nation. The visions have been so compelling! I can only assume that what I've beheld is a probable future."

"If that probable future involves them continuing to bring us breakfast on a platter," Ashangtu opined, "I wholeheartedly support it. It does make me a little uneasy, though, to consider how close they managed to come to us without either of us knowing."

"Shiya-coqui warned me of that," Esperidi said. "She said that the people in this region can basically be invisible when they choose to be—and usually they do. They are hunters, for one thing. And they remember the Manitoh Horde, which was still a real threat to them until just a couple of generations ago and looks to become so again. I imagine we could probably travel from here to the southern ocean—wherever the shoreline may be now—without encountering any of them unless they chose to show themselves.

"Besides, we are exhausted and distracted. And yet... what a vision! I witnessed them achieving peace, a society that valued and cherished every individual within it."

Ashangtu flashed dubious eyes. "Are you sure you weren't seeing only what you wanted to see?"

"So vividly?" Esperidi's expression was equal parts rueful and amused. "I think you overestimate my imagination. No, I glimpsed a future that could be. I'm certain of it. But why did the dream come to me? Why did I participate in its events? You and I must have some part to play in bringing that future about, Ashangtu."

"You'll have to forgive me if I don't relish the prospect."

"Would you rather die, parched and famished, in a barren land beneath a relentless sun? Neither of us were born into this life. We're not prepared for it." Esperidi gestured to the now-empty platter. "We'll probably need this kind of Oskwai hospitality to survive."

"In that case," Ashangtu said, rising, "let's hope their generosity persists. I'm not looking forward to whatever lies ahead. Obviously, the land only becomes more barren if we continue."

"And yet we have to press on," Esperidi said. "We're still too close to Kawli Rainforest. Anyway, we've veered west now. At least there is one advantage to growth becoming more sparse: We can see well enough to navigate and don't have to lament the loss of trails."

The following afternoon—after another meal courtesy of their unseen benefactors—they reached the place Esperidi's dream omens had pointed to. No straight route to the ravine presented itself amid a maze of jutting buttes and hidden sinkholes. Indeed, this stretch of prairie resembled an ocean, its rivulets and dips conveying the impression of waves suspended and frozen. But Esperidi discovered a ridgeline—it evoked for her the skeletal remains of a giant serpentine creature buried in the sands—that passed between two taller mesas. They stared at one another across a narrow, orange wash. Their sides were scarlet and smooth as whetstones.

"Now we know how to interpret your auguries," Ashangtu scoffed. "Just take whatever you remember and turn it inside out, and it'll bring us to the truth. 'Cause that's a blazing sun overhead, not a moon, and it leaves nary a fern-sized shadow throughout the whole stretch of that cut."

But Esperidi, who'd begun to intuit the true nature of those dream-formed shadows, continued walking in silence.

"Wait! What is that?"

Ashangtu drew short as her falcon eyes caught it: an ivory gleam on the ravine's floor, whiter than any sand they'd seen in these southern lands. And it was curiously jumbled, creating a bed that resembled bleached rubble.

Esperidi's eyes, too, were fixed upon the opening. "We dare not tarry here," she whispered. "We're being watched."

"Yes, I know," Ashangtu said. "A dozen primitives, flat on their bellies up on that southern ridgeline. But what do they care what we do here?"

"We're going to need them," Esperidi said. "You and I have reached the limits of what we can accomplish in these lands alone. And how these Oskwai receive us depends entirely on how we meet this challenge. That's why they watch and wait."

"But they couldn't have known we'd come this way," Ashangtu said.

"Not *known.*" Momentarily, Esperidi recalled the

shadowy figures that had gathered behind Raven. "Not known but *hoped*. I think some of these people shared that dream with me. Today, we fulfill an appointment."

"Keep your eyes open for that jaguar, then," Ashangtu said, lashing herself forward while reluctance dragged at her every step.

"I think we'll meet it soon enough," Esperidi said.

As they wound down a sandy slope loosely held together by patches of sagebrush, they saw that the knees of each butte sloped inward for a span of forty or fifty feet until they nearly met. This formed a narrow channel hemmed by high walls.

Then Ashangtu discerned what Esperidi had already guessed about the "ivory" gleaming in the noonday sun. The ravine's entire floor—some ten feet wide and four times as long—was carpeted with skulls lain upon a bed of other bones. This under-bed was broken and splintered as if by many feet.

"This is a burial place," Ashangtu whispered. "Surely they'll kill us if we violate their sacred space by setting foot in there!"

"They venture in there themselves occasionally," Esperidi said. "I returned to a dream echo of this place twice more, trying to clarify my vision. Oskwai dead are left in a flat pan to the west of that ridge from which they now watch us. The bones are piled here once the coyotes and carrion have picked them clean. They've also gathered whatever corpses they encounter across this land—bodies tossed and discarded by the Rupture.

"This marks a place of pilgrimage. One passes through barefoot and lets the voices of the ancestors speak through one's feet. Sometimes, youths walk this ancestral path. It's a kind of initiation. When they reach the other side, the elders pretend not to recognize them until they're given new names."

She faced Ashangtu squarely. "The Oskwai want to see how their ancestors respond to us before they make up their own minds."

She may have dreamed of Raven and Jaguar, but she contemplated that vulva-shaped opening like a serpent coiled around what she most desired and feared.

Ashangtu shrugged. "Look, I don't always agree with your suggestions or conclusions, but you know how to decipher dream riddles. And if this is our one hope of appeasing these people, what choice have we got? Our skins are empty. We've only eaten these last two days thanks to their generosity."

"I know." Esperidi couldn't lift her eyes from the piled bones. "But like you said, it feels so disrespectful, disturbing their dead like this."

"Oh, this?" Ashangtu dismissed her friend's tormenting thoughts with a wave. "Their ancestors aren't actually here, Esperidi. You know that."

"Do we know that?"

"I do," Ashangtu said. "When we come into this life, Ophia clothes us in the stuff of her body. Then, when our lives are through, we return those bodies to Her. It's the humility and respect that we hold in our minds that counts, right?"

"Yes." Esperidi scarcely whispered. She was beginning to sense the true causes of her fear, and a part of her flailed about, searching for an alternative. *But that part of me will die within this ravine*, she reminded herself. *It is the place that resists: It cannot survive in my new world.*

It can't achieve what I need to.

Ashangtu, gauging her friend's determination, said, "If you need a trailblazer..." and started towards the mouth of the cleft.

"Wait! Our moccasins. We have to go barefoot. That part was crucial; I'm sure of it."

Ashangtu bent to slip off her footwear. Then, the two women, moccasins in hand, began stepping gingerly over the mute testimony of the dead.

For a while, the only discernible sounds were the cracking of dry, brittle bones—save for once, when Esperidi cried out, realizing she'd inadvertently crushed an infant's skull by setting her heel upon it.

Ashangtu grasped the woman's shoulders and held her eyes. "It's already gone," she said with unusual tenderness. Then, guided by sudden intuition, she added: "Think of it like a play at the Ambrosine. These actors have all just gone behind the curtain for a costume change."

Esperidi nodded, though the words brought her scant comfort. Mention of the Ambrosine reminded her of the last significant quest—a high watermark of her Sophryne training—that she'd undertaken with Shiya-coqui. The very concept of the theater confounded her in many ways. She wasn't comfortable with the idea that she could simply slip into different roles and play other parts in an unfolding drama. The timid girl still living within her wanted a defined self with clear limits and boundaries.

The little girl...

Her view of the ravine's narrow strait tilted to the right and then whipped back again as if it were a ship's keel in a monsoon. Pale apparitions clogged the ruddy channel, filling her inner ears with warnings and beseechings. Her sense of self—the boundaries that had seemed so dear a moment before—was almost swept away by the force of their presence.

"It isn't the Oskwai ancestors!" she gasped. "We meet our own—the ghosts of a ravaged land!"

Trying to dispel these shades, Esperidi shut her eyes

tight.

When she opened them again, she was balanced on a tree limb over a bottomless chasm, which made her mind swirl like a migraine with vertigo. Wind from the depths swept her precarious perch from under her, and she fell.

Dropping to her knees in a pile of bones and not knowing what compelled her, she cried: "Colleen!"

She was a moment recognizing Ashangtu. "Kawli? Is that what you said? Are you talking about the jungle?"

Esperidi shook her head. The name she'd shouted was already growing cold, like an evanescent dream. But its remnant provoked another memory.

"You were there," she muttered, groping. "You saw the way Tohbin looked at me sometimes."

Ashangtu seemed prepared to follow her friend down any tangential road on the off chance it might ease her. "Like he was trying to puzzle out a riddle? Yes, I did. You know what that was about, right?"

Fearing that she did, indeed, know, Esperidi shook her head.

Sensing her duplicity, Ashangtu snapped, "Shai-win! Surely, you've seen paintings or crystal projections—or her image impressed upon books in the Farsilane library. I noticed it right away. It's uncanny, really. The two of you could—"

"If you say *twins*," Esperidi said, rising in sudden conviction, "I swear by our dear Shai-win that I shall haunt your dreams for the next week!"

Partly amused and partly relieved to see her companion recovering her native resilience, Ashangtu grinned. "I assume this isn't the first time you've heard the comparison."

Fortunately, their banter so preoccupied them thereafter that they forgot to count their footsteps; they became oblivious to the crunching of bones. Esperidi blinked and suddenly realized they'd reached the opposite mouth of the ravine.

The dozen Oskwai she and Ashangtu had sensed on the ridge were standing in a rough wedge a few paces from the opening. Twelve ghostly pallors, the effect of ash smeared over faces and hands, stared back at them like mute testimonials to the vale's dead. Some bore white handprints across their chests like insignia of rank. But their arms and legs were bare, save for a layer of accumulated dust and dirt, and the two Shaini women could see that these people, though their bottom-heavy and somewhat diminutive bodies (none stood much taller than Ashangtu) were akin to Manitohs, were darker, more deep brown than olive.

And their collective *timbre* contrasted with the stoicism characteristic of the Manitohs. These Oskwai were lean and wiry due to privation and struggle, not from asceticism and self-denial. Esperidi surmised that they were capable of frivolity—if ever they encountered circumstances worthy of laughter.

Nevertheless, the voice of the woman standing at the head of the wedge was coldly formal, even severe. "What messages do Ophia's dead bring to the feet of the travelers?"

Though she'd anticipated the question, Esperidi quailed. *It was the voices of my dead I heard, not yours!* Would these Oskwai accept such a response?

Perhaps they hoped for it. They might be eager to receive a perspective outside their ken. They might believe the dead would speak differently to Shaini than other humans.

It had to be risked. But as Esperidi marshaled her courage for this gambit, she was startled when Ashangtu stepped forward first. Offering the traditional sign of peace that the Shaini of Lanore had always used with the traders, the woman bowed with one palm flattened over a fist, signifying the blanketing of aggression.

"Before the great storms," Ashangtu said, "when Sarpienta stirred from his bed, and Ophia was rent from within, an embassy approached my people. Some of the Shetain priests had foreseen what was coming. They'd built an armada of ships which, they said, could carry us to safer shores.

"And so they offered the folk of Lanore salvation if we would but accept their spiritual authority and adopt the Sacred Writ of Toh. I alone argued against the offer. 'Of what use is life,' I said, 'if we cannot think and believe as we choose?'

"And so, Shetain's High Priest, a man of monstrous pride, grew wrathful. My elder sister was taken to the ships. The rest of us were left to face the coming cataclysm. Unable to face the grief that I'd brought upon my family—and their anger—I fled to the Savwain Desert. Thus, I was spared when the waves washed over Lanore.

"You ask what message the spirits brought me in the ravine. Their voices grated on my inner ears, but only until I recognized that this is because I am harsh with myself. They told me that I blame myself for my family's deaths. They reminded me of how I often cannot sleep in the dark, still hours, because I ask myself whether my life was worth the loss of theirs.

"And they challenged me. 'Who are you to think to govern the destinies of others? You paint the canvas of your own life, Ashangtu Lanore. You take no hand in another's portrait. Your guilt, then, is naught but hubris and self-importance.'"

Again, Ashangtu made the peacemaking gesture and bowed. And Esperidi was reminded of how the Lanoreans, because of their position within Old Ophia and their utter dependence upon trade, had valued diplomacy above all else.

The woman's words awed the Oskwai. Some gasped and made quick hand signs as if to ward off—or invite—unseen spirits. Then, their heavy burden of expectation and hope shifted to Esperidi.

Feeling daunted by Ashangtu's intransigence, she stepped forward and offered her own greeting gesture, spreading her arms wide and opening her hands to show that she was unarmed and intended no violence.

"My mentor taught me to walk within dreams with eyes awake," she said. "She showed me a place where the collected knowledge and accounts of other Wakeful Dreamers were preserved. All who find their way there may partake in it. This is how we maintain the legacy of our ancestors. We call it the Sentient Library.

"The spirits of the ravine spoke through my feet. They reminded me that I have been afraid. Since the Rupture washed over Ophia, I have seldom returned to the Library. I mourned my father and my teacher. But so long as I didn't research their fates in the dream Hall, I could pretend I didn't know. I could console myself and say that, perhaps, they were still alive. Perhaps, somehow, they had escaped.

"The spirits showed me how sometimes my mind denies what my heart knows for fear of pain. And so long as this fear governs me, I cannot be the Wakeful Dreamer that my teacher was."

She wasn't sure how much of this the Oskwai could comprehend. Thanks to the efforts of the ancient Shaini, all of Ophia's peoples, from the Sendhi steppes to Sequana's cliff Hives overlooking the sea, shared common linguistic roots. But most of the Hives had also held themselves aloof for great swathes of time, and peculiar dialects had cropped up during those periods. Nevertheless, Esperidi felt *timbres* of relief and vindication. Somehow, she and Ashangtu had offered answers that the southern Oskwai mythos were prepared to receive and honor.

The woman at the head of the cortege had probably seen no more than twenty summers. Her hair fell in dark knots to her waist; her brown eyes blazed with primitive fire. Scantily clad in what looked like tanned zebu leather, she was gaunt and lithe, constantly shifting on her feet and squatting down as if to better scrutinize them from a lower vantage. Then she stiffened suddenly and, pounding a fist against her chest, proclaimed, "Lalai!"

Realizing she was introducing herself, Ashangtu and Esperidi gave their names in turn, imitating Lalai's gesture.

The woman bore a wooden spear, its sharpened stone tip affixed to the shaft with rawhide strips. Holding it near each end so that her arms were spread wide, she offered it to Ashangtu.

Esperidi, intuiting the meaning of the gesture, said, "She means to demonstrate your trustworthiness to the others—to prove that you will not harm them, even when you are armed and she is not."

Ashangtu accepted the spear and held it to her chest.

Another Oskwai stepped forward, bearing a long gray blanket, which he unrolled over the dusty flat.

"It signifies comfort, welcome, and peace," Lalai said. "We do this thing to turn any place upon which we lay it into a home where all those gathered must treat each other as mutual guests."

She glanced at the moccasins the two Shaini carried as she said this. They stepped onto the rug by silent consensus and slipped into their footwear.

Then Lalai turned on a heel. "Come!"

Four Oskwai preceded her. The rest dropped back to stalk behind the newcomers. This solemn procession moved along a well-worn trail. Eventually, it brought Esperidi and

Ashangtu to a scrub flat on a western ridge's farther side, just beginning to be warmed by the sun, where forty or fifty other Oskwai were encamped.

The ensuing night constituted a veritable feast for Esperidi and Ashangtu. The Oskwai had settled around a rill stretching scarcely farther than the shade a cluster of date palms provided, but it would sustain this tribe for several more days. Also, a small pack of deer—gaunt creatures still meaty enough to warrant the effort—had been discovered in a string of tar pits to the south.

"Explains where that venison came from," Ashangtu remarked.

The two Shaini expressed their gratitude repeatedly, as their hosts seemed unappeased until they'd glutted themselves to the point of sluggishness.

Encouraged by this warm reception, Esperidi found a moment alone with Lalai.

"Your coming is a sign from the Great Spirits," the woman said, shaking her gourd for emphasis. "We must call for another Meet—the first since the storms!"

"But what of Shamarai?" a man protested at once.

"How can he persist in his folly," Lalai said, "in the presence of two Shaini? He must learn to see with new eyes. He must learn to read human hearts as well as he reads the portents of coming storms."

"So *you* say," the man grumbled. "He may not see it that way."

Esperidi waited until she felt no simmering tension between the two. She didn't want to instigate a conflict she didn't understand, so she gently prompted Lalai. "Meet?"

"At the stone circle we call Jamurada," the woman said. "Three times we have done this. Many tribes have answered: Yendar and exiled Manitohs; Snake, Jaguar, and Mangrove clans of the Junsa; even some clans from the south, who go by names unknown to us. And we, the Ruhselene."

Esperidi mulled this with growing astonishment. During her years in Farsilane, she'd learned that the Jona-chon, who rode their horses the length and breadth of the Virgoda Plains east of Savwain Desert, employed a similar ritual to create a sense of joint identity.

I wonder if any of them survived, aside from those few I saw mingling with the Vandrene.

But this revelation was not what bereft her of speech. Rather, it was the name Lalai had given her people: Ruhselene. Esperidi recognized the ancient Shaini title bestowed upon all the comparably less sophisticated people they'd sought to enlighten. It meant "Ancient Children."

These Ruhselene were wild, but few were wantonly rambunctious. Some sat by the fire with pensive expressions, hypnotized and enthralled, chewing slowly and seldom emoting. Others were so animate in the firelight that they reminded her of a troupe of marionettes caught in a gale wind. They sniffed the air with sharp inhalations, seeming to rely on their sense of smell almost as much as hearing. Occasionally, they mimicked the sounds of owls and coyotes. Without her sensitivity to their individual *timbres*, it would have been impossible for her to discern their moods, as a cry of pain sounded scarcely different from one of anger or excitement.

Regaining her composure, she tried to frame her question as clearly as possible. "How do you accomplish the summons?"

"All tribes are on the move." With her hands, Lalai pantomimed human migrations. "Who can know where others are camped from one moon to the next? Who can see whether the road to another tribe is made clear? But we have help."

Her eyes beamed at Esperidi. "And now, two more Wakeful Dreamers walk among us."

"I see." Esperidi wondered why the woman used that term so familiarly. Sophrynes had drifted into legend even among Shaini in the decades preceding the Rupture. Vaguely disturbed by the light of idolatry in the other woman's eyes—it reminded her of how Tohbin had sometimes looked at her as if trying to penetrate a mystery,—she tried to invest her voice with a *timbre* of caution. "You have someone who acts as a herald in the dream world, who finds and invites the others."

Lalai pointed to the highest point on the ridgeline, where a ring of menhirs adorned the plateau like a broken crown. "Aye! He bids all Oskwai to meet within the stone circle we call Jamurada. Because it lies in sight of Mordu, the cleft of skulls, our ancestors may listen and bear witness."

Esperidi felt she walked a narrow strait between her fear of offending her hosts and her reluctance to inflate herself to mythic dimensions. She spoke carefully, trying not to upset that delicate balance.

"Can you say more about the people who might come to this Meet?"

"Oke-Jumo is the Singing Chief of the Mangrove clan in the eastern swamps," Lalai said. "They travel in their canoes and have no other chief. And you have heard Shamarai mentioned. He has a fiery spirit, much like this one." She pointed to Ashangtu, who squatted by the fire, wrapping silence around herself like a cloak. "We hear rumors. There is one among them they call the Snake Man. He is Shaini like you and Ashangtu Lanore."

"Snake Man," Esperidi whispered, bewildered. But Lalai did not linger there.

"The Snake clan grew tired of wandering. They settled cliff caves that appeared after the ocean pulled back and the sun dried the land. They dug out the sand and made these places their home."

Aramoye? Esperidi wondered. A *vestige of home?* Geographically, it would conform to what the Singing Chieftess described. But so much had been disrupted, old boundaries destroyed, and new land masses thrust up from the sea....

"To the north and west, other Junsa roam," Lalai said. "They hunt and forage at night, worshipping the owls, and sleep in caves while the sun kisses the land with harsh light. They may not answer our summons," she admitted.

"And we do not know who leads them," the man who'd spoken earlier added. "It has been many seasons."

Esperidi possessed only vague knowledge of the Junsa. She knew that they had been enslaved by the Manitohs during Sanjesota's time and forced to work the Kawli mines. After taking over the governorship of Khempsa, Jain-Toh had not freed them, which had perhaps been an even more egregious violation. They'd been forced to adopt the Sacred Writ of Toh and abandon their worship of Grandfather Serpent Sarpienta, whose cult had dominated Ophia in ancient times.

They likely bear little love for Shaini.

In those dim days, her ancestors had dwelt in caves, such as Aramoye, and relinquished the aboveground world to other, more primitive humans.

"You speak of them like they are a free people," she said. "Are they not still held in thrall by the Manitohs?"

"Ice fell upon the Kawli," the man said. "It covered all in a white blanket that destroyed everything they tried to grow and made the people shiver. Some went to sleep and did not awaken. There was panic. Women, children, and even many men ran in terror, screaming about Toh's wrath, and would not listen to the commands of their chieftains."

Esperidi had only witnessed that event through distant scrying. But she recalled those lightless days in the Savwain when she'd wondered whether the sun would ever show its face again. So many volcanoes had erupted that the ashen sheets blotted her warmth from the sky. Day resembled night. During that time, she'd rarely left her refuge in the Arjena Hills and had nourished her cave-born crops with Sophryne songs.

"The Rupture brought winter to Manitoa for the first time in its history," she said.

"Aye," he said. "Thus, the Manitohs learned to fear Toh, the god of the Shetain priests."

"But the Junsa remembered who they were," Lalai said. "In the confusion and uproar, with none guarding them, they fled."

Esperidi marveled at how the Rupture, which had torn asunder everything of her former world, had also brought unexpected boons. Power dynamics shifted. Master and servant traded places.

The visionary is more valuable to any tribe in these times.

She carried that reflection with her, pouring over its myriad implications as she relinquished herself to sleep that night, fixing her newly budding sense of purpose like an arrowhead. Not until the walls of dream nearly closed over her did she consider a mystery that other concerns had momentarily driven from her mind.

Who is the other Sophryne Lalai spoke of?

꘎꘎

Esperidi and Ashangtu shared a morning meal with the Ruhselene: squash, corn, beans, more venison, and—to their astonishment—baked brown bread that'd been buttered.

Sharing a pensive mood, the two did more listening than talking. The elderly Ruhselenes spoke less than the young, but when they did, it was usually attended by reverential silence as listeners absorbed every word and gesture. Oftentimes, the elders' speech approached chanting or singsong.

Esperidi beamed her appreciation. "We've called them primitive, but the light of their consciousness is not dim," she told Ashangtu. "They are spiritually awake—avid for sensation.

"The Sentient Library preserves lore that relates to the first Shaini. Their world was fluid and dreamlike. These Ruhselene spend much of their lives in a waking dream, too. They seem 'not quite here' to me. They resemble sleepwalkers. But this is not a retreat from the world. See—their bodies are strong and supple; their minds have sharp, discerning edges when directed towards their world."

"Try not to fall in love with them too quickly," Ashangtu said, her lips curling around a mouthful of bread. "We don't know much about their intentions."

But Esperidi's growing sense of wonder swept her along. "Look at that one there." A young man, bare save for a zebu loincloth, proudly bore a tattoo across his chest: four eyes, one pair open and the other closed. And upon his shoulders were emblazoned four wings, two spread in flight and two folded.

"That symbol means one can see when asleep and sleep while waking. And the wings... He flies while at rest and is at rest while flying."

"If you draw a bird analogy..." Ashangtu warned.

Esperidi flicked her tongue at the other woman. "I merely point out that they share our love of dreams. In this respect, they are akin to Sophrynes. They grant dreaming life as much veracity and significance as waking."

Lalai approached them, and Esperidi noticed at once that she was arrayed as if for a ceremony. She wore a plain leather blouse only a couple shades lighter than her dusky skin, but over this, she'd draped a shawl with beaded fringes of gold, sapphire, and scarlet. And her hair was twisted in scores of fine braids, each held together at their ends by similar beads.

The woman stopped a couple paces from them and pressed her palms together before her heart. "Hail, Olen-sa! I recognize the fire of Sorsajna within you! I witness how Ophia cherishes your footsteps!"

The two Shaini, unfamiliar with this greeting but recognizing its importance to Lalai, echoed it back to her.

Appearing deeply honored, the woman bowed low. Then she said: "Today, we will lead you to Pedragira. There, you will meet the man who sang its stones into place. You are called; you are awaited."

Pedragira

Esperidi and Ashangtu followed a beaten path to the topmost terrace of the butte upon which the village of Pedragira spread. As an easterly breeze trailed across the key lime prairie, Esperidi paused momentarily and gazed at this place that tugged upon her subtle senses. After the storms and upheavals of the last two years, all the old maps of Ophia were useless. But this region, like the Savwain, seemed remarkably untouched by the Rupture. The gentle undulations had been weathered by time and wind, not floods and quakes.

I've come to think of Ophia in such terms: lands in slumber and lands in unrest.

These earthen waves culminated in a bare rock butte a hundred feet tall and half a mile long. Even at this distance, Esperidi could see the steps hewn from the stone's outward face.

For days, she and Ashangtu had sensed a population of Oskwai spread across leagues of heather, but Esperidi was perplexed by a lighter, more playful *timbre* emanating from the butte. It grew stronger with every step she took, carrying notes of frivolity and dramatic flair. As dogs in a pack identify one of their own by scent, she sensed the Shaini male whose presence dominated Pedragira's aura. It echoed the half-recalled, evanescent visions that had brought her here.

Her dreams had not been mere wish-fulfilling

fantasies, then—not the imaginings of a woman starved for companionship and aching for vestiges of her lost home.

Ashangtu, boiling with impatience, urged her to keep up. The two Shaini heard several bird calls cast by human throats. The surreptitious callers were invisible, intimately familiar with this prairie's concealing folds. But they felt more curious than threatening.

Lalai had assured them of this. "You must make the final approach on your own," she'd said, "but we will watch and wait."

And the sounds were not mere mimicry. Esperidi felt a sense of *participation* in avian life—identification with all that flew. Perhaps these Oskwai believed they *were* birds or experienced their kinship with birdhood when they made those calls.

She and Ashangtu reached a cobbled footpath after passing through a small copse of redbuds in indigo bloom, the third patch of woodland between this settlement and the Ruhselene encampment. Here was incontrovertible evidence of a Shaini's handiwork. The walkway had not been built but *wrought*. The marble stones were too smooth and uniform to have been carved with physical tools. And only someone with knowledge of *Sacred Timbre* could have made the joins so flawlessly snug.

Their watchers made less effort to hide themselves now, but they remained at least a stone's throw from either side of the road. Their hair was long and ruddy or coppery. They were scantily clad in skins that looked like they'd been tanned. Unlike most of their cousin Oskwai, such as the Manitohs and Sendhi, the males were bearded and generally more broad-chested. Their bronzed bodies, honed by lives of constant wariness and exertion, moved with panther-like grace. Some hopped rather than ran, bending so low that their fingers grazed the grass.

The movements of this largely unseen, milling mass were strangely synchronized, as if they all danced to the same unheard music. But Esperidi could see that they also conveyed information to each other with various hand signs. She was startled to see how closely those signs resembled the hand language she and Shiya-coqui had employed in Farsilane when they'd striven to keep their communications unheard. *The Rupture has rendered us all equals in nature's nest*, she reminded herself. Though Esperidi hailed from the most sophisticated civilization Ophia had ever nurtured, recent years had taught her much about the hunger, thirst, loneliness, and despair that most Oskwai had long been acquainted with.

"See that small party bounding up the stairs there?" Ashangtu called back. "No doubt they've gone to announce our approach to the rest of the settlement."

Clambering onto the stairway put the sun in their eyes, and they could only stare at the steps directly in front of them for a while. Esperidi sensed rather than saw the crowd gathering at the base of the butte, watching their ascent.

At long last, some Ruhselenes exposed their eyes to her sight. The bravest studied her and Ashangtu, marveling at their sharp ears, long almond eyes, and waifish bodies.

This afforded Esperidi another close view of them, as well. The Ruhselenes' eyes were rounded and more deeply set beneath pronounced foreheads. Their noses were broader and visibly flared at times from strong emotion. Having taken a hurried census in one of her recent dreams, Esperidi reckoned that perhaps three hundred folk dwelt here. She was close enough now to feel their elemental presence. Even while relaxed, their energies felt coiled, ready to spring at the slightest provocation.

Whispers of "Shaini" shuddered through their

collective body.

The roadway widened to an avenue, and spears and bows were laid upon its verges on both sides. But this display exceeded mere homage. Furtive eyes met Esperidi's with deference, submission, and awe. None held her gaze for long. As soon as she glanced toward someone, man or woman, they would bow until their brow kissed the ground.

"Damned idolatry!" Ashangtu breathed.

Esperidi concurred. "Whatever myths they cling to... they keep them in awe of Shaini."

"Just for the sake of self-preservation," Ashangtu suggested, "perhaps we should play upon that sense of awe."

Apparently following her own advice, she proceeded with head held high as if she knew precisely where she was going and was as familiar with this settlement as its residents were. Esperidi opted not to chastise her for the pretense. *We have no recourse but to throw ourselves at these tribespeoples' mercy*, she reminded herself.

Rising high enough to see again, she watched the Ruhselene, noting how they walked with legs splayed, swaying as if fighting a squall. Males and females moved with a swagger, arms slightly extended. And they alternately clenched and relaxed their fists as if anticipating conflict.

Two switchbacks finally brought her and Ashangtu to the top, where they faced a broad stone avenue wide enough for three wagons, hemmed on both sides by clusters of straw huts separating bountiful vegetable gardens.

Despite her preparation, Esperidi still gasped when she saw the man. He was dressed like a Vandrene fortune teller, his silken leggings slashed with scarlet and verdigris and his wiry physique only partially covered by a similarly-colored leather vest. A purple scarf concealed his hair but accentuated his ears, which resembled a bald cat's.

She knew him—and saw her astonishment and

recognition reflected in his azure eyes.

"Do I dream? What miracle is this?" Sanyori Mon-Sequestra beamed at his two visitors.

"Those are the thoughts foremost in *my* mind," Esperidi said, mirroring his smile. "Until now, it is only within dreams that I have known you."

The three Shaini clustered together, and although Ashangtu remained aloof and wary, Esperidi and Sanyori stumbled over each other's sentences, eager to disentangle the threads of their life stories and the destiny that had brought them together.

"Where to begin?" the man gushed. "So much to learn, un-spool, and celebrate! I should like to know how you survived, where you've lived. How came you here?"

Esperidi laughed at his exuberance. "Lalai told us another Shaini lived in this region, and as I drew closer to your... capricious *timbre*, I began to suspect who it was. But I hardly dared credit the sensation at first. A heart can be more sorely grieved when it first gives itself to false hope."

Ashangtu rolled her eyes, but Esperidi watched Sanyori digest the implications. "I've learned the same caution," he said. "Perhaps that's why I settled here." He seemed to consider the notion for the first time. "This is a place where my expectations can never grow so high that there's a risk my heart may be crushed!"

He bowed low with a magnanimous sweep of his arm. Rising again, he grinned and closed some of the space between them, arms extended as if he wanted to verify the two women's actuality with an embrace. Then, he recalled his courtesy and merely studied them. Both were dressed for the occasion in cedar bark blouses and skirts that Lalai had gifted them. Esperid had dyed some of the fringes in various blue hues; Ashangtu had opted for red to match her hair.

"And what about yourselves?" Sanyori said. "The toils

of the road tell on you, but otherwise, you're nicely clothed, albeit in a primitive fashion. You look well-fed. I'm amazed you fared so well before the Ruhselenes offered their hospitality. Do your visions lead you to provender?"

"Sometimes," Ashangtu said. "And sometimes, if you possess such abilities, it pays to be cautious around who you tell."

Sanyori's eyes encompassed her sun-scorched face, the sheen of dust that veritably lent her a second skin, and her evident weariness. "Well said! And surely, you require refreshment more than conversation—at least for the moment! I've got two copper tubs in my guest chamber. I'll have plenty of water heated. Bathe once to rid yourselves of grime, then bathe again for repose! Viands will be prepared while you wash—all the finest bounty of Pedragira!"

He glanced along the right side of the avenue to a cluster of huts and made a series of hand gestures and clucking sounds. Esperidi was astonished by the alacrity with which the half-dozen Ruhselenes raced off to fulfill his bidding.

Ashangtu, a native of a Hive synonymous with luxury, audibly sighed in relief. "Now I am the one who must wonder if this is a dream. But tell me..." Her eyes sparkled despite her fatigue. "Does my host and savior have a name? I am Ashangtu Lanore."

"Sanyori Mon-Sequestra." He bowed again—with another flourish. "Be welcome in my village, though it is admittedly no majestic Hive!"

Esperidi laughed. "In this hour, it caresses my eyes like a gilded palace. In case you've forgotten, I am Esperidi of lost Sequana Hive."

"Esperidi Mon-Sequana and Ashangtu Lanore, I am prepared to make reparations for the weariness and hunger of your road. I have offered baths and feasting, and this is but a prelude to the pageantry in store for you. Will you come?"

Esperidi bowed low in gratitude. Ashangtu, slowly won over by the man's effervescent flair, acquiesced with a smile.

The three Shaini continued along bamboo and flax-woven pathways and across two bridges spanning irrigation canals. The broad yards between the end of the avenue and the opening into Pedragira Hive were cluttered with columns little taller than themselves, a riot of russet mushroom minarets bejeweled with indigo bands and jade spheres. They picked their way through these formations as if they were a grove of luminous dwarf trees.

"How did you escape the Rupture?" Ashangtu asked Sanyori.

The man seemed grateful for the opportunity to speak of it. "My troupe and I endured the never-ending winter of the Sendhi steppes to elude the Cordonne. You may recall that Ophian power was limited in its reach even at the height of its sovereignty. It did not extend north to the steppes or farther south than the Kawli jungles. Excepting, of course, Lanore's northernmost outpost—Kublai Hive."

"It survived," Ashangtu breathed. Esperidi heard the effort she expended not to betray any emotion.

"Mostly," Sanyori said. "The mountains were riven, but the *timbres* that wove the Hive were strong and kept it aloft, if slightly slanted. Because of its distance from Ardhid, the first great upheavals did not touch us. And the fires in the south did not blacken our skies as much as others."

Esperidi, distracted by the sculptures surrounding her, lent him only half an ear. The creations reminded her of crystalline shapes she'd made from salt or sugar as a child: her first experiments with *Sacred Timbre*. Indeed, a child seemed to have taken a hand in every buttress, curve, and fluted tower of Pedragira. It burst with creative exuberance like the first Hives in Ophia's springtime, when Shaini focused on the joys of creative expression rather than the application of power.

The structures were lavishly embellished and decorated as if the builders hadn't wanted to stop working on their beloved projects long after their functional forms had been achieved.

"When tidings of its devastation reached our ears," Sanyori said, "we surmised that the power of the Cordonne was broken. What reason had we to stay? We'd migrated to the frozen north to live beyond the reach of our rulers. Now, we froze under gray skies for naught. So we packed what we could fit on a score of runner sleds and made for the southern lands."

A doorway shimmered with lemon-lime phosphorescence like dawn's light refracting off a green river. Its *timbre* suffused Esperidi's inner senses with such a palpable tang that she suddenly thirsted for something sour and sweet. Brightly painted wicker shapes evoking deep-purple comets chased one another over the festooned archway, trailing violet streamers that grazed the trio's heads.

"Clearly," Ashangtu opined, "you are an artist who doesn't know when to stop–or doesn't care to. I wonder... Have you ever produced a play that you considered finished?"

"Before I answer that," Sanyori said with obvious relish, "I'd love to hear more about how my creation speaks to your discriminating Lanorean eyes."

Ashangtu rolled those eyes but then, with a slight smirk, opted to play along. "Taken together, the color scheme seems to assure us that pleasure and fun are permissible here. The lime is tantalizing, the indigo protective and reassuring."

Sanyori shared his appreciation with Esperidi. "You

see why her folk were renowned for their honey? Ahh... she *honeys* my ears!"

Esperidi absently acknowledged this. She was too awestruck to share in the jest. This place reminded her of how starved her eyes had felt for vibrant colors since the Rupture washed so much of Ophia with grainy green-gray hues and choked its skies with ash.

Ashangtu droned on in sly mockery of Farsilane's intellectual elite. "Cool blue veins run down the curve of the immaculately smooth walls like lapis lazuli streams..."

The tallest minaret was as garish and multicolored as a Farsilane circus tent. Indigo and jade still predominated, suggesting precious bands and jewels in the smooth dome. Its upper centerpiece resembled three jade oval pendants nestled together like eggs in a nest, each enclosing a scene from Ophian history. Its right side tapered off into purple root-like shapes that dangled over the opening to a cave with a cozy, rush-woven floor. On the opposite side, ensconced in a thick mound of sod, an ash tree leaned at a crazy angle, clutching to its position with a web-work of roots that made its bed resemble a brain with many folds. The alternating ivory and cerulean cobbles beneath the travelers' feet were fish-shaped, their "fins" interlocking to create whirling patterns that nowhere resolved.

Two-score Ruhselenes sewed, ate, and played beneath the dome's vast shadow. Esperidi could almost hear their collective speculations. *Three of them? What does this portend?*

"Many disparate clans mingled after the storms," Sanyori said. "After a string of volcanic bursts along our eastern horizon, this region was occasionally ravaged by cyclones but little else. About three thousand Oskwai from various clans have formed a loose union between this prairie, the eastern swamps, and the southern badlands. They set their differences aside for the sake of survival. Catastrophes have a way of quelling petty conflicts."

Goaded by a vague memory, Esperidi said, "I never got to see one of your performances at the Ambrosine. My Papa wouldn't allow it. He said you were subversive."

"I saw a few in Lanore," Ashangtu said, "and I can concur with your Papa."

"Subversive to the farthest extent that I dared!" Sanyori said, eyes sparkling. "But I was more concerned with planting seeds for the future than disrupting the Cordonne. I think all of us in the troupe were aware of what was coming. We were circumspect about warning our audiences. At least, until our esteemed Sophryne here showed us another way to congregate."

His remark made Esperidi recall Rona, the young actress whom she'd become acquainted with in several lucid dreams. "Where's the rest of your troupe now?"

"We found some welcome among the Vandrene in the Savwain Desert. Most chose to stay."

"Ashangtu and I both lived there," Esperidi said. "My teacher sent me, knowing the storms would only lightly touch it."

"*Our* teacher," Sanyori clarified with a wide grin. "Aye, and now it's a place where the dispossessed find a sense of community, though there are few Shaini among them. But part of me has always longed to be a teacher, a benefactor. That's why I settled here. Once, I performed on a hill not far from this butte. More than fifty Oskwai eventually gathered. Their *timbre* rang like springtime. And so, when I grew disenchanted with the desert, I was of a mind to return.

"I asked the troupe to accompany me for long enough to help 'sing the stones of Pedragira into place,' as we used to describe such a feat."

"And the Oskwai witnessed it," Esperidi surmised.

"Aye. That's when worship first entered their eyes and voices," Sanyori said. "I'm sure you've noticed. But I think I've made my influence a force for good, too." He indicated one of the garden plots. "It's gratifying to see something sprout from seed, then slowly grow—with careful nurturance—and bear fruit. And then to think that a similar process is ripening within Oskwai minds... and I have a hand in it. No play was ever more fulfilling to partake in."

Esperidi glanced around at the furtive natives. "Is there not a danger in regarding them as blank slates? That's one thought that plagues me every time I debate whether or not to share knowledge with them."

"Danger? There's danger in wielding a blade or withholding your hand. No part of Ophia—if we're still calling it that—is free from the consequences of ignorance and hubris." Sanyori pinched the air. "The most valuable coin in this new realm is a vision of a new way of *being*."

As they moved, Esperidi considered how reserved she felt alongside Sanyori's lithe flamboyance, which imbued his every gesture with gratuitous, dramatic flair. Was this only an outgrowth of his life as an actor? Or had he also adopted such a posture to make himself understood by these folk surrounding him, elaborately pantomiming his words for their sake?

His private home was, like the enclosure, modeled after an Ophian Hive, though it was much smaller: a fluted granite tower, fifty feet tall and broadest at its midriff, its flawlessly smooth walls stitched with amethyst veins.

"The Ruhselene helped us build it," Sanyori said. "But of course, I had to work with the *timbres* of stone to smooth everything, draw out its native luster, and infuse it with song."

"Of course!" Esperidi grinned.

"The upper levels are merely for display," Sanyori

remarked before they entered through the double doors. "Only this ground floor has any chambers and furnishings."

Esperidi and Ashangtu felt spaciousness opening between them and the high ceiling. The oval chamber was partitioned into several sections by stretched hides painted with old Ophian iconography. The walls' immaculate sheen was offset by a thick layer of furs padding the floors, which transformed what might have been an austere and magisterial space into a cozy grotto.

The Hive's undercurrents, however, were rife with other suggestions. Esperidi was immediately cognizant of a *timbre* she could only equate with religious awe in the face of eternal mystery, a sensation she'd only ever received in sacred groves and places of worship, which invited such projections. It was abashed silence before a holy presence, and she knew that Sanyori, if he hadn't encouraged it in the Ruhselenes' minds, had at least allowed it to flourish.

Too tired to consider the implications, she was grateful when Ashangtu said, "So where do we find that promised repose?"

And so two copper tubs were filled for the Shaini women. They basked in warm water for the next hour, scrubbing themselves clean with sea sponges and lemon-scented soap. After dressing, they sat across from Sanyori at a four-foot-long ermine divan in the central hall. A small delegation of Ruhselenes entered with rush-woven platters laden with river fish, corn, beans, and fire-scored slices of tomato.

"If ever there was an occasion that called for wine!" Sanyori lamented. "But alas, we cannot ferment grapes that are not yet grown."

Esperidi momentarily probed his face for signs of underlying intent, wondering if he spoke in metaphor. But this thought was driven from her mind as Lalai entered the chamber bearing another platter. This one was filled with chunks of pineapple, oranges, figs, and small cakes. The woman wore a sleeveless blouse with a low-cut V, its fringe scarcely touching the tops of her thighs. As she set the provender on the table, Esperidi watched as the Ruhselene's eyes met Sanyori's. They brimmed with intimate familiarity and undeniable sexual warmth.

His lover?

The woman gathered the empty platters and bore them away, her awareness of her appeal apparent in the almost insolent sway of her hips.

Esperidi gaped. Her spirits, already wilting as she felt the heat between them, began to freefall. The force of her jealousy appalled her. To make matters worse, Sanyori noticed her look of despondency.

"You do not seem pleased to learn that I've taken some of them for mates."

Some of them? She'd scarcely reconciled herself to the idea of *one*.

Stalling to reclaim her inner poise, Esperidi waved a dismissive hand. "My opinion of your intimate life is hardly pertinent."

"But I am curious to know why you react thus," Sanyori said. He sounded genuinely startled. "There are precedents all throughout our history. Shaini have begotten countless children with Oskwai. This is why many Manitohs, for instance, are so long-lived. And they fortified our own stock, kept us hardy."

"We've always been more vulnerable to disease and hardship," Esperidi allowed. "That's one consequence of living closer to the ethereal."

"Oskwai blood made our ancestors durable, more strong-limbed," Sanyori said. "It lent them endurance and resilience. We sometimes mingled with less civilized humans in ancient times, instructing them. Lalai's people preserve legends of those times. They're accustomed to revering our kind."

"Maybe, San, Esperidi is more concerned with our ancestors' part in *promoting* those legends," Ashangtu said. "They did things to ensure that other humans wouldn't become a threat—like playing at being gods. The homage that woman pays you, is it a lingering vestige of that ancient charade? Sexual tribute, shall we say?"

"I've already seen the awe with which these people regard you," Esperidi said, feeling grateful that Ashangtu had obliquely come to her aid. "It's almost fawning servitude. Anyone entranced by this idea that you're godlike can't be capable of conscious choice."

"It wouldn't be the first time illusions ruled the game of love," Sanyori said. "I could argue that those who disdain the idea of a Shaini-Oskwai partnership have less compassion than I do. They find it distasteful because they believe the Oskwai beneath them."

He punctuated this with a pointed glance at Ashangtu, almost too quick to notice.

"But these folk believe *you're* above *them*," Esperidi pointed out, "regardless of your attitude. Do you encourage them to worship you?"

Sanyori feigned nonchalance. "If we're going to be teachers, there inevitably comes a time when we must be presumptuous. Who decides who can be trusted with knowledge and who cannot? I know there are countless things they can learn from a Shaini. Is it wrong to acknowledge that?"

"The Rupture taught us the consequences of hubris," Esperidi said.

"Or should have," Ashangtu added.

"Knowledge of *Sacred Timbre* enabled us to transform

our world," Esperidi said. "That power opened the doors to countless temptations. It's like you've said: Who among us is wise enough to say where the prudent limits to such power should lie? Would *we* have listened had anyone tried to warn us?"

"We understand the limits of our power because we pushed ourselves beyond those limits," Sanyori said. "That's where our hard-won knowledge becomes a gift. Armed with it, the youthful races don't need to repeat our mistakes. They can sidestep our race's misplaced hungers—with a little guidance.

"You may call it vanity, but when I was a playwright in Ophia, I wrote those dramas to combat the collective apathy of the times. Here, I've found more receptive eyes and ears. And Shaini blood may invigorate the Oskwai as much as any amount of instruction. Indeed, it is the strain of Shaini blood in them, I think, that makes them so receptive to my tutelage."

Then he looked at Esperidi in a way that heated her face. "But we could bring more full-blooded Shaini back into the world, too."

Recovering some of her composure, Esperidi smiled dubiously. *Or am I just relieved to know he desires me at least as much as her? What a tangle!* "You seem to think our mating is a foregone conclusion."

"Well, it is the most logical path for us to take. Only a handful of our kind still live, and I'm sure none of us want to see the Shaini become extinct."

Ashangtu stiffened. "I don't make intimate choices according to the dictates of logic, San!"

Esperidi, however, looked thoughtful. "But do we not bear some responsibility for the continuation of Shaini kind if we are, indeed, among the few females left?"

Most of the conflicts in early Shaini history resulted

from differing attitudes towards the "problem" of sexuality, with its attendant jealousies, possessiveness, attachment, and resentments. Their myths encapsulated their struggle to use that primal energy constructively as they moved from a state of Oneness into a sphere of duality wherein they had to choose: to mate to sustain their species, to pour passion towards one, excluding others...

That springtime age was characterized by the different experiments that various Shaini clans undertook as they wrestled with this dilemma. Their solutions ranged from celibacy to orgiastic celebrations—"Let's re-create that old state of Oneness in the flesh."

What about the idea of family? What about the rare treasure of being devoted to one person for life? The first philosophies posed such questions. Shaini managed the rising conflicts and contentions by congregating around shared ideologies. Hives were created, each of them gradually growing estranged from the others.

Esperidi finally found some stable ground—at least for the moment. "But our disparate attitudes towards the Oskwai would no doubt cause ongoing animosity," she told Sanyori. "And I suspect those attitudes are just one example of our fundamental incompatibility." She sighed. "If I must be alone to the end of my days, so be it. Better that than a contentious life. I've had quite enough of strife."

Sanyori rose, clapping like a master of ceremonies and smoothing over the moment's tension with affected pomp. His homey chamber suddenly felt like a stage in an amphitheater.

"Well, we know where we stand and don't have that question hanging over us. We should be grateful, I suppose. What say I give you a tour of the rest of the settlement?"

Aware of a lingering awkwardness that was far from resolved, the two women followed him to the butte's northern side, which descended in a series of grassy terraces to the banks of a small river where a dozen Ruhselenes spear-fished. The grasslands on the farther side were lusher; more verdant hills rose behind them.

"This originates from Lake Banyomeer," Sanyori said. "You can just make out its blue spread out there to the north. The Rupture spilled it like a teacup. Between it and us lie the Roana Hills. Beautiful territory, indeed. South of here... Most of that region was flooded during the Rupture. It was completely submerged. But the water receded after a year or so. Your old homeland...

"Don't expect to discover much left of the Hive," he told Esperidi. "I've done a bit of distant scrying. I did glimpse the network of caves that filled the canyon north of Sequana Hive, though."

"That doesn't surprise me," Esperidi said. "Aramoye Caverns was created much earlier, built upon existing recesses when our knowledge of *Sacred Timbre* was at its apex. Sequana Hive was created as we entered an era of decadence."

"I never understood why your people did it in the first place," Ashangtu said. "Don't mistake me: That promontory overlooking the sea is gorgeous. But the risk..."

"That was the Cordonne's rallying cry once we'd defeated Sanjesota," Esperidi said. She was thinking of Papa. "We wouldn't cede the aboveground world to the primitives anymore. We would not hide in caves. Ophia was ours. We were meant to be its caretakers. And that's true, but it's true of *all* peoples. The City Mothers and Fathers really meant that *we Shaini* were destined to rule. Even Sequana fell under the pall of that belief."

These reflections made her momentarily wistful. "When I was young, I could say the name 'Ophia' and believe I was referring to the whole world. But I had only really meant the realm of the Shaini and our Hives. I think this was true for most of our people. The world beyond the borders of our outermost settlements was always shunned. It was a land of barbarism and peril."

"And now it is our home," Ashangtu growled.

The waterway became more a part of the land's body along its eastern branch, dividing around increasingly frequent sandbars. The Ruhselenes in that area crossed back and forth at a place where the water was only ankle deep. Some sat cross-legged in the shallows.

Sanyori led the two Shaini farther down to where the waters parted around a jungled eyot thickly draped with moss. The river was some thirty feet wide and appeared deeper here. The few males on the tiny islet had been obliged to swim there while holding their spears in their teeth. Sanyori nodded towards some who were trying to catch fish with their bare hands, occasionally laughing at the comical results. That portion of the river was fenced by rows of fang-shaped rocks, creating a veritable fish trap.

"Now, we must speak of the Meet at the stone circle of Jamurada!" Sanyori clapped his hands like he had in the dining hall. "Your timing is propitious. The spring equinox is nearly upon us, and invitations have already been sent."

"Messengers?" Ashangtu asked.

"Some," Sanyori said. "It's not so safe anymore, between Tumoset's growing power, Shetain reestablishing itself, and Brinstead going mad with superstition. But I haven't forgotten the lessons of our exodus from Farsilance. I've approached the leaders of many tribes and clans in shared dreams.

"The risk, of course, is that congregations can attract unwelcome eyes and ears. My dreams, they have been shadowy on that matter. Likely, my fears make them so.

Nevertheless, I think that this year, we should prepare for uninvited guests."

Then, as if to diffuse the specter of dread he'd conjured, the man pointed towards the fishers and remarked: "I taught them how to fashion better clothes. Many didn't want to wear such garments at first, though."

"Maybe they worried they'd be impersonating their god." As soon as the words escaped her, Esperidi regretted them. She was still grappling with the *timbre* of servility she felt, the way the Ruhselene watched Sanyori like he was something other than human.

She realized that she, too, was eager for the Meet. This morning's conversations had opened her mind to a host of troubling speculations.

"We needed beings to worship once," Sanyori reminded her. "Finally, we outgrew that, realizing we are self-created beings. But would we ever have reached that realization without leaning on our gods for a while?"

"Careful you don't invite more projections than you can bear," Esperidi said. "We can't *teach* them self-knowledge. We can help them recognize the beliefs governing their minds, but they must take the subsequent steps themselves.

"Imagine that we taught some of *Sacred Timbre*'s uses to the Ruhselene so that they could defend themselves. Now, Lalai is a woman of stout heart. She reveres Ophia. But one of her descendants may not be so benevolent. They might use it to conquer the other tribes. How could we bear such a legacy, knowing we helped birth another Sanjesota or Tumoset?"

"What if the Ruhselene insist on paying me homage whether I wish it or not?" Sanyori countered. "What if there's no way I can dissuade them?"

Esperidi was silent, unable to meet his inquiry. She thought she'd reconciled herself to a harsh reality: that she would never experience intimate love. Then, upon this morning, she'd been taunted by the promise of that seemingly impossible dream only to see it snatched away.

A heart crushed by hope, indeed!

She glanced across the river again. Several Ruhselene crouched by the cooled remains of a fire on the little islet and took turns painting designs on each other's faces with dabs of ash.

"I know now that all beings are destined to awaken." She waved towards the primitives, the objects of her fragile hopes. "That's why their independence is so crucial. They must learn how to experience Sorsajna from within—and, feeling that, realize there is no 'without.' The divine fire they perceive in you is a light that never left their breast."

Galvanized by newborn understanding, she added:. "We could help them without threatening their autonomy. In this way, we might atone for the destruction our race wrought."

Sanyori measured her resolve. "You'll have your opportunity to present them with such a vision. Will you join us in the Meet?"

Aware of Ashangtu's eyes on her, Esperidi slowly nodded. "I will be there."

The two women retired early that night. The day's conflicts had wearied Esperidi almost as much as the journey that'd brought her here. If Sanyori guessed at her discomfiture, he was diplomatic enough not to comment on it. He led her and Ashangtu to a chamber adjacent to his where three beds were laid with embroidered quilts.

"I never abandoned the hope that I might find myself in the company of peers again," he explained.

Esperidi tried to convey her complex gratitude with her eyes. She was distracted; her thoughts lingered on the

Oskwai—the Ruhselene. *Now that it's come to it, I don't know how to appeal to these people. I will have to wait until I again enter Beyond Veil-Time, where they can know the heart of my intent, and I can know theirs.*

Nevertheless, she was aware of Sanyori's presence in the other bedroom and the roiling of her unresolved conflicts, and she tossed on the feather mattress for hours before finally succumbing to sleep.

An Oskwai woman brought her food and drink on a rush-woven platter. She was clearly pregnant, though this didn't noticeably hamper her movements. She was as lithe and supple as any of her kindred.

With the awareness that her Sophryne training had instilled in her, Esperidi realized she was dreaming. As if sensing her sudden awareness and regard, Lalai's eyes met hers and held them momentarily.

Sanyori and I keep saying they're the future, Esperidi thought, *but those are the eyes of Now.*

Most of their ensuing communications consisted of wordless sensations translated into stories through internal alchemy. Esperidi was frightened by much of what she perceived. Ruhselene consciousness was steeped in fear, mostly revolving around predators, strangers, disease, and the prospect of starvation and more cataclysms. Thus, they'd entered this alliance with Sanyori willingly, knowing his arts and shelters could buttress them against the dangers and uncertainties of their post-Rupture world.

But Esperidi felt how they were burdened with less past than she was. Her Sophryne disciplines strove to keep her mind rooted in the present moment. Ruhselenes did this instinctively.

Who's really the teacher here?

Ever-shifting landscapes grew around her and Lalai, mirroring their every thought, whether pronounced or subtle, as if the dream was a canvas that each took a hand in painting. They constantly reordered their palettes to reflect their inner minds more faithfully.

Esperidi's creations were often lofty: clouds, minarets, and flocks of birds flying in formation. These symbols expressed the ideals that sustained her: her vision for New Ophia.

Lalai's psychic paintings were fraught with peril and uncertainty. Bears, wolves, and mountain cats prowled; storms erupted without warning; people and animals languished in the mud beneath the pall of various illnesses. The longer she remained in proximity to Lalai, the more Esperidi grew familiar with the mental atmosphere within which the woman moved. Ophia often seemed severe to the Ruhselene, unforgiving of weakness or pain. It was stingy with its blessings and exuberant in its demands. Swept along by the currents of Lalai's inner world, Esperidi witnessed the haunted look of a mother who, noticing ripples through tall grass, imagines her child hanging from a wolf's mouth or bloating a serpent's gullet.

But the dream's atmosphere was not entirely darkened by these threats. Lalai, though wary and defensive, felt most alive when confronting them. She experienced her potency. Love was also a strong component of the woman's thoughts; it bathed the fields and valleys with gentle pink lambency.

And her people understood that consciousness survived physical death. That awareness had taught them the joy and importance of play.

Lalai's relationship with mortality was fundamentally different from Esperidi's. Had she even been impacted by the

Rupture in any fundamental way? When the possibility of death lurked behind every tree and boulder, did it really matter whether it struck in the form of a snakebite or a deluge?

The demands of the hunt had shaped every dimension of their physical province. They could sleep in a squat, identify fish by their splashes, and breastfeed on the run.

Besides, Sanyori could feel the *timbre* of many impending threats and warn the Ruhselene. For that, they were understandably grateful and willing to give him some limited allegiance.

What instruction was needed? The knowledge was instinctive.

Or perhaps love lies behind all instinct.

Esperidi began to wonder whether she sought to "awaken" the Ruhselene woman out of simple arrogance. This sense was sharpened by Lalai's first direct question.

"Why do you pursue me? Is it because you're jealous? I saw the look in your eyes when I served you in the tower."

What are my motives here?

The challenge made Esperidi's dream universe tilt and wobble. First, her mind tried to rally defenses. "This is about *your* liberation! Own your light; it doesn't belong to him!"

But she knew this was not the pertinent point. Unexamined prejudices jostled the vessel carrying her through this dream.

Sanyori is a Shaini; therefore, he must be with another Shaini.

I must be the voice that advocates for the Ruhselene because they can't speak for themselves. A Shaini's reality lies beyond their ken.

Fortunately, a wiser part of Esperidi knew she was

not simply the sum of her prejudices. She was warmed by self-compassion. Everything she'd sought to achieve—in Farsilane, the Savwain Desert, and now in Pedragira—had been inspired by underlying altruism, even if her means were sometimes shortsighted. Ultimately, Esperidi wanted all beings—including herself—to realize their promise.

A flicker of springtime streams passed through Lalai's laughter. Her question about jealousy was, in itself, a symptom of her internal awakening. She questioned the dynamics underlying love, sexuality, possessiveness, and freedom as her people understood these concepts.

Eventually, following Lalai's *timbre* through the dream environment became too challenging for Esperidi—the Ruhselene woman was in a constant state of transition, of *becoming*—and she forsook the struggle.

She opened her eyes to Ashangtu's shadow, leaning over her bed.

"You tossed and groaned so much," the woman said, "I feared you'd taken ill." Fighting palpable inner uncertainties, she laid her hand against Esperidi's forehead. "You don't seem hot—"

"It was just a dream."

"A dream?" Ashangtu's dubious expression was so comical that Esperidi almost laughed. "Would you care to describe this 'dream'?"

"If I do, will you explain why you look like you find the idea so preposterous?"

"Fair enough. But you first."

Bemused but comforted by her friend's proximity, Esperidi related all the details she could recall of her encounter with Lalai and her internal struggles.

"Now it's your turn," she said. "Why're you so incredulous?"

Ashangtu folded her arms across her chest as if guarding her heart from deception. "You realize you often snore, yes?"

"All right..."

"Well, you fell asleep, and amid all that moaning and groaning, you snored maybe five or six times. Then you opened your eyes again. I thought you'd fallen into a fever. But you attribute it to some epical dream you had between two strikes of a gong."

Esperidi chuckled with the force of her sudden comprehension.

"Haven't I told you, many times, that when we dream, we step outside the framework of Time?"

Scarcely visible in the dimly moonlit chamber, Ashangtu's lips formed a wordless "Ohhh."

"Anyhow, I have no heart to explore it right now," Esperidi said.

"Oh, so now it's the teacher playing the fool," Ashangtu said.

"What do you mean?"

"None of it is a big mystery to *me*," Ashangtu said. "You haven't been aware of it—or you're just unwilling to examine it. These hidden expectations you've nurtured... You came to this place hoping to find not just another Shaini but a partner. Loneliness and loss have compromised your sense of reality. I get that. You wove fantasies around Sanyori before even meeting him."

Esperidi, still fresh from her dream, pondered her lucid journeys and the heart-warm wonder they stirred in her, how she would awaken feeling that all things were possible. Then, invariably, she would try to grope with her all-too-human hands, which were never formed to hold such contact.

"That's the heart of my difficulty, isn't it?" she

acknowledged. "I want to question Sanyori more about what he's doing with the Ruhselene, but I don't know how far I trust myself. What are my real motives?"

There were some wounds that her journeys and visions could not assuage.

"I consciously chose to be a healer in Ophia, but now I question whether I've truly healed myself. I believe in the integrity of the Sophryne way. But I'm terrified—half-trained as I am—of the thought of leading anyone astray. More people learning from me means my misconceptions can *deceive* more people."

Ashangtu's mental footing was undisturbed. "How could anyone be led astray by self-awareness and responsibility?"

"Well, any teaching can become distorted...."

"That's not your fault!"

"I am liable if I'm doing it all in response to some unanswered need within myself," Esperidi said.

"The need for closeness," Ashangtu suggested. "Satisfying your desires—a young woman who *wants*—"

"Yes! I've conversed with beings from countless places and eras as I journeyed across the Partition," Esperidi said. "But I can neither touch nor be touched by such beings. Now, I have to accept that a desire for intimacy lured me to Pedragira. I was goaded by loneliness. I have to relinquish that fantasy of partnership and union—at least for now. And my heart is sore and heavy."

Contemplating such matters in the dead of night, with naught to distract her mind save for the stars overhead and owl calls and peepers, Esperidi was confronted by fantasies that made her flush. She jumped out of bed and began pacing. "Ah! Shiya-coqui told me that I shirked the Sophryne Way because I worried it would condemn me to a life of loneliness. But that's exactly what's happening!"

"It isn't just about being a Sophryne," Ashangtu said. "There aren't many of us left. Maybe Sanyori is just being practical. What other opportunities have we? Most of the few surviving Shaini we've heard about are aligned with Shetain."

Then Esperidi gasped as the woman grabbed her shoulder and halted her in mid-stride. Ashangtu leaned in with rare tenderness.

"I know it wouldn't be the ideal solution you're looking for," she whispered, "but I'm here. We do have each other."

Esperidi felt her body pressed close, and for a moment, her mind swarmed with fantasies, and her body teetered on a half-formed "yes!"

...curling up beneath the blankets that Sanyori had given them... held tightly with all the passion the woman possessed—even if nothing else happened—

But she couldn't sustain the fantasy for very long. She was forced to acknowledge that Ashangtu's only real appeal was that she was close at hand. Otherwise, the Lanorean woman left Esperidi cool. Aloofness and caustic armor did not moisten her. She wanted someone eager to reach her inner sanctum, someone with whom she could divulge its secrets.

She shook as the realization penetrated her. She'd never considered the matter very deeply before; she'd never been in a situation wherein she *had* to clarify her feelings.

"It... doesn't work that way for me, Ashangtu," she breathed, trying to draw away without making it seem like she was repulsed. "I think I only respond that way to men."

That could just be her natural inclination, of course. But as she pondered the idea in this half-conscious twilight hour, Esperidi wondered whether her particular life situation, with her Papa always close at hand and yet, in his way, as aloof as Ashangtu, had made her crave the idea of surrendering to a man both forceful and responsive. Someone who *wanted* to know her and plumb her depths.

Suddenly, the full momentum of the moment caught up with her, and she was seized by panic. "Ashangtu! You won't... pull away from me now, will you? We have been companions, and I truly care for you—"

Ashangtu was still shaking her head and rolling her eyes as she returned to bed and pulled the covers over herself.

"You Sequanans! You're not nearly as bad as the Shetains, I'll grant you that. But you get awfully stuck in the muck about these sorts of things!"

Esperidi wondered how she could ever sleep again amid the room's atmosphere, thick with so many unnamed insecurities. She sighed audibly when Ashangtu spoke again.

"What do you know about the Rainbow Wars?"

Though the subject made her uneasy, Esperidi was grateful for any conversation. "Shiya-coqui told me a little about it. Before that, I didn't really want to know. The first time Shainis slaughtered each other en masse? It doesn't make for pleasant reading."

"But what did she tell you?"

"Just the legend... Shaini entered Ophia via the Rainbow Bridge, and then arguments erupted around where, exactly, that rainbow had touched the ground. Each side wanted to declare different lands sacred."

"That argument was a pretext," Ashangtu said. "Most of the conflicts in our early history revolved around sexuality and all the possessiveness and attachment that goes along with it. The first Shaini myths tried to grapple with all that.

"It was a huge shock, at first, moving out of Oneness."

Esperidi nodded at this reprisal of her earlier meditations. Shiya-coqui, too, had told her that early Shaini history was sexual history, characterized by different experiments that various clans undertook as they wrestled with the dilemma.

"That's how we split into Hives," she said, fighting a yawn. "That's when Shetain began preaching celibacy."

"And Helwen proclaimed orgiastic celebrations," Ashangtu said. "Let's re-create Oneness in the flesh. And I need to clarify one thing." Her tone sharpened. "Shetain didn't preach *celibacy*. They preached that sex was debasing, an act disdained by their new god, Toh. That's a gaping distinction."

Ashangtu vaguely waved to indicate Pedragira's inhabitants. "There's no way you could describe this to an Oskwai. And it's hard for even us to understand. But the first Shaini were born much more aware of their origins. That seed of silent knowledge about their nature and identity was potent. The sense of Oneness... It was a sore challenge, sacrificing that. And before long—"

🌿🌿

Lalai skirted along the edge of a pine forest with a dozen Ruhselenes. The sky was bleak. The wind carried hints of oncoming winter.

Where are we? The Sendhi waste?

This question—the thought itself and the act of witnessing it unfold—made Esperidi recognize her true situation.

I revisit a dream, but it is not the same. But then, how could it be? I am not the same dreamer as before. Also, there is another mind contributing to the panorama.

Instinctively, she glanced down at her hands to verify this truth. They constantly fluctuated, shrinking or expanding as if with indrawn and outdrawn breaths. She turned them over. The purple dye she'd applied to her nails in waking was still there.

Esperidi hovered at the verges of the party's sight, wondering how she could get Lalai alone. Then, a name floated into her consciousness.

She whispered "Suskhana" several times, watching the wind carry the vibrant vowels to the woman's ears.

Lalai, overcome with curiosity, turned to follow the sounds to their source. Her companions, forgotten, dissipated like mist from the dreamscape. The woman stopped within a pace of Esperidi and crouched, eyes wide with unabashed curiosity and wonder.

The art of conscious dreaming was the most demanding discipline Esperidi knew. It was seldom forgiving of mental or emotional ambiguity. Psychic atmospheres were wild, sometimes savage, storms. Distinguishing their patterns was an art akin to mariners reading sea currents and sky portents. Esperidi could only navigate that turbulence if she clarified internal conflicts. Her mind had to be calm—and her heart eager.

Shift.

She and Lalai stood by Pedragira's tilled, autumnal gardens. "Why do you all walk barefoot?" Esperidi asked. Then, guided by an intuition she didn't logically comprehend—and realizing it was spring in the waking world—she added: "Is it because of the harvest?"

Lalai smiled. "Indeed. Ophia gives birth, so we must tread softly upon Her body."

Communication within a dream was simple and direct; language and other mental constructs formed few barriers. A significant portion of it was telepathic. One's intent was simply *known* to the other. Esperidi had learned to rely upon this for dream interactions with beings on the other side of the world (or on other worlds) whose waking language was utterly foreign to her.

Thus, it didn't shock her when Lalai "spoke" without moving her lips. "I, too, have vivid dreams. I ache throughout my days because those dreams call me to reflect their glimmer, but I do not know how to do this. I yearn to express things that there are no words for."

Her dreams reminded her of a time when animals and humankind conversed. Esperidi witnessed this as a panorama unfolding before her like an Ambrosine play, where the actors sought the beasts to learn the uses of plants and healing arts.

The Ruhselene can't be content as merely instinctive creatures, she realized, *yet they can't articulate the new freedoms they sense. They are humans caught between two worlds. They behold a new realm of choices, yet don't fully understand "choice."*

"The tribe has named you Lalai," Esperidi said, "but now I feel how this name does not conform to your idea of yourself. I'm unsure what to call you."

The entire landscape was diaphanous, and emotional undertones bled through its fabric like sunshine and moon glow streamers.

"You said it already. I want to be Suskhana," Lalai sent.

Esperidi quivered as the name's deeper import penetrated her. Could it possibly be coincidental? "Suskhana" was derived from the ancient Shaini tongue: It referred to someone who hunted on the far side of the Partition: a dream stalker.

"Dream-stalker," Suskhana echoed. "Like you."

That statement carried an unmistakable *timbre* of pride. Esperidi suddenly regretted every moment she'd wasted projecting jealousy toward this woman. *She sees what I do here and wants to emulate it!* She felt obliged to repay that sweetness and generosity somehow.

"I want to tell you some things you may not know about my people, the Shaini," she said. "Our lifespans are longer than yours: That's one obvious difference. We are... not as deeply rooted to Ophia as your kind. Part of our being exists always in a more subtle dimension. But we must eat, drink, strive, love, and eventually grow old as you do."

Esperidi couldn't discern how much of her monologue the woman could receive and organize according to her native storehouse of symbols. The contours of Suskhana's mind were still exotic.

"So you identify yourself with that sound: Suskhana. That can be your name henceforth if you choose. Leastways, that's what I will call you.

"And I tell you now that there are many ways in which sound manifests. One can be heard with our ears." Esperidi used her mouth to repeat Suskhana's name, making it audible. "Another can only be felt using inner senses. It embodies something of the essence of that which is named. It is why most beings know their names before they can say them. This is the art that Sanyori drew upon to build Pedragira Hive."

Utilizing dream matter to flesh out her concepts, she staged a demonstration:

"This *timbre* embodies learning...

"This one, growth...

"... enhancement...

"... discovery"...

"My people thought they'd perhaps opened the doors to an age of innocence again when they discovered *Sacred Timbre*. Ophian civilization revolved around it. It permeated every part of our lives. Even children were taught how to recognize the distinctive *timbres*." Esperidi motioned as if pinching the air. "'Mental and emotional qualities birth these inner tones and determine their forms. They manifest all physical phenomena. With their insight into the core nature of reality, the Shaini created a civilization of wonders."

She paused a moment to rehearse how to proceed, and that question conjured Shiya-coqui's voice from years earlier.

Do you prefer if we call it the kiln, the garden, or the cocoon?

"When you learn to perceive these inner sounds, you'll translate them into symbols you can understand. They may not strike your ears as 'sound' at all. Instead, you might see a gentle waterfall and feel a sense of peace.

"But consider the dangers of swift manifestation! Intense self-awareness is required to use *Sacred Timbre* wisely. Anger, fear, jealousy, resentment, the desire to dominate others... these things can materialize as easily as anything we *want* to create. The invisible forces of life can only truly be respected if we understand the inner mechanisms through which they work. We must be sensitive to those forces. And sensitivity and discernment had grown decadent in the age preceding the Rupture. That's why, more and more, we Shaini witnessed *Sacred Timbre*'s destructive side.

"But if you hearken to that one word of caution, I can help you to become fluent in this inner language."

Now, Lalai-Suskhana was alight with eagerness and wonder, sensing the new worlds opening up before her. She clutched that awareness to her breast and bounded away, eager to explore the reaches of this new inspiration. And Esperidi lost her.

※ ※

Esperidi was relieved to see the Ruhselenes, by and large,

beginning to accept her. They let her join in their tasks, breaking and tilling the ground, mixing in rich, composted loam, and digging clay from the river's basin to bake into bricks for hearths, baths, and to line the water and sewage systems Sanyori had conceived. Traditional roles prevalent in other parts of Ophia had not taken hold in Pedragira. Males sewed clothing with bone awls alongside females. Hunting parties were equally divided.

Suskhana disappeared into the prairie, and after a few days, even Sanyori seemed troubled, especially as the time of the Meet drew near. Esperidi suspected that her dream interactions with the Ruhselene woman had jolted her into deeper self-awareness, and she'd gone off alone to try and assimilate that unprecedented experience.

When Suskhana finally returned to Pedragira, she remained aloof, laboring alone. Esperidi surreptitiously watched as the woman continuously worked with a section of birch trunk and a strip of goat rawhide. If other Ruhselenes cast Suskhana inquisitive glances, they didn't draw near to examine her handiwork. Their sounds and movements suggested disquiet, uncertainty, and wariness in the face of something they didn't understand.

Suskhana awaited her tribe the following evening as they returned from hunting and fishing along the Banyomeer River. They kindled a fire in a pit a short distance from the top of the gardens and formed a ring around her.

The hunt had taught them the power of a closed circle.

Ripples of excitement shook the gathering as Suskhana held aloft a drum she had fashioned. Many of her kindred reacted to the sight with wariness and suspicion. Some visibly flinched. What was this unknown witchery? They'd heard stories of Sendhi and Manitoh Singing Chiefs who used drums to converse with fell spirits.

Suskhana ignored their various reactions. She sat cross-legged on the ground, set the drum between her legs, and started thumping on it with her open palms.

The Ruhselenes were quickly bewitched by the sound. Some of them, already squatting, bounced on the balls of their feet. Suskhana's rapture was palpable. She'd seized upon the idea—nurtured in dreams shared with Esperidi—that her inner self could be expressed. She could discover the sounds to articulate what she felt, the sounds appropriate for the things named and the perceiver of those things. Self-awareness had been strengthened within her, and now it required a voice.

So Suskhana sang.

The joy within her song needed no justification. It was an innate characteristic of Sorsajna, the source of life, and reverberated within every particle of her being.

Its words disclosed their meaning to Esperidi's inner senses:

"It is safe to awaken," the flowers say
My home and thought-body are one
My heart-soul hums
Lands and people echo
My essence joins Sorsajna
See! It names me anew!
Lalai in daylight,
Suskhana in twilight
Dreams birth all landscapes
and horizons
And there go my thoughts: See them growing
Reminding me of promises made to myself
Sorsajna, Suskhana, and Lalai are one!

Sanyori's eyes flickered between the woman he'd

known as Lalai, in her ecstasy, and the other Ruhselenes with their cries of assent. Some seemed to intuit the song's meaning: they joined in as if from long familiarity with its refrains.

Esperidi, standing beside him outside their circle, turned to the man and smiled mischievously. She had to shout over the Ruhselenes' clamor. "Perhaps she'll no longer be a docile mate after this, but I'll wager she'll be a more inventive one!"

"Assuming she'll still have me!" Sanyori returned.

"Through their dreams, they learn the language of their souls," Esperidi said. "I was merely the catalyst for something inevitable. We must remember that all consciousness seeks to expand its reach, San. Do you not want to nurture the potential that we see in them?"

"Have you glimpsed... Do you know where this all might lead?"

"Consider their name."

"Ruhselene?"

"Yes—Ancient Children. But also, you heard what Lalai sang. She calls herself Suskhana now. Dream Stalker. She dreamed it. See how they respond to her! I suspect they will ask her to lead them from this day forth. The Ruhselene are fresh to the world, in a way, yet they're aware of its heights and abysses. And they know their place within the cycle of life. Maybe they will have the wisdom to prevail where our kind could not.

"Indeed, we are all moving forward now into unprecedented futures."

Esperidi nodded toward the audience. Suskhana was winding down her song.

"What makes us more than instinctive creatures, San, is not our architecture or mathematics or codes of laws... not even our language. And by 'us,' I mean every Oskwai as much as every Shaini. What distinguishes us all is our capacity to dream."

Sundered Roads

Wakeen opened his eyes to a bark roof held aloft by arched wooden poles. It was loosely woven with reeds and rushes and appeared higher than he could reach were he standing. A profusion of litter cluttered the muddy floor—animal bones, crude tools, a hatchet, and wood shavings—confirming his impression that this shelter was hastily constructed. Indeed, he guessed the builders had been anxious to flee the place as soon as their work was completed. But furs cushioned his back, and a slim measure of warmth and light emanated from a burning brazier upon a wooden tripod in the wigwam's center.

"That thick pole in the middle... the top of it is carved to look like a rattlesnake's tail. I think they meant to pay homage to you and your friend."

Wakeen glanced to where Jemcay stood by the wigwam's doorway. Dire recollections of the previous night's events began to swamp him, and he focused on her face to stave off the memories.

Noting the intensity of his regard, she approached, bent beside him, and offered him a waterskin.

"There's a creek nearby where the water flows fresh," she said. "These Oskwai built a fishery there where they trap catfish and pike. They don't have much food, but they mean to cook what's available to honor us."

Wakeen swiped a hand. "I don't want anyone starving on my account. We should tell them to stop."

"I tried," Jemcay said. "I don't think there's any way to convince them not to revere the Snake Man. I sense that the Shetain priesthood has only had a passing influence on this community. They'd been exposed to the Sacred Writ. But they gravitate more towards—"

"Sarpienta," Wakeen groaned. "He who lives within Ophia. Toh rules with laws and guilt. His mouthpieces use the rhetoric of shame. It's a kind of hypnotism. Such tactics will never be as persuasive to these nature children as old Grandfather Serpent's tremors beneath—"

He cut off as Jemcay bent close and, with her other hand, offered him a lukewarm mug made of baked clay. The aroma of the liquid inside was pleasant but strong enough to sting his nostrils.

"This is Puli, their favorite intoxicant," she said. "Since my constant chiding failed to loosen you, I thought perhaps strong drink might do the trick." She chuckled. "And lest you envy me for my time outside this tent... I spent the morning burning leeches off my thighs after taking a swim and the rest of the day repelling mosquitoes." Her smile ventured towards a leer. "I notice you've enjoyed my aroma. That is just for you. I exude a much different scent for insects that covet my blood."

Wakeen stared down at his chest. "I'm not used to a woman—"

"Being so forward?" She knelt beside him, and her tone softened. "Perhaps you don't realize the appeal of a man with a big heart who strives so much to hide it. Some women welcome such a challenge."

Embarrassed, Wakeen accepted the mug and considered its dark amber contents. He recalled how beverages such as this had been demonized by the priesthood he'd grown up in.

"It'll be another slap in Father's face," he decided—and sipped.

"They brew it from agave plants," Jemcay said, "which were plentiful in the more arid region they came from. Apparently, they enjoyed it. They hauled sacks of it when they migrated."

"Who can blame them?" Wakeen said. "If I had to exist in this lightless swamp day after day, picking leeches and swatting flies, with white-skinned zealots on one side of the border and the shadow of Shetain on the other, I'd be drinking myself senseless, too. But are you talking about the Savwain Desert?"

"No, someplace south of here," Jemcay said. "I never traveled farther than this, so I only have a vague idea of what kind of land was there before the Rupture. Much of it was under waves for a year or more, and the salt ruined the soil. They found a cave refuge there for a time, not far from the shore, where they could fish. But eventually, one of Shetain's priests found them and told them that the place was an abomination, that a curse would follow their people for generations if they stayed."

She reflected for a moment. "The more they talked about it, the more it sounded like the ruins of a Shaini Hive."

"Well, we can rule out Sequestra," Wakeen said. "That's the Hive Father claimed and refashioned into the Canted Citadel. This place–"

"Fetu Swamp," Jemcay said. "That's what they've named it."

"Well, Fetu Swamp is a drowned portion of Sequestra Forest." Wakeen delved into the geography he'd gleaned from Shetain's library. "Sequana, maybe? That lay along the southern shore."

"That shore extends many more miles now," Jemcay

said. "A lifeless tract of sand, stones, and rotting ocean life."

Wakeen took another pull of Puli and winced his appreciation. Grunting, he stared down at his now half-empty mug. He realized he had decided to get drunk. "Is there more of this?"

"It seems to be the one thing that the Junsa have in plenty," Jemcay said. "And they're prepared to offer us the best from their stores. But–" She posed the question delicately. "Don't you want to meet our hosts and thank them?"

Wakeen grimaced, recalling the two Junsas abandoned at the ziggurat by their kin. He momentarily wondered whether he'd be able to keep his drink down. For Jemcay's sake, he blunted the edges of his rage.

"Why don't you tell me what you've learned? Then I'll decide."

Jemcay had to compete with the sounds of Junsa frolicking. Between the shadows cast on the tent tarp and a nearby river bank, the air was full of their commotion as they discharged their evening energies: shouting, laughing, arguing, and splashing.

"Shamarai is the chief of this Jaguar tribe. In another tribe, he probably would've been called Singing Chief. He earned the Junsas' trust by warning them when storms would come. He knew to follow the movements of the animals. When the herds sought higher ground, he understood that the valley or plain was no longer safe.

"So Shamarai's reputation spread, and other tribes peacefully allied with the Jaguar. I think they all loosely refer to themselves as the Snake People now. But they grew weary of constant flight. Some asked whether these upheavals might be appeased. They began listening to the priests, like Konatep, who told them that Toh sent the Rupture. The people asked, 'What have we done to deserve this wrath?

How can we make amends?'"

"And let me guess," Wakeen fumed. "Konatep told the Oskwai that Toh—this capricious god of wrath, a god that plays favorites and keeps score—could be placated with blood."

"He said that Toh is easily displeased and hard to placate," Jemcay acknowledged. Then, her lip curled around another recollection. "These Junsa, it's said they had some contact with the folk of Sequana near the southern ocean and the forest people of her sister Hive, Sequestra. Before they were enslaved. The Shaini of Sequestra Hive even befriended them in their furtive way, teaching them things, trading with them.

"But Sequestra Hive is now no more, like you said. And when the pale settlers arrived on the ships, along with the remnants of Shetain, they drove the Junsa out of the surviving woodland. I've learned this much since we've been here. They were forced into flooded places like this. They learned to fish and forage. Meanwhile, sickness killed many of them. The Rupture has poisoned much of the land and water."

"I'd hoped they'd break free of Shetain's yoke after the storms," Wakeen said, voicing his core anger and disappointment. "Men and women should not live under such bondage of fear."

"Their devotion has only deepened since. After a blanket of ash and dust blotted out the sun... cast Ophia into night... and then Kawli Rainforest beheld something it never had in their history when the snows fell. It couldn't be Sarpienta's doing, right? He dwells within Ophia. The ground's tremors are his movements."

"Right," Wakeen muttered, catching the trail of her logic. "They must've asked what happened to the sky, the loss of the sun and moon. Surely, those were signs of Toh's displeasure. Maybe they were being punished for their lack of faith and should have heeded my father's teachings better. That's how they'd interpret it."

Jemcay paced for a while, wrestling with some inner deliberation. Then she straightened with sudden resolve. "We should lead all the Oskwai into the refuge, to what's left of Elmicora. The Sendhi in the north. These Junsa. Anyone we can find."

Wakeen shrugged. "Much of it was destroyed."

"Farsilane was destroyed, but its Great Central Pyramid still stands. And we know that many of the passages that connected Kublai Hive, up in the snowy wastes, to Mangoyen are intact."

Wakeen nodded. "It would be a start. A faint hope. But we are far from Mangoyen. And what you've told me of Helwen... that's the first I've heard of any part of old Elmicora left intact aside from the remnants of Shetain." He scrutinized her and posed the question softly. "Jemcay, how many of your folk survived?"

The woman closed her eyes and began to pace again. "A few score," she said finally. She waved outside the wigwam walls. "We number fewer than this tribe."

"It will be hard for anyone to search for us in this swampland," Wakeen considered. "You could make your way back to Helwen"

"But traveling north would bring us close to the Conhuera Mountains," Jemcay pointed out.

"Yes. Those heights are riddled with bandit encampments now," Wakeen acknowledged. "And to avoid the mountains, one must contest the Kawli."

"Not all those who came over on the ships wanted to swear allegiance to Shetain, apparently."

Wakeen barked a mirthless laugh. "That's the narrative Shetain feeds the survivors. It's what my father and his priesthood want them to believe. Trust me, it's a mutually beneficial arrangement. The bandits make the Oskwai tribes feel endangered, and then they turn to Shetain for security. What they get is slavery.

"Meanwhile, New Shetain and what we call the Bandit Kingdom both do thriving trade with the Vandrene and the Sendhi. Believe me, Jemcay; the priesthood leaves nothing to chance. If profits are being made somewhere, you can be assured they have a hand in it."

"It seems like so much of the Rupture's devastation worked out in Shetain's favor," the woman reflected. "It has deepened everyone's devotion, for one thing."

Instinctively, Wakeen gazed southwards. "That's why the white settlers, the Brinsteaders, are so fanatical. They believe that Toh reached his hand down to shelter them from the Rupture and then guided them safely to these shores. He did so because they are his chosen people."

"It is a dangerous line of thought," Jemcay considered. "To begin believing that any creator would favor one people or even one species over any others..."

"It's easier to sacrifice those whom you believe your god has already rejected," Wakeen said. "But these Junsa did not stumble upon such a belief by happenstance. It was planted and encouraged. My father has been in this game for a long time, and there is no more consummate master of it in all these lands."

With a gently chiding smile, Jemcay said, "What does our Sage Serpent have to say about all this?"

"Hush, woman!" Wakeen snapped. "Do not name such beings blithely. Forces exist beneath Ophia of which you know naught, and none of them are to be trifled with."

Jemcay made an effort to sound contrite. "Your pardon. Again, I err in your august presence. I meant to say I'm curious to know Sarpi's opinion."

Wakeen, encouraged by a *timbre* of sincerity beneath her subtle mockery, replied: "He says that illusions easily fool humans because we trust too much in our eyes. We'd be more discerning if we relied more on our sense of smell and–" He faltered. "Touch."

"Perhaps we should experiment with his idea right now and see if it holds any validity," Jemcay suggested.

Smiling down at Wakeen, she placed two fingers on his eyelids and slowly closed them over. Then she began humming into one of his ears.

Wakeen gasped at the pristine *timbre* that rode along the soft melody and penetrated his inner mind.

"If it is a question of trust," Jemcay whispered, "I could make no clearer a declaration of trust than this. Helwen's *timbre*. I have given you the key to open its gates and all its inner sanctums. I am more bared and vulnerable to you now than if you had already conquered my womanhood."

Wakeen, knowing her intent—and realizing he had already acquiesced to it—offered no protest. Nevertheless, he shuddered when he felt Jemcay's palm against his chest.

"Don't you understand that you shrink from me because you've only ever understood sex as a means of control?"

This idea gave his defenses something to rally around. "Is that not what you tried to do with the Manitoh Chief of Chiefs?"

"I didn't say that I don't understand the method," Jemcay said, "or that I would not avail myself of it if I felt I had no other recourse. But for an adept of Helwen, the kind of sexual control that Shetain practices is child's play. What is the ability to limit a being, weighed alongside the realms of limitless possibility and wonder that can be opened by two flames conjoined?"

"It's not that I don't believe you," Wakeen said. "It's

just that I don't know how to make my emotions obey my mind."

Then he was forced to open his eyes, as her laughter carried such a note of merriment that he had to seek its source.

"I'm well aware of your struggle," Jemcay said. "That's why I brought drink!"

Trying and failing to echo her humor made Wakeen scowl. "I say I cannot make my emotions obey my mind, but now even my mind is besieged—at war with itself. All these thoughts—"

"Let me see if I can guess a few," Jemcay said. "Let's see. 'She is from a permissive Hive, the most permissive in Ophia's history. Therefore, she wants to sleep with me because she wants to sleep with everyone. And even if she did not, even if she wanted me for me, I must resist this because what if—just what if—those stories I grew up with are true? What if I *am* tainted? Won't I just deepen this taint if I give in to pleasure? What if pleasure itself is evil? What if, after crossing this line, I'm never able to hide the horrible truth about myself?'"

She bent closer. "Well, have I hit close to the mark with any of that?"

"Much," Wakeen admitted. "Sadly, there is much more."

"Then let me add another note to that symphony," Jemcay said. "If they number so many, what difference can one more make?" She paused until she noticed the subtle indications of his body language asking her to continue. "'What if I move through this doorway, and it exposes all those lies for what they are?'"

This image found a chink in Wakeen's armor and began to worm its way into his consciousness. Throughout the last year, maybe longer, his dominating passion and obsession had been to escape Shetain at all costs. But he understood, now, that the formative years he'd spent there had taught him to deeply distrust his power, and he would need power if he were ever to be truly free.

As if she'd read his thoughts—and perhaps she had, considering how loudly their *timbres* rang within his own mind—Jemcay said, "If it were not truly a window into empowerment and freedom, then why would your father try so hard to control it among his flock? Sex is the hub of the human wheel, the vehicle through which we can travel to the heart of our being. We can reclaim our center if the union is entered into with trust. And you're a man whom I trust, Wakeen, whom I would give myself to."

For a delicious moment that he wished, ever afterward, he could have preserved in amber, Wakeen basked in the afterglow. His body was sated, filled with yea-saying contentment and gratitude, the likes of which he'd never known. And his soul swelled with plentitude that lifted him far beyond his body's limitations. It evoked from deep within him a sigh like his very cells rejoicing.

But as Jemcay's leg crossed his, her chin nestled against his chest, and he felt her breath, *cold* swept through his being like a sudden blizzard. It was so vicious, so certain in its condemnation, that he feared it could suffocate him. As he lurched to his feet, Jemcay gasped. Wakeen heard pain and startlement in her outcry. But he couldn't face her. He stared at the thin tarp against which shadows of the Oskwai fires played and clutched himself.

The soft swishing of buckskin warned him of her approach. A moment later, Wakeen felt her hand against the small of his bare back, and he stiffened. He had to say something. She deserved that much. But the words froze in his throat. All the warmth he ached so badly to express had been stolen away.

"This was your first time?" Jemcay asked.

He nodded. Even that rudimentary response required effort, but he forced himself further. "Aye—and likely the last, too."

He forced himself to turn, but as his eyes met hers, he wrenched his face towards the ceiling. "It's not something... I'm just not capable of it, Jemcay."

"You're as capable or incapable as you believe, Wakeen."

That drew his gaze, and he saw some severity mingled with the compassion in her eyes. But she laid a gentle hand on his arm. "I would not say that if I didn't know you were ready—or some *part* of you wasn't ready—to hear it."

Wakeen grasped both her shoulders, and for a moment, he didn't know whether it was to draw her into a rough kiss or thrust her away. "Fangs and blackest venom!" he hissed. "I believe I've committed an act of spite against Toh! I don't even *believe* in Toh!"

"You've managed to escape Shetain, but still, you carry its shackles," she said. "But this is something we can remedy."

Wakeen wanted to believe her. At that moment, he might have severed one of his hands to grasp what she suggested in some tangible way. But he could not accept it. The very concept baffled his imagination. He couldn't equate it with anything he'd ever experienced. Who would he be without that ever-present voice of condemnation? He proffered this question to the universe and met with nothing but the silence of the void.

Finally, filled with self-contemptuous thoughts too

severe to tolerate any witnesses, he thrust her away. "Go back to your people," he said. "Be with those who have never known this taint. They're the only ones who can live free of it. Its roots, they reach down into the core of me."

"If you believe that," Jemcay persisted.

Her unwavering kindness left him with no rock to crawl under. Wakeen wanted to curl up in a fetal position. He might have, had he not felt Jemcay's eyes on his back. Kneeling, he dug his fingers into the rush mat, seeking the ground's pulse to steady him, remind him that his very existence was not an affront. But it was too far away. The knit rushes foiled him. He wanted to rend them along with the skin tarp and the totem pole wrought with mistaken piety—anything at hand that could be made to pay for his lost humanity.

No wonder he felt such an affinity for serpents. Ophia had always spoken to him with a forked tongue, condemning his natural grace while extolling the virtues of venom.

Jemcay's words reached him as if across a gulf of worlds. "Why do you torment yourself when there has been no violation? Listen to me! Anchor yourself in my voice! Do I sound like a woman who believes herself wronged?"

The point of reason within Wakeen could understand what she was saying. It recognized the logic of her appeal, but his body rejected it. *He* was wrong, his actions notwithstanding. Malignancy claimed the greater part of his being. He had no right to bring that to another, to touch in that way.

He shot upright as if the ground had jolted him, provoking Jemcay's panicked cry. Wakeen wanted to scream, but once again, the woman's presence inhibited him.

He had to get away—*away!*

He couldn't contain it. He needed an outlet for this rage against his past and the overpowering sense of futility it'd bequeathed upon him. But here, there were no statues of Toh to topple, no tapestries to burn, no chapels to desecrate. His mind flailed about, searching for something that might provide the release that lust had denied him: some tangible, physical embodiment of his revulsion whose destruction wouldn't sink him into deeper shame and remorse.

He could think of only one thing near at hand.

The half-dozen Junsas nearest the wigwam fell back amid scattered cries of alarm as Wakeen emerged, his brow a thunderhead. But then they crouched, spears poised as if against the onslaught of a horde, as starving wolves will do when pride forbids them to concede ground to a grizzly bear.

Wakeen glared at them. "'Hinder me, and I'll call upon the snake!' he shouted, hoping they wouldn't realize he had no heart for such things, even if he knew how to carry out his threat.

Regardless, it was soon obvious to the Junsa that their village was not the object of his rage. The enigmatic man in their midst stalked through thick swamp air full of curious whispers, past family tents where moonlight illuminated the whites of furtive eyes, over a mound of drained ground where, evidenced by markings and statuettes, they returned their dead to Ophia's muck and mire. Wakeen sloshed through an orange, stagnant stream, heedless of water moccasins and alligators, deaf to the low, self-communing gargle of the swamp, as the crude pyramid the Junsa had erected drew into view.

He'd found it instinctively. He had a lifetime's acquaintance with the filthy *timbres* of such places, where good men and women forsook their sense of personal power, attributing it to judgmental and bloodthirsty gods.

Burn, burn, burn!

The mounded edifice began to quake long before

Wakeen reached it. The vehemence engendered by twenty-five years of forced self-denial found its quarry. Waves of force bounded from the Shaini, slapping against the bulwark as if his heart was a catapult. But he realized he could not lay his physical hands upon the object of his fury. His battering psychic force—*Sacred Timbre* run amok—had destabilized the ziggurat's foundations. As a sinkhole widened beneath its feet, the structure tilted to the left like a mockery of New Shetain's Canted Citadel. Concurrently, a portion of it fell away, so its top half resembled a ravaged, zigzagging spire. Unable to bear its misshapen weight, this portion froze at the top of the promontory for a moment that seemed to still the world and then slowly toppled over the steps, nearly effacing them on its way down.

Wakeen didn't know how to rein in the power coursing through him. He couldn't fight the personal apocalypse he raced toward. A part of him welcomed it.

Then Jemcay's voice snatched him back from the edge of the abyss. "Is this how you'll conquer your false guilt, Wakeen? By invoking another Rupture? Do you even recognize the difference between destruction and self-immolation?"

Wakeen felt the *timbre* of concern in her voice, the love that he knew not how to answer or allow into his inner sanctum, and he sagged. The terrible toll of his exertions was rapidly catching up with him. He hadn't felt this exhausted since slaving in the Kawli mines. As the ruins of the ziggurat finally settled—a half-sunk and pummeled knob of stone and mud—he sank to his knees in the spongy grass and wept.

Jemcay caught up with him, but she did not press him. She allowed the silence to linger, merely laying a hand on his shoulder to show that he needed to fear no recrimination from her. Wakeen's heart slowed to a rate more congenial to human rhythms. He drew what seemed like his first breath since his personal tempest tore him from the wigwam.

"You are a good person, Jemcay," he whispered. "Forgive me for having judged you. My life has taught me how to do little else."

"I forgive you gladly, Wakeen," Jemcay said, "if you'll reciprocate that pardon. I regret pushing you to claim more than you were ready to."

But then, noticing that his rigidity did not waver and his eyes made no allowances for hope, she shrank into sorrowful recognition. "But maybe I *should* go. I thought my presence might help liberate you, but it seems to do naught but peel your scabs and smear salt in the wounds."

"I have to leave, too," Wakeen said, dodging her prophecy of imminent pain with pragmatism. "Maybe Sarpi can teach me how to hide. Everyone in the priesthood, all the Inooks, know the face of Jain-Toh's son. I have to find another path." He glanced vaguely westwards, and his pallor, drained of nearly all the flush of life, spoke more eloquently than any words. "I must get as far away from Shetain as I can—scores of leagues if there's enough land left in Ophia to open my way. Perhaps to the Savwain—live among the rest of the freaks!"

Slowly, he grew aware of Sarpi's presence at the mound's perimeter. The snake's forked tongue tasted the air avidly as if the man's extravagant apocalypse had laid a banquet before it.

"But I don't trust myself to choose," Wakeen said. "What little I know I have learned from nature's heart, and it has ostracized me from the only world I was ever familiar with."

Turning towards the edge of the mound, he called: "And so I leave the choice of road to you, my brother! Where you go, I will follow—until some semblance of reason returns to me!"

☙❧

"Well, since the three of us so seldom get the opportunity," Sanyori said, "I thought we might exchange dreams."

Ashangtu, aimlessly wandering the chamber—which she recognized had been modeled after Farsilane's library—stopped before a bookshelf and feigned interest in the titles, going so far as to graze her fingertips along the bindings. She roiled with restless energy. "I'd welcome any distraction at the moment."

But Esperidi sighed heavily. She knew Sanyori was distracted, anticipating the Meet on the morrow and merely making an idle suggestion. "I was hoping for a break from that. Honestly, my dreams of late haven't often been of the relaxing and comforting kind."

"Well, I'd like to offer one," Sanyori said. "It seems I never get to *talk* about dreams unless I'm in the midst of *having* one. These Oskwai—" He waved vaguely in the direction of the river. "They tend to think I'm handing them a sermon or a prophecy."

"You might want to cultivate the habit of calling them Ruhselene," Esperidi said. "And if the *Ruhselene* want prophecy, they're more likely to seek it from Suskhana."

Ashangtu leaned closer to the bookshelf to hide her chuckle. Esperidi had often been terse with the man since her romantic fantasies had been dashed.

Sanyori heard the subtle repudiation, too, but his reaction was empathetic.

"My lady of Sequana, do you not think this is what Shiya-coqui would have wanted us to do? Besides, any omens that might foreshadow what's in store for us at the Circle of Jamurada would be invaluable."

The woman waved a hand, appearing keen on sinking into the indigo flax-woven floor. "Very well."

Sanyori, long schooled in diverting his thoughts so that his performance wouldn't get derailed by an unenthusiastic audience, proceeded as if she'd veritably begged him. "I'll describe last night's foray while it's fresh. It was simple but powerful. I ran straight across the Rudowine Ocean. The waters were choppy. Each time I took a stride, my foot caught the crest of a wave, giving me just enough traction to push myself forward. So I sprinted as if hounds were on my heels until all the shorelines disappeared, and I could see naught but water.

"It was exhilarating! Such an empowered feeling—though I was also aware that if I ever slowed down, I would sink. It was only my speed that kept me aloft."

Esperidi was thoughtful for a long moment. "It's hard to find a richer symbol than the ocean. And that's often the core question, isn't it? When do we skip along its surface, and when do we risk a deeper plunge?"

Ashangtu scoffed aloud. How quickly the ambiance had shifted! Now, she heard notes of subtle condescension, a kind of bourgeois smugness.

Or am I just conjuring echoes of home?

Her eyes pinned Sanyori. "But there's a much simpler explanation, isn't there? You're trying to exceed your limitations, and you fear that if you can't sustain that—or if you ever cease to run beyond those limitations—then you'll sink. You'll become something less than human."

She nodded towards Esperidi. "She does the same thing all the time."

Sanyori's face went blank with surprise momentarily and then transformed into a beam of appreciation. Grinning at Esperidi, he said, "In lieu of Sophryne Masters, we must learn from one another. Sorsajna's boon! That the two of you

393

found each other—"

"If you really think so," Ashangtu called, "then you might want to pay some heed to what I'm actually saying. What happens when you run out of stamina and can't outpace your life anymore? What happens when you discover that you're just as human as the rest of us?"

Sanyori studied her, sensing the *timbre* of personal bitterness underlying her tirade. "Are we still talking about dreams?"

Ashangtu scowled at the books in front of her one last time, stiffened, and then stalked out of the room without glancing toward either of her companions.

Sanyori began to rise from the long table, but Esperidi waved him down. "This isn't about us, San," she said, though her eyes followed Ashangtu's retreating back as if she wished she could find some way to forestall her friend.

Perhaps I have to accept that Ashangtu is an ocean that I can't sprint across, she decided.

A moment later, however, the fur partition was flung aside, and the woman strode back. She glowered as if daring them to comment on her change of heart and then moved aside for Suskhana.

The Ruhselene woman took two long strides into the room and stiffened, her chiseled face flushed and sweating, her spear held crosswise across her chest. Clearly, she'd arrived at a run. Her eyes found Sanyori. "Our people are arrayed along the circle's southern side," she said, "and a handful of Junsa have already come. They camp in Jamurada's eastern shadow. Peace offerings have been exchanged, and vows have been given, but another group comes..."

She paused to process her startlement—or to conceive of a way to describe this unexpected delegation.

"There are maybe half a dozen Pale Faces from the Brinstead territories. I saw them as they began to circle the edge of Mordu, Cleft of Skulls, and hastened here. A Manitoh priest leads them, and at their head is a young woman, fair-haired, in a robe like blue sky."

Suskhana turned at a sharp intake of breath from Ashangtu but then shrugged off the interruption. Shaini were strange folk. Who among the Ruhselene knew how to interpret their reactions? "Perhaps she, too, comes to preach the Sacred Writ. Toh has chosen not to denounce Jamaro but to honor Him as a patron deity, Jain-Toh has said."

The three Shaini understood the reference. Jamaro was worshipped in the Chonnen lands across the sea. Some of the Rupture's survivors had brought over holy relics and effigies for his worship, thinking, at first, that these actions were hidden from Shetain's eyes. But Shetain's Sovereign Priest apparently welcomed this potential "rival" of Toh and encouraged the Brinsteaders to continue their worship.

"Should we welcome them?" Suskhana asked Sanyori.

"I doubt we have a choice," Sanyori said. "Not without bloodshed. Tell me–" A note of trepidation crept into his voice. "Are any in their party dressed differently from the others?"

"Aye," Suskhana said, "four of the Shadowstalkers, the unfeeling ones, their faces like vultures hidden behind brown hoods."

"Inooks," Sanyori breathed. "And four of them. It sounds like this priest is the same one I encountered in a Sendhi longhouse. If so, he'll not remember the meeting fondly." His sigh seemed to expel his last reserves of fortitude. "Well, if nothing else, at least the shadow lengthening over my mind and heart now bears a face."

Rising, he clapped his hands in crowd-rousing fashion. "Our Sophryne training has taught us to dispel shadows! And yet, our lives beneath the Cordonne taught us discretion. And so we must do what we always have done:

feign obedience, offer whatever assurances might appease them, and hope they leave us in peace. Unfortunately, we may now have to withhold knowledge that we would otherwise have shared."

Suskhana patted her spear as if conveying a promise, turned, and ducked under the tarp again. "I will await you there," she called over her shoulder.

"Where is Ashangtu?" Esperidi said.

Sanyori whipped his head about, and then his eyes found the partition on the room's farther side, still rippling as if from a breeze. It opened onto the hallway connecting the guest bedrooms and bathhouses. He raced over, flung it aside, and probed the passageway, but his eyes found nothing but polished basalt.

"Must have gone back to her quarters," he remarked. "She was apparently not pleased by the news."

Esperidi shouldered past him and headed down the hall. She found Ashangtu in their shared bedroom, hastily throwing her few belongings into her leather satchel.

She began speaking without lifting her head. "Blue was always my sister's color; she loved the ocean. It seems the priesthood can make allowances for personal taste, after all. Or maybe they just want to soften their new favorite pet some more."

Then she turned and allowed Esperidi to see her moist, reddened eyes. "I can't face her. Not after all that's happened."

Esperidi grappled with the vague clues she'd been handed. "Her? Sister?"

"Don't ask me to explain. I can't." Ashangtu gripped her satchel until all her knuckles whitened. "Look, I never promised this was going to be forever!"

"No, you didn't," Esperidi allowed. "But it is customary among friends to say goodbye and offer an explanation."

"I know who that priestess is," Ashangtu said, "and I can't let her see me. I don't want her to know that I'm still alive. Let her think Islinn washed away with the rest of Lanore!"

Now Esperidi juggled a three-word riddle. Her–Sister–Islinn? But she shrugged this all aside. "Can't you wait for me here? It's not likely they'll want to come within the walls of Pedragira, not with all the Ruhselene about. And surely, if they do intend to come here, or if Sanyori must offer them hospitality, you'll know beforehand."

"Esperidi, I have to go!" Ashangtu shouted. "I don't share your vision. I don't believe we can build Ophia anew with the Oskwai as our tools!"

"I use no one as a tool!" Esperidi said, discovering some steel of her own. Then, reading the resolution in her friend's shoulders, she cooled to compassion. "Where will you go?"

Ashangtu merely grunted.

"How will you live?"

"I don't know. I suppose I'll have to rely upon what you've taught me."

"I didn't get the chance to teach you much."

"I can hunt within the world of dreams as well as any Oskwai can hunt with their eyes and ears." Ashangtu failed to sound convincing, even to herself.

Suddenly, Esperidi strode forward and hugged her from behind, pinning the other woman's arms against her sides and leaning her chin against one shoulder.

"I worried that if I asked for it, you might deny me," she explained with a hint of a smirk. But she couldn't sustain such forced levity. Intuiting that Ashangtu's overtures towards her a few nights ago had been rooted in love, expressed through the only channel free to the Shaini at the time, called forth an ache in her breast.

She stepped back and gave her friend room to turn. Ashangtu's eyes were running freely now.

"I have to meet this delegation," Esperidi said. "I *must* be there. There are things I can share with the chieftains that no one else knows about, not even Sanyori. I really wish you would delay, at least until I can tell you where you might find me, should you ever want to again. I don't think I will know that until after the Meet."

"I know your generous, self-sacrificing *timbre*," Ashangtu said. "I doubt I could ever mistake it in a thousand streams of dream."

Esperidi wanted to embrace her again, but she saw Ashangtu teetering and feared another emotional display might unbalance her. "Then you must look for me there," she said.

And an internal echo made a part of her want to wail: *If I'm the one who must go, can I count on you to find me?*

"I suppose I could bemoan how quickly we're parting ways," she said, mastering herself with effort, "but then, it's nearly as long as *my* apprenticeship was."

Ashangtu was suddenly intent. "Be careful, Esperidi. You may not be as acquainted with their ways because you didn't have as many dealings with them in Sequana, but we did in Lanore. The Shetain priesthood would be keenly interested in what you can do. They'd use your gifts to serve their oppression if they could. And failing that, they wouldn't hesitate to destroy you."

"And while I'm looking over my shoulder," Esperidi persisted, "where will *you* go?"

"Away," Ashangtu said. "I can't face Ildriss. You have no idea what Shetain did to her, to all of us. It would not surprise me if she turned me over to the priesthood for my own good if I showed my face.

"I haven't the heart to bid farewell to Erawen. So for

now, I'll just say goodbye to Sparrow."

Then, after some visible effort to conquer her defenses, she hugged Esperidi.

"Your allotment of pain is more than sufficient for any human being," Ashangtu whispered. "Quit worrying so much about the rest of us." A quick breath escaped her lips, which might have been a mirthless laugh. "But then, if you did that, you'd cease to be who you are, wouldn't you?"

"I can't believe how hard it is for me to let you go," Esperidi muttered. Though she'd settled into a daily practice of rigorous self-examination, she'd begun to lean upon Ashangtu in ways she'd never suspected.

"This isn't easy for me either," Ashangtu said. She turned to place the last couple of items into her sack and pull the cords tight. Again, the walls were erect and implacable. "It's just necessary."

With that, she slung the sack over her shoulder and stalked out of the room without another glance at her friend.

※ ※

Esperidi stared at Ashangtu's bed for a long time. The tousled quilt and sheets bore mute testimony to the restlessness that had so often characterized the woman.

"May you find some measure of peace somewhere, somehow, Islinn Ashangtu Lanore," she whispered.

Usually, in a similar situation, she would have said, "Rest in the arms of Sorsajna," as Shiya-coqui had taught her. But she suspected that she and Ashangtu had many more leagues to travel before either of them could really rest.

She slowly grew aware of Sanyori's presence behind her.

"This is not the way I would have chosen for her to leave," the man said. His voice was carefully diplomatic. "But you know, it is not wholly without cause. Perhaps it would be wise for you to—"

"What?" Esperidi said. "Run? I fled Farsilane; then I fled my teacher's sanctuary under Mount Veneer. Then, I fled the Savwain and the Kawli Rainforest. What happens when I'm all out of places to run?"

"I always did suspect that Shetain would eventually take an interest in our Meets," Sanyori allowed. "For the last few years, they've tried to take a census of all survivors in Ophia, and they don't want anyone congregating unless it's by their edict. This is the first time we've risked it since the storms. But we pose little threat to them right now, and their energies have mostly been consumed in rebuilding their power. For this priest to have such a vested interest in attending the Meet, I suspect—"

"He *knows*," Esperidi said with sudden certainty. "Ashangtu and I traveled with a couple of Manitoh traders. I had to succor one of them, else rattlesnake venom would've stilled his heart. And he, Tohbin, revealed that Shetain has eyes and ears in the Savwain."

"You know all this, and yet you choose to stay?"

"How can these people ever awaken," Esperidi said, "if the only voices they ever hear are the ones that want to hide their history from them, teach them guilt and penance, teach them to revere a god who is revolted by their very existence?"

"Remember the Sentient Library," Sanyori urged her. "Remember what you and Shiya-coqui and Rona accomplished there. You can do much more in the world of dreams."

Esperidi mulled this for a moment. "That is true. Nevertheless, I've run out of hiding places—or soon will. I don't exist *solely* in the dream dimension, San. I'm also a being in a body, and this body has its limitations."

"I suppose you're right at that," Sanyori considered. "I've always been rather averse to limitation. Pesky prohibition! It spoils theatricality, to say naught of invention." His grin was disarming. "Well, I sense that the Ruhselene, at least, have developed a sense of loyalty towards you. If you're threatened, I'll wager they will defend you."

"The priest would not come if he believed he was in any real danger," Esperidi said. "Besides, I don't want any blood shed on my account."

She moved over to the bed that had been Ashangtu's and stretched herself upon the woman's discarded bedding. Folding her hands over her sternum, she drew a few long breaths and closed her eyes. Ashangtu was not here to sing for her this time. Shiya-coqui had no voice on this side of the Partition. Esperidi would have to trust herself more deeply than she ever had before.

Then, recalling something that might aid her, she sought within the folds of her cloak until her hand closed over the amethyst that Tohbin had given her.

Gripping it, she said, "I cannot let this priest of Shetain silence me, San. I *must* be there. But first, there's something I have to know."

The man moved beside the bed and bowed over her. "Do you need anything from me?"

Esperidi shook her head. She could already feel the bond she'd formed with Tohbin asserting itself through the crystal she clutched, and she feared the emotional ambiguity Sanyori stirred up in her might disrupt her concentration.

As if sensing this, the man said, "Then I'll learn as much as I can from Suskhana. If you're committed to going, we'll need to make preparations soon."

Esperidi merely nodded. Already, she was sinking below the threshold of rational consciousness. Her surroundings felt less urgent and pertinent. Within a handful of breaths, she descended into a scene of fear and pain—and hovering over it all, a cold will that fed upon such things, delighted in them. Tohbin and Kunsei's faces were illuminated by a baleful white light that filled a chamber with an immaculate domed ceiling and perfect joins. The chamber's acoustics amplified the low hum of the staff a priest leveled at Tohbin's chest. Its head clasped a quartz ball carved to resemble a human skull. The cold light emanated from this crystal, a light that made Tohbin howl and Kunsei cry out with sympathy and stifled outrage.

"She wields Sorsajna!" Tohbin gasped in the moment his will finally broke—after enduring extravagant pain. "It is true! She is one who dreams awake!"

Esperidi intuitively trusted this augury. Manitohs often spoke of the creative forces of life in this way. The Shetain priesthood had taught them to do so. Just as they preached of a god, Toh, who existed separate from Ophia, they tried to divorce Sorsajna from individuals lest people discover their personal power. Sorsajna, they claimed, did not exist *within*. It was not the breath of life but rather an alien power existing outside the self, something to be usurped and *wielded*.

Gasping as if she'd emerged from deep waters, Esperidi opened her eyes. Slowly, she recognized Sanyori's face and realized the man had returned.

"How long? she muttered.

"It's been at least an hour," he said.

I lapsed into dreams afterward—dreams of her again!

"If you're still intent upon doing this," Sanyori said, "it must be soon. To make the equinox, we must leave well before dawn."

Esperidi nodded. What she had glimpsed had only deepened her resolve. "He was not slain," she said, mostly to reassure herself. "They hurt him. The priest made him talk and thus betray his integrity. But Tohbin is still an asset because they know he's trusted in the Savwain. So they got what they wanted out of him and then let him and his son go."

Grasping at this slim consolation, she rose to follow Sanyori.

From Colleen's Journal

Sensations once imprisoned by names burst into new worlds.

How do I find my footing in this place, poised on the cusp of infinite skyways again, immobilized by boundless choice?

How many rewrites can my narrative absorb and still cohere?

Questing for the center of an ever-changing orbit, my house meets its architect—and both are altered by the exchange.

"Sage Serpents," the good doctor mused. His voice was chummy, with enough notes of derision to get my hackles up.

"Yes! Ever heard of the Naginis of ancient India? Communing with serpents just might be the oldest religion on the planet!"

"Right. And then they all convinced us to eat fruit from forbidden trees."

Whew. Deep breath. Give me a moment to get my bearings, Mister Visinsky, and rehearse the acrobatics I'm gonna have to perform to get through this next hour with you.

I'm supposed to entrust my life and sanity to you and your colleagues. And according to you, a nightmarish, haunted house lurks just beneath the surface of my mind, all these ghosts clamoring to get free and wreak havoc. And the ghosts are <u>me</u>. But I will expose my innermost thoughts to you, and, with an innocuous smile, you'll assure me it's okay because I'm in a safe space to do so? When the entire philosophy you live by insists that our universe is anything <u>but</u> safe, that we are constantly beset upon by terrors, both outside and inside?

And, assuming I <u>did</u> listen to you and decided to play along with the game and pretend that I am in a safe space and can trust you and be totally transparent, where would you lead me? It doesn't sound like you've seen many comforting shores yourself.

But Dr. Visinsky waved a hand to ward off the mustering storm clouds. "Let's move on. You talked about drawing regularly after your sister died."

"<u>More</u> often, yes."

"Do you think there could be some connection there? I mean, a connection with <u>what</u> you drew?" He waved my sketch of the "Sage Serpents."

I searched my memory and was startled to actually uncover something. "There was a rhyme we made up."

"Do tell," he said. He seemed to relax for the first time since the session began.

I tried to compose myself—I was trying to convince him of my emotional balance and rationality, right?—but as soon as I began, the energy was irrepressible. I burst into singsong.

"Losers, winners
Saints and sinners
Last one to Cora gets

snakes for dinner!"

"Interesting." Dr. Visinky's smile never wavered. "And Cora?"

"Cora was the name of our magic world we could go to, a place only we knew about. Sometimes, it reminded me of a faery land, like Avalon."

"And other times?" he prompted.

That was all the syrupy condescension I could endure that morning. "Other times, it reminded me of Wonderland, where everyone goes around grinning from ear to ear, but secretly, they're all effing psychotic!"

That stung him enough to make me instantly remorseful. "I'm sorry."

He dismissed this with a wave, banishing all that "unquantifiable human pain" from his eyes.

"The issue isn't whether you or I think any of your childhood games were silly, Colleen. The issue is whether or not you've ever been able to really let them go. It's not that unusual, you know: clinging to childhood fantasies to insulate yourself from trauma."

Then he delivered the gut punch. "Trauma signifies the <u>death</u> of childhood, basically. Tell me, Colleen... Are you still trying to live in Cora?"

Lingering guilt from my previous outburst spurred some candor. "I wouldn't know how. I only ever knew how to go to Cora when Stacie and I were together. When she died, it's like that whole world died with her."

"So it's not just a fantasy world, but a <u>dead</u> fantasy world. Don't you see how dangerous this is, how crucial it is for you to let it go so you can get back in touch with your real life?"

"Doctor," I said, "last time we were in session, you lectured me about how love and compassion were chemical reactions in the brain. And now you're going to enlighten me about 'real life'?"

"You were drawn to that tree over the gorge," he pronounced, as if his logic was unassailable, "because it symbolizes, for you, a threshold that you've never been able to cross. A threshold into mature adulthood."

See, we make this "science of the psyche" our rock, even though the whole conception doesn't have a stone to stand on. It's become the most radical thing in the world for anyone to pose questions like, "What if we're just innately good, all of us, without exception? What if nothing prevents us from doing good at every turn save for the contrary ideas that we constantly insist are true about ourselves?"

Now, to appease a Western mind, particularly one with a few extra letters stamped on the end of its name, one must occasionally twist one's own mind hither and thither into a pretzel.

I mean no condemnation. I merely call attention to the delicate mental gymnastics involved. That morning, my sweaty palms kept slipping off the trapeze bar because this voice inside me persisted: "What if you're wrong about all this, Colleen? What if they're right?"

Like Western psychology, I hadn't a stone to stand on.

But I railed on. For the sake of your puppy-dog eyes and the kindness I see shining behind them, I'll do my best, Doc, to describe what keeps me turning in my bed at night as if on a bed of coals. And while I'm at it, maybe I'll be able to paint a picture of the world that "mature adulthood" has created for us.

Most of the world's "duly elected leaders" (just try and convince me that any of us still have legitimate elections) aspire to be dictators for life. So before you go to bed tonight, parents and kiddies, don't forget to set your clocks back three hundred years.

And why, exactly, are these "leaders" meeting in places like northeast Mongolia and Antarctica?

This company here is trying to pollinate flowers with cyborg insects after their pesticides decimated the bees. This one manufactures artillery shells that explode into Taser shrapnel or emit pain waves. This billionaire is dumping psych meds into the water supply. This one's spewing chemicals into the atmosphere to combat the damage caused by... er, chemicals. This one argues on live TV that national security would be easier to maintain and enforce if we were all implanted with computer chips.

Economies melting down, coming food shortages... What better time to outlaw growing crops on the front lawn and arrest anyone who collects rainwater? Not that we can afford homes anymore, anyway.

If there's a conflict of interest, your android housekeeper will end your life to save her own. Kill-bots win wars we didn't even know were being fought. Hacking and cyber-spying are such the norm that we're a hair's breadth from an utter stalemate, everyone leaning towards their computer screens, just waiting for someone, somewhere, to get up and do something so everyone else can track it.

Give me a person's name, and, in fifteen minutes or less, I'll tell you the names of their kids and parents, the schools, churches, and football games they've attended, their favorite restaurant (and what they typically order), and the names and IP addresses of their servers.

This journalist claims that North America will be ninety percent depopulated by starvation and cannibalism over the next decade. This one claims the school shooting last week was staged; he provides some compelling evidence. Anyway, it's easier for a kid to get ahold of an assault rifle than it is for him or her to find a sympathetic ear. Easier to score painkillers on the street than to go to the hospital. Easier to fast when the "wealthiest Nation on Earth" can't afford to feed its people because all of its "surplus" goes towards keeping banks and yachts afloat.

Countries keep their soldiers busy in covert wars abroad because they know they can't house or feed them if they call them home.

Besides, most of the "food" on store shelves isn't food at all. Not even closely related. Not even second cousins once removed on their mothers' side.

The looming Civil War, an unprecedented ice cream swirl of class, race, and border wars, is shaping to be the furthest thing from civil. But it might be entertaining, at least from the safe remove of a phone or TV screen. A Sith lord and his apprentice will bankroll both sides of the conflict and give us a good show of opposition, much like world politics, in general, has done for longer than I've been alive.

Homes have moved away from waterfronts. Every developed nation has nuclear capabilities. We must submit to electronic retinal, rental, and rectal scans every morning while we brush our teeth.

And so on.

Oh, and Doctor Visinsky? I've been getting messages every night from a place called Ophia. Hopefully, I've already addressed why I might occasionally fantasize about going there. But I don't think it'd be an improvement overall. They're not doing too well, either. It's just a different version of the same malaise.

But these communications <u>have</u> opened my eyes to some truths that all our world's headlines tend to overlook:

That life's mystery and promise elude us in the places where they're most often sought: in chemical soup and cosmic debris, frozen strictures, and high-flying dogmas.

That we should listen, rather, to how the universe speaks in the surge of a parent's pride in a child's first steps and words. A miraculous promise finding its feet. That young one's cry of wonder at spring's first violet or a sparrow alighting on the sill.

Love in the eye, recognizing the grace in another. Never repeated, never to be replaced. Love in a still hour, bridging lifetimes and worlds. Embodied once and for all in the cherished being whom the soul's eye descries in a forest of drifters.

And when life's unseen currents sweep people into a quiet sanctum, and their hearts alight with recognition, awakened by that specific glance and smile, that unique timbre in the voice of the beloved—

Who lifts the Veils from your eyes when doubt casts its glamour upon your star-spun grace—

Peering past a thousand facades to find the face you hold in trust—

In night-sea journeys where only the heart's GPS is unerring—

Walking side by side to that sun-speckled pinnacle or deepest caves warmed by the lambent well—

Wandering awestruck into a world still wet from the dream that birthed it—

Hail, Sorsajna! Source of all! Your satyr hooves sink deep into verdant red earth, and your fingers curl skyward!

We'll dance within your primrose circle as your meadow bowl in eternal springtime uplifts us like cupped hands, bearing its twin treasures: freedom and permission.

Permission to be fully ourselves. To be this world's mirror. To be love's reflection in the eyes of another.

As the whole human panorama of joy, uncertainty, struggle, and victory tumbles forth in the wake of our footsteps. As we surmount the mountain's pinnacle, pledging our fidelity.

"To share my home, knowing you already carry it with you."

"To share my life because your presence was its missing piece."

And the path winds to a place consecrated by trust, where we all join hands, proclaiming, "Let it be this union, this peace and community, that announces to the world what the road stretched out before us already knows: that we will walk it together."

<u>That</u> is what is real for me, good doctor. Realer than the realist realty that ever reeled.

Awaken the Singing Stones

Konatep rode over the meadow that gradually sloped towards Jamurada's Crown with an eagerness that almost made him giddy. His patient maneuvering was coming to fruition, though he hadn't even suspected the latest developments until his informants had brought word a week before.

Every piece of news he'd received since then had only whetted his anticipation. Such a cadre of unbelievers and savages, all gathered in one place! And ready to hear the words of the Sacred Writ—or die if their ears refused it. This day's events would quell all doubt about who was second in power behind Jain-Toh in Shetain's priestly hierarchy.

All the tribes of the region, including even the furtive ones from the swamps, would be represented, along with three Shaini. He even had Ildriss the Chosen walking before him—Shetain's new face of "mercy"—to wrap the proceedings in a seeming blanket of tolerance. Everything conspired to deliver him the perfect coup, one that even his Master could not have anticipated.

It was almost enough to make him believe in Toh's Providence. Of course, Konatep was an initiate of the Sacred Writ's inner mysteries; he knew how that text had come into being. No one with such knowledge could ever be a believer in the way that the rest of Ophia was—and was *required* to be.

Toh, Jamaro, Shai-win, and Sarpienta were names that superstitious and fearful folk gave to forces they feared they had no power over. Konatep *used* superstition to leverage control over these less-informed natives; he was never a slave to it.

It signified little. He had been appointed to bring Truth to their dull and lifeless ears, and today, that service would bring him everlasting glory.

His sense of exaltation clouded momentarily, though, when he considered the Jaguar delegation amassing on the hill. By all accounts, the Jaguar tribe were fierce hunters and warriors, and their prowess had emboldened more Junsa leaders and their attendant guards to attend this Meet than Konatep had expected. Nearly a score.

The Junsa were undecided in their allegiance. As for these Ruhselene, they had spurned all his invitations to treat with the priesthood. Konatep's hastily assembled party was outnumbered, and the Brinstead Pale Faces who marched with him were hardy but not particularly skilled in the killing arts. But they bore Shetain's steel, which would turn the tides should this meeting go awry. Also, four mounted Inooks flanked the priest, each constituting a veritable war party.

Besides, there was that hesitancy in the heart of even the most backward native when confronting a mouthpiece of Toh. They always seemed to know when they were in the presence of their greaters, and that hesitance often turned the tides of a conflict. And who could say how these unbelievers might turn if violence erupted? There were a lot of ancient animosities simmering beneath the surface here, blood feuds and racial prejudices—long nurtured, of course, and encouraged. That's why Konatep had summoned the Manitoh party to this meeting. It was easy to make people forget themselves, neutralize the threat they represented by simply reminding them to *hate*.

Identify their suffering and tell them who was to blame for it. Stoke those flames. Even Shetain's acolytes understood this tactic.

Konatep lifted a hand to halt the procession and then turned to the nearest Inook. "We wait here. Let them sweat and wonder while I take the pulse of this 'council.' Then, each of you will lead a horse to the ring. But wait outside the stones until I signal for you."

For the first mile, the road out of Pedragira was flanked by tall, crenelated poplars gently swaying in the pollen-thick breeze. This row of trees ended shortly beyond the last cultivated fields, where broad cottonwoods spread their green arms to embrace the tranquil spring in languid repose.

Volcanic ash and weathered basalt spewed forth by the Rupture had produced incredibly fertile soil in this region. The Ruhselenes had leagues of arable land. And, thanks to Sanyori, they were familiar with various crops and what songs would coax forth their inherent vitality. They knew how to cultivate and cook them. Roana Road was little wider than its wagon tracks, but the Ruhselenes were loath to trample the cultivated plots and small canals on either side, so they stretched their line.

An hour later, they reached higher, drier ground. From this vantage, Esperidi could see the gentle spread of the Roana Hills, rolling northwards, and the long, lightening shadows of Lake Banyomeer cupping their furthermost border like a silhouette. The yellow-green hills were mostly bare save for occasional patches of rock or pine.

Slowly, the circle of Jamurada came into view. The menhirs peaked at varying heights, but four men standing upon one another's shoulders could not have reached the top of the smallest. The thirteen stones—one (arched, miraculously, from a single piece) in the center and twelve on the periphery—seemed to enclose an eternal mystery. The stones at each cardinal point were connected by a bell-shaped arch, creating the semblance of a portal.

Esperidi could cross the distance from one end to the other in probably a hundred paces, but she doubted she could ever span the true breadth of that world within the circle.

She asked Sanyori why the Meet was always held during the spring equinox.

"The sun centers perfectly within the central archway but twice a year," he said, "the other being in mid-autumn. As to the significance of that, I think it's best to ask those who come to meditate on the spot. But now, it has a deeper resonance. Despite all the Rupture's rages, these stones still stand, and the sun's position has not changed. We are reminded of a kind of permanence that endures amid all of Ophia's upheavals."

Esperidi felt like she looked upon the Sentient Library rendered, as distinctly as possible, as a physical construct. It was a microcosm containing the entire immensity, drawing seekers into that central mystery from all corners of Ophia. Deep affection for the circle of Jamurada stole over her, wordless awe and reverence.

She leaned towards Sanyori—to offer reassurance or grasp it for herself, she wasn't sure which—but the man flinched away.

"Your pardon," he said with an enigmatic smile. "I seem to be on edge." Then, as if seeking reparation, he added: "A dream guides me this morning. Perhaps it was Shiya-coqui. Who can say? I am prejudiced: Whenever I hear a voice of wisdom, I assume it is hers. Regardless, this voice was in my mind as I awoke. It told me I am the forerunner of the dawn. You are its bringer."

Esperidi frowned at his obvious duplicity. Sanyori held his arms behind him, fingers interwoven by the small of his back as if he was reining himself in for diplomacy's sake. But Esperidi didn't feel caution emanating from him. Rather, his *timbre* felt faint and opaque. His somewhat beatific smile dared her to probe deeper and uncover his true thoughts.

It seems that his prowess as an actor extends beyond the stage.

She resisted the bait. "Very well," she said. "Then tell me more about the people gathered here."

Sanyori seemed reluctant at first. "Many people alive in Ophia today owe their survival to Jain-Toh. This you know." He tried to dispel the shadow that name conjured with a self-deprecating smile. "He is, perhaps, the only one more adept than me at manipulating myth. But no priest, however crafty, can hold power alone. And so he is also astute in recognizing others' gifts.

"Twin brothers, of an age with myself, were born in the Kawli. Jain took a keen interest in them, for one was a formidable warrior, and the other was exceedingly cunning in statecraft and subterfuge. Jain offered them a place on the ships before the storms came."

"Tumoset and Konatep," Esperidi whispered.

"Aye. The Second Scourge and Shetain's new protégé. The two fists of the priesthood, one reared by Inooks and the other tutored by Jain himself."

Sanyori raised his gaze northwards, above the line of hills, and shuddered. "We are safe from Tumoset's Horde only because of their pride. They covet the horses of the Virgoda Plains, and the Jona-chon horsemen taunt and defy them. So Tumoset is occupied to the north.

"But Konatep comes to convert the Ruhselene and further pressure the Junsa, who seem ready to cave to his will. Brinstead's governor, another of Jain's 'salvages,' is with him, along with a small entourage: the new settlers, whom the natives call Pale Faces. Most of Brinstead's honest folk have already joined the Vandrene, and its opportunists fled to the bandit colonies. Those who remained in the eastern settlement, what used to be Sequestra Forest before it burned, are a superstitious lot. They eagerly embraced the edicts that came down upon their settlement from On High."

"High on Jain-Toh's holy brow, I suppose you mean," Esperidi drawled. She intuited Sanyori's underlying bitter *timbre*. Sequestra had been his homeland.

His gesture reminded her that he could make even a shrug appear flamboyant. "These we cannot hope to ally ourselves with. This is the best outcome I can foresee: They will deem us and everything we do here as beneath their concern.

"Suskhana and the Ruhselene are good people—and you apparently have already won their loyalty. So who remains? The various Junsa tribes hail from a place they call Fetu Swamp. This, also, was a portion of Sequestra. Spared by the fires only to be flooded. Shamarai of the Jaguar tribe seems to have united them.

"Alas!" He lamented suddenly. "That the Sendhi, our dearest allies of old, cannot join us! But they've just completed their pilgrimage to Mangoyen and are exhausted from the journey. And Mangoyen is far from here. But it warms my heart to think of their reverent souls warming that mountain home."

Alerted by a tremor of love in his voice, Esperidi probed him with raven eyes.

"Yes, I have taken an apprentice," Sanyori said. His smile was strangely sheepish. "Perhaps I'll tell you about her sometime. But for now, her humble heart sustains me through this trial." And with that, he aimed his clouded eyes towards their destination again.

As the gentle slope carried them towards Jamurada's Crown, Esperidi sought to understand the invisible forces working beneath this critical moment. She used Sanyori's voice as a guideline and opened her percipience as wide as possible whilst staying rooted in her body and the feel of Roana Road beneath her feet.

The Ruhselenes fanning out behind her were fairly at ease. They encompassed Yendar, Junsa, Ibwe, and even Manitoh within their bloodline; their heritage, in and of itself, dissolved many racial tensions. Moreover, they aspired to their adopted name—Ancient Children—to *be* children, fresh to the world, dragging no past behind them.

Like the Vandrene, Esperidi thought.

But she was nearly overwhelmed by the ancestral misunderstandings and hatreds roiling within the stone circle. Those Junsa who had retreated into caves during Sanjesota's decades of terror had a hunted, haunted look—eyes that might never learn to trust again. The male chiefs of seven different clans were present, but they all seemed to defer to the man Sanyori had identified as Shamarai.

The one who became more militant after the death of his life-mate, Seribu.

Shamarai's Junsa eyed Suskhana and the small embassy flanking her with wariness and a hint of grudging respect. Their apprehension paled, however, alongside the *timbre* of hatred—almost an audible roar of repudiation—that all the people arrayed along the plateau's perimeter hurled towards the Manitoh cortege, which milled along the butte's spine. The Junsa had labored under the Manitoh whip for over a century. In their minds, every dweller of the Kawli jungles who wasn't a slave was a slaver. Esperidi thought of Tohbin and Kunsei, and her heart ached for this misapprehension.

And these Manitohs did not strike her as enviable. Esperidi read echoes of the Cordonne's fanaticism in their eyes. Their presences carried faint *timbres* of secrecy and shame, like the malignant thoughts that pursue one in the small hours and never relent. They were the ghosts of their own self-abnegation.

Esperidi understood better now why Sanyori had been so keen on having her and Ashangtu attend the Meet. In a gathering this rife with tension, one of the few things that might quell boiling tempers would be the semi-mythical awe with which all Oskwai tribes held the Shaini. And the Shaini legacy, fortunately, allowed her and Sanyori to sidestep ancient animosities. Their people had been, by turns, benefactors and recluses, but they had never been oppressors. Even Jain-Toh's governorship of the Manitoh capital of Khempsa had only happened in response to Sanjesota's wars—if the official histories were to be believed.

These simmering tensions on the summit were counterbalanced by the arrogance sauntering at the head of an approaching wedge: the gray-robed priest, whose staff glared from its crystalline head as if from two skull eyes. As for the four men flanking him... Esperidi shuddered like a cold wind from the Sendhi steppes had whipped through her soul. She wasn't confident she could describe those four figures as *men*.

Reaching the summit, Sanyori strode at once into the center of the circle and raised his arms high. Esperidi wondered why he didn't wait for the priest and his Manitoh and Brinstead entourage, but then she realized that that group had not drawn any closer. They milled about a few hundred yards to the north of the plateau.

To this Konatep, she thought, *everything we do and say here is but a preliminary. He will come when he decides that all are ready to hear the "one word" of authority and Truth.*

Sanyori was undoubtedly aware of the subtle dismissal, too, but didn't allow it to dampen his effervescence and dramatic flair.

"My friends! Betimes, we gather like this and then appear too astonished to speak. We meet in New Ophia, not the Ophia our ancestors knew—what *we* once knew—and we aren't sure how to make greetings in this strange age sprouting up in the Rupture's wake.

"I am Sanyori Mon-Sequestra. If I feel any strong point of commonality with you all, it is this: We believe our fates are bound to the people we serve. And if there is any difference there, any discrepancy, it is that I do not give my allegiance to any one tribe. Not Junsa, Yendar, Ruhselene, Sendhi, Manitoh, or any other. *All* of Ophia is my tribe. It is the welfare of all humankind that concerns me. And so I dream of a Nation wherein representatives from all corners of Ophia may gather, and all may have a voice where crucial decisions are required. May this Meet serve as a model for how such a Nation should conduct itself!

"But I'll not try to deceive those who don't already know me. I am no lawmaker or governor. I manifest my visions on the stage or with paper and quill. Fortunately, there is with me today a Shaini who is much more adept than I at preaching to the hearts of the scared and dispossessed. And so, delegates of Ophia's free peoples, I give you Esperidi Mon-Sequana!"

Like most Oskwai, Shamarai knew little for certain about the Shaini. And what stories had been handed down amongst his people recounted scarce interactions. The accounts reached no consensus about whether they were even human. The Shaini were a remote race who held themselves aloof from other people. On that level, Shamarai felt a certain kinship with them.

They were credited with bringing language to all of Ophia's people. But the two Shaini who had stayed with his tribe for two nights and a day had done little to illuminate such mysteries. The woman had been inquisitive, asking many questions about the Junsa and Shamarai himself, but she'd revealed scant hints about herself or her lineage. The man had merely issued two commands: Cease your sacrifices and do not worship or follow me.

Only one thing was fairly certain: Few of their kind had survived the cataclysms. Nevertheless, Shamarai knew that one group, of whom this man Sanyori was the last representative in the region, had settled for a while in the Sendhi waste. That Hive, according to dim rumor, was now a slanted ruin.

The Olen-sa moving towards the circle's heart wore a robe draped with sky-blue fringe, and though its cowl was pulled down, it draped over her hands and moccasins. She was probably sweltering in it, but Shamarai supposed she was loathe to bare more of herself in front of so many male eyes. Something about the way she regarded him made him stand up straighter. It reminded him to claim his portion of Ophia's ground, air, and sunlight. But he would give his trust when she proved herself worthy of it.

And he was distracted by the group behind him, waiting and watching. He could feel the Manitohs' eyes at his back. Shamarai had heard tales of monkeys dwelling in the Kawli forest. His grandparents had seen them during the years of captivity. When one of them was beaten by a stronger monkey, they would turn around and look for a weaker one to abuse. It had been this way in Khempsa. The

Manitohs, humiliated by their subjugation, had victimized the Junsa in turn.

He thrust his fears aside, forced himself to focus on the Olen-sa's almond, almost reptilian eyes. Shamarai could tell that this Esperidi Mon-Sequana had never spoken in a circle before. She felt somewhat abashed at being thrust into the position by her male companion. Such a mood could overtake even the boldest among the Junsa. Esperidi was in its grip now.

Armed with this awareness, Shamarai was not as caught off guard as he otherwise might have been when the Olen-sa suddenly faced him and, investing her half-smile with all the compassion her eyes and lips could convey, said "How may I honor you, Shamarai? Or, failing of honor, how can I at least set you at ease?"

Shamarai had heard Sanyori speak before. The man reminded him of Coyote, a wise creature who was not born to lead but rather to teach others with tricks and cunning. Of this woman, he knew nothing. Therefore, he was not prepared for her affability. He saw a smile radiating warmth and compassion where he'd expected imperiousness.

"My people preserve stories from before the great captivity," he said. "They spoke of other ages when Grandfather Serpent turned in his bed, and mountains tumbled and burned. We survived in deep caves; we ate vermin and blind fish and drank from streams never warmed by sunlight." He mastered himself with clenched fists. "How can we trust Shaini? We know that the construction of your cities was not wholly achieved with the sweat of your labors. You invoked forbidden powers—"

"*Sacred Timbre.*" Esperidi nodded in acknowledgment. She did not appear concerned that she uttered blasphemy; she was only surprised that Shamarai, too, understood the concept. "Yes: I cup a fire within my hands that can warm or devour. But this fire is not the province or privilege of Shaini-kind. *All* beings are heir to it. All of us bear the responsibility. What use will we make of this fire that Sorsajna has gifted us?"

Shamarai winced. Junsas had been whipped and flayed by the priesthood for even using that word: *Sorsajna.*

"Those forbidden powers, as you called them, saved my life," Esperidi said. "My teacher, Shiya-coqui, felt disruptions... She called them forces of amok. She felt Ophia groaning beneath her feet. She felt the wind's wrath and the ocean's avarice. So she sent me into the Savwain Desert, knowing it was one of the few places that would avoid the coming upheavals."

"You call her teacher," Shamarai said. "What did she teach you?"

"She was a Sophryne, the last of her kind." Shamarai shook his head; the term meant nothing to him. But the Olen-sa hastened to assist his understanding. "Her knowledge preserved much of the old arts—how to travel beyond the Partition. She was adept at conscious dreaming. And she was fluent in the lore that lifted Ophian civilization into its golden age: *Sacred Timbre.*"

Emboldened by the Ruhselene, who now fanned out along Jamurada's southern arc, Esperidi projected her voice to all those present. "There are more affinities between us than differences. *Beliefs* cause strife. I seek to undermine those beliefs. The only antidote to fear is the knowledge of our power: the power we have to inscribe the stories of our lives. Fear can never be conquered if we are unwilling to extend ourselves, to use our abilities to their furthest extent, to give ourselves at least that token of trust in ourselves. You cannot know the worth of power until you allow it freedom."

"Ophia provides for the Junsa," Shamarai said. "We have no use for power."

"You have use for it if you possess life," Esperidi said. "It informs our breath; it lends our thoughts and feet mobility. Your fear, Shamarai, has less to do with the nature of potency and more with the trustworthiness of those who wield it. I believe that humankind is worthy of trust, regardless of the errors of its history."

"So you are human?"

"Yes, Shamarai. The Shaini are human in all the ways that matter."

Ascending the hill in Ildriss' shadow and approaching a gap between two stone monoliths, Konatep felt his equilibrium shaken by irritation. The Shaini woman standing within the circle's center, a slight and swarthy figure... Some self-delusion held her upright and lent her an air of authority.

Toh's mouthpiece scowled. He was accustomed to his arrival at any longhouse, wigwam, or Meet received by silence and gnawing uncertainty. He held any congregation within his hands when he could speak first. But this signified little. If he could not silence an infidel, well, he'd learned another tactic in the years of his indoctrination. If allowed to speak for long enough, such people usually condemned themselves. Then, Konatep merely had to act in his condign role as the hand of divine justice.

However, another man in the entourage lacked his patience, and his voice rose above the din. This Brinstead Pale Face, bald save for thin wisps above his ears, wore a sabine robe. Over his chest hung a fist-sized jade medallion the priest lent him for this occasion. It bore the image of Jamaro, the Chonnen thunder god, naked to the waist and thickly muscled, one foot on a giant serpent's head.

Smiling inwardly, Konatep thought, *We pretend they are twins. Jamaro and Toh exist in a state of truce... for now.*

Spasms of hate and fanaticism twisted the man's visage. "I am Havar!" he shouted as if his name was a title. "Minister of Brinstead by Jain-Toh's appointment! I speak by Shetain's authority!"

Esperidi tried to mask her distress when she saw this minister and the similarly pale-skinned men spreading out behind him. The folk of Brinstead were professed devotees of the Light. But the light in their eyes was even more diminished—obfuscated and confused—than the Manitohs moving alongside them in a more solemn procession. Esperidi sensed a veritable ocean of pain and conflict within the white settlers. The seven Manitohs, men and women, were held rigid by a collective *timbre* that commingled awe and stoic resolve. The Brinsteaders were gripped by something more frightful: shame.

Then Esperidi was distracted by the savannah-haired, willowy woman walking beside Konatep. The Junsa, sensing her Shaini heritage, shied from this woman like birds from an asp.

Surely, she is Ashangtu's sister, Ildriss!

Konatep, striding at the head of the Manitoh cortege, veered toward the woman so they passed between two monoliths side-by-side as if opening a bridal threshold.

Esperidi caught something startling about Konatep's eyes. They were strangely lifeless, like openings into pits—though when they first found Sanyori, they darkened with venom. But then, as if the High Priest recalled a subtle advantage, he beamed again with smug elitist pride. His smile even more solicitous (and subtly condescending) than before, he raised his arms, forearms pressed together, and then separated his hands so they formed a wide V.

Esperidi bowed slightly in response. Sanyori merely

nodded. Neither wished to return this particular salute.

"This is joy unlooked for," Konatep said, sounding like a man who rated joy the very least of life's offerings. "So many tribes gathered in joint purpose. And two Shaini.

"I am Konatep, High Priest of Toh and counselor to the Chosen." At this last title, he inclined his chin towards the woman. As if on cue—and briefly grazing her haggard eyes across Esperidi and Sanyori—she responded: "Hail, Olen-sa! Hail, Oren-ta!"

But Konatep dismissed this with a brusque gesture. "We in Shetain have new names and titles now. Ties to the past have been swept away. Reviving them brings naught but pain."

He tore his gaze away to address the gathering. "My friends—brothers and sisters in this war!" His tone suggested that he believed all present were part of his flock. "Toh has a plan for us all, though we may dislike what He reveals. We have fallen far from the destinies He intended. This is our sore heritage. I recognize our failure in each of you because Toh has taught me to peer into that depth of failure within myself!"

The throng that had followed this man to the summit responded: "Respect for Truth makes the whole world of lies an ill fit!"

"To deliver unto you this Truth, I will risk your displeasure and hatred. When darkness is not confronted, it can sow its corruption forever. But the uncovered and confronted darkness can be seen for what it truly is: only an obstruction of Toh's love."

His assembly responded: "I spurn all familiar watering holes, for lo! A far different thirst afflicts me!"

"I want no man or woman by my side," Konatep said, "who believes that the life they've hitherto led is worth defending. Toh does not deal gently with such."

Then, he dropped his hands to signal the end of this ceremonial prelude. He paused, seeming to relish the pervasive silence and attendant tension. Ildriss stepped closer to the central stone, glanced at Esperidi, and immediately stiffened as if that brief look had betrayed her. Halting, she spoke in a monotone so emotionless that Esperidi couldn't discern its underlying *timbres.*

"Stewardship of Ophia lies in the hands of those who would obey Toh's will. Our world will ascend into His light or be utterly extinguished. The hand of fate will be decided by steadfast adherence to the Way."

Then Ildriss lapsed into wide-eyed dissociation as if she'd stumbled into a wall of blankness or heard a contrary voice that she didn't know how to dispute. Esperidi wailed inside. *She is so broken! Ah, Ashangtu! I understand now why you couldn't bear to face her!*

Konatep, however, did not find his devotion to Toh so burdensome. His eyes and feet bounced with eager buoyancy as if to combat the dour air surrounding him.

"But we are remiss in our sense of ceremony, Sister Ildriss," he said. "It was the Olen-sa's turn to speak." He encompassed the gathering again. "But before we proceed, some truths must be revealed. Lies must be unmasked."

With long strides that sent his cloak whipping behind him like a sail, he bolted towards Sanyori, who watched his approach with a quizzical smile. Konatep paused for a moment, allowing his audience to witness his triumph.

"There's a lesson here for all of us—a reminder that unbelievers may wear fair guises! But the hand of Toh exposes them!"

Then he swiped an arm, and the assembly gasped as it passed through Sanyori's form. The evanescent semblance of the man rippled as if it was a reflection in a pond that, until that moment, had been undisturbed. For a few seconds, the image flickered: there one moment, gone the next. Then, it snuffed out entirely, an extinguished candle.

Some Junsas gripped their spears and cast their eyes about as if more witchery might strike at them from a blind side.

"The lies of the deceiver!" Konatep shouted.

His flock responded as one: "No illusions can withstand Toh's light!"

But Esperidi moved towards the central stone again as the commotion rose. Though startled, she was not as utterly dumbfounded by "Sanyori's" disappearance as the other spectators. She'd already begun to suspect the nature of the figure that trod beside her to the Meet. His *timbre* had felt tentative, reminding her of someone too distracted by thoughts of past or future to sustain a conversation in the present.

Once he finished dispensing with Sanyori's shade, Konatep eyed Esperidi's movements but mostly panned his gaze along the circle of onlookers. Esperidi saw the four Inooks entering the circle, leading horses, in response to the priest's subtle signal. But Konatep made a placating gesture to one who seemed on the verge of intervening. Then, without meeting her eyes, he aimed the indulgent smile of a patient parent toward Esperidi.

"Let her speak," he said, as if everyone present had been waiting for his permission. "I have already dispelled a Sophryne shade before their eyes. Surely, they will not now be fooled by the lies of a Sophryne witch!"

Esperidi ignored him and anchored herself in the beseeching *timbre* she felt emanating from Shamarai. He wanted something from her. He was waiting. Her lucidity sharpened as if an invisible hand had tapped her shoulder or the breeze carried a whispered reminder to her ears. But for the moment, she hovered in an in-between place. And though this expanded her senses far beyond their accustomed bounds, it did not inure her to the vestiges of instinctive mortal clinging.

She did not believe Konatep would allow her to live after she'd spoken her piece.

In that moment of anguished recognition, she thought of Ashangtu and Sanyori. *My allies abandoned me!* A part of her wailed. *I'm all alone!*

Then, Esperidi heard Shiya-coqui's voice as distinctly as if the woman leaned behind the nape of her neck.

Perhaps they knew that they had to. Perhaps they understood a truth that you still try to conceal from yourself: that this step of the journey is yours alone.

Esperidi nodded in response to this voice. If her life was forfeit, she could at least spend it in such a way that Oskwai lives might be spared—and they would understand some of the true causes of their suffering.

Turning towards the promontory's southern lip, where the Ruhselene milled, she shouted: "Your people need you, Suskhana! Promise me you'll not interfere if I am threatened!"

She didn't wait for a reply. Esperidi felt presumptuous, raising her arms to call attention to herself; she was too self-conscious to lift her voice above its natural swell. Nevertheless, as soon as she began, the summit quieted. Faces probed her. Konatep's eyes momentarily flared like the glint of sunlight off daggers, but he held his peace.

"You've been fed lies by the Shetain priesthood concerning the Rupture and your culpability," Esperidi said. "They've urged you to sacrifice those dear to you to expiate sins that are not yours. Everyone who experienced the cataclysms indeed took a hand in creating them—else they would have been untouched by the destruction. But my people, the Shaini, are largely to blame for all the ill that was wrought.

"With the exuberance of younglings, we ruptured our civilization through our over-eagerness, employing power without regard for cost. We had to learn about our limitations by overstepping them to such an extent that those actions could never be recalled."

Even a fully trained Sophryne would be daunted, venturing into a realm where all stood revealed: the buried sorrows and rages of people who, driven by extremity, sacrificed their own to appease the darkness. But Esperidi had resolved not to run; she wasn't spurred by guilt or regret. Sorsajna depended not on the pathways she strove to open. But to partake in its light... Ah, that required self-awareness. And forgiveness.

"All beings in all times must become aware, in their way, of how they participate in Creation. Otherwise, Sorsajna could have always remained One and need never have expressed itself as Many. Every act of shunning nature costs us the awareness of a portion of our inner life, our true heritage. But even our apparent catastrophes are lessons clothed in pain. We learn we cannot separate from the world that nurtures us and still hope to find our hearts."

Esperidi had yet to encounter a tribe that the Rupture hadn't injured. And it was these inner abilities she spoke of that enabled those people, in one way or another, to survive, whether they were conscious of that providence or not.

"How might Ophia transform if we can even consider the idea that the reality we experience is an extension—an illustration on a three-dimensional cave wall—of who we are, growing from the inside out?

"Armed with my warnings, can you avoid the pitfalls? Can you hold onto these lessons after I'm gone? Can you cherish peace in your hearts?"

Esperidi now approached the crux of her sermon and needed to choose her words carefully. If the onlookers felt they were being preached at, they might seal away their hearts, rejecting the message.

"My people thought to utilize *Sacred Timbre* to shape the face of the land according to our desires," she said. "We overreached ourselves in ignorance and pride. We groped towards the heavens while racing toward a precipice. Amok swept across lands beyond the horizons of our sight; we disrupted the very foundations of life. It never occurred to us that Ophia's inner tones, evoked without reverence and humility, could destroy Her. Thus, the same forces we utilized to order our world tore it asunder.

"Let this be the lesson that steers the humans of this new age away from a similar fate! Shai-win's mercy! Let me wring that much hope out of the ruin of Ophia! If I am the last Sophryne, the final keeper of the flame, let my example light the way over the abyss. Our world need not plunge into its depths a second time!"

Esperidi continued to open herself to the furthest extent that her native ability and training allowed. She poured her last ounces of love, hope, and honesty into the Meet she shared with the tribes. Sorsajna, the source of life, could ask no more of her.

"And so a cycle begins anew! Let humankind's capacities flourish under a new sun! You are Ophia's heirs. Within you lives the promise of stewardship. And your dreams flow out of an infinite wellspring. Remember that. If you understand this endless source, available to all, then why act out of greed or lack? Why hoard Ophia's bounty or deprive anyone else of it?

"We are *all* birthed from Sorsajna, from which all blessings flow!"

Konatep turned to one of the Inooks and signalled. This man, swift as a viper, rushed to Ildriss's side and grasped her shoulders. The woman gasped with an expression of utter dismay and confusion as she was ushered towards one of the horses so swiftly that, at times, her feet scarcely grazed the ground.

Ildriss rallied herself for one futile protest. "But I was to be our peace ambassador!"

"There will be no peace today," the Inook droned as he hoisted her onto the horse. He mounted behind her a moment later and spurred the beast down the butte's gentler western side.

When Konatep reached Esperidi, his face was aglow with triumph.

"Toh entrusted His message to me," he told the assembly. "We are the only ones deemed worthy of deliverance from the Rupture. We are tasked with building Ophia anew: a country and people devoted to His word. As for the others... If they have indeed eluded their fates, they could only have done so with the aid of sorcery. And now—"

His index finger denounced Esperidi. "From her own mouth, this Olen-sa condemns herself! She was forewarned of the Rupture through divination! And this is hardly the extent of her transgressions. She is a Sophryne—aye, by her own admission. She will not forsake *Sacred Timbre*, the discipline of arrogance that shattered Ophia, but she *will* embrace the madness of dreams! She'll seek worlds that Toh's Light has forsaken! I tell you, Chosen—You see the roots of terrible devastation before you!"

Esperidi made no outcry when Konatep grabbed her hair and pulled her head back. She didn't protest. At that moment, Konatep's reality seemed to impinge upon hers only tangentially, and she couldn't understand her reaction at first. Did she merely wish to deny the priest the satisfaction of seeing her tremble and plead for mercy?

"We bear the burden of judgment!" the priest railed. "Toh has delivered her into our hands. Will we allow her freedom when she bears powers that once rent our world? Are we worthy of His great faith if we ignore obvious evil?"

What Konatep did or did not think of Esperidi was not pertinent. Having spoken her truth, she now felt wrapped within it. And this sensation deepened the conviction—beyond anything she'd known before—that her life was hers, that no one else could elevate or condemn her truly. The only judgment she needed to fear was her own.

She'd been prepared for repudiation. She'd marked the lost fanaticism in the wounded eyes of most of the onlookers. These people possessed nothing aside from their devotion. Dogma and obedience were the only available answers to the riddle of their pain and loss.

Thus, she was shocked when a few Junsa voices rose to defend her. The trauma inflicted by the Rupture had not silenced them all.

Shamarai gripped his spear until his knuckles whitened. But he wavered where he stood, like a stiff tree lashed by a harsh wind. He felt the readiness and outrage of the men standing beside him. He knew that they would join him, to a man, if he chose to fight. But he also knew how lethal the Inooks were. They'd lost one of their number, but this would scarcely slow them. And the fell power that Konatep wielded through his staff... The eyes of that baleful skull had already claimed the lives of a half-score Junsa who'd dared defy the Manitoh priest. There was enough death on Shamarai's hands already.

Suskhana, too, was acquainted with tales of the crystal skull and of the Inooks' lethal hands. And the Olen-sa had commanded her not to interfere...

Also, a faint, almost imperceptible hum had begun to

issue from the stones in response to the first sun's rays striking the central arch. The sound soothed Shamarai and Suskhana, urging peace, bidding them to stay their hands.

Konatep bent to hiss in Esperidi's ears. "Repeat this if you dare—if you think anyone here will trust your word over mine. Consider it in your last moment and despair! Your adopted people—those savages, those chattel made in an image fit to mock Toh—will slave for the glory of New Shetain! And you! Sophryne!" He spat the word. "Bah! Did no dream warn you that you would meet your death here? You verily leaped into my net of your own accord."

Recalling the Cordonne and its fate, Esperidi whispered: "The world is your mirror, Konatep. Every net eventually ensnares its caster."

The Manitoh priest shook her. "Where has the other Shaini gone? The third!"

But Esperidi drove the priest from her thoughts. She had no time. She had to settle deeper into the Sophryne state, though she accepted that even it could not save her life. Evoking an inner tone that embodied the essence of "mobility," she fought against the heavy inertia that held her down.

Sophryne consciousness might at least allow her to escape pain.

But Esperidi wasn't certain what impulse spurred her to dive inward. Was it merely fear of death's sting, of whatever harm might bring her to that culminating release? Or was it that instinctive longing—every Sophryne was acquainted with it—to part the Veils and become utterly immersed in the humming, loving Creation that existed beyond and within this camouflage of transitory forms? That longing made her almost impatient with death's cumbersome transition.

I'll shed Ophia like Sarpienta sheds His skin!

That thought reminded her of the morning practice she'd adopted while traveling with Ashangtu—and the dream that had inspired it. *Yes! It's time to withdraw my hand from the serpent's head!* And as Esperidi mumbled a Sophryne song, she envisioned that pocket of dream reality, anticipating the moment when the rhythmic motions of her fingers no longer lulled the great snake to quiescence. The moment its eyes opened and, smelling prey, it lashed at her to deliver the liberating blow....

Esperidi inclined her head towards that blow. It was time. Feeling the serpent's restlessness, she lifted her dream hand.

Shiya-coqui's voice rang again. "Remember that your consciousness is free! It is independent. It is not bound to your body. Recall what I taught you. You can relinquish the house of your five senses."

With a convulsive effort that spewed an aged groan from between her tight lips, Esperidi fell to her knees, staring at the ground as if it were her life's final obstacle. The effort cost her the remainder of her consciousness. She did not feel Jamurada's smooth cobbles or Konatep's fingers clenched in her hair. For her, the fall was much farther, a plunge into a nebulous chasm wherein the myriad terrors and dreads that are the heritage of all humankind dwelled.

The Partition of materiality folded back. Her consciousness swelled to a dimension that felt expansive enough to contain Ophia and yet cherish every dandelion, every pebble.

Slowly, a figure took form in the void of no-time. At first, Esperidi thought that she looked upon Raven. She recognized those penetrating eyes, the sharp beak that struck her inner senses like a sword of discernment. But as the being coalesced, she saw that only the face was that of a raven. Though draped in ebony feathers, the body was human: erect and magisterial. Probing deeper, Esperidi realized she couldn't determine its sex. It seemed to embody both, mingling the *timbres* that she usually associated with the masculine and feminine into a seamless whole with different qualities coming to the fore from moment to moment.

Overawed, she shrank before its immensity. But at once, a voice made itself known.

"Why do you kneel before *yourself*?"

The question confounded her. "Erawen," she said, "I kneel because I failed. I need you to forgive me."

Peals of laughter emanated from the figure like ocean waves. "You cannot fail! You bear Sorsajna within you, the light that can never be extinguished!"

"But Esperidi Mon-Sequana *did* fail. I understand now why she was born into Ophia. But this body, this vehicle, could not complete the task. The forces ranged against her were too great."

"Their *resources* are great," Erawen said. "Their manipulations are strong. But strength divorced from love is a paltry thing."

Suddenly spreading its hands wide, Erawen said, "Come closer, child!"

Esperidi did so as if answering the deepest bidding of her heart, and after a few steps, she felt the figure grasp her shoulders.

"There's something you must understand," Erawen said. "Put your faith in this, if naught else. Our universe leans towards supporting the flowering of life. This impetus is alive within every conscious being. And this is why your enemies can never surpass your Vision. In seeking to control life, they remove themselves from the very source of true potency. Their ambition blinds them to the light you carry—the light that also lives within them, though they have forgotten it."

Releasing her, Erawen smiled as if appeased.

"And now, there's someone I wish you to meet."

꙰ ꙰

Esperidi rose with such force that Konatep was momentarily unbalanced. But she did not face her accuser. Instead, she fixed her eyes upon Shamarai, and the light within them seemed not her own. The Junsa chieftain, recognizing it at once, stiffened with wild amazement.

"Shamarai, my love," she intoned, "I have leaped upwards into the ocean that encloses our Ophia like a womb! I have met the stars once writ upon my palm; I've walked upon the face of the moon that followed me along the canyons and swamps of Aramoye!"

Shamarai glared at the speaker, hoping to pierce the Shaini facade and see Seribu's face. Some of the phrases she used were foreign to his ears, unlike how his life-mate had spoken in life, but the particular lilt and cadence evoked Seribu's presence powerfully.

He was so enrapt in trying to penetrate the mystery that he didn't wonder at the warm yellow glow that began to illuminate the plateau until it was strong enough to make him squint. Shamarai gazed skywards, but the sun was not bright enough to account for such luminosity. And he was warm as if he stood within a circle of campfires. The soft hum was more insistent. The megalithic stones seemed to converse with one another, sharing a protracted "aauuummmmm" that felt like an utterance from Ophia's heart.

Everyone gathered stared about in wonderment and confusion. But the Inooks seemed to shrink from the light and sound as if it diminished them in some essential way. To Shamarai's eyes, they seemed to tremble as if with ague.

Seribu's voice—he was now somehow certain it was, indeed, her—held him affixed to a *timbre* of love hurled across the Partition.

"I borrow the Olen-sa's voice so you may know that I yet live! Grieve no more! Nay! Not for a single seed that fails to take root in a garden forever preserved, for all seeds will find their right time and place to flower."

Then, that voice was cut short.

The priest Konatep did not seem to suffer from whatever afflicted the Inooks. His staff's pale glow defied the warm light of Jamurada's stones. Now, the Manitoh priest bent that baleful argence down upon Esperidi's brow.

He cannot! Shamarai railed within the stunned confines of his mind. *She delivers Incora!*

"Hold!"

This command was shouted by the grizzled and bearded head of a man just cresting the eastern lip of the gnoll. Much of his tangled mass of auburn hair was dyed the green of jungle leaves. He was broad-shouldered, somewhat hefty, and walked with a peculiar lurch like someone constantly lashed by an internal primal force he was reluctant to respond to.

"There is one voice yet unheard by this council!"

This man and his audacious interruption provoked Konatep's snarl.

"And whose voice shall we hear, Wakeen? That of a man who, when all the treasures of Shetain are laid at his feet, spits in Toh's eye and flees his birthright, an infidel and coward?"

"You gather to decide Ophia's future," Wakeen said, sounding utterly unperturbed. "Should you not heed a voice from the heart of Ophia Herself?"

Konatep's laugh rose to a maniacal pitch, and spittle frothed at the corners of his mouth. "Again, who?" he raved.

"You have no home either on the ground or in the heavens! You've forsaken both, and both revile you! Go back to the Kawli mines, where your befouled hands can find their condign use! Or find a heathen tribe who will worship you in your vanity!"

"Nay, not me," Wakeen said. "I can think of a much worthier representative."

The gathering stilled as the big man looked over his shoulder, waiting. Finally, he remarked to the space beyond the lip, "After you, my brother," punctuating this with a solicitous wave.

A gargantuan head emerged onto the cobbles, yellow and turquoise eyes glaring from a cranium larger than a bull's. Length upon length of the reptile's scaled body drew a sinuous S over the crest of the plateau to bask in its light and draw warmth from its stones.

The horses the Inooks had brought into the ring reared and bolted with squeals of terror. Brinstead's Pale Faces went whiter than cotton sheets, pressing their backs against one menhir as if wishing to dissolve into the stone. The Manitohs in Konatep's entourage immediately hurled their spears aside. They prostrated themselves, invoking names old even before the fashioning of Khempsa, Khampalu, and Brune—among them, the ancient word for Grandfather Serpent: "Sarpienta!"

Espying something that quickened its interest, the giant snake soon outpaced its companion. The muscles beneath its thick skin, alternatingly black and glittering, like steel scorched and cracked until its underlying gold shone through, were taut with the anticipation of rapture and violence. Its softer-ribbed underbelly was emerald, lime-green, and yellow in places.

As the three Inooks dashed the five or six paces that separated them from the creature, Shamarai, already outraged by the priest's defiling of *Incora*, was pushed beyond the edge of reason. *They would slay the serpent!* Snarling his fury, he rushed the nearest Inook, stone axe held high overhead.

The Inook's response was almost too quick to follow. Catching Shamarai's axe hand just below the wrist, he drove three stiff fingers of his free hand into the Junsa's sternum. The blow seemed to snatch all the air from Shamarai's lungs. In the time it took the Shetain assassin to accomplish this, however, two other Junsa, who had followed at Shamarai's heels, were upon him. One managed to wrap thick arms around the Inook and, as the ruthless minion struggled within the glare of Jamurada's Singing Stones, which sapped his strength and will, another Junsa clubbed his head three times with a stone mace until the thick bones of his skull crunched, bathing the crude weapon in a wash of crimson.

Shamarai recovered himself and straightened. As he did so, however, he saw that the other two Inooks had already been dispatched. One lay on the other side of the moving, scaly wall, his head and body separated by a Manitoh axe. Over another stood a wiry Ruhselene woman, her feral eyes alight with fierce triumph. Noticing Shamarai's regard, she shouted, "With his last breath, finally he *felt* something indeed!" Then she removed her spear from the Inook's breast with a savage grunt.

Konatep stumbled in a half-crouch, glaring about him with a rabid light in his eyes, nearly in a paroxysm of fury. "Infidels! Defilers of the Writ!" he cried.

He'd become aware of two facts simultaneously. There was no mistaking the snake's intent. As it propelled itself across the plateau, its feral eyes were fixed upon Toh's mouthpiece. And no support remained around the priest. Even some of the Brinsteaders were kneeling now.

"Fools!" Konatep cried. "This is no god! We *made* this

creature!"

The depth of his fanaticism mastering his fear, the foremost of the Pale Faces, Havar, rushed forward and grasped Konatep's tunic, shaking the priest in his outrage. "By Toh and Jamaro!" he rasped, "Would you defile the Sacred Writ to preserve your own life? Is this the depth of your faith?"

But then he gave back with an outcry as the snake feigned to strike at him, deliberately pulling short a few feet from the ashen man. Havar stumbled and fell backward in his terror. Then, he scampered on palms and feet towards the stones at the northern side of the circle.

Wakeen shoved the man as he passed. Havar tumbled to the dirt but picked himself up almost in the same motion and ran. The remaining Brinsteaders, seeing their leader so unmanned, hurried after him, hysteria alight in their eyes.

Konatep stood alone. With no other recourse, he leveled defiance at the snake.

"We made you! Shetain is your *master!*"

The priest clutched his staff in both hands and raised it by his head like a broadsword. "Aye, you remember this, don't you?" He taunted the giant serpent. "Its bite is as agonizing as yours, all the more so because it doesn't kill. Rather–"

The creature regarded him curiously for a moment and then, like the lash of a whip, made as if to lunge towards his legs. Konatep brought the staff down to meet the strike. In almost the same instant, though, Sarpi lunged towards the exposed flesh of his neck. The impact made Konatep's body ripple like a doll shaken by its head. He fell to his knees as if paying the same homage as the other Manitohs.

Still, he managed to glare contempt. Through lungs quickly constricting, he grated, "You were always an abomination!"

Sarpi, seeming agitated by his prey's persistence, struck again.

Now, Konatep trembled with venom from head to foot. He made no more outcries. Feeling his heart racing towards an explosion, he had time for just one bewildered thought.

The beast made a feint! How?

Then he went still as a petrified tree. His eyes glazed, and the last thing those eyes bore witness to was the soft pink of Sarpi's throat as the great serpent loosened its jaw and extended its mouth to receive Toh's priest. Moving half the body towards its gullet, it lifted its head, an almost gleeful light in its eyes, so that gravity could help its muscles pull the lean body down.

Wakeen casually moved around the circle's circumference. "It seems Sarpienta has spoken," he remarked. "We can only hope that those who might inflict their beliefs upon others against their will might take heed of this omen."

Then he took a place in the circle's center and, revolving slowly, strove to meet as many eyes as he could. "We leave now, and you will not follow us. And you will abase yourselves no longer. Old Sarpi here moves along his belly, but he does not come kneeling. Neither should any of you come kneeling!"

Then he picked a random direction, and the Manitohs and Junsas in his path parted like a tide. In a moment, he and his serpent companion, bloated with Shetain's High Priest, were gone over the dip of the hill. A hush as profound as a religious experience followed in their wake.

Opening her physically-focused eyes, Esperidi vaguely groped towards the man's retreating form, mouthing a wordless protest. With the portion of herself that had remained attuned to her surroundings amid all the internal maneuvers that had allowed another voice to speak through her, she understood that he had intervened and probably saved her life. But his rigid back was immune to appeal, and she was left to wonder at the immensity of the reptilian tail—

Suskhana had mentioned a "Snake Man," but Esperidi's memory of that remark had been swept aside in the rush of ensuing events.

—weaving over the last few feet of the plateau before disappearing over its face.

Both Sides of the Mirror

Esperidi opened her eyes to a pink-domed ceiling whose transparency admitted dawn's strengthening light. She was prone on a low-lying bed. Slowly, she recognized the room she'd shared with Ashangtu in Pedragira. Before her, several Oskwai squatted in silence.

As Sanyori leaned over her, she rallied enough to mutter, "How long?"

"You've slept for the remainder of the equinox and a night."

"A day and a night," she marveled. "I remember no dreams."

"Perhaps you dreamed enough whilst awake on Jamurada," Sanyori said. "You'll be ready for a big breakfast soon, methinks."

Esperidi reached out and tried to verify his tangible presence. She recalled seeing his image vanish when the priest Konatep had touched it. Sanyori allowed her to graze her fingertips across his cheek.

"I was aware the moment my projection was dispelled," he said, "but it's a long run from Pedragira to the stone circle. Much evil might have befallen there before I could have reached you had other forces not intervened." He swallowed hard. "Please forgive my deception. I believed my image would be more convincing if naught knew of it but me. You see, Konatep and I have encountered each other before.

Or perhaps I should say he's encountered my shade. He was... not pleased overmuch by the outcome.

"I considered going out there robed and masked. But I'm not altogether sure what kind of training these priests have received, how versed they are in *Sacred Timbre*. Perhaps he could have sensed my identity. He surely would have tried to kill me if he'd known I was there. A man like that does not appreciate having his pride slighted. And with the Inooks by his side, he would've accomplished it easily."

"This was not the first time you've projected yourself like that," Esperidi surmised.

"The third, in fact," Sanyori said. "I've been an actor since adolescence, so when my knowledge of *Sacred Timbre* deepened—" He extended an arm to illustrate. "Sending a doppelganger out ahead of me was a natural extension, so to speak.

"I first accomplished it when we escaped Farsilane. To distract the audience, along with a couple of Cordonne lackeys in the wings, I returned to the stage for a long soliloquy after the rest of the troupe had left. Only, I wasn't actually there. I'd already hopped the boat.

"The second incident occurred about a year ago, shortly after we left the ruins of Kublai Hive. I did it to save a young woman: Kanchi, my apprentice, now Singing Chieftess of the Sendhi in Mangoyen." For a moment, his eyes had a faraway cast; they glittered with almost parental pride. "It's amazing, isn't it? What we're capable of when we have a strong enough impetus?"

"I had never imagined that another being could speak through my physical body," Esperidi marveled. "That startled me."

Sanyori mulled this and then, recalling a more urgent concern, thrust his myriad questions aside. "You know, I'd hoped the two of us would have more time. I'd meant to sit down with you and discuss some things I discovered during my forays to the Library."

Esperidi dismissed this with a nervous wave. "I think I already know what you would say. It's about *her*, isn't it?" When his eyes failed to contradict the supposition, she added: "I'm not ready, San. Not yet. This trial has tested me sorely."

Sanyori squinted at her and then offered a commiserating smile. "It sounds like you do suspect much of what I was going to say."

"Ever since my apprenticeship with Shiya-coqui began, I've anticipated that, someday, I'll need to contact someone beyond Ophia's bounds—and that I have a strong connection with this being. But right now, I need to find my footing *here* again."

She returned his smile. It was easier than she thought it'd be. "We'll just have to promise to meet up again, and then you can tell me your tale in full."

"I'd readily agree to that, tale or no tale."

One of the Oskwai suddenly stood and approached, bowing low before Esperidi. She recognized Shamarai.

"One of the Inooks escaped with that new priestess of Toh, Olen-sa," he said. "It will not be long before Shetain knows all that transpired on Jamurada. This place will not be safe. Where will you go?"

Sanyori's expression brimmed with the same urgency. "That giant snake who wrought your salvation... There's a rumor that the folk of Shetain bred the creature to serve as the living incarnation of the godhead, a way to cow those who still cling to old beliefs. Konatep proclaimed as much, hoping it would spare his life. If the priesthood suspects the secret has been revealed, they're liable to hunt down everyone who attended the Meet to silence them."

He turned to Suskhana, whose keen ears strained

towards this exchange, but the woman stiffened—with palpable, undaunted pride—before he could speak. "We love the Roana Hills! Our dreams have awakened every ravine and crest into story and song. *Never* will we forsake them!"

"Then, at least take to the caves until things quiet in the land again," Sanyori urged her.

"How far back do these caves go?" Esperidi asked, suspecting she already knew the answer.

"There are walls." Suskhana extended a flattened palm to pantomime encountering an invisible barrier.

Esperidi intuited the perception that the woman was trying to convey. Though she didn't understand their true nature, Suskhana knew something artificial had been created, forbidding access to deeper recesses beneath the hills.

Sanyori confirmed this. "Like most natural caverns that survived the Rupture, these were sealed off. There must be an entrance into Elmicora somewhere in there, though I haven't investigated the possibility.

"From what I've gleaned, five gateways to Elmicora endured. My apprentice discovered the passage within Kublai's ruins that connects to Mangoyen, whose depths cradle Elmicora's heart. The others, I surmise, are connected with Helwen Hive, Magda's Oasis, Roana Mountain, and the canyon caves outside lost Sequana—Aramoye."

"Then Roana is worth exploring further, don't you think? For the sake of the Ruhselene?"

"It'd be fruitless," Sanyori said. "For us, anyway. Recall your history. The portion of Elmicora that would run through the Roana Hills was wrought by Shetain Hive, which hoped to use it as an expedient route to the Kawli when Jain-Toh was governor there."

Esperidi's lips curled in contemplation. "Of all the Hives, Shetain kept their lore most private, safeguarding it against Ophia's other factions."

They'd never shared it until their Hive had been integrated into the Cordonne, and to her knowledge, no Cordonne member had survived the Rupture except for the Sovereign Priest.

"So only Jain-Toh would understand the woven *timbres* that could open those portals," she concluded.

"He or his children, who were no doubt taught the inner keys," Sanyori said. "For all his arcane mastery, Jain isn't going to live forever. And I suspect his progeny were all sheltered away from the worst of the cataclysms on Chonnen shores."

Esperidi recalled what Ashangtu had confessed to the Ruhselene after they'd passed through the ravine of skulls.

Sanyori nodded vaguely eastwards. "In fact, our snake charmer of the swamp may be one of Jain's children, a young man who fled in defiance. It's rumored that his older sister did as well."

"I urge you to take to the caves anyway," Esperidi told Suskhana. "They'll at least give you some shelter from predators and raiders, even if they can't safeguard you from the priesthood." Then she smiled somewhat abashedly. "I realize I'm not your chief and have no business advising you."

Suskhana threw back her head and laughed. After all the recent days' losses and upheavals, it sounded like water frothing out of spring's thaw.

"Sometimes you are *too* humble, Olen-sa," she said, "and even more so for a Dream Stalker! Who wouldn't welcome the counsel of one such as you?"

Embarrassed, Esperidi wanted to dismiss this praise, but as she started to speak, she realized that the warmth of Suskhana's trust and admiration nourished places within her that had long felt starved. She would need such trust if she was going to build a new home... somewhere.

Shamarai was growing impatient. "Where will you go?" he repeated.

Esperidi probed him with quizzical eyes. "Tell me one thing first, Shamarai. Why did you so readily believe that it was your Seribu who spoke through me? How could you know it was not a ruse?"

He seemed amused, and much of his previous tension dissipated. "From your lips came mention of two things she loved most: the ocean and the sight of the moon from Aramoye. Also—" He grazed his fingers across the back of his hand. "The group of stars that make the shape of a bow..."

"D'yangi," Suskhana said.

"Yes: D'yangi the Huntress. Seribu had these stars tattooed beneath her knuckles." Shamarai's eyes bore into Esperidi as his hands articulated his incomprehension. "You could not have known such things."

Esperidi digested this as quickly as her still-waking thoughts allowed. "Where do *you* want to go, Shamarai?"

"All the Junsa desire to return to Aramoye," he said. "The priests called it a domain of evil, but they lied about many things. These others—" He indicated several Manitoh men and women standing by the bed that had been Ashangtu's with a nod that could not disguise his distaste. "They wish to join us there. I will not forbid it if they have your blessing."

"Mine?" Esperidi marveled at the thought but then awakened to the reverence with which everyone in the room held her. She had performed *Incora*. "I forbid no one to live where they choose to live," she said. "And I agree that the Shetain priesthood has filled your ears with many lies. But the Mirrors of Aramoye are something you must be wary of. My Papa left Sequana because he could not bear what the cliff caves reflected. He argued that the passages should be sealed—that we should bury the entire canyon and its memory. Most Sequanans disagreed. So he and I departed for Farsilane, where he hoped to find more sympathetic ears."

More to herself, she mused, "I think he was eager to escape a place that held nothing but pain for him anyway. My mother—"

Reading her emotion as she faltered, Shamarai said, "Still lives, as does my Seribu. You proved this to all of us at Jamurada."

But Esperidi's inner equilibrium was too disrupted to find solace in his assertion. *I'm haunted by a woman I never knew. And Papa's been dead nearly three years now, yet his shadow still hovers over me, making me shrink within myself when I think of him. Can I never be free of this?*

Shamarai sought to convey with his eyes a complex loyalty that he had no words for. Then he stooped slightly and offered his hand. "What say you?"

"I long for Aramoye, too," Esperidi admitted, rising with the clearest certainty she'd felt since the idea had first visited her. "It is all that remains of the place that most closely resembled home for me. What if its heart could be revived? And if others shun the place out of superstition—and the Inooks fear to go there—all the better."

"What sticks out in my memory now," Sanyori said, "is that Aramoye was the first settlement—the *only* one ever in our history—to abandon its armories."

"That was its great leap of faith," Esperidi said. "I didn't know that until I delved deeper in the Sentient Library. I wanted to understand better where I'd come from. Not that I believe a place *shapes* you into who you are, mind you. But there are *inner* reasons why we gravitate to those places. Reasons we choose the hour and place of our birth...

"It's easy to rail against those decades of Cordonne rule and say that there was always war or the threat of it. But war is spurred by this underlying idea that, given the chance, others will do their worst. That it's in their nature to hurt us to the fullest extent that we allow them to. Therefore, we must rally defenses. In such a climate of belief, who possesses the courage to lay down those defenses and thus be an example for the rest of Ophia, a living embodiment of what peace can be? That's what Aramoye accomplished for a while.

"That's why I was unsurprised to hear that the inner sanctums survived the Rupture. They were formed with such an intention. They embodied the very *timbres* of peace. And they were wrought with the understanding that we would not project our internal conflicts upon others and make them enemies.

"That's why I feel I need to be there." Her eyes appealed to Sanyori for understanding. "There was a moment after we left Tohbin—and before Ashangtu and I found you—where my heart and mind unraveled. Acknowledging my need to devote myself to Ophia's healing enabled me to start feeling whole again."

"The Cordonne's Mothers and Fathers were motivated by similar ambitions," Sanyori cautioned, "and look what they wrought."

"There's always that danger if we pursue such an ideal," Esperidi said. "One's tempted to think, 'I know what's best for others. I know what path they ought to take.' If Aramoye is still what it once was, if it does still embody those *timbres* that formed it, it can keep me grounded. It can return me to myself whenever I start thinking there's a battle somewhere outside myself that I must contend with."

"Which makes Aramoye the ideal place for any Sophryne to live, I suppose," Sanyori said. "Any Sophryne concerned with the responsible use of power, anyway. Because you know, Esperidi, some natives will confer power on you whether you wish it or not. You'll have to accept that if you live among them."

"But maybe if I refuse to participate, and they feel the the canyon's influence, they'll see past that. In the meantime, though, I will *let* them lean on me as their link to Sorsajna."

"Their wounds are deep," Sanyori warned.

"This is the best way to address some of that hurt. I will act as their Singing Chieftess so that what is now hope and faith may flourish into surety within them. It'll help them to develop new myths to replace their tales of savage gods. Yes!" Esperidi laughed. "The more I explore the question, the more convinced I become. Aramoye is the place to risk such an experiment."

Then she searched her friend. "Will you come?"

"Oh, I doubt it's the place for someone like me," Sanyori confessed. "I *revel* in the contrast. That's why I love the stage. That's *my* mirror, where I can see my reflection diffused among a score of characters. And I can also offer that mirror up to any who'd want to peer into it.

"And, as much as Ophia lies broken and bleeding, I still long to see her. Nay, I think it's time I found a troupe again and traveled! I'll spread the myths far and wide, always trying to stay one league ahead of the Shetain priesthood."

"And the Ruhselene?" Esperidi asked.

"Many have already left," Sanyori said. "Suskhana here remains, though I suspect it's only because she wants to say goodbye to you before she goes. The Ruhselene want to settle in the foothills around Lake Banyomeer. Build a city, even. Which is either the most foolhardy or naively hopeful thing one can do in these times."

Esperidi looked to Suskhana to confirm her inner hunch. "You're attracted to the energies of that place, yes? Those hills lie along one of the lines where Sorsajna has found a place—" She fanned her hands several times to illustrate— "to pour its energies into Ophia and renew her. I'm sure that's what attracted the folk of Shetain, too. It inspired them to create their portion of Elmicora beneath those hills. That's probably what sustained the region through the cataclysms."

"But Jain-Toh, no doubt, has not forgotten," Suskhana said. "We dare not hope he'll eschew all ambition to reclaim the place."

"There are no safe havens anymore," Esperidi told her. "This is partly why I have to go to Aramoye. I have to deepen my practice and learn to trust my visions more fully if I'm to be of any help. I can't learn anything more merely by studying the pieces already laid on the board."

Then, having unburdened herself of so much hope and fear, at least in naming those things aloud, Esperidi rediscovered her courage. A *new dawning is possible now—for all of us!*

From Colleen (As Preserved in the Sentient Library)

In the days that followed, the frequent, vicious sandstorms painted southern Ophia in a sickly yellow haze. The wind howled in the travelers' ears, and the sand penetrated every loose stitch in their clothes. They fought for breath as the air's vehemence hurled a desiccated land into their faces or side-swept them from left and right. Esperidi was grateful for Sanyori's foresight: He'd provided them all with shawls.

She was forced to march at the head of this precarious procession. Only her inner vision allowed them to navigate. But she was close enough now to feel the *timbre* of Sequana, her home, calling to her heart like a beacon. Its body was broken, but its spirit still lingered in the land it had sanctified, whispering secrets about her inheritance that her younger self had seldom dared fantasize about.

During the storm's first lull, she sat with her companions and taught them an old Sophryne prayer, hoping to emphasize their kinship with nature's forces so they wouldn't look upon these storms as their adversaries and feed them with spite.

"This body, housing airy spaces, communes with the winds.

"This body, sustained by rushing veins and cleansing wells, imitates rivers and seas.

"This body arises from Ophia; to Ophia, it shall return.

"But it houses a fire that can never be extinguished."

The following day, moved by a tender impulse, she focused on the line about air elementals and developed it into a chant. Into this, she cunningly wove tones that approximated the inner timbre of peace, providing it with a material echo. She taught the tune to her companions, and they hummed and chanted through the thick cloths protecting their faces.

Esperidi was beginning to remember what the ancients knew, what her people had forgotten: They flourished when they were givers, distributors of the life force to other peoples and realms.

Perhaps, in time, that recognition could restore balance to all of Ophia.

Soon, Junsa and Manitoh alike felt peace emanating from them, communing with the surrounding air, the air that sustained their lives in every moment. And that sustenance responded like a purring creature beneath a petting hand, calming and subsiding until, by the third day, it became mere wind, vigorous rather than vehement; exuberant, not malign.

In truth, Esperidi had oftentimes been grateful for those storms. The immediate peril had diverted her mind from ancestral tensions within the ranks and her own sense of apartness. She worried about the possible futures her choices could set into motion. Was she prepared to relive the parade of culture with its myriad faces? Could she bear to witness that panorama—tribal bloodshed, the rise of monarchies and tyrants, the growth of convoluted and stifling bureaucracies—as people groped their way through history anew? Knowing the decadence, pretense, and spiritual malnourishment that civilization could foster, did she truly want to unite the disparate tribes and thus set them upon that road? Were there other roads that humankind might take? Was she wise and prescient enough to find them?

But the closer they drew to Aramoye, the more she and her party were overcome by a curiosity stronger than both personal and hereditary dreads.

Futurity was not a question that needed to be settled in the present, Esperidi decided. Had it been more accessible, the lore she learned from Shiya-coqui could have saved Ophia. Her people would've survived. If they'd better understood the nature of their inner selves, they would have used Sacred Timbre wisely. They would not have given their power over to the Cordonne. Instead of existing in thrall to the Weaving, they would have lovingly embraced their capacity for connection and unity.

Of course, there was no way she could ever test these theories.

But thrusting such concerns aside, Esperidi gasped in wonder and joy when, at long last, she and her companions filed into a subtly luminescent cavern and heard their footsteps echoing beneath Aramoye's vast, immaculately smooth dome.

The humming welcome of Sequana's ancient cliff caves was nearly audible.

—My last entry before leaving the hospital.

Marguerite's was a bohemian café. Aside from the best (in my humble opinion) coffee in Sadenport, it offered Panini sandwiches, Mediterranean salads, focaccia bread, and artisan bagels topped with any of a dozen spreads. If a poet had to work in a coffee house, this was his or her best downtown option.

I was grateful and relieved when they hired me as a server and cashier a few months after my release from the hospital. Although I was often merely drifting through my days, for a while, interacting with the public helped to ground me. I felt I'd rejoined the human community. And the place had a familial vibe—no egos, little undue drama. So, I was saddened when, after nearly two heart-warm years, the owners told us they planned to sell the place to one of the big chains.

We were assured the new managers wanted to keep everyone on when the turnover happened. No one who chose to stay would lose their job or swallow a pay cut. The Ascendian would take them under its wing.

I knew little about The Ascendian Café except that it'd begun in a small town in New Mexico. But after receiving the news, I researched them as thoroughly as I could online. Saint Santiago, the birthplace of the first store, used to have a population of a mere six hundred and fifty. Back then, the Ascendian was the only place to eat (or even get coffee) in town. Within the last couple years, however, the region had swelled to over eight thousand residents. Construction had been relentless throughout that period of growth. New adobe homes, paved drives, cobble roads and pathways, and power lines sprouted constantly. Scanning via a Maps program, I noticed an unusual number of vegetable gardens and livestock farms, all apparently communal.

They opened a second restaurant in a neighboring town to meet increased demand. From there, the franchise rapidly spread up the West Coast.

My co-workers and I turned from baristas to carpenters and decorators in preparation for this transition. The eight of us completely transformed the space within a few weeks, using some photos of the original Ascendian as guidelines. We carried in plain, unpolished wooden tables to give it an Old World feel. We set up new table tents with black and white pictures of a witch at her cauldron—albeit with bandana, overalls, and cowboy boots replacing the traditional black dress and pointy hat. We strung several dream catchers across the ceiling, some as long as six feet. Later, when we prepped the first steamer pans, the place smelled of mint and roasted pinons.

The night before The Ascendian's regional manager arrived to oversee the turnover, I dreamed I followed a lady into a crowded cave. I commented on the wave of people there. At times, they waded waist-deep, circling a subterranean pool. The crowd's movement eventually created a whirlpool. And their numbers swelled with a constant influx of newcomers from the opposite opening.

"The power we generate when we all move in the same direction!" the lady enthused. I kept trying to leave; I felt like I didn't belong there. But each time, she would intercept me.

Finally, I eluded her. I made it outside and began

walking along a river. I wanted to call out to some Undines or water spirits to help me, but I knew they wouldn't respond unless I could remember their names.

I carried this feeling of struggle and futility over into the morning. My sense of loss and foreboding shadowed the Big Day.

Nadine Milagro, originally from Mexico City, arrived directly from Headquarters in Saint Santiago, New Mexico. She wore a one-piece black dress with lacy patterns that somehow de-emphasized her femininity even as it hugged her figure. I guessed she often wore this outfit to "casual" business meetings. Her black hair was tied in a tail that whisked to and fro (literally like a pendulum) when she walked, brushing the small of her back. She must've spent hours as a kid practicing how to shift her weight to get that perfect swing. And I wondered if she always greeted the whole world with that show of teeth.

The timing of our first meeting could not have been worse. The "end of an era" reality had finally sunk in for me, and I was swamped by the realization that I'd used this cozy coffeehouse as a port in a storm, a place to keep my head down, surround myself with familiarity, and not think too much about anything. I was about to lose this sanctuary that I'd clung to in the years since being given a "clean bill of health." Some of my co-workers, whom I'd grown close to over the months and years, would not continue with the Ascendian.

I hid in the empty break room as tears welled up, tears I couldn't repress.

Oh, God, not here!

Nadine waltzed in, having obviously already learned my name, and started talking before she got a look at me. "Good morning, Colleen. I... oh!"

I hastily swiped my tears. "Sorry," I stammered. Then,

as if this needed useless elaboration: "I'm not always like this."

Nadine waved a hand as if I'd merely spilled some batter. "Oh, you need no apologize for feelings. Is good we know you're alive and not robot." Her eyes flared with crafty light. "It is personal? Or you are sad about the change that is happening?"

"A bit of both," I blurted without thinking.

Nadine acknowledged my emotional confusion with a kind of brisk empathy. "Is tough for everyone here, but maybe, for you, more so, no? Margueritte's has been like home?"

Normally, such a question—coming from a veritable stranger—would have felt intrusive. But I was too vulnerable to do anything but nod.

"You seem—" Nadine hugged her chest to illustrate the concept she was groping for—"on your guard. Suspicious, maybe?"

Believing I'd probably already jeopardized my position in the Ascendian, I forsook diplomacy. "You just seem a little forward, is all. You talk like we already know each other and are used to confiding all these things."

She seemed to relish this opportunity to enlighten me. "Oh, see, it is like this: I am a stranger to you, yes, but you are no stranger to me. Let us see—"

With head tilted toward the ceiling and a finger at her temple, she pantomimed rummaging through her memory. "Suicidal ideation. Three months in a psychiatric hospital. Doctor said—" She groped for a key quote. "You get lost in fantasy and sometimes cannot tell the difference, what is real and what is not."

There was a limbo period there where I wasn't sure whether what I was hearing was going to shatter my paralysis or deepen it. I gaped at Nadine's expression of...

Inquiry? Amusement?

Finally, the dam broke. "What the hell is going on here? You've read the police report? You have access to my hospital records? So much for that doctor-patient confidentiality BS!"

It's hard for me to describe this moment without resorting to clichéd terms like "nothing was real" and "the walls were closing in." A couple years before, during a more naively optimistic time, I'd written about peering past a thousand facades to find the face you hold in trust. Now, it seemed there <u>was</u> no trustworthy face. Pulling back one facade merely exposed another.

Run!

Run where?

See, I needed to find a point of stability. I'd seen where a free fall could land me, and I intended to never know that depth of horror again. Come on, Colleen. If there's no bright, shining road, at least find the one that's least dark.

"What's it matter, Colleen?" Nadine asked as if appealing directly to that point of conflict in me. "We help you in ways no doctors ever could. This is more important, no?"

"We?" Tossed like a ship in a storm, I circled back to my first demand. "How do you know about me? And <u>why</u>?"

She handled me like a flailing child. "Is our business to learn about people we notice are... gifted. I would come sooner, but business back home... We had to clean house, let us say. But listen! You must no be ashamed of what you've been through. This pain makes you wise. Oh, I could tell you stories! And the world needs more female... empowerment now. Empowerment, yes. Is up to people like you and me to be the messengers. We must embody the Truth so that others may see.

"Those at the hospital, they would label you crazy.

They think you a danger to you and maybe everyone else. I believe you are no danger except to unbelievers. I think you just want something more than all this."

She waved at the world outside with an air of disinterested dismissal.

"See, people give this big importance to the self. Then, they try to outsmart the Maker. When does this ever work?" She leaned close until I could smell her minty breath. "The Maker saved you that day when you stood over the gorge, ready to jump."

Her hand dove in imitation of free-fall.

I tried to evade her eyes, but they were relentless.

"You have been happy working here?"

I managed a numbed nod.

"If you work for The Ascendian, and it feels just as much like a family, you like this?"

I repeated the same mute gesture.

"We'll be happy for you to keep working here," Nadine said. "Most people no work for bosses who understand. Becoming awake nowadays... is like you see truth about yourself and the world, but then you are alone. No one else knows. They believe the illusion."

This kind of talk, coming from a corporate higher-up, confounded me. Wasn't everyone in the establishment invested in it? I mean, Nadine wasn't the owner of a mom-and-pop bagel shop. She was the regional manager of the fastest-growing chain on the West Coast.

I vaguely recalled being warned about spiritual rhetoric. "It is like any other kind of script: It can be turned to all kinds of purposes depending upon people's motives." Saul, the first human being to throw me a lifeline since I lost Stacie, had said that. I tried to resurrect other words. "Earned knowledge isn't merely something teachers possess; they've become an intimate part of it through their inner awakening and transformation. That's the difference between a medicine man and a doctor."

But Nadine spoke more like a medicine woman than a doctor, right?

"Still pretty, even when you are sullen," our new manager remarked. "You are a writer. Probably that explains it."

"Oh yes? Explains what, exactly?"

Nadine screwed her face into an expression of mock profundity–the Deep Thinker. A fist under her chin completed the caricature.

Then she threw me off balance again. "Do you think it just coincidence that we meet like this today? Those ready to receive Truth feel it inside. They move towards teachers who live this every day. Works like gravity, no?

"The veils between worlds are not so thick." Startled by this echo of things I'd confided in my journal, my breath caught. But Nadine diffused the tension with a merry twinkle. "Is just we human beings–" She reached across the table to rap my forehead with her knuckles–"who are thick! U.S., other countries, they get everything backward. Evolution, heredity, how this universe was born." She tapped her chest. "They are faulty, and they no speak to the heart. You know how to solve the chicken or the egg question? Learn to ask a different question."

When I shied from responding, she added: "Those doctors no care about your heart and soul, only what your body looks like under X-ray. The one I spoke to, he said I would be wasting my time with you. Said you're convinced you have all the answers already. And that you're one of the most stubborn women on Earth." Her smile widened. "He made this sound like a fault, but for me, is something to be proud of. Hey!" She lifted my chin. "Wouldn't you rather know how the Maker sees you than how these doctors and shrinks see you?"

Maybe I was fighting for some vestige of autonomy. Maybe I was speaking on behalf of my pride. I can't be sure. But from the depths of my confusion, I mustered a shallow protest.

"Doctors give you drugs. Spiritual groups harp on and on about how you need to turn everything over to a Higher Power. What's the difference?"

Nadine grinned "You no like the idea of God that much, eh?"

"It seems to me," I said, "that whenever someone uses the word 'God,' it's either a shortcut or an excuse."

"Is not so at the Empty Vessel," Nadine said. "We say this word with love. But I prefer to say 'Maker.' No matter! You call it this or that, it is still a slow process, no? Waking up from living like sleepwalker?"

Something within this idea saddened me. "I'm too young to think of trying to transcend a life I've hardly started living yet!"

I sank into a kind of paralysis again. My life felt like a movie unfolding before the helpless eyes of a voyeur.

"You think you find salvation some other way," Nadine whispered, "go ahead—try it! Listen!" She knuckled her chest. "I see myself in you." Suddenly, she sounded like a confiding sister. "You know what it's like, feeling connected to something the rest of the world no understands. Like you crashed here from another planet, no? What the Ascendian does... It gives people like you a place to be. Where you feel safe, surrounded by those who <u>know</u>. No money worries. You earn your salary without bosses and customers driving you loco. You can know what you know, believe what you believe, and no one judges."

Then, she handed me a blue and white pamphlet. I'd been too startled to realize she'd been holding it this whole time. Gripping it, I glanced at the title: "Our Vision," written in a rainbow arch over a plain silver goblet that faintly glowed.

"Read it tonight," Nadine urged me. "We talk more tomorrow."

I went into work the next day feeling like I'd fallen off the Earth. That pamphlet read like something out of a cult sci-fi movie, only it was corroborated by so much that had happened in my personal life. It was my own reflection in a circus mirror. I'd had trances less surreal than The Ascendian's history and mission statement.

Somehow, I mustered the courage to pose the questions that most terrified me. "How far does your influence go? Did you arrange for my release from the hospital?"

My family had certainly done nothing to advocate for me.

"We have this understanding with people in psychiatric field. Some people they cannot help. The gifted ones, like I told you. These people need a spiritual solution."

"And they're also the only ones the Ascendian hires!"

We were alone at one of the dining room tables. The Grand Opening was still a week away.

"This you have backwards, Colleen. Seekers follow the path of their own free will, and talk about it with who they choose. It is like this: Whenever there are enough believers in a place, a strong core group, we open up a new store."

"It's a whole chain of restaurants, every employee indoctrinated into the same friggin' cult!"

Nadine's poise made me sound like a petulant child.

There was this place of unassailable rectitude in her. I may as well have tried to wear a mountain down by whining at it.

"There is a sub shop in Albuquerque; I know the owner," she enunciated. "Probably two out of every three employees you see there are people he recruits from church. These people are no afraid to ask other workers if they accept Jesus as their lord and savior. I will ask you: What is the difference?"

"Well, the reach of the Ascendian is a hell of a lot bigger than this guy's one store, for one thing!"

Honestly, I wasn't sure what my argument was anymore. These were just verbal flares meant to hold an eerie sense of encroaching darkness at bay.

"Devotees of the Flame worked at the Ascendian ever since first store opened," Nadine persisted. "That was the idea. A few hundred people follow Master Santiago. All these people he gathers around himself because his words and wisdom draws them. Then this number grows and grows. All these people sick and tired of the profane world."

I didn't care for the way her lips twisted around that word: profane. It sounded like she'd practiced pronouncing it in front of a mirror.

"One of our earliest disciples, he says, open a restaurant that will be haven for believers; offer them support and money. Where they'd no be looked down on but feel free to be themselves."

I thought of the testimonials I'd read in the pamphlet. Like some of Nadine's arguments, they'd sounded like memorized articles of faith. "It bugs me, Nadine, people just spewing out a script..."

"What script you rather they repeat?" She adopted the tone of a counter clerk so adeptly that I could almost see the paper hat on her head. "'Would you like to make that a combo meal?' 'Is that going to be on white or wheat bread?'

'Paper or plastic?' 'You want fries with that?'

"All these lines they must say, day after day! Handed down from Corporate! Is better if the script be about finding their beauty, or filling emptiness, or knowing the Maker, no?

"Colleen," she said, "I do believe in right thought and action. I want to be—" I watched her reach again for an English equivalent to her thought. "Deliberate creator of my life, not at the mercy of what the world throws at me. When I woke up this yesterday, I say, 'I intend to find someone, another suffering soul, someone who'll benefit from this Truth that has saved me.' And I meet you!

"No, no... never would we refuse to hire someone because of their beliefs," she hastened to assure me. "Someone works at Ascendian restaurant for years and never even hears about becoming Devotee of the Flame. Also, this work no good for some followers. They no like working with food, or they are awkward around people. Some already have careers. These people, they may volunteer on farms or in our plants. Carpenters and painters and plumbers, we have all these people who travel all the time. When a new store is built, we contract them."

"I've heard warnings about religion and politics riding in the same cart," I snorted, "but religion and fast-food? The implications are dizzying."

Nadine's smile indulged me. "Much dogma hides in ways people eat. Always it is this way. We are more obvious, maybe. Many people, they say, 'I will become vegetarian or vegan or want to eat organically'—all this ties to spiritual beliefs. They have ideas about food and karma. They say, 'I will eat a lower life form, not a higher.' See, it is like this: Maybe when someone is obsessed with what they eat, when they try to hold themselves to this diet or that, what this really means is a wanting to be pure on the inside.

"Most workers who come around to teachings, they

no need persuading too much, Colleen. They have lived in this way, a paycheck to a paycheck. Such a life makes you question. Just as much as... oh, I don't know... the death of someone you love will do, maybe."

I mustered another weak protest. "They weren't going to be working those kinds of jobs forever."

"Oh yes? You can promise people this?"

"A few years of college—"

"Oh, dear!" Nadine hoisted an eyebrow. "Sift through piles of resumes in our stores sometime. People with degrees—engineering, computers, programming; people spend years in culinary school, work as chefs or food production managers. In they come, begging for work. Some say will do anything, wash dishes... 'Just give me some hours!'

"We must face this, Colleen: The service economy is here. And it no look like your Daddy's American Dream."

"But how could one of America's largest chains host its own religion for years, and scarcely anyone knows about it? Is there secret training? Are your employees <u>told</u> to keep quiet?"

Nadine's smile was fainter now, her expression surreptitious. I wished I hadn't caught that.

"We must be... discrete, yes. When someone learns that there is philosophy behind the Ascendian, already we must feel that they make personal commitment to the Way."

"What? I...I haven't made any commitment!"

For the first time since this conversation began, Nadine sounded vulnerable. "With you, I take chances."

She rushed to cover her moment of uncertainty. "Why is important for anyone to know beforehand? You need to know the number of Christians in the world before you start the reading Bible?"

Suddenly, her English flowed much more fluently.

"The Maker has a message for all of us, but we can only help Him deliver that message if we're willing to be empty vessels. No Self interfering with what He is trying to pour into the world.

"Few are called; even fewer answer.

"Now, if you be ready to change your life—if really you are set to do such a thing—anything in the world can bring you the message."

Her eyes danced on the edge of cunning. "You love archaeology, no? There have been visitors: Emissaries of the Light come down to check on us, to look how we make progress and encourage us. These are our founding fathers. They build pyramids. They leave stones on Easter Island. We are descendants. You let the Light burn away everything within you that keeps you living in illusion, you know what this means.

"Santiago has—" She spread the concept with her hands— "direct pipeline to Emissaries! Like radio. Think of this! You no spend another day doubting, not knowing. What you love most? Your writing? He tell you where it comes from!"

Her eyes sharpened. "Did it scare you, first time?"

Somehow, I knew exactly what she was referring to. Lulled by the privacy of the moment, I answered without thinking. "Oh, hell yes! I thought I was schizophrenic. Was this God? The Devil?"

"Suppose it was a good thing, but you always around people telling you it is bad?"

It was getting harder and harder for me to raise an objection. If all there was in the universe was the consensus reality... Well, I had nothing to ground me here anyway: no supportive family, no lover, nothing but a past littered with dead loves and the debris of a thousand missteps.

Suddenly, it seemed I'd spent these years at

Marguerite's suspended in midair. I needed a place to land. Preferably....

We are the people with no past.

Yes, like those gypsy folk I'd written about: the Vandrene. Desert dwellers. I'd lose myself in the Southwest like Esperidi lost herself in the Savwain. Like her, I'd emerge with a deeper understanding of my true calling.

I had to believe! The alternative—that the world had finally caught me, and there was no more room even to wiggle—was intolerable. It'd been easier to engage in a mock battle with psychiatrists and hospital staff than to step back into the actual struggle that comprised my life.

And I was more bereft than I'd been at any other time since leaving the hospital. Only a month ago, Daddy had finally lost his battle with "self-medication." No more trailing his slowly capitulating body through the sands of an unforgiving world and bearing the cost of living.

As if some instinct guided her to my point of sorest vulnerability, Nadine said: "You no want to find your true family?"

Job security. A support network. People who didn't judge me for believing in my psychic experiences. A place to land. Family.

And so, like Esperidi, I made a tentative step towards my life's new calling. Only mine was a concession to darkness. "All right," I said, "I admit I'm curious."

Nadine looked both relieved and cautious. "We can no more talk like this—casual," she said at last. "You want to know more, you come to headquarters in Saint Santiago. You say yes, and I see you get transferred. We even pay for flight."

Then she patted my shoulder, her smile acknowledging her victory. "You think about all this."

Cascades of Light

The sun cast a dim reflection upon the clouds west of the mountains, mustering one last show of defiance before she was extinguished. Across the land below, night fell. It was *always* night here. A mile down and twice as far away, a frosted sand bar spread, a thin bastion sundering raging waters.

With the inevitability of a recurring nightmare, Pallides Mon-Sequana looked upon Ardhid, the land bridge, bathed in lights like a sea of fireflies. His Lore Masons conjured witch-fires across the snowy plain, making a thousand Shaini campfires appear as tens of thousands to Chonnen eyes. He would waste no men on a small sortie. Let the invading host amass their full force upon that slim rock and ice tract—and face their reckoning.

Anticipating blood, his nostrils flared, pulling faint odors of salt and decay. Avaricious waves ground sand and rock at his perch's feet.

"Begin!" he cried.

The Lore Masons' chant was both sonorous and menacing, carrying portents of crushing, tearing, and exploding force. The sea began to boil and churn as if lashed by a whip. It latticed Ardhid in so many of its low-lying places that the land bridge resembled watery ribs.

The cry of the Chonnen army was audible even over Farsilane's chant. They realized their peril now.

Suddenly, the ground tilted and swept Ophia out from under them. The Rudowine Ocean drank thousands of gray-eyed soldiers in a gulp. Somehow, Pallides registered their collective terror and pain. His world drunkenly lurched. The rumbling came again like a titan had stirred in Ophia's bowels. And he was alone. The peninsula's tip had fallen into a chasm—which, in turn, was effaced by merciless waves.

Another tremor split the ground beneath him. Fissures opened in every direction. The shore-bound hills collapsed—sand castles trampled by a tantrum-throwing child.

There was nowhere left for him to go. He was forsaken on a tiny island amid a violently revolting sea.

"Enough!" he shouted, clenching his eyes shut.

When he opened them again, the vision they afforded was no less hellish than the scenes he'd been forced to relive over and over. Magma poured off the three distant hills; the prairie crept towards his feet in baleful red hunger. The outlines of the surrounding mountains were stark and black; there was no world beyond them. The middle distance was choked with ash, dust, and scorched sand.

Pallides shook his head as a disembodied voice seemed to narrate his plight. "Look! His emotional upheaval shudders within the very bones of the land!"

This voice was answered by another that sounded remarkably similar. "Ghastly region! I'd likely have suffered tremors myself if I'd been convinced of its reality."

"But look how he resists!"

I'm going mad, mad, mad.

The former Cordonne Father had long black hair—tightly restrained—and a lean, stoic face. He was a grim man in the autumn of his life. Insolent eyes glared above a belligerent mustache. His fists were clenched so hard they shook.

How do I examine myself? I see no mirror!

The whispers came again. "He still holds to the appearance he formed in his most recent expression."

"He is as disassociated from the environment surrounding him as he is from the violence that brought him here. See! Scarcely does he notice his apocalyptic backyard. He regards it like a dream in a fog."

Mad! Mad! Mad!

Pallides gazed across a parched, blasted landscape continually reborn in fire and ash. The distant tumult—there seemed to be a thousand volcanoes out there, demarking his horizon—occasionally shook the ground beneath his scorched sandals.

This again!

But he wasn't afraid. He *ached* for the ground to open up beneath him, to swallow him and end his slow anguish. But he knew it would not. For this, too, was a scene he'd been forced to relive countless times.

"Have I not suffered enough?"

But he discarded this idea as soon as he posed it to the hot, merciless air.

No. No penance suffices for what I have done.

Hearing footsteps, he hissed; suddenly, his every muscle was taut. Since coming here—a span of time and space that he couldn't measure by any form of reckoning—nothing had disturbed his pristine, complete loneliness.

The figure stood about five paces from him. It was shrouded in an azure cloak with a long cowl that completely obscured its face. Its feet were bare—inexplicably, Pallides thought, considering this rough, unforgiving terrain.

He wondered if someone had finally arrived to condemn him. Part of him was relieved to no longer squander the minutes and hours awaiting Judgment.

But the low female voice did not sound accusatory or even reproachful. "I heard that you've been having difficulties with your transition. You keep recreating old torments in this place and don't know how to release them and move on."

"Heard?" Pallides scoffed. Equal parts outraged and ashamed, he would have dismissed this phantom if he'd been able. "From whom? I haven't spoken with anyone since I arrived here. There's no one to speak to! Who could know about the agony that binds me here, rooted to its source?"

He sensed rather than saw the figure shrug. "Perhaps a nearby river told me before you consumed it with fire. Does it matter *how* I know? Tell me you are well and that this experience is not causing you undue suffering, and I'll leave you alone."

The force of Pallides' inner need caught him utterly by surprise. "Please don't go!" He nearly groped for her. Now that he'd been reminded of other sentient beings and his ache for connection, losing that contact seemed unendurable.

"But why do you want to help me?" he demanded. "Is this what you do?" He groped for mythic images from his previous life, trying to orient himself. "Are you some sort of gatekeeper or guide?"

"Only *you* get to be that," she said. "Here, you are lock, key, and locksmith. Maybe, before we're done here, I'll have convinced you that this was always true of your life in Ophia as well."

"Ophia!" Memories of the Weaving passed over him like frigid shadows, and he shivered. "How could you know where I lived? Are there ways of peering into that world from this one?"

"Of course. It's possible to peer into any point in the universe from any other point. And by 'universe,' I mean all realities we can conceive. You begin by realizing that you are always standing in the center. There are—theoretically, at least—an infinite number of planes, realities, probable dimensions, whichever description—" she seemed to grope (or listen) for something; then she delivered a comparison incomprehensible to him—"floats your boat! Hehe!

"But in truth, my wanderings have only *grazed* across most of the dimensions I'm aware of. They are like the flickering shadows that catch your eye in a dream, and then you forget all about them amidst the next shift in the dreamscape."

"Normally, your riddles would irritate me," Pallides admitted. "But... I welcome the distraction."

He scrutinized her shadowy form. That cowl should not have concealed her face so thoroughly. But he could discern no trace of her features. It was as if naught but a ghost inhabited that robe.

"So is that what you did then? From here, you peered into Ophia and spied on me?"

"Do not attribute the Cordonne's guile to me! I do not live in this place," she said. "You belong here more than I do. You're bereft of a physical body, and I still possess one. Safely ensconced in a bed, I hope."

Her *timbre* sang with an unmistakable note of merriment, much like when she'd said, "floats your boat." Such humor confounded Pallides. How could anyone muster the heart for laughter in a place like this? "And yet you have watched me. You've admitted as much. So what do you conclude from what you've seen?"

"Your consciousness seeks healing and communication between its estranged factions. One side clings to numbness; the other denies what it indeed knows."

"More riddles!"

"Here, then, is one you might find easier to read." The

figure pointed to where a newly-formed lake spread its blue blanket across the barren, convulsing pan. "Water is life. Here is hope!"

"But scant hope when it is so black and cold!" Pallides retorted, not knowing what made him so convinced of this.

Again, he sensed movement. The figure seemed to shake its head. "You know, you cannot sustain this charade forever. The pressure of your inner knowledge continues to mount. See how the landscape shifts and groans in response to your every turn of thought! Come now, Pallides... You cannot help but realize that you are Toh Himself here!"

Skipping transitions, Pallides found himself weeping. His throat was clogged with so many denials that he gagged on their futility.

"Yes: Rinse the memory away. Flood the fire of this plain with your own deluge. It is temporary. And soon, you will know that the source of this pain is an illusion."

Eventually, Pallides sank to his knees in the hot dust and settled into the quiet, nearly thoughtless space that often arrives after giving pain its due. But then, he remembered that this stranger had witnessed his abjection. He glared at her. "Maybe you ought to introduce yourself, no?"

"I have gone by many names in many times and places. Wouldn't you rather know *why* I am here?"

"Fine, then. Why?"

"To help you understand and accept what has happened. To lead you out of this hellish labyrinth you've woven around yourself."

"I don't want anyone leading me anywhere," Pallides insisted. "I wanted it *over*, ended."

His back repudiated her as he wandered aimlessly, his sandals kicking up trails of black soot to mingle with incarnadine fumes like irredeemable phantoms.

The cloaked figure followed at a respectful distance. "Yes... because you perceived the world as something you were the victim of, not something you had a hand in creating. You relinquished the idea that thoughts have power. Violence is always the result of a sense of *powerlessness*. But you believed it was more potent than love. In your mind, there was no way that kindness could contest with the force of a spear, a Cundra, or an ankh."

"You speak of thoughts. What makes you so privy to mine?"

"Perhaps this furnace wind whispers them to me."

Pallides scowled, but he couldn't find a potent retort. He didn't know what he was fighting for or what walls he should defend in this place.

Such matters had been simpler in Farsilane.

And the breeze carried the confounding scent of renewal. Spring fought to emerge into his parched hell. Green growth pockmarked the horizon. Stark rock slopes gentled with grass and loam. No longer spouting from hot geysers, water settled into cool, placid streams.

Alongside this startling pastoral, the woman lofted a snatch of tune:

> Around the bend and as far as I can see
> There's no resting, forever, for me
> All our knowing
> keeps growing
> Shaping new stars over far-flung countries

Finally, Pallides peered down and beheld the miracle unfolding at his feet. He acknowledged the tiny buds, the patches of grass, clover, and dandelion. His ears found surcease: The previous uproar subsided to a mere legend of a storm that'd passed.

But he was still neck-deep in pain—pain made more keen, perhaps, by the present contrast. The tranquil sights and sounds were peripheral, lapping against him like waves his toes were numb to.

Lashed by grief, he began to ramble.

"After my wife died, I forsook the work I loved. It was too strong a reminder of her. Eventually, I moved to Farsilane and took on the mantle of City Father—a functionary of the Cordonne." He pronounced that word like it'd become synonymous with damnation. "But I had already decided that Ophia was not a world I wanted to live in. I thought it entirely corrupt, sick, and doomed. I verily existed in perpetual darkness. Though I drowned in those first convulsions, it was an act of suicide. I entered that invocation intending not to survive it."

He didn't realize he'd languished on the ground once more until he mustered the courage to face his companion again and found her gazing down at him.

"Do you see now that you have always been an idealist in your heart throughout all your lifetimes—even this last one, which seemed to go astray and end so tragically? You would not have been so disturbed by your perception of Ophia had you not nurtured a vision of how She should look in Her springtime of life."

"Vision! Hah! And look what it purchased me! Keep everyone in step: living, speaking, and thinking in accord with the Cordonne's *guiding ideals*."

But his belligerence expired after that last flare. "It doesn't matter now. It's over. I'll accept my punishment."

His companion merely waited, knowing Pallides' protests could not persist much longer amidst the growing pressure of his inner recognition—especially here, where all camouflage had been stripped away, leaving his spirit naked to bathe in Sorsajna, the fire at the heart of Creation.

"Would you accept punishments for all your other expressions as well? I think by now you must suspect that not only do you not have to answer for his deeds, you no longer have to *be* Pallides! Ah, yes." She chuckled. "I can almost hear you thinking, 'If I am not *him*, then who am I?'"

This idea of *other expressions* made the former City Father brighten at a sudden, obscure thought. "I once fashioned Singing Bowls, you know. I had little understanding of the principles behind their workings and little desire to know, but I loved the craft. I'd hold that tiny spool steady, vibrate it with the inaudible sounds—"

"*Sacred Timbre*," the woman said.

"Aye. It could make red sandstone run like syrup and render granite soft and malleable as wet clay."

Momentarily, the scene Pallides described superimposed itself upon the burning prairie. His hands enacted a virtuosic dance, softening and shaping the stone he'd once transformed into elegant bowls.

"And my bowls were resonant and vital! Four of them could move one of the greater pillars in Farsilane!"

But his effervescence vanished as if a thunderhead had eclipsed it. "It was enough for me that the power worked, that it achieved results. I did not question *why* power was to be used. In the service of what vision, what values? Zaire Mon-Sequana often asked me this. Others among our people posed such questions. I considered them frivolous."

"Zaire was your wife?"

"Aye. She died in childbirth." His visage contorted; his hands, folded together as if in benediction, trembled; thunder roiled overhead. "Power! It avails us naught when we need it most!"

Then he squinted as the figure across from him wavered like a reflection upon the surface of a rippling pond.

For a moment, he experienced the uncanny sense that she was as buffeted by sadness as he. However, when her form solidified again, she seemed even more vibrant and insistent.

"I would very much like to hear more," she said in a voice wet with the *timbre* of longing.

Pallides shook his head. "You're enjoying this, are you?"

"I never enjoyed seeing you suffer. I always wished I could show you how needless so much of it was."

"Always? Needless?" Pallides teetered on the edge of realizations that threatened to plunge him into oblivion. "What could you know of my pain, woman?"

Though he couldn't discern it behind her cowl, his companion bore a fragile smile, equal parts shy and determined. "Perhaps a little bird told me about it."

The former City Father gaped at her for a seemingly interminable moment and then shook as the revelation rattled his foundations. Had every day he'd ever lived, in every life he'd ever known, suddenly revealed itself to be naught but a dream?

His voice trembled with a realization that he hardly dared credit.

"Sparrow??"

The ground of his being tumbled and groaned, even as another part of him chased the recognition as if it were spring's first birdsong.

Esperidi Mon-Sequana strode three steps towards Pallides, stopped, and slowly pulled back her hood. "Hello, Papa."

She regarded the man who'd been her father in silence for a long time—though she was well aware that, in this place, "time" was a contrivance. No minutes manifested here, only the gaps created by her and Papa's shared uncertainty.

The landscape settled into a curious stasis as if Pallides' "afterlife" evinced bated breath. Its two sole inhabitants understood the path this must take, and neither felt entirely ready for that commitment.

But Esperidi acted within an arena that her entire life had prepared her for; that surety enabled her to embrace their destiny before Pallides could.

"I do not think you'll be able to escape this place of torment," she pronounced, "until you've named the guilt that wrought it."

"Have I not done so already? We seeded the Rupture! All that blood and ruin—"

"You know that's not the guilt I refer to."

Her eyes pinned him to this moment of reckoning, exposing all his hiding places, leaving no avenue for retreat.

"You must acknowledge how you threw yourself into the Cordonne's Great Purge because you really sought to purge something within yourself."

Pallides intuited what she was alluding to, and he stared back, wide-eyed, with a stricken expression such as Esperidi had never beheld upon his face in physical life. "What?! You mean for me to confess it... to you?"

Esperidi folded her arms across her chest, marshaling her courage—and, she acknowledged, perhaps buttressing her heart. "Who better to bear witness than me?"

Unable to answer her courage, Pallides turned back towards the ravaged landscape, panning his gaze across its tormented sweep as if somewhere he could find an egress, an escape route from himself—forever.

"It is condign that I should writhe in this nest of flames," he decided.

"Perhaps I should be the judge of that," Esperidi said. "If you cannot forgive yourself, Papa, give *me* the opportunity."

She stepped closer and pressed her appeal. "Why did you suddenly decide to become a City Father and throw yourself into the pursuit so zealously?"

"I welcomed the distraction!" Pallides shouted. "Are you happy? Or will you not be content until I debase myself utterly?"

"Distraction from *what*?" Esperidi persisted, ignoring his spout of melodrama. She could not relent: not now. He was so close to release! "These shadows thrive in silence, Papa. They swell with every denial. When we name them aloud, we rob them of their power."

"I needed to avert my eyes from the woman you were becoming!" Pallides' anger, lashed by age-old shame, lent him the fortitude to face his daughter again. "You blossomed by the day. More and more, you resembled *her*. At moments... wild thoughts escaped." As if pronouncing his own fatal verdict, he inclined his head toward the heavens and screamed: "A part of me wished you could take her place!"

Esperidi acknowledged this with a nod like the slow toll of Time. "Does it help to know that a part of me cherished the admiration that glowed in your eyes when you forgot to guard it—like a flower cherishes the sunlight?" She took another step closer. "These things happen, Papa."

Pallides head shifted like a boulder back towards the writhing horizon. "Condign that I should burn for such thoughts," he persisted.

"You never acted upon them," Esperidi reminded him. "I never felt unsafe with you in that way. The only side of you that ever frightened me was your fanaticism."

Suddenly, she sounded wistful—or deliberately disarming.

"Once, I was a man in a city called Sadenport. You were a strawberry and cinnamon girl who broke my heart and left your face etched in my memory for years. In ancient

Sequestra, you were my male child and suckled at my breast beneath the banyan trees for your first seven months of life.

"Do you not see how absurd all your self-recriminating beliefs are in this place, all your notions of straight roads and empire paranoia? No human being's nature stays confined within such narrow straits—and no thoughts, in and of themselves, are so ill."

A memory from her waking life arose, provoking a chuckle. "We shed lives like Sarpienta sheds his skin."

Then her eyes returned to Pallides with renewed focus. "Of course there were times when you thought of me as the woman of the house. I was the only woman living under your roof!"

Pallides clenched his jaw and then released it with visible effort. Finally, he landed upon words to etch his astonishment. "You don't abhor me for it?"

"What hurt," Esperidi acknowledged, "was how you withheld your affection from me from then on. You froze inside. Your heart atrophied. Like the time you castigated yourself for your body's natural response when, in a carefree and thoughtless moment, I hopped onto your lap—"

"Enough!" Pallides cried. But his walls were fast dissolving now from the force of his inner clarity. He'd tasted reprieve; perdition could never hold him like it had mere moments before; it could never again feel as just and inevitable.

"No, I recognize what you're doing," he said. "And you're right. The burden..."

"These things feel much less cumbersome once we call them by their right names, don't they?" Esperidi suggested.

"Yes." Pallides sat with this revelation for a moment and then shrugged. "But what do I do with it? Where do I go from here?" He fruitlessly groped for the source of his inanition. "What *now*?"

"Now you forgive yourself, relinquish this horrendous self-imposed sentence, and give yourself permission to live again."

"Live?" His laugh was clipped and befuddled. "I've *died*, girl!"

Esperidi slowly shook her head as if marveling at his density. "You've been awfully lively company for a dead man, Pallides. I must say."

She stepped close enough to offer him her hands. "Feelings and thoughts," she said, "can be moved through—much like this landscape—once they are acknowledged. Let's walk through them together until you realize there isn't a single one that holds any power over you anymore. We're bound to find your garden bower ere long.

"What now? Now, you follow your heart until you understand how it might like to clothe itself anew. The universe is forever discovering itself and its potential, Papa, and we exist at the forefront of that exploration. And you will have the support and guidance of many who have known and loved you before—and who *you* have loved!"

For a moment that could not be measured, Pallides assimilated this at the pace his old mind was accustomed to. "So... you do this?" He tried to ferret out the words for a host of intangibles. "This is like a vocation of yours? You do it often—serve as a guide like this?"

"I suspect I may do it every night," his daughter said. "I can't rightly say. I oftentimes don't remember, after I wake up, what I've been about."

Pallides spread his arms wide.

"I'm your father. It seems unfair that I should presume to let you guide me."

"You *were* my father," Esperidi said. "And the best one I could have hoped for, in light of what I'd hoped to achieve and how I ached to learn and blossom." Confronting the doubt marshaling in his eyes, she added: "You taught me to discern where I could expose my heart and where I should hide it from cruel eyes. You helped me to gaze into the heart of our people's true predicament. You lent me all the impetus I needed to commit to the Sophryne Way and learn to fly!"

Suddenly, she appeared shy. She blushed in a manner appropriate for the form she'd adopted. "But if you still feel that the debt lies heavier on your side, we could barter."

Pallides' lips curled in a half-smirk. "Afterworld bartering?"

"Yes!" Now that the idea had taken root, Esperidi spoke with growing conviction. "I'll help you through this transition. And in return—"

Suddenly, years retreated from her face, smoothed her skin nearly to the point of innocence. Her raven hair wove itself into twin, waist-length braids as her body shrank. Pallides blinked, and the girl before him stood scarcely level with his chest.

"In return, nine-year-old Sparrow gets to spend a last moment with her Papa before he leaps into his next adventure."

Pallides' grin broke into a wild smile, astonished by slow-rolling tears. "So it seems those tales of a paradise awaiting us after death have some validity, after all!"

But he faltered there, and his surroundings failed to cohere. Colors ran; shapes and shadows merged and separated. All of reality swirled. "What is this?" he wondered aloud.

Esperidi tried to smile for him, but the expression was somewhat marred by pain. She'd never seen him look so vulnerable before, so forlorn in the face of Immensity. "The Rupture's waves have finally subsided. Now, we wait."

Pallides clutched himself and shivered. He felt

insubstantial, diminished by the weight of Creation. His former daughter's words implied *change*, and it was difficult for him to conceive of any other reality besides *ruin*, which had long seemed the defining fact of his existence.

"Wait for what?"

"Another wave draws nigh, bigger than all the others," she said. "Its crest will brush against the sky and wash over all the land." Her anticipation of what was coming soothed her thoughts, and she smiled more freely. "It will be brighter than the sun, but it will not hurt your eyes. You can stare into its heart if you wish."

For a time, Pallides wrestled with this concept in silence, marveling at his former daughter's stature and weighing his own. He seemed to shrink beside her, but for once, he rejected this attack of inadequacy.

"And you'll stay with me?"

Leaning her child's head against his shoulder, Esperidi grabbed his hand and squeezed it. "Until it washes over us, Papa."

And so they stood side by side as an inconceivably vast light roiled across the horizon, growing as it devoured leagues of broken land like thousands of luminous yellow horses hued with joy and affirmation. Pallides chuckled aloud, realizing it was just as Sparrow had described. In moments, he could see naught but that encroaching Light. The very ground he stood upon pulsed in time to those luminous hoofbeats. Like a diver preparing for a deep plunge, he drew breath and held it as the immensity engulfed him in its loving stampede.

꽃꽃

Esperidi opened her eyes and inhaled the spicy aroma filling the amber cave. The small of her back was sore. That same place! Her feather mattress didn't quite pad her against the floor's bulge, and the twined carpet was nearly as hard as the fig wood beneath it. The space beside her was cluttered with a few quaint reminders of Old Ophia: a baked clay rendering of Sequana Hive, the shape of an ankh woven from dry, yellow reeds, sculptures of two Singing Bowls, and a chest full of herbs and trinkets.

For a while, her face bore a faraway expression.

I should attend to that lump. I keep telling myself that.

But she pushed this trivial concern aside as she raised her eyes towards the rush-woven food tray and the man who held it.

"Oh, Shamarai, you needn't do this!"

The man bent and laid the tray on the short wooden tripod he'd built for her. "It gives me great pleasure, Olen-sa," he averred. Then he straightened and studied her. "Troubling dreams?"

Esperidi rubbed the vestiges of sleep from her eyes. "Troubling only insofar as I'm having difficulty remembering them. There was a girl—"

"Your twin?" the Junsa suggested with an irreverent curl of his lip.

Esperidi's eyes shone back with playful derision. "I was an only child, Shamarai. You are speaking nonsense."

"'She looks just like me!' Always, you describe her thus. And you have dreamed of her many times."

"Yes, well, she was only there at the beginning, I think, and it was very brief. She helped me find the place I sought... and then waited nearby in case I failed of courage."

Courage for what?

"We said a silly rhyme together beforehand."

Something about snakes for dinner!

Suddenly, Esperidi detected a subtle scent amid the tangle of tantalizing aromas. Grasping the stone mug set beside the food, she drew it closer to her nose and inhaled sharply. With that breath of astonishment, almost incredulity, she said, "Jasmine?"

Shamarai looked pleased. "You taught us a potent song, Olen-sa. A patch now grows near Sarpienta River."

Esperidi sniffed again. "And honey?"

His smile widened. "Several trees house beehives near that place."

Esperidi's mind drifted backward. She knew she could lose much of a dream's import if she became too distracted by the day's events. Therefore, she didn't ask Shamarai how many people were waiting to speak with her, seeking advice, counseling, and comforting. If this day was like any other, there would be a great many.

Instead, she posed a question to herself: *What was I doing before I awoke?*

Out loud, she said, "Papa was there, I think—in a great meadow. Sometimes, it was burning. At other times, plants grew before our eyes, and birds began singing. It felt like springtime."

Esperidi cupped the mug and tilted it towards her friend in gratitude. "Perhaps I shall recall it all better after this cup of tea!"

Shamarai bowed deeply and turned to leave the chamber as if he'd been waiting for this cue. As he drew the tarp entryway aside, however, he paused. "How long do I tell them to wait?

"Give me an hour," Esperidi said. "Then I will see them."

Shamarai bowed again and exited.

Esperidi sipped her tea, savoring the flavor she'd missed since those days—it seemed an age of the world ago—in Shiya-coqui's home. Then she retrieved her leather-bound journal and quill. Flipping to the nearest blank page, she scribbled the first word she could salvage from her morning's dream that she hadn't already voiced. She recalled that it'd been uttered in a tone of astonishment.

"Sparrow?"

Esperidi sighed and took another sip of her tea. "Well... I guess it's a start."

Here ends "Ophia's Sister-Soul"
The saga continues with "Gossamer Veils"

www.ingramcontent.com/pod-product-compliance
Lightning Source LLC
Chambersburg PA
CBHW052331110726
47901CB00005B/1205

* 9 7 9 8 9 9 8 6 7 7 2 0 5 *